White Nights, Black Paradise

White Nights, Black Paradise

A Novel

Sikivu Hutchinson

INFIDEL BOOKS
Los Angeles, CA

Published 2015 by Infidel Books
Copyright 2015 Sikivu Hutchinson

Hutchinson, Sikivu.
White nights, black paradise / Sikivu Hutchinson.
pages cm
ISBN-13: 9780692267134
ISBN-10: 0692267131

1. Jones, Jim, 1931-1978—Fiction. 2. Peoples Temple—
Fiction. 3. African Americans—Guyana—Fiction.
4. Jonestown Mass Suicide, Jonestown, Guyana, 1978—
Fiction. 5. Social movements—Religious aspects—
Fiction. 6. Jonestown (Guyana)—Fiction. 7. Historical
fiction. I. Title.

PS3608.U8595W45 2015   813'.6
QBI15-600109

Cover images courtesy of the California Historical Society

To the victims, survivors, seekers and travelers from the African diaspora who gave their hearts and lives searching for home

Jonestown Children, California Historical Society

TABLE OF CONTENTS

The Promised Land
Dover AFB, December 11, 1978

Hinterlands
(November 18, 1978)

IN THE FIRST expressions of my grief I reproached my fate, and wished I had never been born. I was ready to curse the tide that bore us, the gale that wafted my prison, and even the ship that conducted us; and I called on death to relieve me from the horrors I felt and dreaded, that I might be in that place where slaves are free, and men oppress no more. Fool that I was, inur'ed so long to pain. To trust to hope, or dream of joy again.

—Olaudah Equiano, 1789

CHAPTER 1

Taryn and Hy Strayer, California Highway, 1975

THE DRIVE FROM Modesto to Livermore was six degrees of cow dung, a deep rich funk for each rest stop. They drove scrupulously, bonded in discipline, determined to make good time. Taryn fought to keep her pinched clothespin nose, inherited from her father's father's Afro-Scottish mishmash, from surrendering to the shit kingdom outside the window. Her sister Hy had had an abortion two days ago and was still nursing cramps, babbling in white tides of fitful sleep.

They had been driving for over five hours with only pit stops, and now it was time for a real one. Time for Hy to change her pad while Taryn stretched and thought about what came next. They'd powered through the first several hundred miles with shots of coffee, Taryn's lime juice tonic, and a tape player cribbed from their mother's collection of battered black machines that she'd used during her dabble with investigative journalism in Greenville. If they had a brain in their head they got it because of her, their mother said. They didn't come from fried mush or monkeys they came from big brains.

Hy had to pee bad. Taryn wanted to push through and drive as long as the gas held out, but the car was stuck behind a row of fat semis tethered together in the fast lane like circus elephants.

"We'll stop and squat," she said.

"I want to use a toilet."

"We'll stop and squat. Saves time. The next rest stop isn't for thirty miles." Taryn pulled out a roll of paper towels from the glove compartment.

Hy sank back down into the seat and squeezed her legs together. "Fuck it T. Just pull into a fucking filling station. I gotta go now!"

3

"If we push through we can make it in two hours."

Taryn looked at Hy's grimace, ignoring her appeal, jerking the car roughly onto the shoulder. Dark flat fields rimmed by slivers of barbed wire stretched out beside them. Hy got out of the car and squatted next to the passenger door. She wiped herself with the paper towels, scraping brown blood off her thigh.

The abortion room was pure, every tile on the floor bleached to white picket fence perfection. The walls burst with Hallmark card flower portraits from ghost gardens, the sheets rubbed so hard of blood stains that they bled again, brown as her nurse's hairy birthmark branded right above the bulge of her Playtex gloves.

It was Hy's second abortion and the pain made the first seem like licking the bottom of a bowl of French Vanilla ice cream. The first time she was gloriously stoned, out celebrating her birthday and the sweet liberty of the pending procedure the night before. Taryn had worked overtime doing books for a Chinese restaurant to lend her the money. Then she got hired to teach Catholic school trig and dropped her hours at Deng's Garden to part-time, paying for the second abortion outright with no strings, lectures, hectoring, or rebuke.

"This is a down payment on your future, Hy," she'd said, licking fried rice off her fingers.

Taryn had whipped Tom Deng in poker and everything was semi-right in the world. With the gambling she had three income streams and they could make their rent, gas, dental bills, and a few extras while Hy was looking for work.

Her cramps stopped around the time they hit Livermore. She slept in snatches between the news reports, the weather and the check cashing ads. They were coming back from L.A. after crashing at a cousin's apartment in South Gate, their stuff crammed into the trunk and the backseat. She'd had two dead-end interviews there, and one a week before at an accounting firm in Hayward, a graveyard of grim houses and thirsty lawns. Somehow she'd gotten hired at the Hayward company.

She was the math whiz they didn't know was black on the phone, now the official fly in the buttermilk. Hy teased her about her sandpapery, Carol Channing, closet Negress whisper, how it dipped and rose a few octaves whenever she was bored or scared, a reluctant understudy to their mother's. Their jaws dropped when she walked into the office, the white secretaries trying to assimilate her into a phantom slot for a cleaner or fairy-godmammy flipping pancakes in the break room. She was too tall and thin for them to go far in that flight of fancy, the slither of eyes across her body sending her back to elementary school when the cheats and the molesters were out in full force trying to feel her up and steal her answers on the math test.

It was third grade now, sitting at the desk with her hands clasped in front of her. The McCrary boys had just been paddled for cheating, six metallic thwacks for craning their necks to copy her, for signing the answers to each other in their special twin language. Theirs was the smart class, the brown-paper-bag test-passers with a few token full-blood Negroid digressions like her. The twins jeered every time she walked past, teasing that she was praying mantis skinny and burnt to a crisp.

But she had a head for numbers. What were they going to do with this bright as new money anomaly? This credit to her race, who corrected the teacher on her nine times tables, never had to use her fingers, count under her breath or wait to be saved by the bell?

In third grade she learned the unreliability of the Lord. She called on him to annihilate the cackling, drooling pinheads who wanted to see her fuck up. What was the Lord God Almighty good for if he couldn't pull off a small favor after a week's worth of goodness from her, of sucking down the hot coal of her mother's insults and the steamy paint peeling stench of the bathroom they shared with the boarders from Minnesota. Everyone else in her class was blessed with a nice white toilet to sit on in quiet contemplation. Everyone else had real toilet tissue instead of the week old Negro newspapers rolled and pressed into service for every ass cheek in the house.

In the waiting room of the accounting firm under the watchful eye of Miss Ann Becky Sue she willed the run in her stocking to stay put until the interview was over, counting how many generations back that Becky Sue's ancestral nigger in the woodpile went; scoping out the telltale bend of her nostrils, the sub-Coppertone sheen ripening on her arm from fingertips to elbow, the betraying kinks at the base of her porcelain neck.

She surveyed the evidence over the top of the *Time* magazine she'd snagged from a pile of moist Wall Street Journals opened to an editorial about the assassination attempt on Gerald Ford. It was axiomatic that he'd be spared, that the dumb shit Manson family zombie who tried to shoot him wouldn't know how to aim a gun. There must be some kind of math equation to capture the probability that a warmongering old white man would take a bullet and live on to dementia versus a good young one dying instantly. God moves in mysterious ways, she thought.

On the road Hy was always pegging stalking candidates. After they'd taken a break at thirty mile rest stop she watched a man with a bible lope toward a teetering camper from the side mirror.

"I think that fucker was following us," she volunteered.

"It's all in your head," Taryn said. "Go back to sleep. We'll be home in a few more hours."

At the interview they kept Taryn waiting long enough for her to finish the entire magazine and start a word search: fun facts about frisky felines. Every few minutes Becky Sue mumbled apologies, wilting with boredom under the stack of un-alphabetized files and past due invoices she had to chew up and spit out before day's end.

The week before, Taryn had read in a tabloid that one of Becky Sue's soul sisters had gone to court in Louisiana to protest being categorized as Colored on her birth certificate. She'd taken to bed in mourning for three days after she'd found out she'd been born tainted, and revived by the ghost of Hattie McDaniel with some smelling salts and a hot kerchief to soothe her throbbing forehead. She fielded disease-of-the week movie offers from Hallmark—working title, "I went to bed a virgin and woke up a Negro, a tragic story of loss and redemption."

The receptionist's phone buzzed and she gestured for Taryn to follow, blazing a trail of lavender toilet water, a pink message pad full of doodles clenched in her fist. The company would be moving to San Francisco to meet a growing client base. Boxes, potted plants, lamps and appliances were stacked in the hallways. Betty Sue opened the door to one of the offices and led Taryn inside.

"Have a seat, Mr. Malloy will be right with you."

Malloy's walls groaned with diplomas, pictures of shit-eating grinning white men and a child's artwork. She searched for the inevitable family photo and found it, Mom, Dad, Spot; the beaming towheaded six year-old prodigy of the tightly bound threesome launching a kite into the sky. Everything in the room was fastidiously shoed into its place; pencils, calculators, rolodexes, annual reports categorized and corralled into military order, all snapping to attention when the door swung open and Malloy walked in.

"Dan Malloy," he said, extending his hand, his expression vapid, the telltale sign of having been briefed of her blackness. He settled down behind the desk and opened a manila folder with her résumé in it, scanning the page, skeletal fingers pressed together in cathedral form.

"Hayward, a strange choice for a young, talented person like you," he said.

Outside of an interview the searching glimmer of a question would've been reasonable enough. But within this context, it was potentially treacherous. White men, professionals who were "amazed" by her credentials, always had a stratagem.

"I've applied all over the country. California, the Bay Area, is a preference."

He nodded approvingly. "Lucky for you, or whoever we hire for this position, we're moving to Frisco. Beautiful place—once you get past the spoiled flower children and their like. Certainly beats down south with the smog and Hollywood crap."

She waited, forced herself to smile and nod, watching the ascent of a tiny spider on the wall behind him, weaving its way between the picture frames. She had never mastered the cadence of small talk, its cunning, or façade of casualness.

"Yes, well," he continued, tugging at his wedding band. "You'll find that sleepy Hayward has few surprises and even fewer charms for an ambitious young person like yourself. So Miss Strayer, you have three years crunching numbers and doing taxes ... worked at a Chinese restaurant, a development company and an air conditioning outfit. Looks like you built up a nice client base. That shows initiative." He scanned the résumé again. "Math teacher?"

"I enjoy teaching."

"I was a teacher in another life," he said, "Reading, writing, science and a little bit of 'rithmetic to dirt poor white kids in Lexington Kentucky then in West Virginia. Two and a half years trying to keep sharecropper and mining kids in school when most of the parents didn't even go past sixth grade. Hardest job in my life."

The spider made its way across the family photo, suspended between the tail of the kite and the little boy's grasping fingers. Taryn shifted in her seat, running a rocket launch count until the interrogation began.

Malloy closed the folder and picked up a framed photo on his desk, robin's egg eyes narrowing behind the shield of his bifocals. "There were days when I came home so tired all I could do was fall down on the couch and sleep for hours. It never got as bad as that in law school or even when I got my CPA license. All of the round the clock cramming couldn't hold a candle to dealing with those kids every day. So I commend you, if you were good, and I'm assuming you were."

"I received high evaluations."

"I know. I spoke to your principal."

She looked at him, suppressing her surprise. She had deliberately not put the woman's name down as a reference because of their rocky history, the dreary marathon of bucking her, an imperious East Coast Quaker who considered herself an expert on the plight of downtrodden ghetto children and flaunted it proudly at every school board and parent meeting.

"There wasn't a lot of love lost between you and her," Malloy said. "She said that you have a sharp tongue, are demanding, don't take shit, but came early and left late." He sat back in his chair, studying her over the rims of his glasses. "When I was a teacher I went and did home visits. You'd have eight, ten kids living in Walker Evans' shotgun shacks with the mother, father nowhere to be found, the whole lot of them scrambling for peanut butter sandwiches and Kool-Aid for dinner. Now these were white kids, mind you. They'd come to school the next morning either hopped up and cocky or falling asleep bored, challenging every word out of my mouth and invariably there would be one kid, bright as a lodestar, the most sullen, withdrawn and pugnacious of them all, just ready to set the class on fire if I looked at him wrong. Brilliant, brilliant kids hopped up on sugar with old geezer teeth rotting out of their mouths. Condemned before they even got a start in the world."

Hy was going to miss her check-up at the doctor's. Taryn was supposed to pick her up immediately after the interview. A half hour had passed with no mention of the job or its duties and her skirt was disintegrating into a sweaty smudge on the seat cushion.

"Are you a religious person?"

She hesitated. "I don't think you're allowed to ask me that."

"I know. But I did. It's your prerogative to answer or not. I happen not to be, but there have been various points in my life when I believed that there might be some kind of entity out there. I rejected it after the evidence said otherwise. I ask primarily because part of our client base consists of what one might call religious, spiritual or quasi-spiritual community organizations. If you're hired, your personal beliefs should have no bearing on the business of this company or its dealings with these organizations."

"Of course."

"Most of our clients navigate delicate financial conditions that require the utmost confidentiality."

"When I worked for the development company it was similar."

"And what of the school? What was the most personally trying situation you dealt with?"

"I would say limited resources and an aura of fatalism, mixed in with a misguided missionary complex coming from the leadership."

Malloy perked up, taken aback by her candor. Why the fuck did she say that? This would doom the interview; bashing the former employer being bad form, a preview of potentially mutinous behavior down the line.

Malloy came from behind the desk and extended his hand for her to shake. "I've got a delivery coming at four. Thank you for your time. Elaine will validate your parking if you need it."

Taryn muttered a perfunctory thank you and walked out into the hallway, forcing her face to go slack, flattening her rage as she calculated the waste of gas, dry cleaning and the endless mock interview sessions with Hy, bored shitless and pitching softballs just to be contrary.

In the reception area the secretary was hunched over a file cabinet slurping on a cup of coffee, feigning ignorance of Taryn's presence. The door swung open and two white women entered, cradling packages. The first one flicked her hair and smiled, betraying a mouthful of horsey piano key teeth, a chorus of cheap bangles announcing her every move.

"Hi Elaine, can you sign for this quick please? We're double-parked outside and it's fixing to rain. Be a sweetheart." She extended a clipboard with a packing slip on it.

Mr. Malloy appeared at the doorway. He walked briskly over to the women and took the packages, as the first one turned and smiled at Taryn.

"Hello."

"Thank you, Mariah," he said.

"You're welcome. We gotta get goin'. It's gonna rain buckets and the traffic report is saying the Nimitz is jammed. The Reverend is doing his radio show in an hour and we're having a group listening session in Richmond."

"Snowball's chance in hell that you'll make it that far with the rain and the traffic. Quite sure it'll be rebroadcast several times before the night is over."

"Yeah, but that's not the same as hearing it live." The second woman chimed in quickly.

"No. Of course not. Can't say I've ever had the pleasure of hearing a live sermon from the good Reverend."

"Well you should try and come sometime," Mariah said.

"Separation of church and state," he retorted. "Not prudent to muddy the waters."

The women followed Taryn out into the lobby toward the elevator. The quiet one looked at her and smiled. "He thinks he's got it all figured out. Hot shot rich guy in a fancy office out here in the boondocks."

"Property taxes are lower here," Mariah commented. "Don't be too hard on him Deb. Father must halfway respect him otherwise he wouldn't give him our business."

The elevator doors opened. Mariah motioned for Deb and Taryn to go in first. Muzak washed over them.

Mariah hummed a few bars, watching the lights on the floor panel flicker. "I hope you get it."

"Excuse me?"

"The job. I hope you get hired. I don't ever think I've seen an Afro-American person there except maybe a temp."

"No, not even that," Deb said. "Which is why I'm not sure why Father is doing business with these bigots."

Mariah paused, biting her lip. "Must be some method to it."

They reached the ground floor. Mariah dug into her bag, pulled out a brightly colored pamphlet and handed it to Taryn.

"Here, check us out sometime if you're interested. We do freedom circles about social and political issues and we have cultural events every weekend. Do you have kids?"

"No."

"'Cause we have activities for kids and families too, if you got any nieces, nephews or cousins you take care of. Fun bits mixed in with the socially relevant stuff to help you get your bearings if you're new to the area. I'm from the Midwest. It can be a little overwhelming getting used to California."

"I am too, and it hasn't been difficult for me at all," Taryn remarked.

The white women were hovering, trying to seem like they weren't, quietly proud of their pamphlet filled with multiracial scenes of kids frolicking by a pool, adults assembled in heated discussion, a band and a chorus of mostly black people swaying on a church stage, all framing the center image of a white man named Reverend Jim Jones in dark glasses with a thick black bowl haircut wielding a microphone.

Taryn put the pamphlet in her purse. "I don't believe in God," she said.

Deb took some Vaseline out of her pocket and dabbed it on her lips. "Well, actually, some of us don't believe in God either…In fact Father, that's him, Reverend Jones, is quite flexible about people's beliefs in the church. He welcomes all views. Our community is a mix of belief systems."

"From each according to her ability, to each according to her need," Mariah chimed in. "Doesn't matter whether or not you believe in heaven or hell, it's all about doing good right here right now."

When Taryn got to the car she put the pamphlet in the glove compartment and forgot about it, fishing it out weeks later after receiving the junior accountant offer from Malloy. Hy took an interest in it, putting it on the list of things to explore when they got to San Francisco, full of vigor after the abortion, enlivened by the novelty of the move and unsettled by the makeshift closeness it summoned between the two of them.

"So you think those white women had something to do with you getting hired?" She asked Taryn.

They were an hour outside of the city, bombing past dark houses, gas stations, open trenches littered with tractors and dump trucks fashioning the bones of new subdivisions.

"Doubt it. These were glorified couriers going out of their way to make it seem like doing business with Malloy was a necessary evil."

"Like it was all for show? White women always want to make themselves look more down and revolutionary when they get around us."

"That was the tenor. But it was something more. They were claiming their outfit was non-denominational, sort of a mix of secular and religious. I don't know if they were saying that to appease me because I told them

I don't believe in God. You know I don't have any tolerance for magical shit."

Hy frowned, irritated. "Why does it have to be shit? If people are getting something real out of it, then it's not all bad."

"What's real is highly subjective when you're sitting up in church around the clock."

Hy grunted, looking out the side mirror for stalkers. "Mind if I drive?" She asked.

A forty miles to San Francisco sign flashed in front of them. "The last time you drove you got into a wreck. We're almost there."

CHAPTER 2

Little Jim, 1943

FIRST IT STARTED as a booming, a thumping, a rumbling of ten thousand feet stomping the bottom of a tin boat. The whole First Redeemer church rocked off its foundation and thrust up into the white sky like Auntie Em's Wizard of Oz house spiraling in the eye of a Kansas tornado. Wriggling under the boy's rain coat, Muggs, his baby pet monkey, always got excited, heart beating ninety miles an hour, fur standing straight on end. Jim had gotten Muggs from a carnival barker after the man was going to leave him for dead; one eye clouded with glaucoma, belly bloated from a diet of cornmeal mush.

"Take that fucking thing," the carnie said. "No good rabid mange. Hell, I should pay you to take it off my hands. Prob'ly got the plague."

Muggs was his first love. The special one. The one who stood up for him when he was about to get the shit beat out of him by his daddy, fired again from another job after coming in lit. Whenever his daddy came at him, Muggs bared his teeth and spit and rared up like King Kong. Then his daddy would go after Muggs with a baseball bat, tearing up the house with his muddy boots, screaming for revenge.

The boy prayed to the Lord every night, wishing him dead like his daddy before him—pushing up daisies at forty nine with no mourners and a trail of racetrack debt left behind to a sour widow. His daddy Big Jim bet on the dogs, the cocks, the frogs, on anything that ran, hopped, skittered, crawled. Next to a bottle of Jim Beam it was his adrenaline rush, his religion, rumination and revelation; the only time Little Jim thought his daddy was remotely making an effort at something.

Muggs especially liked the cockfights, licking his lips at the pudding of warm blood and marrow when the loser went down, reveling in the spill of cash on the ground as the owners sparred about the amount. Big Jim paced on the sidelines, quiet, friendless, chewing a homemade antacid of licorice and walnut down to the nub to quell his stomachaches. He'd never been past the state line of Indiana and wore it proudly in the flat arid pasture of his accent, summoning his Rebel ancestors with every boast, toast, and hazy bet.

He had a system, he told Little Jim and Muggs. "Watch me and get educated. Someday we'll get rich working this circuit."

Little Jim saw Muggs listening and taking notes in his head. No way that chimp wasn't human. Nights when Muggs fell asleep in his arms and the whole house was dead he dreamed Muggs' dreams, and he his, unsettled by the damp a.m. gift in his boxers.

They'd sneak into First Redeemer, the Negro church, and hide in the broken corner pew bound with masking tape. Muggs stayed calm if Little Jim brought candy; the smell of it, the promise enough to keep him mute, drunk with anticipation. The first service began at nine sharp. The deacons opened the side windows an hour before to air out the weekday must. Returning servicemen in uniform sat in front; minds and bodies busted, drifting away from the pro forma prayers and asking God to deliver them decent jobs now that He had spared them from the war's carnage.

For Jim it was good as gravy, the pastor hooking him with whiplash brio and nail-biting tales of heroism against the Germans. Like a radio show come alive and wriggling in 3D right before his eyes. When Prophet Zeke spoke, it was as though they were the only two in the room. The rustling burgundy robes of the choir evaporated into butterflies. The organist thumped in silence; his father's grimy truculence held at bay for a blissful hour of sweaty call and response. Zeke commanded the stage with the Good Book bleeding in his meaty grip and not a dry eye or nodding head in the house. Jim escaped the drear of his parent's apartment, flew away from the fights, eviction notices and endless kitchen table get-rich-quick schemes.

15

"I'm smarter than your mama," his daddy would say out of nowhere. "Just 'cause she's holding down a regular job don't make her any smarter than any man. It's easier for these girls anyway. All they have to do is show a bit of leg and some two bit horny bastard will give them a job. Now your mama ain't young or good looking enough to have that kind of power, but it's still easier for her than me. A man who don't take no shit will get beat down in a second. Beat down to a nub to make him cry like a little girl, make him run with his tail between his legs. That's why I don't last at these penny ante jobs. Nobody is the boss of me. Remember that boy. Nobody is the boss of you except your daddy, while I'm living, and God."

Big Jim had all kinds of maladies, real and imagined, that kept him out of the service.

"Your daddy was in the broom closet hiding," his mother Odessa said, "while every other boy in his high school got called up. After the war was over the Army brought their ashes to their mothers in a jar. But your daddy was still cock of the walk spry and able-bodied."

Odessa was folding clothes and handing them to him to put up. It was their Sunday ritual, after he and Muggs got back from church, the afternoon spreading out in front of him like the Gobi desert. She brought her shift at the paper plant home with her, mimicking the dull as dishwater Southern Indiana accents of the line supervisors, the canned adages and flubbed off- color jokes of her crewmates. She performed to pass the time as the pile of underwear, socks and t-shirts mounted and she had him rolling on the bed laughing, thick shiny black hair flopping over his eyes.

His grandmother was a straight up full-blooded Minnesota Creek Indian, a warrior with a twelve-gauge shotgun who protected her farm from marauding white men. Any new friend he made he let them in on his secret ancestry, a favorite dessert to share with whipped cream and a cherry on top. They were special if he told them. Except that there were no Creek tribes in Minnesota and his parents were third cousins who despised each other on first sight and still did.

"If we'd been any closer kin to each other you would've turned out retarded. All the kings and queens in England did it and the kinks didn't show up until generations later."

Hiding in Zeke's church pew he blamed his migraines and delicate stomach on their sundry blood tie, hating every floorboard in the dingy cubbyhole of his room. When they were both gone he staged his own sermons, putting on his mother's robe, lowering his voice like Zeke. Muggs went wild, egging him on with a lopsided leer.

One night, when Big Jim staggered in early and caught him in the robe, he made him strip and preach naked, muttering queer, faggot, punk in the ribald taunt he used on the sidelines of the cockfights to distract the animal he was betting against.

"Talk about Samson and Delilah," he wheezed. "Spread some knowledge about that." It was the only shit he knew from the Bible, the only scripture that he saw himself in, as a warrior with golden hair, scraping his ass, shown up by the fucking whore who betrayed him. He called Little Jim queer, but he was secretly bemused, fascinated by his voice, his budding command, the way he sprung up from his usual guarded posture of watchfulness into blazing theatrics.

They were not church people. Big Jim had married his mother at the courthouse. He got his religion from the smell of bloody cocks, though he wielded God like a chainsaw, imploring the Almighty to spare him when he was doubled over with cramps and diarrhea in the bathroom, his gut rotting one hundred proof through his skin.

Prophet Zeke lived in a stately brick house with lions reclining on each side of the front steps. Their eyes watched Jim as he walked by, sniffing him out as friend, foe, or betrayer, wondering what that white boy was doing in this neighborhood. Surely he'd been warned.

But he knew even the littlest white baby had command over the oldest Negro.

On Saturdays a steady stream of visitors and supplicants came by the house bearing hamburger casseroles, oven fresh coconut cakes, pots of greens and maudlin confessions. They sidled up in groups wielding crumpled bills. All the bus drivers, janitors, washerwomen and school teachers in Negro Indianapolis lined up one after the other for an audience with the Prophet in his powder blue parlor.

Each session was timed to the minute by a deacon with an emerald stopwatch, punctuated by the bawdy squawks of Maisie, Zeke's geriatric macaw who'd been liberated, like the rest of his animal menagerie, from the jungles of Africa. Prophet Zeke was a world traveler. A collector of the finest silk ties, cigars and first edition bibles, a hoarder of currency from over fifty countries, kept in a safe guarded by two Dobermans in his basement suite. His second wife Prophetess Gloria ministered regally at his side with a new hat for every scripture in Ecclesiastes, batting her light golden brown eyes at Zeke when the congregation swooned.

Prophet's feet, hands and loins had holy powers. Little Jim fixed his mind to get some of that, to get inside the blue parlor and have Zeke tell his fortune. He'd never seen a white man go inside though. Whites used the neighborhood as a short cut on their way out of town, barreling down the streets with the tops of their cars open, knocking past stop signs expecting Negro drivers to give them the right of way.

A month after the war began, a hung-over white boy glee clubber, on the way back from his senior prom in his daddy's new Edsal, hit a five year-old black boy crossing an intersection in broad daylight.

"How was I supposed to see that spook in the dark," he asked, as the police led him away to the station, cleaned him up, doused him with Old Spice, called his daddy and bid him adieu right in time for his next singing gig.

With his oil slick hair, Little Jim stayed outside in the sun and got brown enough so people would think he was Spanish and not one of the pasty-faced German-Irish mutts that went to St Ignatius Catholic School instead of the publics with the rest of the crackers. They envied him because he spoke so well, had no accent you could place, his tongue wriggling out of the grave his father had dug.

It was he who was going to bust out of the primordial muck of generations of Indiana hayseeds who never knew more than the perimeter of their front yard, the church gossip and the exact shade of the Negro they caught undressing Lucinda with his eyes. Summertime and all the dirty blond princesses on his father's side called him Tar Baby, while they wore their widest brimmed hats and carried parasols everywhere. In exchange he had Muggs greet them with his perfect finishing school hiss, baring straight white Miss America teeth that glowed in the dark and scared the living shit out of the princesses.

"Monkeys are us," he told them. "They understand everything we do 'cause we're cousins."

"Shut your dumb stupid mouth," cousin Lucinda jeered. "We didn't come from no monkeys. Our daddy says we're in God's image and that monkey stuff is blaspheming against his name."

He liked the rise he got out of them when he said it. Knowing the poetry of Genesis backward and forward, setting a goal to read a new book in the Old Testament every month so he could stop the dumb motherfuckers in class dead in their tracks. How can the world only be several thousand years old? Did Adam and Eve screw each other to have Cain and Abel? Where can I get me a talking serpent?

When the teacher sent him out of class for cutting up, he jumped the fence and went straight to Prophet Zeke's neighborhood, feeling a comfort there, a visceral sense of ease settling over him the minute he hit Milligan Avenue. The world spread out in front of him. He walked past the hodgepodge of shops that anchored the Negro downtown, lingering in the windows of the pharmacy, the sundries store, the barber, slinking into the antiquarian bookstore preceded by a growling stomach.

Paradise was an hour with volume one of Horatio's African diorama or Carter G. Woodson's *The History of the Negro Retold*, deep in the silverfish funk of marked up pages. The first time he went in the grizzled man behind the counter looked at him warily, running his hair, his posture, his clothes, through his brain like long division in a calculator.

"Go home boy it's your dinner time. Won't your mama be looking for you?"

"Don't have one."

"Daddy?"

"Nope."

Every muscle of Jim's face betrayed him when he lied; mouth twitching, dark eyes thumping like a snare drum. He wanted the Negro to see him as an orphan, his calling card and secret sauce.

If I have no past I can be anything, he said years later to his People, standing before the congregation as he gathered the crippled black woman up into his robes, kissed her on the head, and set her walking, straight as an arrow. I can be God Almighty and the devil himself all rolled up into one.

CHAPTER 3

❧

Mariah, San Francisco, 1975

THE GLEAM OF the Breck girl's hair bounced off the skyscrapers. I am Breck, hear me roar. She shook out her hair in the midst of the city's bustle. Loved running her hands through it, feeling it blow in the breeze like Rapunzel jamming her finger in a light socket, electrified for a glorious moment of blissful control. Surely that was one of the reasons why The Reverend Jones chose her from the clamoring line-up of other women in the sanctuary.

Mariah had landed in San Francisco as part of a dare. You won't last no more than an hour outside the city line of Cicero, her mother warned her. They were watching the Republican political convention on TV and she was knitting winter caps and sneering about all the peace and love horseshit on the tube. When Mariah came to the City she panhandled, worked in a gift shop by the wharf, swept floors in a bank until she found a situation with Uri, a fifty-five year old Croatian trucker whose non-negotiable was biweekly blow jobs in exchange for her own room and two square meals.

She discovered the Temple when the movie she was going to see one night in the Fillmore district was sold out. She walked past the noisy lit up church building and peeked in. It was the first time she'd seen black and white people mixed together in a congregation. Little black kids mingled with white adults in the pews. A teen group with all races performed a skit on the Montgomery bus boycott and the March on Washington. The church band played a few strains of Marvin Gaye's "What's Going On" for the minister's entrance, keeping a soft undercurrent of sound throughout his sermon. He glided to the pulpit under a tower of shiny black hair, arms raised in conductor mode. Dark aviator shades framed his plump face, glistening with warmth and bemusement at the music, the hushed crowd.

Buckets strewn about the sanctuary caught rainwater leaking from the ceiling, the syncopated drops giving his speech a nice little backbeat. He riffed on the Ford assassination attempt, its implications for the U.S.' imperial missions in Latin America, and whether Squeaky Fromme was just a misguided mentally ill pawn or an agent of liberation. Every so often one of the elderly black women would rise, give a little bow, wave her arms up to the sky asking for deliverance as Jones crescendoed to her outburst.

"Nothing like a little Motown and Brother Marvin to get the juices flowing," he said, grasping the mike with both hands. "Forget all that sanctified mess you hear in the other hallowed institutions of religion this is real music for the mind and spirit! If Paul can be a prophet then certainly Brother Marvin can too, right? C'mon all you sisters in the front it's ok to lighten up and smile. I got word today that a delegation from an apostolic freedom mission in Jackson, Mississippi, Ole Miss as the Confederates like to say, is going to visit us next month to get pointers on how we administer our human services programming. We're going to need tour volunteers and goodwill ambassadors to house some of these folks."

Half the room clucked support for volunteering, stunning Mariah. In most churches she'd attended, volunteering was met with half-hearted compliance. A white woman with two biracial children toddling around her legs stood up and offered her home across the bay in Antioch. A black and Latino couple holding hands said they'd give up their bedroom for the visitors and sleep on the floor. One by one people piped up to volunteer homes, time, food and donations to help with the visit. The minister smiled and drank it all in, asking the church advisers stationed in the front at each side of the aisle to jot volunteer names on a clipboard.

Even among the sea of people in the congregation, she had not gone unnoticed.

"I see we have visitors here this evening. Welcome to you all, welcome to our Temple family of humanity. There's no need for airs and social graces in our house of worship. When we say everybody is welcome we damn well mean it. No qualifiers and no exceptions. Drug addicts and street workers alike. Hell, our addicts and streetwalkers are more respectable than most of the so-called County supervisors supposed to be running things here in San Francisco. No matter. When nuclear Armageddon comes, everyone in this joint will be safe and protected because we got a shelter for the whole Temple family."

Only the diehards stayed after for his special communion and prayer circle. Diehards and others seeking refuge from the pissing rainstorm—bleary-eyed fence straddlers quaking at the prospect of a private audience, wallflowers with a love-hate relationship with being noticed, families queuing up for the buffet of rice, beans and baked chicken beckoning at the back of the hall. Diehards and Mariah.

"What's your name, sister?" He'd asked in the warm lilt that he'd honed for softball questions, his eyes crinkling when she mumbled, the slow catch of her Midwestern accent knocking him back to miserable bug-dripping summers in Indiana.

She could count every pore on his broad flat face. Ride the rollercoaster cheekbones that swerved right up to his eyes, nestled meekly behind tinted glasses. Measure every inch of the scavenger's nose, poised to suction like an anteater.

"Mariah was one of the blessed," he said, "One of Magdalene's ten sisters. A pious woman with a tooth for nectar and ambrosia. That was her undoing and her downfall. Died of a fucking tooth abscess at thirty-five. That was old as Methuselah for folks back then. Once you got past twenty-five and you were female? You were put out to pasture. Dried up and obsolete according to the macho sexist pig propaganda of the day. And if you didn't have no kids, then fuck you twice."

The Reverend wore dark shades every waking moment but when he spoke to her it was like she was the only one in the world, like time had narrowed down to a pinpoint and it was just them, two angels dancing on it. But he didn't believe in frivolous superstitions like angels. No spirits, hoodoo voodoo, haints, fairies, jinnis, tree sprites or other ethereal emblems of the afterlife that good perfumed men of God regurgitated Sunday mornings.

"False prophets," he declaimed, rubbing calamine lotion on his ankles, dimpled and pink as a mewling newborn. "All that madness is as good as Casper the Friendly fucking ghost. I do healings for my people but that's between me and them. Can't say exactly where the power comes from, shit, I've always had that natural predilection."

He slathered calamine on himself at the slightest itch, a preemptive strike against the invisible regiment of fleas and tiny miscreants from the insect kingdom poised to devour his sensitive skin. He bruised easily and was always huffing, moist with anticipation of the next misguided query or plea from the throng of parishioners waiting expectantly after he finished his social gospel hour sermon.

She became his envoy. One of the ones he could count on to intercept visitors or new members who weren't properly educated on the church's rules. From six to twenty she'd been strictly Croatian Orthodox, reverent of the long cast off sect that her father cleaved to in defiance of her mother's grinding Catholicism. She was Jesus' shiny-eyed child. His fire lit the way for every major step in her life, smiting the turmoil of uncertainty when she decided to leave and go West.

Father, as the Reverend was called, was impressed with her moxie, her lack of a plan, the scrap and grit she'd shown traveling cross country by herself with no money and no connections. She'd lied about the arrangement with Uri but somehow he managed to find out, like any good oracle would. He just knew things, intuited them. He had a direct line to the secrets of the universe. That was what separated him from everybody else in the world. She saw how gently he treated even the casual seekers and newbies waiting in line to speak to him. Listening, counseling without judgment. Where her mother and father would smack her down as the dirty whore the Bible said she was, Father was patient, curious about every obscure nook and cranny of her young undistinguished life.

"I've got something to learn from everyone here," he said during an after-session when the crush of seekers was thickest, bouncing a black baby and a white baby on each knee. "Look at these little things. They're the wisest ones in the joint. Only Satan would defy me on that one. That is if he exists," he said to murmurs of delight, while skinny white women hovered over him with lemon tea and honey for his raw throat.

She got a position in the Temple kitchen doing home deliveries to shut-ins and the disabled. The hours were long but she enjoyed the work, relishing, in her loneliness, the chance to linger and talk to the older women who spoke vividly about their lives before and after joining the congregation. They hailed from all over the country. From the East Coast, to the Deep South to the Midwest; Father had stirred them preaching justice and equality. Now they had found a kindred home. Something about the rhythm of manual labor and conversation exhilarated her. The menial task of assembling the meals, packaging them, labeling them, moving them to the truck, clambering through the streets looking for addresses in the warren of little houses and apartments in the Fillmore district and temporarily beating back the looming dread of going back to Uri's cold miserable flat.

Father's lieutenants noticed her dedication, her attention to detail, the painstaking care she took with the elderly, their faces glowing when her truck pulled up to their curbs. Calls had been placed on her behalf, lauding her willingness to go above and beyond. How she drove an 85 year-old amputee to the hospital when an errant grandson didn't show. How she replaced the rubber no-slip pads in the bathtubs. How she changed the support hose of a woman who hadn't left her bed in six years.

Saint Mariah, one of the lieutenants dubbed her, acidly noting the growing length of her closed door sessions with Father. For four consecutive weeks she was the gold star employee, her quiet industriousness cited as a model for the church workforce, rippling with lazy jealousy. Anyone who was in favor with Father was in celestial orbit for awhile. For a short while until he'd rubbed their Achilles heel into blisters with gripes about how many hours Tom was putting into his work assignment versus slacking Dick and Harry.

Father was world-renowned for his healing powers. The first time Mariah saw the majesty of it the congregation was wilting from a plague of back-to-back days of freak ninety degree heat. Even the band couldn't thump enough to get a rise out of the dead sanctuary. Father stepped up and called for a laying on of hands. Somebody in here is aching, he said. Somebody in here needs me real bad. Somebody in here is trying to get to Canaan's Land without us.

A woman with sunken cheeks and a bowler hat clutched her side and came forward, moaning about a ruptured spleen. "It's keeping me up nights, Father. It's making me loony. None of the medicines the doctors gave me have made a darn bit of difference. I can't do anything with my grandbabies, can't walk like I used to, the Devil's going to run me into the ground and make me into a vegetable."

"Now we can't let him do that, can we? You still got a lot of life left in you, sister." The Reverend Jones turned to the congregation. "We can't let the devil have his way with this good woman, can we?" He spread his big red hands on the end of the pulpit and rocked it back and forth. "Shame on the devil," he said, pensively. "The devil, as you've heard me say, is only as big and as mean as you make him. When you're struggling look into yourselves people. Look deep in and see what kind of affliction of the heart, mind and soul is troubling you and making outward manifestations of sickness rot your bodies. This sister has maybe a ruptured spleen, maybe an ulcer, got some kind of gastrointestinal madness down in deep that's eating at her. It's not just her problem it's all our problem as a family, as a community to deal with. But the Lords of Capital don't want you to see it that way. Hell, they don't want you to even see her. Far as they're concerned she's a burden, a modern-day leper, or, how do they say in the parlors of the Rockefellers' tenth country house in Switzerland—a symbol of the permissiveness of the welfare state. She's a leech to those who've never done an honest day's work in their entire lives. And man, wouldn't it be nice to earn one hundred K every second for just taking a shit ... You walk from the counting room to the crapper and presto! You've made one hundred thousand dollars in interest quicker than I can say bullshit.

Who's taking account of *that* up in "heaven"? Which one of "God's" bookkeepers is keeping score on that heresy? There shouldn't be a world in which our sister here can't afford half a hospital bed and the DuPont's are cranking out Monopoly money and salting away in Swiss bank accounts! No way, no how, it's damn obscene!"

When he finished the congregation rose to its feet; little kids, old women, gangly bearded young white men in barely starched button down shirts, a row of amputees in wheelchairs waiting for their bite at the apple. An ecstatic tremor from the first pew to the last.

Mariah bonded cautiously with these people, instinctively attracted to the weakest and neediest. She'd prayed to God to make her interest in them innocent, but she knew it was not. If her messages to Him went deep enough she would be delivered from the superiority, the satisfaction she got from being the savior when relatives slacked, friends evaporated and doctors failed. They took her face in their hands and called her their sweet angel. They waited for her with tins of special treats. The darkest Negro woman she'd ever seen stroked her lustrous hair with tenderness, awe coiled up in her like a wet spring.

"You're like the Spanish flamenco doll I had as a child. Had alabaster cheeks and jet black hair and deep dark brown eyes you could stare into for days."

Around the old Negro ladies Mariah was careful to wear her hair down so she could see their eyes glitter when she came in. Wondering in bed at night if it was envy or contempt. Being in the company of so many of them regularly was a new exciting phenomenon. Some buzzed with disdain, asserting independence. But administering to their needs was her passport, the only safe bet she could make on the strange ambition clawing at the pit of her stomach. She saw the way that Father looked at them, the way he treated them with care and dignity during the services. He opened his arms and took them in, while the world treated them like the damned. She knew that she must make them the bedrock of her work day, shuffling from residence to residence, meal to meal, bedpan to bedpan, keeping her ear to the ground for the next opportunity to be bumped up the ladder.

The first time she met alone with Father, it was to discuss the organization of the home meal delivery program and how soon to start serving the two hundred new members he'd recently recruited from black churches in Richmond and Oakland.

"Call me Jim," he whispered, modest, eyes cast downward, polar opposite of the fury he exuded from the pulpit, dark helmet hair quivering with its own velocity. His humility moved her to speak in an octave lower than normal. The Minnie Mouse semi-whine with a perpetual question curlicueing at the end of her sentences disappeared, and Mariah teetered along a tightrope of fitful confidence, gobbling down his praise. Only she had the capacity to make the program a crowning success. Only she could integrate the new people in seamlessly, ensure that their dietary requests were heeded.

"Saturated fat is killing black people. It's poisoning the ghettoes," Jim said, slurping down a macrobiotic shake. "That shit is just another form of corporate anesthesia, salted down and cheesed up. You know what a Big Mac does to your frontal lobe, Mariah?"

"Uh no," she stammered.

"I suggest you study up on it."

The meals program would take the edge off her homesickness and doubt; provide the sticky sweet glue for the dedication Father demanded in exchange for the church's soothing embrace.

"One more thing. You should beware of all that hair," he said, brushing a few moist strands from her forehead as she sat next to him sifting through a pile of grocery receipts. "It's a potential curse, an albatross. It will bring you down with covetous men and jealous women. They'll look at you and that's all they'll see. They'll eat you alive in their minds and fuck you to death with their eyes and our message will be neutered. Cut it."

He said no one should be attached to the temporary shine of this world. The cars, the homes, the TVs, the clothes, the trappings and pacifiers of a comfortable life were mental parasites sapping the radical impulse. His impulse was towards socialism, a curse word to her parents.

He lived simply with his wife and children on the top floor of one of the stately nineteenth century brownstones the church had bought and rehabbed. Ten families were crammed into four units, the building festering with the pell-mell energy of multiple generations. The church promoted communal living. It provided more social cohesion and stability among the membership, Jim said. Rent and three square meals a day in the church's cavernous basement were free, but it was understood that all income, Social Security, disability benefits, veteran's benefits and work salaries would flow to the gatekeepers, the Planning Commission church trustees who scrupulously invested every penny to make the dream of utopia possible.

She used to look forward to her paycheck on every second and fourth Friday. Now her yearnings for the diversions that she bought—movies, cherry soda, pinball at the arcade on the wharf—made her tingle with shame at her selfish juvenile fixations.

She moved into an apartment with toothpick thin Carol Phelps, the head of the Planning Commission, and two other vaporous white women who worked sixteen hour days in the church-owned Laundromat. Like many of the elite guard, Carol had left her privileged left-leaning white family and immersed herself in service to the Temple, having coasted into activism with a background of international travel to the Alps, impressionist summer art camps, Marcuse lectures and aid missions to starving children in Biafra.

As the new roommate, still low on the totem pole of church staff, Mariah was uninitiated into the women's byzantine rites of conduct. The persnickety arrangement of soap and towels in the bathroom. The precise order for drying dishes. The purchase of toiletries and feminine hygiene items that everyone could use equally. Niggling transactions all monitored, noted then dissected in Planning Commission meetings.

Carol preferred sanitary napkins to tampons. When Mariah brought a package home, she snarled that she wouldn't shove those dirty little things up inside her because everyone knew they caused crabs. She ruled the house with paramilitary cool, talking sisterhood and tolerance in one breath and snickering about the ingrates and knuckle-draggers at the laundry the next.

Her room was a dead white sanctum, denuded of all personal effects, the detritus of past mementoes shackling her to her other phantom life as the shy, wallflower daughter of Norwegian immigrants. Anyone who didn't get up as early as she did was a slacker, fucked up, shiftless, insufficiently dedicated to "The Cause".

"It's a crime to waste an hour to sleep when there's all this work to do," she said, stacking up the chipped breakfast dishes. "But I understand some people need more rest. They get recharged from sleep, but hell—I just lie awake thinking of what's next."

There was always a sliver of light at the bottom of her bedroom door, strains of Procol Harum, Traffic or Jefferson Airplane filching from the thin walls. She bragged about knowing Classical Spanish guitar, doing fingerings on tables, chairs, her arm, carrying a pocket tape recorder on her at all times, ostensibly to listen to music or dictate mental notes in a rare lull.

But Mariah caught her taping their small talk when the four of them were hanging out in the common area. The tape shut off with a loud click in the back of her pants pocket. Their ears pricked collectively. The other women went quiet as Mariah shifted in her seat.

"Are you taping us, Carol?"

"No, but what if I was?"

"This is our personal space, our *private* time. Why would you do that?"

"I said I wasn't, Mariah. You have a really bad habit of belaboring things. Instead of projecting your paranoia onto me you should be more worried about your ability to pull your own weight around here."

"What are you talking about?"

"I'm talking about your habit of expecting others to do your work for you. Many of us work long hours at the Temple and when we come home, we expect the schedule we've all mutually agreed on to be followed. You shouldn't expect to be cleaned up after like a child."

"I don't … I'm not. When have I not cleaned up after myself? And I work just as long as you do at the laundry, plus I'm managing the meals program for three different cities. The leadership has recognized me and I'm going to be up for a promotion soon."

Carol grew still. She got up from her seat and reached into her pocket, pulling the tape recorder out. "The milk expired yesterday. Were you aware? The milk expired and the dishes were left in the rack for two days. You were supposed to have taken care of that stuff."

Sally coughed, embarrassed for Mariah, as Carol went on. "We thought you might be considerate enough to consult our list of allergies and off-limits items before you buy things. We all came here from long distances, different backgrounds, different life experiences and nobody should feel superior, should feel that they can outshine anyone else for petty bullshit like what they wear, or what race they are, or how long and beautiful they think their hair is."

Carol and Sally looked at Mariah. Allison, the other roommate, who worked in the Temple daycare, kept her eyes down on the table, channeling all her energy and attention into a crumpled packet of green Jello.

"I heard that Father made a suggestion to you about what to do with that hair."

"That was between him and me. It's nobody else's business."

"No, it's everyone's business. You're in the shower longer washing that hair. It clogs up the drain. Soon we'll have to get a plumber in here to deal with it. That's extra time and money."

A baby cockroach skittered down the napkin holder and Allison suddenly came alive, smashing it with the tissue in her hand.

She got up and threw it in the trash. "I sorta agree, Mariah," she remarked, fingering the stumpy brown braid sticking out from her head. "Maybe you weren't there when Father was preaching on it a few weeks ago, but it's really just a bunch of bourgeois bullshit wearing your hair that long."

The neighbor kids were jumping Double Dutch outside in the courtyard that connected their building with the one next door. The four women listened for a moment to the syncopated rhythm, the clip clop of the girls' feet reverberating against the swish of cars pausing at the stop sign on the corner.

Carol smiled gingerly and leaned back in her chair, legs crossed, a bony sliver of ankle peeking from the bottom cuff of her frayed jeans. The girls pounded hard, chanting:

Five little monkeys jumping on the bed, one fell off and bumped his head. Mama called the doctor and the doctor said, no more monkeys jumping on the bed.

"Such a beautiful sound to hear on an ordinary day. I couldn't jump rope to save my life. I was always the klutz missing the beat and getting tangled up in it. To jump like that, with such joy." Carol got up from the table, shaking her head. "What I wouldn't give to go back there. No worries, no cares in the world."

She walked across the room and opened one of the counter drawers, taking out a pair of scissors. "Here, use these tonight," she said, handing them to Mariah. "No one needs all that hair to feel like a real woman."

Taryn & Hy
Fillmore, San Francisco 1975

The first sound Hy heard every morning was the man in the next door unit running in place. At 7:00 like clockwork the running began; disciplined, droning, obliterating her need for an alarm. It was rumored by the mailbox gossips that he'd been a champion marathoner for the East German Olympic team. Then a double agent who'd defected and was now working security for Peoples Temple church. After Taryn was hired by the accounting firm they'd gotten a tip on the apartment from one of her co-workers. A few months later the Peoples Temple Planning Commission had started managing the building, challenging rent increases by the owner, a corporate developer out of Seattle.

Most of the residents were fastidiously quiet, keeping to themselves with the polite mien of charm school children. A mixed family of eight lived right above them, the mother wrapping leftover meat scraps, gristle and bone in the front page with Gerald Ford's face on it, the kids divvying them up in the backyard to the roving pack of neighborhood mutts.

The front window looked onto a vacant lot piled with mattresses arranged fort style by the kids. For three blissful hours in the morning light streamed through the side windows, receding into gray at noon, when the toddlers upstairs scampered into the kitchen for their piglet feedbag of peanut butter and jelly and banana.

Hy burrowed into the throwaway papers for jobs; clerical, telemarketing, dog walking, anything. She wasted twenty dollars applying to an envelope-stuffing scam guaranteed to net thousands for housewives looking for supplemental income. Her calls to the local retail stores went unreturned, applications tossed into the circular file. She spent her afternoons kicked back on the stoop wrecking her teeth with Orange Crush, voracious with envy of anyone that had a job, who could justify waking from the dank clot of dreams that quicksanded her into the green flea magnet sofa the previous tenant had bequeathed them.

She wrote up a schedule and put it on the refrigerator so Taryn could see she was being productive. Shit yeah she was planning, researching, organizing, taking charge of the slow grind of mind over matter and not just flitting aimlessly from whim to whim.

She made sure to be out when Taryn came back home at 6 o'clock, mapping out all the libraries that were a short bus ride from the apartment, ranking the ones with the most comfortable chairs, the least snoopy attendants and the fewest mutinous white blond kids running amuck from their cooing mothers. The local library crawled with a plague of children underfoot in the stacks, fighting for stuffed animals and knick knacks, pawing at the brightly colored pop-up books the librarians put on display in the new readers' section.

It was kids and idle men, eyes boring into her over withered stacks of *Sports Illustrated*. Every wastrel in the city seemed to watch from the card catalogue. Leches in league with the library interns who glowered by the paperback carousel, judging her shiftless and drifting like the rest of the reading room fixtures.

The one clear saving grace about moving to the city besides the milder weather was the streetcars that tied each end of the bay together in a bow. From the back cars she could see all the neighborhoods unfold in kaleidoscope. From the shiny Nob Hill citadels to the weathered gaze of Peoples Temple's Geary Street church. Every morning she followed the labor negotiations between the transit union and the mayor's office. A strike would strand her, stifling her escape from the slow sucking death of sharing the tiny apartment with Taryn. Ever since Taryn started her job she'd horded the car, unilaterally deciding that drives during the week were a dangerous extravagance given their budget.

"You spend so much time in the library," she proclaimed, "have you tried asking them about openings? They've got plenty of people working there without a degree, part-time students and the like doing filing."

"It's a dead-end."

"Well, have you asked?"

"Yeah, yeah, of course."

"'Cause once you get in, you're eligible for employment throughout the entire system."

"Which means Big Brother is watching you."

"God, Hy, that's dumb. If you get hired by the city you get more opportunities at other jobs. That's all I'm saying."

Taryn opened the front blinds onto the street. A man was submerged under the hood of a parked car at the curb, sweaty torso gleaming in the sun. An ice cream truck jingled at the end of the block, as waves of children stormed past the window to catch it on scooters, skates, bikes. The man jerked out from under the hood and wiped his forehead with his t-shirt, watching the procession dazedly, fingernails shellacked with motor oil.

"Andy get me an Eskimo pie!" He yelled, cupping his hands to his mouth.

"Say it don't spray it!" A girl on a ten-speed retorted back to him.

"He's like fucking neighborhood watch. Always on duty," Hy said.

"Seems unemployed. These damn amateur mechanics like this corner for some reason."

"They throw all their messed up tools into the lot over there. I think he's one of those Temple commune people."

"No. Not him. Word is they have a problem with letting gay men who're out into their shit. At least when it comes to the leadership."

"What do you base that on?"

"A rumor from a guy in the office who got involved and left because it was too strict on the men. Said something about certain men being stigmatized as too oversexed."

"I take it lesbians are ok then?"

Taryn looked at her annoyed. Hy had never been supportive of Taryn's love of women, her few fleeting relationships through the years having aroused a studied territorialism in her sister. She ignored the dig, pulling the curtain back on the window to watch the scene outside.

"That mechanic guy is always hovering like the Pied Piper of Hamlin with that entourage of little urchins of his." She paused, taking her nylons off and resting them on the radiator. "You look at the listings in the Laundromat? Sometimes they have ads for babysitters tacked up on the boards."

"Yes, I looked. For the hundredth time. None of those white bitches want a skinny black woman looking after their brats. They want Hattie McDaniel so they can pay cheap and play Scarlett."

Taryn pursed her lips and rolled her socks into a tight ball, digging her feet into the matted carpet. "Have you even called any of the listings? Or have you psychically determined that everybody who puts up an ad in the laundromat is a white bitch?"

"I can tell by the last names, the prefixes. No Negroes live in Pacific Heights or Nob Hill. That's delusional."

35

"Is it delusional to want you to be self-sufficient, to get a job that pays something, as opposed to floating around here all day eavesdropping on the neighbors?"

"I have a schedule. I enrolled in those two community college classes but they're packed with assholes just trying to get financial aid. Just 'cause I don't want to bust my ass cleaning shit off toilets doesn't mean I'm not looking."

"But yet, those that are cleaning shit off toilets are getting a paycheck every week, while you're sitting here railing about white bitches. Right now you've got to take what you can get, take the classes, transfer to a four year college, get your degree, then you'll be able to reject the menial stuff." She went into the kitchen and peered into the refrigerator, methodically taking out tortillas, cheese and a container of sour cream. "Think of it as an endurance test. Like holding your breath underwater. You were always good at that."

The cool tang of chlorine slithered up Hy's nose, as her frog fingers spread out before her and she dove down to get the lost treasure on the floor of the white people's pool in blistering Indianapolis. The white financier's family opened their yard to underprivileged Negroes once a week during the summer. They were all enthralled by the way Hy willed herself to be an amphibian; so titillating an entertainment that a young Negro knew how to swim. The father of the house threw car keys into the bottom of the pool. Whichever sister fetched them first got an ice cream cone served up fresh in his study.

Hy snorted. Drawing the sound out in the way that she knew got on Taryn's nerves. Taryn ignored her, putting a frying pan on the stove, turning on the burner. The grindingly familiar clatter of the upstairs neighbors streaming out from the bus and into the building pierced the air, making Hy's skin crawl with an abject, bottomless hatred of oblivious humanity.

"Motherfucker," she whispered. "This place is so loud."

"I saw a flyer at work from the independent mayoral candidate advertising for paid canvassers. Why don't you call them up before all the slots get filled?"

"I hate saying canned scripts a million times. Knocking on doors, talking to old people and shut-ins, that shit's tedious."

Taryn laid the tortilla in the pan to fry, one eye on a trail of ants marching between the pineapple shaped magnets on the refrigerator. The Planning Commission had promised to send an exterminator but a month had passed and the insect kingdom still conspired in the kitchen and bathroom.

"I think you'd be good at canvassing; talking to people about issues that is," Taryn said. "Even if it is a spiel you can improvise, liven it up, get your feet wet in that world. It wouldn't hurt contacts-wise either. You could contribute more around here. Who knows, maybe it could lead to something."

She took the fried tortilla out of the pan and spread sour cream over it. The entryway door opened and shut, as residents wrenched open their mailboxes, rifled through the junk circulars, propped up strollers and bikes along the back of the staircase for the evening. Someone shoved a piece of paper under their front door.

Hy picked it up and skimmed over the short message. Five sentences in the bold industrial font of a practicing typist. "The Temple is officially buying the building," she said.

"So that's why we've been seeing more of their folk moving in here."

"Doesn't say anything about a rent change or whether somebody's going to come out here and exterminate these bugs."

Taryn motioned for Hy to give her the notice. "The upside is they'll make sure our rent doesn't jack up sky high. I've read that they're buying up other buildings to expand, so this makes sense. I'll call tomorrow to check it out."

Hy shook her head. "Sounds like another land grab. A church empire or something. They're probably scheming to put us right on top of the eviction list because we're not part of the faithful."

"That's not going to happen. The Temple is one of Malloy's special clients. I work with their people sometimes on returns and claims. They're generally straight shooters, not like those Podunk Iowa televangelists raking in millions. Most of the stuff they do is community-based, like food drives, providing free medical screening, leading protests. They got their people out to rally against all those thug police murderers in the East Bay right before we moved here."

"Good," Hy said, throwing the notice in the trash. "Just as long as they don't fuck with us."

CHAPTER 4

The Prophet, Indianapolis, 1946

FRIDAY'S WERE PLASTIC slipcovers pinching Jim's ass as he sat in Prophet Zeke's living room waiting for the Joe Louis fight to go off the radio, romanced by the smell of bacon and greens stir frying in a cast iron skillet. Friday's were women in impeccably pressed updos and clip-on heirloom earrings, bending down to serve the men, starched button down shirts pent up with secrecy. Friday's were the Prophet's boys scrubbed siren bright in pin-striped suits synchronizing their anodyne smiles in the sanctuary mirror.

The Prophet had built the congregation soul by soul, sniffing out sickness, marital conflict, firings, and missing children like a bloodhound in heat. Going door-to-door with his dusty King James and gold scepter to steady his bad knee, he sprinkled scripture with tales of landing at Normandy with his all-Negro regiment. A do-right man married to the same woman for forty-five years and not a dime of government subsidy, his valor swallowed up in doing outhouse detail for a cracker's greasy spoon. His parting salvo was to never wait for what the white man is going to do next.

"You'd do just as good waiting for the devil. It'll lead you to wreck, ruin and derangement. The only thing that's promised to us as Negro people is hard work, suffering and a small helping of glory on the side if we're man enough to fight it. Positive or negative, don't look to the white man. That's Satan's path."

In the city, Prophet Zeke's Divine Global Ministries was a power on the north side. It had four Sunday services—members seated on one side of the aisle, newcomers on the other; truth seekers, skeptics, throwaway paper journalists and those who came to lap up the cheap entertainment with a biscuit straight from Jesus.

The seating arrangement made it easier for church volunteers to divvy up and categorize the proceeds from the collection plate. Phone banking for new contributors began at 9 am sharp Monday morning. Follow-up calls to congregants at 12:30 after lunch. Each envelope had a prayer check-off box and a price. Higher contributions got a premium personal prayer from Prophet and the Misses. Lower tithes netted a prayer wish from deacons, ushers, Sunday school youth or auxiliary members. The Prophet made sure that there was something for everybody, everywhere, 24/7 365. Where other churches shut down Tuesday to Saturday, Divine Global Ministries was a ubiquitous machine, a power, a visceral force wormed into city council meetings, bar dives, dance clubs and bridge groups.

The Prophet had clawed his way to the top of the Negro bourgeoisie's food chain. He bought two old Tudor homes on Spook Hill and had them razed to build a health center. It became a revolving door for runaways, manic depressives, and terminally ill patients who pored over the barrage of tonics and good luck charms sold in the commissary for the slightest shred of hope.

Zeke and Mother P took all of the city's Negro wayward under their wing, founding a separate institute for faith healing, peddling intricate training techniques for the laying on of hands to aspiring preachers looking for a niche market. It was their policy that no one be denied treatment even if it was suspected that they were part of a rival congregation sniffing for dirt or trying to steal the Prophet's methodologies.

The Prophet did five healings every service. Taking the smaller ailments, the niggling aches and arthritic pains of the elders first; climaxing with big ticket cancers and deformities that would whip the crowd into a chanting, dancing frenzy.

Jim watched it all from his favorite spot in the balcony. After the first month, the novelty of his silent white boy shadowing had worn off, and everyone but the children had stopped giving him wary once-overs and lingering stares, accepting him as one of the Prophet's many pet projects.

At the downtown movie halls the Negroes could only sit in the balconies for matinees, pretending to piss on the heads of the delicate white flowers below. On the rare occasions Jim had money to go, he tucked his baseball cap down on his head and stole up to what the crackers called nigger heaven; dodging the zealous teenage ushers, nestling in a seat by the railing as he waited to be enveloped by the flood of the cartoons. In the darkness he could slip in unnoticed and unmolested, savor the anonymity of mistaken identity. For sixty blissful minutes he could be a ghost emissary from another world. Thoughts of his parents, the cage of his tiny room at the cramped apartment receded into the drunken squeals of thumb-slurping kindergartners gaga over Woody Woodpecker.

He had formally asked to be the Prophet's apprentice, reveling in the odd jobs that gave him a chance to see the city, delivering balms to dying patients, gathering life histories from the motley gaggle of invalids the deacons scrounged up for Sunday healing bonanzas. At first he did most of his errands on foot, ignoring the sneers from the row houses, the ancients in their walkers gawking down from screened-in porches, the women sucking their teeth at yet another green ass white motherfucker come through there sniffing around the ghetto for prostitutes like they were all jungle whores.

He started carrying his Bible and a tin of ginger snaps as insurance, flashing a big Pepsodent grin to disarm passing skeptics. He smeared Crisco on his hair to make it blacker and slicker to accentuate his wannabe Indian-ness, and fantasized that the corner boys playing stickball itched to jump every bone in his white body.

Before he left in the morning he made sure he was correct: shirt collar, pants, black socks, clip-on tie starched and creased to a crisp. Shoes buffed to gleaming out of respect for his position as a representative of Divine Global. Above all he was there to lift up the Prophet's reputation, the delicate business of saving souls. He imagined spies watching him, scrutinizing his clothes and conduct for the slightest deviation.

He loved the Lord, but guarded his stealth desire, the dull insinuating ache for the fat earlobes of Aaron Vincent, the allergy-ridden know-it-all who sat in front of him at the Wednesday evening recitation and discourse for junior deacons. Aaron loved to argue First Corinthians and Timothy, teetering around the room on his tiptoes, declaiming with zeal about why women should be seen but not heard in the church. He was constantly trying to outshine the others, special animus saved for Jim, the white interloper. Jim just sat back and let him grandstand, imagining the earlobes as Christmas ornaments tinkling under his tree.

"It's a sin to have a woman speak before mixed congregations. The Bible lays it out clearly. You don't want to mess with that. If it wasn't true, you wouldn't see the natural divisions in all human societies and civilizations, the way men and women act differently, are built differently, want different things."

"What kind of mess are you talking?" Mother P said, sticking her head in the room. All the women deferred to Mother P, imitating her Marshall Fields' wardrobe on less than a shoestring, smearing their faces with foundation two shades too light to capture the golden glint of her Hollywood skin. When she did her ritual walk down the aisle at the beginning of Sunday sermon she tossed out rose petals from a basket while the women devoured every strand of fried hair, wisp of chiffon and crinkle of white lace. Mother P called the flowers her rose petals of peace and women strained to catch some for good luck and longevity.

They sucked up all the mincing pageantry to her face; but ripped her vain pirouettes and legendary stinginess behind her back. The hand-me-down clothes she tried to pawn off on poorer congregants, the compulsive penny-pinching of toilet paper, soap, napkins, kitchen plastics.

"Mother P is a national treasure," Zeke said. "She keeps Divine Global balanced and in the black. She ain't nobody's rib. She's an equal partner, a beacon in the night of womanhood, the financial brains that's keeping this boat afloat. She could've gone to Yale in mathematics but there was no money for poor Colored women from Greenville, Miss in the twenties. She helped me build this empire from scratch with no formal education or book learning. Due to her counsel with the Lord, we now have three women's auxiliaries ministering to the poor and the sick around the clock."

On cue ushers bowed their heads in unison, snapping their white gloves in salute. The women's attraction-repulsion flowed through the sanctuary as Mother P ascended the stage, sat on a blue velvet throne and looked down at them beneficently, smoothing her raiment around her with maximum pomp.

An attendant handed her a microphone and she leaned forward, spitting into it in a disciplined rasp, "There's evil in the hearts of some of you in the first row now I can feel it. Umm, I can smell it. There's virtue in the hearts of some of you in the second row now I can feel it. Yes, I can smell it. Second row turn to the first row and say good morning sister-brother praise God we can lick this evil. As children of Father and Mother Prophet we can lick this evil. As a family united in the eyes of the Lord we can lick this evil. As a tribe united against sin and hate we can lick this evil. As a nation rising up in response to God's call we can lick it. Second row trade places with the first row and let me see your shining beautiful faces ready to serve Divine Global's mission for the Lord. First row know that we have a lot of work to be done and the road is long, hard and rough but if you let Him know your evil intentions, He can save you from the Devil's workshop of idleness and sloth."

The first row was filled with large donors, assorted relatives and career sycophants who got Zeke an honorary chairmanship on the United Negro Insurance board. But it was well known to a select few that Mother P's speech was intended for the woman sitting in the front row who gave Zeke spiritual massages to help ease his arthritis. It was well known that he had a succession of spiritualists who serviced him from head to toe; that he and Mother P secretly dueled with each other to see who had the most captive, cunning and unswervingly loyal entourage of incurable gossips and obsessives; that being a magnet for the lost and the searching was a burden of greatness which he, and she, by extension, would have to bear for their entire lives. It was said that after the birth of his youngest son the Prophet's penis shriveled down to a peanut and he and Mother took solemn vows of celibacy.

"For the good of the family and the congregation I sacrifice my earthly self to be divvied up into a million little pieces."

Fatigued to the bone he was in perpetual demand as a speaker, as a source of gentle motivation for the undecided Negro voters in the city's limp electorate. Every March and November the aldermen shuttled him from event to event so he could bless the proceedings. Jim and the foot soldiers ate their rubber chicken dinners in the basement, ears cocked for the last speech, fanning out like roaches amongst the politicians to ensure the unimpeded flow of plump donation checks to the church building fund.

"Our jewel in the crown for 1948 is the construction of thirty new senior housing units, each equipped with individual bathrooms, box fans in every window, no-slip bars in the tubs and the best heating system in modern history."

Every week Jim assumed a new responsibility, edging up in Divine Global's brain trust. His whiteness diminished as a barrier. He wondered if his mother would be pleased. Church inner workings repelled her, so he omitted the details of his escapades from their night chats. At ten o'clock she came back from the fruit canning plant stretching her stumpy legs out on his bed in a sprung coil of hyped up exhaustion, their time together a precious island.

She had become shop steward after the company threatened to fire any women they suspected of being pregnant. The prior steward had been a spy for management, snooping around watching for signs of nausea and fatigue. Who was getting fat around the middle, who was running to the toilet to pee every fifteen minutes. Who was potentially knocked up and resisting the operations manager's back office gropes.

"I tell these new girls to keep their traps shut and not blab to every-body about their business ... They'll just as soon sell their grandmoth-ers to the highest bidder if it was going to get them ahead. These same men you see sitting up in the Methodist church praying and carrying on turn right around and rape and pillage at work. Big men crushing ants, acting like the universe was made in their image, making a mockery of what it means to be a man."

After years of working at the plant her ankles were swollen with edema. He massaged them with one of Zeke's special rosemary and eucalyptus elixirs, nodding rhythmically to her loud soliloquies. As thin as the walls were, they never woke Big Jim. The more active she became in the union, the more he receded into reveries about scoring big with cockfighting, telling everyone in the apartment building that he was grooming his own animals for national competition.

Jim's mother Odessa ignored him, shuttling from her makeshift bed in the bathtub to work in a cloud of deep disdain. "I don't ever want to catch you being a deadbeat that way Jim," she declared. "Contributing to the overpopulation problems of this world by swinging your pistol around indiscriminately. The Negro and Spanish women making less than us at the plant have it ten times worse. They only pop babies out because no one's talked to them about birth control or spacing their procreation."

"You think there's a conspiracy, mother?"

"Conspiracy about what?"

"To-to keep them down like that."

"Speak slowly, James. If you speak slowly and deliberately your tongue won't get caught with that stuttering."

"Ok."

"All you have to do is look around you and see who gets stuck in the rat slums with no electricity. You can't expect people to do better and improve their lot if you don't give them a decent way of life."

"One of the boys in my class is going to college through that new government program for the soldiers."

"Good for him. If the government can help them get that crazy Nazi-killing mentality out of their heads then all the better."

"I think I can get a scholarship through one of the churches in town."

"That means they're good for something then."

"Why did you and Pa never go to church?"

"Why? To be lectured to by a bunch of illiterate fools about fairy tales while they line their pockets with my money? Getting mixed up in theology is a waste of your talent, boy. Anyone with the right amount of cunning can master it, throw up a storefront and rope in the herd. Preaching is a lazy man's game. The kind of brilliant mind you got you need more rigor."

"It's not a lazy man's game. Prophet has three degrees from different colleges and universities. He's been to Africa and Asia on missions, knows how to speak Cantonese, or at least I think that's what I heard him speaking. He developed a special ministry for amputees coming back from the war."

"So he's a learned man and a saint."

"H-he's a g-good man."

She pointed to her mouth. "Calm down, son. Take a breath before you speak. I didn't mean to suggest none of them are good. Just that you should beware, should question would-be miracle workers. I understand that this Prophet of yours has a beautiful home with a wrought iron gate around it."

He nodded.

"Have you been inside?"

"Yes."

"And why does a prophet need an iron gate around his house? To keep out god's children? To make sure other Negroes in the neighborhood, the cursed ones, same flesh and blood as him, don't steal the riches he got from his worldly travels?"

"They're not cursed."

"What?"

"Negroes aren't cursed."

"What word would you use James to describe the misery that those people have been allotted?"

He paused, breathing from his stomach as she'd instructed. His father shuffled out from his room to take a leak.

"I don't know."

She sat up, pointing to her ankle, pain in her eyes. "Can your prophet heal this?"

"I think so. I've seen him work on people with all kinds of cancers. A deaf man who'd never spoken before got up all the sudden from one of the back pews in the church and started reciting the Gettysburg Address."

The toilet flushed down the hallway. She pressed her hands together in mock prayer. "Can Prophet tell me when your father is going to die?"

He spent all morning after church crafting a makeshift altar from a shipping crate and blankets. Then he made a size 12 shoe box into a casket big enough to fit the ferret's dead body, his mother's bathrobe pulled around his neck like a cape. Today would be the send off for the dearly departed animal, and he needed an audience. There was a group of orphan kids that he'd been watching for awhile, a posse he always seemed to run into whenever he made his rounds for Divine Global. He lured them into the barn with the promise of cigarettes. The four of them lazed around on the hay bales relishing forbidden hits. Elijah, Calvin, Skeeter and Blimpo; voices cracking between boyhood and manhood as they snickered about farts, girls and aborted acts of bestiality. He had sized up Blimpo as the most malleable, Elijah as the resident skeptic, and Calvin as all-around apathetic, his duck eyes only flickering to life around food or baseball cards.

Solemnly, he gave the ferret last rites befitting an emperor.

"What does ferret hell look like, Jones?" Elijah chortled.

"C'mon Jones, raise him from the dead!" Blimpo yelled.

Calvin took a drag and handed the cigarette to Skeeter. "Yeah, you such a genius, make his spirit talk!"

"Sorta looks like your grandmother, with the greasy little whiskers," Skeeter said to Jim, pinching the zit on his chin.

Jim threw an empty pack of cigarettes at Skeeter. "Fuck you," he spat.

"When I die then I'm dead and in the ground and that's it," Elijah said.

Calvin rolled his eyes. "Naw, there's gotta be something that happens."

"Who says?"

"Plenty of people, genius. The Bible, that book the Indians use, most of the world."

Jim sprinkled holy oil over the shoebox casket, motioning for them to be silent. "Shut your fucking traps, blasphemers. You want this animal to come back when you're asleep tonight and roust your asses from your pissy little wet dreams? Being human don't mean you're superior to any other living thing on God's green earth. They got just as much of a right to safe passage into the next world as any of us."

"And how're you gonna know they get there, Reverend Jim?" Blimpo sneered. "God talking to you? He keeping you warm at night?"

Skeeter went into one of the empty stalls to relieve himself and Blimpo counted down as he peed, whooping when he hit the ten second mark. He lurched over to the altar and picked up the shoebox, dumping the ferret's stiff twisted body onto the ground.

"Oh look! This bitch was about to have some babies!"

Elijah poked at its stomach with a stick. "No shit. You the daddy Jones?"

Jim stepped toward them, the cape flapping at his ankles in tatters. "A ferret isn't a bitch. That defies logic son. Just like a human female can never be one unless she stoops and degrades herself like your mother did when she had you."

"I don't have a mother, asshole."

"How did you get here then? A turnip truck? Parthenogenesis? Every mammal has a mother. Few more years of evolution though will probably make daddies obsolete. You all better multiply while you can. Spread your seeds before that shit dries up and becomes unusable."

He picked the ferret up by the tail and put it back in the box. "Yes, this poor beast was about to have a litter."

Elijah snorted. "So you accepting paternity?"

"Matter of fact I am. Remember that when you wake up in the middle of the night and start itching. Might be one of this 'bitch's' hatchlings giving you a love bite."

Skeeter's fingers crept self-consciously up the side of his neck, raw from scratching and rubbing. He was one of the syndrome babies born after a chemical explosion polluted the water supply near the homes just off Imperial Way. All of the "syndromes" had skin conditions and epic fits of itching.

Jim looked sympathetically at Skeeter. "What if I told you I could get rid of all that crap?"

"How?"

"Keeps you up at night does it?"

"How are you going to get rid of it?"

"He ain't," Elijah interjected, kicking at a hay bale. "Bright boy thinks he's sanctified. You don't fucking fool me with that black magic shit."

"Who said I was trying to fool you, asshole? I know you sleep on your back with the night light on to ward off asthma attacks."

"Who told you that? How'd you fucking know?"

"Sleeping in that position ain't gonna help you, son. There's no cure in medical science for your condition. Here." He stretched his hand out to Elijah and gave him a few brown colored pills.

"Take this and give some to Skeeter there."

"What's this?"

"Sleep aids to help with your nocturnal afflictions. They'll knock you out like a baby and have you up on your toes in the morning all brand new."

"They stink."

"It ain't milk and cookies, son. You too much of a pussy to swallow something that smells bad? The worse it smells the better you'll feel. One pill before bed at night with a pinch of sugar and it'll keep away all that panting nastiness you dream about that makes you cum in the sheets."

The boys cackled.

Jim grinned and stroked the ferret's twisted ribcage. "That's right, cum! The stuff you spend half your life thinking about, beating off to squeeze out. Wouldn't it be nice to be like this little fucker here? Never having to be obsessed with that madness eating you up inside? In the

49

animal kingdom the females go in heat and you just do it. Over and done with. None of this torture about a piece of ass you can't have. Sounds like heaven don't it Blimpo?"

"Maybe."

"Remember boys," Jim said quietly, a crease of amusement on his dusty forehead. "God has a plan for everything. Nothing, not a single solitary thing is left to chance. You being here at this second, this moment—it's all part of it."

"That what that nigger preacher teach you?" Elijah asked. He snapped his fingers at the boys, motioning for them to leave, then walked over to the altar and snatched off Jim's cape.

"This'll make a good dish rag for our foster mother Miz Carter. *That's* in God's plan."

He balled the cloth up into his fist and started walking out, the rest of the boys falling into line behind him like a drill troop. Jim watched them go. He took some matches out of his pocket, lit one and set the ferret on fire, his penis stirring inside his pants as the flames grabbed at the rafters.

CHAPTER 5

The Temple, San Francisco, 1975

IT WAS ONLY Mrs. Townes' second Sunday at the Temple. Now she stood before the congregation at the microphone in her best Dinah Washington wig and crushed satin chrysanthemum hat.

"And I said to the Lord Father Jesus, take me now! Ten years with the pain and sleeplessness, take me now! Medical bills piling up and the collections people hounding, calling at all hours. Take me now, take me now, take me now! I went to all the clinics and straight up begged to be treated the pain was so bad. They wanted to pack me off to an old folks' home down in Augusta Georgia. I tell you that was no better than putting horses out to pasture! There is such goodness in this room I can feel it! Women that have suffered like I've suffered I can see it! Children that want to lay down and die for their mothers, they're in so much pain. I can feel it! When I was down in Los Angeles at this Presbyterian hospital they strapped me to a gurney in the hallway while the nurses did triage. It was just like being in a filling station. Sick people kept coming in with no way to pay and no insurance, patching themselves together like rag dolls. What way is that to live in this so-called rich and most powerful country in the whole wide world?! What way is that to live in this country supposed to be made in the image of God?"

"Father Jim give her strength!"

"You helped me once, Father. Now there is a recurrence. There is a recurrence."

Jim stood at the top step on the stage, his hands pressed together. "The cancer has come back? Approach sister, approach."

She squared her shoulders and met him on the top step. "I prayed and still it's come back."

"Prayer is a fool's errand, sister. You're praying to something you don't even know exists. You're laying down your deepest secrets to a Sky Daddy going to come down and save you from the everyday failings of your body?"

There was silence.

"Th-that's the way I was taught to believe."

"The way you were taught to believe is wrong. Else why would a merciful, all powerful and all knowing God let poor black people starve on the streets in this great rich country? Answer me that? Why would he in his ultimate beneficence let mothers have to put their babies down crying and dirty and hungry night after fucking night?! I say that's sacrilegious, that that's an abomination in the eyes of any so-called merciful God that claims to be all powerful. I've looked into your soul sister and know you're a good person. I know all the good works you've done for the community, buying clothes and school supplies for little homeless children, children in some of the worst foster care homes in our city. That's no way for those youngsters to live. That's no way to grow up and become an educated thinking adult in this depraved society. When's the last time you had solace sister? Real solace? Come here let me give it to you."

Jim Jones put his hands on the woman's temples and the room erupted. She bent down, cupped her hands to her mouth and spat out a small brown growth. A slight white woman named Mariah darted from the audience, scooped it up with a towel, and put it into a paper bag.

The room was in a state of rapture. Children of all shapes and shades hopped out of their seats, jittering up and down the aisles and knocking against each other like bowling pins, as the adults surged forward in the pews, oohing, aahing, squealing, and exhorting Reverend Jim to deliver the woman from her misery.

He drank it all in, whipping off his dark shades for a second to polish them on the sleeve of his robe. "No all powerful God would let this good woman suffer!" He bellowed, grabbing the mike in both hands. "My children, you must ask yourself what kind of laws of the universe do we live under if a goddamn Sky Daddy is gonna sit in judgment of this pillar of the community and keep her wallowing in pain like a pig in shit."

"Give it to her Father, heal her, give it to her good!"

Jim clutched the woman's head against his chest, sweat dappling his pasty cheeks. The organist ripped off a few arpeggios, pumping the foot pedals through the floor while a white man in a pleather jacket passed out fans on the side aisle, pressing them knowingly into the outstretched hand of every elderly woman who beckoned.

"Have you ever seen anything like that?" The woman next to Taryn and Hy whispered. "I grew up in Christian Science and there were never any straight up miracles like that."

Taryn coughed and edged away. She went through her purse, cataloguing the wreckage, sleeping pills, sanitary napkins and spearmint gum sticks, interspersed with an unopened fruit cup, leftover from the office when she'd worked late getting ready for a pending audit of several big church clients. Everybody at work was in overdrive cursing the IRS bloodhounds.

When Hy had suggested going to the Temple's service as an outing, she consented partly out of curiosity, partly to penetrate the gloom her sister had descended into after taking a middling part-time job to help with the rent and bills. Between working at a take-out pizza place and folding clothes at the Laundromat, Hy was too fried to go to City College. She brooded that nobody would hire her as a secretary, a receptionist, a file clerk or any kind of front office person.

"You just have to be white, skinny and fuckable, that's the only criteria," Hy said, after job interviews that were abruptly aborted when she walked through the door.

Now, Taryn watched her sway to the organ, a bizarre sight given her disdain for the gospel gorges of their mother's church. Hy gripped the pew in front of them, peering into the heads of a married couple holding their Bible, arguing bitterly over the din about whether they should stay or go.

"Its blasphemy what he's saying. Taking the Lord's name in vain like that," the husband snarled. He took the bible and headed for the aisle, plowing through the crowd with it pressed against his chest like a shield.

Jim noted the commotion and stopped. He beckoned the organist to lower the volume, releasing Mrs. Townes for a moment, his robe drooping damply around his body.

"You're leaving us so soon, brother?"

"I'm not your brother."

"Not blood brothers but spiritual brothers," he said, soft, plaintive. "We're all here on God's green earth. We should all share in the richness of it equally so that makes us brothers and sisters under the skin."

"You took His name in vain. How can you stand up there and call yourself a Christian?"

"Well I thank you kindly brother for coming out in the community to see for yourself what we're all about. I live the example of Jesus Christ. I take no salary, I drive a beat up old car and I live with my people three hundred sixty five days a year. Now a lot of my brethren, some ordained by the most prestigious religious authorities and divinity schools in the country, don't do that. A lot of them are good men but they don't live and breathe the example of Jesus. You see them driving around in their big cars, rolling up to their big houses, wives decked out with every jewel in Persia and life is good for them, but what about their lowliest sickliest parishioner, struggling to pay their light bill after shelling out ten percent to the collection plate from their disability check? I know you're a man of conscience and I know you've asked yourself in quiet moments why God permits that. Why there's so much ungodliness among his so-called highest servants."

Jim turned back to Mrs. Townes, taking her hand again as he leaned into the mike.

"Sister I know you've wondered this too, in your darkest hour."

"Yes Father, yes Reverend Jim, I have."

"And where did your questioning lead you?"

"I came to the conclusion that kind of big gap wasn't right."

Jim turned toward the man again. "What kind of divine spirit would countenance that obscenity? Would tolerate going against the example of Jesus for one second? That's why we study the bible brother. We learn it inside and out but don't take it as the gospel truth. For far too long the white man has used his religion as an instrument of oppression to downgrade and debase black people and people of color. Used it to rape, steal, murder and plunder with impunity. We see white people living up in the hills with serious capital and riches, and black people living in the ghettoes with barely a collective pot to piss in. The fascists want to tell ya'll that you're lazy but they're in collusion with the Judeo Christian 'God'."

The man shook his head and continued toward the exit, glancing disdainfully back at his spouse in the center pew. The air filled with mocking hisses, teeth sucking, and admiring clucks of support for Father. Jim's white wife Mabelean stepped out of the front row, smiling sweetly from under shellacked blond hair as she cradled a fussy Asian baby.

Jim waved his hand for calm and resumed his makeshift sermon, focusing his patient, enveloping gaze on the man's spouse. "It took a lot of courage for you both to come here today. There are forces in this country that want to destroy us because of our resistance to the power structure and the work we do for the poor."

Mabelean nodded and stepped to the mike, balancing the baby on her right hip.

"Why, even yesterday, in one of the so-called community papers, we were subject to a vicious attack by the journalist Ida Lassiter, a woman who used to be a leading activist for justice whose sole purpose in life now is doing hit pieces on us. So we thank you from the bottom of our hearts for daring to take a chance on us."

"Thank you Mother Mabelean," Jim said, his gaze shifting to Hy and Taryn. "I see more newcomers here who've made the bold decision to find out what we're all about for themselves. Know that whatever walk of life you come from, whatever misgivings you might have you have a home here with the Temple. We don't screen or judge people according to what some higher power says is valuable. We don't scrutinize you for your bank account or how much you can tithe. This ain't no fancy pants congregation, this is a ministry of your neighbors, your kinfolk. You come as you can, with no judgments and no airs."

Mrs. Townes gasped ecstatically, taking Jim's hands in hers, face flush with gratitude. "Thank you Father, thank you. I say to everyone here—let him lead the way, let him do for you as he did for me. A great weight has been lifted off me and tonight I'm going to go home and sleep soundly for the first time in months!"

Applause roared through the church. Jim smiled, his gaze lingering on Taryn and Hy for a moment then floating warmly upward into the rafters.

At the end of the service the sisters followed the flood of people out into the cold sun, walking silently to their car, wedged between two over-flowing trash cans at the end of the street. Taryn balled the program up into her purse and got behind the wheel. A car swooped in behind them and hovered, waiting to take the space.

She frowned. "Horde's already massing for the next go-round," she said. "Wonder how much they rake in in a week."

"What did you think of the service?"

"It was a good circus. It's like the damn UN up in there so how could all of them be wrong?"

Hy stared out of the window at the unbroken chain of dumpsters snak-ing down the curb. Dogs skittered in and out of the clutter, stopping to paw at fast food wrappers smeared with chili cheese—a panting, sniffing sub-nation making its way through the city.

"They do a lot with animals. They've got a shelter system for monkeys and ferrets that get thrown out by zoos and rich people. So it's not just charity for people."

"Uh-huh. What's up with the Elvis shades he was wearing indoors? And the wife with the beehive toting the Asian baby? Nice staging for the cameras to have all that local color around."

"I didn't see any cameras."

"Types like that have to cultivate some kind of mystery to keep the gravy train going."

"I think the cancer lady was genuine."

"Right."

"You heard her, she'd tried everything, had no money, her condition was recurring and she couldn't sleep at night."

"That's what she said. Probably as healthy as you or me."

Taryn tapped the horn at the car in front of them, just barely ambling through the intersection as the light turned red. "Impaired motherfucker. Sleepwalking through the light."

"They wait in line for hours at the county hospital and get told they're only going to live a few years anyway, or that the illness is all in their heads, so why bother with aggressive treatment. Then they go to the down home neighborhood Baptist church and get told God is going to watch over them and bring them home to heaven."

"Thought we left fucked up driving back in Indianapolis. Come the fuck on!"

"The family upstairs invited me to a potluck Friday. Want to come?"

"I might have to work late."

Taryn rolled down the window and dangled her arm out, motioning for the driver behind her to let her in. The car relented and she sped up to the crosswalk, stopping just short of an elderly man hobbling through the yellow light with a bag of groceries nestled against his chest. She shuddered and drummed her fingers on the steering wheel.

"A city full of old people and their only refuge is church or the morgue. Damn travesty. I'd rather be shot."

"You heard him. You've seen the congregation. It's not like a traditional church, with people begging to get saved and waiting for heaven and all that."

"Yeah, yeah, I got it, they're anti-establishment. That's half of the city when it's sexy. But faith healing, Hy? The woman coughed up some weird shit and now she's cured? And the church doesn't exactly run on goodwill and peace on earth. The nonprofit arm raked in thousands last year. I don't work with that account directly but I see the bank statements. All of these outfits, even the most supposedly grassroots ones doing pure charity, are profiteers and schemers."

"All? I heard they were paying medical bills and rent, serving three square meals a day. When you have to give somebody a blow job to get a good place in line at the soup kitchen, getting fed in church sounds like a fucking good deal."

"Yeah but what do the members have to shell out for all that benevolence? Ask those old ladies how many checks they write a month for the Emergency Relief Fund or the new housing project or the Pastor's Orphan Campaign just to get a chance to be 'cured' of cancer."

"Better that, than gambling or some frivolous shit."

"How is being able to control how you're going to spend your own money frivolous shit, Hy?"

"Who's forcing them to spend money on the church? And if it goes to helping the community why are you trashing it?"

Taryn sped up. "Criticizing not trashing … You're being naïve if you think all they're doing is getting some crippled kids wheelchairs."

"Handicapped. The term is handicapped. And how do you know what they're doing, or what any church is doing for that matter, when all you do is hang up in that office with those white people. Just because you have a steady paycheck it doesn't give you the right to act like you're more moral than anyone else. There's no social value in doing a corporation's taxes."

"Most of our clients have less than fifty employees. They're hardly rooking people for the kind of money the Temple is raking in. It's a business Hy. Get that in your head. All that community stuff is just a ruse to reel in the weak and the searching. These church types, whatever the denomination, are good at sniffing out Achilles heels, clamping down with their fangs and holding on tight for blood. Doesn't matter what the community concern is, they'll accommodate it. You got a bunch of drug addicts and dealers in need of rehab? They'll set up a treatment center to cure them just so long as there's a profit margin."

They were almost home. Fruit and knick-knack vendors patrolled the western corner of the street, waving bags of oranges, bananas, psychedelic kids' toys flashing and clacking into the wind. A series of police shootings and confrontations had rocked the neighborhood.

Signs from protest rallies in the city square flapped from the telephone poles for one solid mile. Some bore the face of a dead tenth-grader from the local arts school, murdered by white cops after his paintbrushes were mistaken for a gun. In death he was a coke snorting thug and unholy menace, the fallen poster child of a network of feral black boys terrorizing ghetto denizens and gold cufflink stockbrokers alike.

Hy watched the signs flicker by, guilty that she hadn't gone to any of the protests, nauseated suddenly by her sister's untroubled profile.

"You're wrong about those people," Hy said. "You're so smug about their gullibility. You have the same allegiance to that accounting firm. At least the Temple people are involved in some type of movement that goes beyond all this. At least they're trying to change conditions, make some kind of impact on the world. It's easy to sit on the sidelines and criticize when you don't have anything at risk."

"So you're the revolutionary now after going to one service? What qualifies you to trash me for getting up every morning and going to a job that pays the bills and that I'll be able to get ahead in instead of some minimum wage crap job with no benefits?"

"And you think those white boys are really going to let you run that office someday? You're crazy."

"You don't seem to understand that being in that kind of environment is all about access. It's all about watching and learning the modus operandi of the white world, so when the time comes I'll be ready to start my own business. That's why we came here remember? This is the big league in comparison to Indiana and the clock is ticking. How many times have I told you that you've got to be *strategic*. You aren't a white girl. You can't afford to be messing around taking a year off trying to find yourself dabbling in piss poor jobs with no plan. If something happens to me tomorrow we've got a little bit of savings and that's it. If we get evicted there won't be a decent place in town we can relocate to."

Hy turned to face her, eyes flashing. "And you're getting so lost in all that you can't see yourself. What are you going to learn from them other than how to assimilate and be the good Negro they can stick on company brochures trying to look liberal? You look down on the Temple but you're like a damn zombie when you come home. How is that different from being stuck back in Indiana dealing with the white trash at the temp agency who thought you were a genius just 'cause you could add and subtract in your head?"

They pulled up in front of the apartment. Families who'd taken the trolley from the church service streamed down the street, throngs of young children dawdled behind shadowboxing, whining about candy, the adults shining them on, haggard, wrung out. Hy jumped from the car and rushed to the door of the building, slipping on a bundle of throw-away papers that had been dropped on the stoop. She picked one up and examined it. The byline of the writer Ida Lassiter floated over a picture of Reverend Jones talking to a group of Temple protestors at the Housing Authority.

Deb, a fussbudget with a pouf of salt and pepper hair who lived in the communal apartments walked up chomping on a green apple.

"Hi Miss Hyacinth. It was great seeing you at the service." She slurped on the apple and grinned. "God this is so juicy. I've got more at my place. Want one?"

"No thanks. What's this?" Hy asked, tapping the article.

Deb frowned at the crumpled front page. She bent down quickly and scooped up the bundle. "Garbage."

CHAPTER 6

Ida Lassiter, Indianapolis, 1948

THE BODIES WERE stacked five deep, whole generations of invented families greeting each other in silent communion, year by year, decade by decade, until the plot had been exhausted and the gravedigger moved on to find fresh accommodations in the dirt. Infrequently, he was called upon to exhume a body that was believed to be out of place; a white woman that was exposed by a relative as one quarter Negro, an orphan baby revealed as the bastard of a serial rapist pissing in the gene pool.

Lelyveld, the white gravedigger, predicted that the cemetery would run out of room before the next presidential election, when Truman would be kicked out. By then, he reasoned, the country would be ready for a socialist administration, weary of the milquetoast promises and concessions of the Democrats and the FDR establishment. He began his day at 5 a.m. with the newspapers spread out at his feet. It was important to know what the mainstream was doing, the super-elites and the corporate stooges with their fingers on the levers of the machine. This was the oasis in his daily routine, his mind churning with delectable presentiments of doom that powered him through the tedium. At 5:30, he was out of the office with his gloves on, patrolling the grounds to ensure that the residents were undisturbed, checking for signs of nocturnal visitors, reviewing new requests for burials as he awaited the arrival of Kedrick, the mortuary director, perpetually late, perpetually harried, perpetually thirsty for his counsel.

"Has the Negro woman been by?" Kedrick asked.

"What Negro woman?"

"Some charity woman hooked up with one of those do-gooder groups."

"A lot of them snooping around."

"They want to get us cited for violations."

"Violating what?"

Kedrick sighed, slouching down into his rumpled dun-colored suit. "The grave stacking. They think if they get us on that, then they can make a case for that other thing. Shifting the Negroes into the white cemetery."

"Cold day in hell when that happens."

Coffee formed a moat of tar on Lelyveld's tongue, the minutes pounding a countdown to lunch into his temples. It was a rogue struggle to keep from looking at his watch to check the march to 12:00. He'd cleared most of the older plots of weeds when he heard the sound of Kedrick arguing with someone.

A tall thin Negro woman in black gloves and a wide brim black hat walked out of the building heading a trio of white women. They stepped out of the gate and onto the grounds. One scribbled vigorously into a notepad. He could tell from her movements that she was taking dictation from the Negro woman, who strode across the grass in full command. Kedrick trailed behind, brow furrowed, fly unzipped from having scrambled off the toilet to catch up with the visitors.

"This should be a few feet wider," the woman snapped. "It's a clear code violation. None of the white burial grounds have this small a berth for graves. Make sure you get the exact measurements."

"Excuse me what exactly do you think you're doing? This is private property, you're not authorized to be on these grounds."

The woman turned and held out her hand. "I'm Ida Lassiter, don't believe we've formally met."

Kedrick frowned and offered his hand limply.

"I'm afraid you're mistaken about the restrictions for being on this property, or perhaps you're being purposely obtuse," she said.

He stiffened, sucking his gut in, flicking invisible pieces of lint off his shirtsleeves.

"Tours are conducted with authorized visitors between the hours of 3:00 and 5:00. I don't recall receiving a request from you and your group. So I'm going to have to ask you to—"

"This is public domain. I met with the land use department yesterday morning. You have no enforcement power over this jurisdiction." She turned and gestured toward the white women. "These are representatives from the orphanage, the Twelfth Street soup kitchen and the War Widow's society. Ms. Baines, Ms. Castro, Ms. Winslow. Their families have all contributed substantially to Sam Stimson's campaign chest and he's well aware of their participation in this research. We'll need another thirty minutes to complete our survey of the grounds."

Kedrick stared at her, pallid cheeks flushing. Any mention of Stimson's name, permits, or jurisdictions was like a slug of kryptonite for him. Lelyveld knew he was skulking around waiting for the alderman to make an ethics charge against one of his white funeral homes quietly go away, knew Kedrick had been fucking a mortician who was unlicensed and getting paid full- time for part-time work. He had no stomach, time or patience for the rough, picayune small city politics of permits and jurisdictions. But to see Kedrick hoisted up wriggling, his umbilical cord cut from his bloated belly in the cold light of day would be Christmas, Thanksgiving and Easter rolled up into one for Lelyveld.

They could do nothing but stand around and watch while the women barreled through the grounds. When they were done, Ida Lassiter stopped in the reception room and took three business cards from the desk and passed them out to the white women. They dropped them in their purses and said a curt goodbye to the secretary, piling into a parked car in front of the building.

"Bitches," Kedrick grumbled. "Look at her sitting in the passenger's seat being chauffeured around like the Queen of Sheba. It's a damn travesty. There'd be none of that kind of behavior in Mississippi. The niggers there are a different breed. Respectful, know their place, know not to overstep."

They watched the car pull onto the street and drive away. Kedrick smoothed his tie down, uneasy for a moment in the silence. Lelyveld just nodded and went back to the grounds.

He didn't care for all that nigger talk. Just tolerated it because it was expected. He'd seen the Negro soldiers come back and get the shit end of the stick. Even the bravest ones, the ones that had saved whites from the Krauts in the heaviest combat. He stretched his toes in his shoes, thanking god that they and every inch of him was white. He finished his work ploddingly, the sucker punch of March air stiffening his joints to where he could barely move at the end of his shift.

On Wednesday, he ate dinner immediately after he got off work and took the train to the meeting of the Syndicate, a communist-aligned worker's group, a few miles away. Mercifully, he'd arrived late enough to miss the highlights of last month's minutes, members milling about scraping stale cookie crumbs from the table, white faces ragged with worry about the prospect of exposure for being there. All he cared about was the pending motion to organize cemetery workers by the crafts guild. He'd been asked to make a brief statement on behalf of the forty or so workers in the county. It was a small but significant step for the Syndicate, which jockeyed with other radical organizations for visibility, position and membership against the savage chest-beating tide of commie witch-hunting.

The core of the group was mostly younger men; loud, bruising and in a hurry to assert themselves, watchful of each other, mindful of the shifting sands of micro-status in this uneasy brotherhood of dissidents. The older guard did the agendas and correspondence with national and international chapters, calling tactical briefings, convening relentless theory and practice sessions that bled night into day. Lelyveld was eternally in the middle, mid-age, midstream, his mind defined by vacillations. The Syndicate was a life raft launching violently at him. A last ditch chance to be sure, to be certain, to wrest purpose from the lockstep of burying bodies.

A few men had risen above wariness and secrecy and taken the time to welcome him, feeling him out in their limited, fumbling way. At his second meeting he'd noticed a young man who looked barely older than a teenager hovering on the margins with a notepad. The lieutenants had shaken him down to make sure he wasn't an infiltrator. Rather than get indignant the boy seemed to like the attention, grinning coolly through the pat-down search with his dark matinee idol hair as he watched the members form a wolf pack around the refreshments put out by some of the women. Embarrassed about the interrogation, Lelyveld went over to offer him some punch and was intercepted by Mike Shuster, one of the young-old guard, stout, 46, wispy red over-stroked goatee; a sly nail biter and righteous teetotaler who worked at the refinery.

"Ol' Jim Jones here is our resident college boy. Says he wants to study the law. Ain't that right now Jim? When the capitalist thugs throw us in the brig he'll be our one-man boy wonder legal defense."

They let him keep his notepad. The officers even began relying on his skill of nearly total recall when a fact, figure or reference was hazy. The boy had memorized Das Capital, showing off his grasp of dialectical materialism like a shiny new car. The membership scorned eager beavers but his earnestness bore through the grizzled reserve of the chairman, a Danish-descent pipefitter always railing against the malfeasance of the union locals, how they sucked up big salaries and big dues, how they were doing everything in their power to keep out the Negro worker.

That evening Jim Jones was practically at the chairman's elbow, sizing up the membership with big brown saucer eyes as a battle about an overdue light bill ensued between the secretary and the treasurer. Lelyveld sucked in his gut nervously, rehearsing the fine points of his speech for the thousandth time. They'd put him on the agenda after a guest speaker on the lynchings of two black schoolteachers in northern Indiana.

Shuster and some of the others got to grumbling about what it had to do with the business of the Syndicate.

"Every time our boys go on strike they ship in busloads of Negro scabs to break it." Shuster spat. "The bosses go 'round scooping up every idle semi-able bodied nig—uh, Negro sitting on a bus stop, apartment stoop or street corner. Most of 'em can't be trusted to do an honest day's work on their own and when the bosses get hold of 'em and promise twenty cents an hour, well naturally that shit looks like gold."

"The representative from the Regional Negro Trades couldn't be here due to a time conflict so we have a replacement ... a Miss, uh, Ida Lassiter," said the chairman.

Ida Lassiter walked up to the makeshift podium and looked around at the ripple of white faces, expressions stoic to vaguely bemused. The men on the perimeter of the room continued their side conversations in low ponderous registers, leaning into each other in a grand show of exclusivity, ignoring the chairman's limp call to order. Two white women counted the proceeds from raffle ticket sales at a card table near the kitchen, while a third bustled around vigorously picking up stray cups and empty plates.

Ida popped a cough drop into her mouth, searching her purse for a napkin. "May I trouble you for a napkin?" she asked the chairman. Wherever she traveled she made sure to take her own supplies.

"Thank you for allowing me to address you this evening. My colleague Warren Deverell had a last minute commitment he needed to honor so it's my privilege to replace him. As some of you may be aware the situation here in the state of Indiana has reached a crisis point with the rash of terrorist attacks against Negro citizens. Last week, two schoolteachers were hanged and killed in Noblesville after the entire community was ransacked by white mobs. A month ago Negro tenant workers received threatening notes from their landlord after it was rumored they were attempting to organize his farm crew. Statewide, Negro workers are being threatened with violence, with the rope, even with imprisonment if they insist upon exercising their rights as hardworking, taxpaying, law-abiding Americans trying to put food on the table for their families. These unconstitutional atrocities go against every standard the U.S. has attempted to set for itself abroad as a so-called defender of and beacon for global freedom. We've watched the Syndicate take baby steps toward becoming a force in the trade union movement and would like to extend an invitation of partnership in the common cause of workers' rights."

"Baby steps?" Mike Shuster snorted. "Like hell we're taking baby steps."

The chairman waved his hand for order.

Ida grasped the podium, drawing herself up to her full height as she waited for the outburst to recede. "I meant no insult *brother*," she said. "It was simply an acknowledgment of the immense maiden effort the Syndicate is making to champion the dispossessed and the disenfranchised. I'd hope that some of that organizing muscle could get behind our cause. That we could rely on the Syndicate at key moments to raise its voice, write letters and be at pickets and protests as a valuable ally when the situation calls for it."

Shuster and Tennyson Ailes, another ironworker, rocked back on their heels in unison, arms crossed tightly over thick chests.

"Don't hold your breath, lady," Ailes said. "You familiar with the Lowndes strike? Fourteen-fifteen hours a day, that's the time I put in. Some of my brothers here did more. Out there two solid weeks doing shifts and none of the papers or the politicians gave a rusty fuck. You give me one good reason why me and my boys should stick our necks out for Negroes who swoop in and play scab for the bosses while we fucking starve in the cold?"

A few men murmured in approval. One of the white women nodded her head. "That's the God's honest truth. Saw it myself and it was ugly. Turncoat police out in full force treating them like less than a dog and proud of it. Made me even more ashamed to be an American than I was before."

Ida came from behind the podium. She took a cracker from the refreshment table and crumbled it in her hand. "You talk of the police and the politicians and how corrupt they are but they will crush this movement down to a nub if there is no alignment, if it isn't broad enough. You're right to be angry, to feel rage for the dirt that they do. But it's misplaced. All the bosses know is divide and conquer. That's the only language they understand and the quickest way to play you for fools is to pin it on the Negro working man."

Applause came from the back of the room. Lelyveld turned and saw Jim Jones clapping his hands together exaggeratedly, hair whipping against his bulbous forehead.

"Well said, ma'am. Well said." He looked around and smiled, feigning indifference to the pinpoint scowls and stares of his comrades. He rubbed his hands together then cracked his knuckles, waiting for Ida to resume, eyes glowing, moth to the flame of the hot contempt pulsing through the room.

Shuster rattled a keychain strapped to his belt. "Nice show boy. Gotta get you a membership to the NAACP. This lady will be ready and raring to sign you up afterward to get their numbers of bleeding hearts up."

"I don't represent nor am I affiliated with that organization," Ida said. "As I stated, I'm here for one purpose and one purpose only and that is to ensure that Negro men *and* women—that Negro lives are protected within the full extent of the law. The real question is whether you, this movement, white working people, will stand in solidarity with the Negro and against the carnage that's right at your doorstep."

The chairman looked at his watch and cleared his throat. "Thank you Miss Lassiter. It-it is 'Miss' right?"

The men in Shuster's corner snickered. Thom Judge, a stenographer and one of the disputed founders of the Syndicate came forward. "I second the thank you Miss Lassiter. Your courage is appreciated. Took a lot to come in here and put up with the boorishness of some of my brothers who seem to have left their manners in the outhouse. Can you tell us what you're asking the Syndicate to do in the immediate?"

Jim Jones walked up and gave her a cup of water. She took a few quick sips and handed it back to him. Lelyveld saw how Jim was sniffing around her and wondered what kind of extra points the boy was trying to score. He fidgeted and watched the minute hand drag around the clock again.

The more time devoted to the drama of the Negress, the less time his item would get. The last train left at 10:00 and the men would start stampeding the door at half past nine, leaving the stalwarts and the partisans to sop up the dregs of the meeting.

"Er—chairman sir haven't we had enough time on this item?" He asked wobbly-voiced, angry at his timidity; but the men stirred in agreement and Ida Lassiter glanced at him bemusedly, a dim hint of recognition flickering on the half- moon of her face.

"To answer the gentleman's question we're staging several protests and meetings over the next several weeks. We'll go to the district attorney's office as a token first effort but our main target is the feds, the Department of Justice."

Mike Shuster howled, "This lady here wants us to join up with her to change it but that ain't our fight. When there're one hundred motherfucking Negro scabs taking food off my family's plate I got bigger things to worry about than looking noble at a NAACP convention with a bunch of white do-gooders that went to Harvard and got a thousand bucks to give."

Jim looked at the chairman. "Call a vote."

"What?"

"Call a vote."

"Who the fuck you think you are, junior?" A man with a paint brush bristle mustache and blond brows said, twisting a chewed up straw between badger teeth. "Still don't think this little pup got all his shots, Mr. Chairman. He's nipping too close to you. You catch what he has you might give it to all of us."

The chairman winced, turning to Jim, "You're out of order. This isn't a matter for a vote, it's for committee deliberation." He rapped his gavel again on the podium. "Thank you, Miss Lassiter. The committee will take this up and get back to your organization with our decision. Jim, please make sure Miss Lassiter gets to the train station safely."

Ida folded her notes up and waved him off. The room churned with unease, the watchful, titillated suspense of a circus audience, their hungry eyes riveted to the vertiginous flash of trapeze artists hurtling towards each other in blinding light.

"I can make it on my own, thank you. These aren't the roughest wilds I've been in, not by a long shot."

Jim rushed to her side. "No, please, allow me. I was headed out anyway," he cupped his hand in a whisper. "This is my third meeting. It was tedious until you got here."

They walked out of the hall and into the empty street. He quickened his pace to keep up, a few inches shorter than she and unaccustomed to walking briskly.

"Your chivalry is touching," she said. "I'm good from here young man."

"I appreciated everything you said in there. You reminded me a little of my, uh, mentor."

"And who might that be?"

"Prophet Zeke of Divine Global and First Redeemer."

She laughed. "Now that's rich."

They'd reached the station. Ida paid her fare and swept into the gloom of the tunnel, watching every move of Jim and the other whites hovering around the platform.

He wobbled backward, pained, fumbling through his pocket for a tissue to wipe his nose. "I-I didn't mean any offense."

"None taken. I'd expect no less from a greenhorn like you. How did you happen to land in Zeke's orbit?"

"Started volunteering at the church a few years ago."

"That so? I know Zeke is gratified to have a young white boy among his foot soldiers. If nothing else you're learning from the master how to zig zag, glad hand and still come up smelling like roses. Maybe you weren't aware that for three years your mentor was on the payroll of the Pullman Company as part of an organized effort to make sure Negro porters wouldn't unionize. Remember those sermons where he preached against the unions ruining Negro job prospects? According to ol' Zeke Negro men were supposed to consider themselves lucky to be working in an industry where they all got called George and made less for fifty hours than white part-time janitors."

Jim blushed. "I think that was before my time."

"Of course it was." The streetcar to Indiana Avenue was approaching. "But I won't revoke your honorary Negro credentials. I'm quite sure the Zeke experience will be useful for you somewhere down the line.

CHAPTER 7

⚜

The Alliance, 1948

SNOW HAD BEGUN to fall, the first anemic flakes nipping her cheeks as she walked to the bone cold office, weaving past the zombies of 6 a.m. Ida liked to be out early, before the throttle of Detroit tankards ruined the stillness. The golden hours of productivity were between 5 and 8. After that everything went to shit.

The rent on her office was paid up until the end of the year by Van Doren, a conservative tabloid owner philanthropist who veered left in private and kept the thermostat at a miserly 60 degrees. The military grayness bothered Ida more than the cold. The cold kept her hand moving. If she wrote quickly she could wear the day down to a nub, outrun it, have a clear space to think.

There was a knock at the door and her co-editor Harrison tumbled from his chair to get it, frowning at the pinched face of a bareheaded young white man.

"Can I help you with something?"

"I'm here to see Mrs. Lassiter. I heard this was her office." He shifted nervously, working a breath mint through his mouth. Snowflakes lit up his black hair, guarded eyes darting from Harrison to the hallway behind him.

"And you are?"

"Jim. Jim Jones. Mrs. Lassiter and I met at a meeting last month."

Harrison called warily to Ida, "A white boy named Jones to see you. Claims he was at a meeting you were at."

"Yes, he's one of the young Reds at the Syndicate I told you about. Let him in."

Harrison opened the door, stepping out into the hallway to make sure Jim hadn't been followed. He waved him to Ida's office.

"Good morning, Mrs. Lassiter."

"Mr. Jones. What brings you to this side of town?"

"Please, call me Jim. I read your editorial the other day endorsing the hotel workers' strike. It was very inspiring."

"Oh? Now that's special. I didn't know I had an audience with the boys in the Syndicate."

Jim grinned sheepishly. "Some of us know how to read down there. It's not all barbarianism."

"I'm assuming you didn't come all this way to fawn."

"No, although, as I said last month, I admire the work that you do. Your courage and integrity, battling those glorified Northern crackers to the bitter end like that. If the boys in the Syndicate had an ounce of what you have—"

Ida picked up her pad and started to write again. "I'm on deadline, Mr. Jones."

"Jim."

"Seems you've got out your butter knife. If you admired me so much you'd know not to waste my time with preambles. State your purpose and get on with it."

As though he'd anticipated her sharpness, instead of tensing, he relaxed slightly in his seat, delicately avoiding the gash on the right side of the cushion with a gymnast's skill.

"I felt awful about what happened at that damn meeting last month. But I know you probably expected it. Even though they're good soldiers for Communism that kind always feels like their struggle is the real one and everyone else's, especially the Negroes', is counterfeit in some way."

She kept writing. "I went there for one simple reason and that was to get visibility for our issues. I didn't expect to be welcomed with open arms. Your 'boys' certainly didn't disappoint on that score."

His voice softened to cream. "I don't want to waste anymore of your time. I realize that this might be a lot to ask but I was wondering if you would be open to supporting this community project I'm working on."

"What is it?"

"Well, one of my callings ma'am … My main calling that is, is to preach the gospel."

She looked up. "So you want to take a page from Zeke and start your own congregation."

"That's right ma'am. I've got a few hundred saved up for rent on a place on Hennepin Street. Plan to move in next week."

"That's a strange calling for a communist."

"I believe if you read the gospel correctly you'd conclude that Jesus was a communist in many ways. Living like a poor man, wanting everyone in the world to have the same right to food and shelter. Most of these preachers don't know the real meaning of Jesus."

Snow salted the window, obscuring the brick monolith of the building next door, a sweat shop masquerading as a dry cleaners. Harrison hacked and coughed from the common area.

"Nothing novel in that analysis and I know the gospel quite well, thank you very much. I've left several congregations during the course of my life, known my share of malfeasant preachers. Put as much distance as I could between me and them. What distinguishes you from that lot?"

"I expect to be judged by my deeds, not my words. I've listened to your speeches. There's nothing you don't say in them that you don't live and act on. I'm a white boy who came up dirt poor and despised, but I can still clean myself up, walk through the door of any bank in Indianapolis and get respect and a loan if I speak the bosses' language. I have no communist illusions about that, Mrs. Lassiter. The first goal with this church is to provide something in the community that's going to bring the races together in real fellowship. First two services I had were half Negro and half white. We'll be the only church in Indiana, and I dare say one of the only ones in the country, to have the races sitting together, worshipping in God's house."

"That will change as time goes on. The whites will get tired and go back to their Jim Crow churches ... They'll be able to say that they got out before they became part of your little experiment and whatever name you're trying to make for yourself. Some of the Negroes will stay because they'll be so grateful a white man is paying attention to them."

"And why are you so sure I'm trying to make a name for myself?"

"Aren't you?"

"My goal is to serve meals five days a week, no questions asked, no cross-examination or waiting list or hoops to jump through. From there I want to give the poorest families assistance with their utilities. We need a recreational center in the backyard to ensure that our children have someplace safe to play after school and we need educational programs for seniors, as some of them are shut-in and isolated during the day."

"All to the tune of Negro and white in harmony. Your church is on Hennepin correct? Are you aware that a ten year-old Negro girl was followed home by a car full of white thugs and threatened with her life last week? Or that several maids who wait at that bus stop are regularly passed up by half-empty buses and wait in the dark for hours before a driver deigns to pick them up? No Negro family can touch that neighborhood with a ten foot pole if they're not chaperoned by a white escort or working for a white family. Even the most affluent of us—no realtor would show us a house."

"Well maybe I can help."

"Help?"

"We can set up a sting. You have your people go to a property and submit an application. I come after them posing as a buyer or renter with worse financials than them. The realtors fall all over themselves trying to give me the property and we nail 'em."

"Just what, exactly, do we 'nail 'em' on, as you say? Restrictive covenants are still in force, exposing bigoted landlords takes time, work and this so-called sting would hardly have those people paralyzed with fear of litigation. That's the typical response of youth. Uncoordinated actions like that will never have a ripple effect. If we got an army of people focusing on specific properties, documenting their experiences, staging targeted protests at the board meetings and conclaves of these organizations, writing the kind of editorials that we did in the thirties on tenement conditions—now *that*, that is something I could back."

"You say uncoordinated actions will never have a ripple effect and yet you took on city transit on your own and won a lawsuit."

"Well now you've inverted your history. What I did was hardly uncoordinated. It was part of a larger movement of organized action spearheaded by Negro women. Yours is the short view, ours is the long; decades, centuries long. I don't have time for radical white boys looking to make a splash with the huddled masses, or yet another preacher with hat in hand."

"You say radical like it was a swear word. Is that how you see me ma'am, as a vulture? I regret that I've given you that impression. But I know it's unavoidable, given what's happened here, what's happening every second and every minute in this country to the Negro people. My ignorance isn't as deep as it would seem, and I'm teachable. Hell, the people I minister to have taught me more in one year than I ever learned in any institution of higher learning."

The phone rang in the outer office. "I'm glad that you feel you've been schooled by the commoners," she said, reaching for her dictionary.

Harrison knocked on the door then came in. "There've been more arrests of strikers at the Hotel Majestic. Thirty-five in all, most of them Negro."

She rose from her desk. "Thank you, Harrison."

"Also, the babysitter, and master Sturges have arrived." He bowed his head in mock deference and went back outside, leaving the door slightly ajar. Ida paused, irritated by the disruption. The sounds of her nephew Sturges, four years old and bubbling over with questions, echoed through the room. She was watching him for a week while her sister recovered from a hernia operation.

She closed the door, towering over Jim for a moment, pinched black patent leather shoes resting against the wheels of his chair. "Now," she said quietly. "I have a proposal for you. The city council is, as we speak, scheming to expand the no loitering ordinance to apply to workers on the sidewalk in front of private buildings. Some of the folk will be in court for a preliminary hearing next week. Be there. You and your people. The more white faces sitting in the audience the better. We need law-abiding white church folk to be front, row and center staring those barbarians dead in the eyes. We also need people to go sign up for public comment, do leafleting, anything to let the council know that they're being watched by other groups besides the Negro organizations."

"Yes, yes, that's the only symbolism they understand."

She bent down in his face. "I'm not looking for symbolism, Mr. Jones. I'm looking for conviction. Everyone you bring with you has to know what they're there for. The white press picks it up, starts snapping pictures and taking statements, I can't afford to have a whole gaggle of folk acting discombobulated."

"Ok, what should we do?"

"Your people need to get trained. If you're serious, you have ten of your best ones here at this office on Sunday at nine o'clock sharp. The session goes for two hours and we don't serve tea and crumpets."

"Yes, ma'am."

"Don't mock me. If your propaganda is as good as your preaching then you might have a long career ahead of you. I fancy a good stem-winder sometimes. Bring your Bible."

Jim got up to leave. Outside the door in the sitting area the babysitter chirped and cooed. Sturges wriggled away from her, swaddled up to his cheekbones, mesmerized by the mysterious doodads of the printing press, hot caramel eyes glowing, crumpled daisy mouth in an upside down question mark.

Ida had not wanted a child, any child; had rued every queasy retching second of the brief surprise pregnancy she'd had in her late thirties, despite being told it was a Godsend, a final shot at redemption for an old maid. The prospect of a child's perpetual presence had unnerved her, the attraction-repulsion of new motherhood, the dread that they would be imprisoned together for life; she, a shoddily divorced Negro woman, an object of whispered ridicule, bald-faced pity and bad fortune for all the lusty Sunday morning moralists at her church.

The miscarriage had been sweet deliverance, a gift tinged with the barest, tiniest smidgen of regret that it had not been her sole choice, that God had heard her and acted on his own.

Jim walked out, brightening when he saw Sturges. "Hello, little man," he said, bending down to his eye level.

Sturges jerked away. Jim reached into his pocket and pulled out a yo-yo. He dangled it in front of the boy, snatching it away playfully as he grabbed for it, squealing.

"Little man's going to rule the world someday," he said.

CHAPTER 8

❧

Jimmy Jr., Indianapolis, 1963

IT WAS A game that Jimmy Jr. made up to pass the time. Every passing car filled him with hope and anxiety. The ones that slowed killed him with their ambivalence. Every car was a tiny island. Couples intertwined in the front seats. Families shifting behind the windshields in their Sunday best. Old white people, stone-faced, praying to make it alive out of the wilds of the ghetto. Jittery, he willed them to slow and stop, carving his initials into the window sill with his penknife as they rumbled past, a mechanism to let off steam. When the new white man and woman came to take him the initials would be the last trace of him left in the house.

That week he'd bragged about the adoption to the other foster kids. His mother was going to be as beautiful as Betty Grable, platinum blond hair piled high on her head. His father would be tall and rangy, a fount of candy, money and comic books. Every night he'd fall asleep tucked in with their gentle hands, velvet green grass rippling outside the window of his very own bedroom.

Of course, he'd been too small for these things to have happened. His parents Jim and Mabelean had adopted him when he was a baby, plucking him from the midst of other Negro children who'd waited longer, tried harder, suffered more. Fate tantalized, tortured him. Why had God chosen him and not them? There had been nothing said about this in Sunday school, in his mother Mabelean's rousing little side sermons or the pre-schoolers' picture book lessons on the Underground Railroad. Whenever he was tempted to smack the shit out of his brother Demian he chastened himself, saying if God was giving him this good thing then he would show that he deserved it.

But then, Demian was always trying him like the slave catchers tried Harriet Tubman.

"They should've changed their minds," he sniped. The white child. The real biological one. His face a twisted little ugly little angelic map of Mom's and Dad's.

"Shut-up! You're just jealous!" He swung back around and grabbed Demian by the neck, putting him in a headlock. Demian wriggled and squealed, kicking at his ankles. They tumbled onto the floor in a heap, a silken voice echoing above them as two hands pulled them apart.

"Now, boys, that's no way to act on the Lord's Day."

Jimmy Jr. straightened his shirt and looked up into the face of his dad, his dark eyes twinkling, the skin at his neck sunburned, bunched up under his pastor's collar.

"You beat each other to a pulp boys you're doing just what society expects you to do."

Demian panted. "Huh? What're you talking about?"

Jim turned to Jimmy Jr. and took a dollar from his pocket. "Here you go son. Demian, I overheard what you said to your brother and I want you to apologize right this instant. Jimmy, I know you want to spend this on candy but think about saving first. While everybody else is goofing off squandering their savings you'll be building up your piggy bank."

Jimmy crumpled the dollar up into his fist and muttered thank you. He paused, staring resentfully at Demian. "Demian thinks he's smarter than everybody, but he can't even read."

Demian lunged at him, Jim pulling him back, his voice ringing through the cold room.

"Watch it, son. You all are blood brothers no matter what anyone says. You should always have each other's back. When I was coming up I would've given my right arm to have a brother to talk to, to horse around with, beat the crap out of. You feel anger toward each other now, but that'll evaporate once you get out into the world and see what it's really like to be without any kind of family."

Demian shook his head. "*He's* the dummy, he can't even write his own name."

Jim put his hand on Demian's shoulder. It was always the same hurly burly between them after church service. The same taunting and bloodletting before they all piled into the car to do recruitment canvassing in the Negro and poor white neighborhoods. Mother Mabelean would sit in the front seat while the three of them went up and down the block, moving from house to house with their flyers. If there were men present she'd make them feel uncomfortable, his dad said. Some had never been in the same room with a white woman, so she stayed in the car tallying the sign-up cards of new members.

"How many times did the cops stop and ask if you were ok?" Jim asked her when they got back.

"Only once. It was one of the nice ones, a younger one, a bit chubby, has some kind of accent. Pollack, Slavic, one of those. We've seen him patrolling around the church before. He didn't mean any harm," she swiveled around and smiled warmly at Jimmy and Demian. "Why look at the both of you! What handsome young men you are. You've got legs for days and I'll bet you'll grow up to be just the same height." She reached out and touched their cheeks.

Jimmy flinched, dropping his eyes to the car's ratty green upholstery. She blushed, picking at her chapped lips. Jim looked from one to the other in quiet assessment. He folded the remaining pamphlets and put them in the glove compartment. A couple pushing a baby carriage ambled past, tracking the scene of the white family with the little black boy over their shoulders.

Jim kneeled down in front of Jimmy, nodding over at the couple. "Little man, what did I tell you about paying too close attention to what other folk say or do. They don't love you. They don't stay up half the night worrying about you. We do. Me and your mother. You don't owe them nothing. Not embarrassment, not shame, not nothing." He guided Jimmy into the backseat, motioning for Demian to follow. Mabelean started the car. He gave the couple a pointed look as they drove away, his voice softening in reconsideration. "Ok little man, I don't blame you. Maybe I'd be scared to death too if black folk thought I belonged to some strange white people."

Jimmy watched the neighborhood as the car rolled down the block, the houses melting and shifting.

"I see Miss Ida's got an editorial in the newspaper this morning about the Negro porter's union and the Communist Party snubbing it," Mabelean said.

"She mention our church?"

"No."

"That's a curious omission given our support for the union. She knows how hard we've been working to keep the profile up on this. Hell, I'm practically the only white pastor in the state to stick my neck out for it."

"I'm quite sure next time—"

"I didn't tell you last week May, but … I got another death threat. I didn't want to upset you, what with all the stress you've been under taking care of the kids and managing the new members."

"You underestimate me. They underestimate us. They can't run us out when we're doing God's work." She glanced over her shoulder at Jimmy and Demian. "Boys I hope we're not scaring you with this talk."

Demian ignored them, making a battleship with his two fingers, steering it down the back of the seat. Jimmy scrunched himself up and pressed his body into the car door, counting the number of Buicks he saw. Mabelean's floral print dress exploded into an open poppy field. She was always put together, stately and composed in the eye of his father's storm.

Jim brushed some stray strands of hair from her shoulders. "Your hair's growing like a weed, May. Time for a haircut. What do you think, Jimmy? Should your mother get her haircut?"

Mabelean looked anxiously at Demian in the rear mirror. "Demian, what do *you* think?"

Demian shrugged, crashing the battleship into the window.

Jim swiveled around to face Jimmy, eyes twinkling. "Look under the seat there. See that package? Open it."

Jimmy opened the silver package and took out a yo-yo.

"That was mine when I was about your age. I could do those tricks you see the real experienced boys do, walking the dog and loop-de-loop and all that crazy stuff, but the real thing was if anybody messed with me they got beaned upside the head. Turn right up here May, right by the stop sign. You think you can walk the dog with that scrappy old thing, little man?"

Demian dropped the battleship, nudging his brother for the yo-yo. "Ooh, I-I want one too, Dad!"

"Well sweetheart, I originally meant for you all to share it. But since you were too preoccupied to answer your mother and so hellbent on sassing your brother after Sunday school maybe next time you'll know not to put on airs. You have to work for every damn thing in this world, Demian. It won't be handed to you just because you think you're better than everybody else."

They crossed over the railroad tracks, leaving the Negro neighborhoods, plunging back into the gray whir of tattered residential streets wedged between a scrap metal plant and a police uniform factory. They parked in front of a three-story house with chipped shutters and bathtub planters plopped down on an overrun lawn. An apple-cheeked white woman with horn rim glasses and knitting needles rose from the porch, peering at them in the noon glare. Jim bounded out of the car and waved.

"Good afternoon ma'am, I'm Reverend Jim Jones of Peoples Temple church." He gestured to the knitting needles. "That your preferred method of self-defense?"

The woman laughed and laid the needles on the chair. "Very pleased to meet you Reverend. Is that your wife there?"

"Yes, and those are my boys. Come on out Mabelean and meet Miss Seymour!"

Mabelean emerged from the car and opened the door for Jimmy and Demian, bending down to coax them out. Jimmy grabbed tentatively onto her arm, shielding his eyes as she guided him onto the sidewalk and into full view of yet another strange white person. Jim walked over and put his arms around them. "Miss Seymour, this is my wife Mabelean and sons Jimmy Jr. and Demian."

"Pleased to meet you, Mrs. Jones." She paused, blinking at Jimmy. "You know you're the spitting image of a young Sammy Davis Jr.."

Jim charged ahead up the front porch. Miss Seymour and Mabelean stared at each other for a moment in a tight circle of pinched smiles. Mabelean tried to lead Jimmy toward the house. He dug his fingers deeper into her wrist.

"Ow, shit!" She yelped, snatching her hand away, red welts rising on her freckled skin.

Miss Seymour gasped, "Oh my, are you ok?"

"Of course she is," Jim interjected. "No harm, no foul. The boy's just nervous."

"Fraidy cat," Demian muttered behind his hand, so his father couldn't hear him.

Miss Seymour led them through the front door and into a bright parlor lined with newspapers meticulously stacked and catalogued by name, date and subject of interest. A parakeet in an overhead cage squawked at them as they entered, pecking at its droppings, dynasties of bird funk ripe in the blue-green feathers baked into the bottom of the cage.

"Sit, sit, make yourselves at home. I'm generally not one for baking but the mood struck me last night." She nodded at the banana loaf gleaming in the middle of the table as she poured Mabelean a glass of water from a plastic jug. "You all are to be saluted for taking in this boy. Doing what you did, that's God's work right there. If there were more people in the world like you."

Jim cut a piece of bread and stuffed it into his mouth, eyes lighting up ecstatically.

"Outstanding, just fabulous ma'am. This is positively sinful on a Sunday! I wanna take a few slices for the road to give to my deacons. Most of 'em don't have time to pause to get a good home cooked meal, much less a delicacy like this."

"Oh now come on!" Seymour said, blushing.

"Honest to God. I haven't had anything this good since I was a boy in Lynn. May's not one for sweets but I know my boys'd like a piece."

Miss Seymour got a plate, cut a few slices and put them down in front of Jimmy and Demian. She disappeared into a back room and reemerged with a small wooden cage. A baby monkey stared glumly through the bars.

"Here she is, the poor thing. Appetite's been off for the past week and her eyes are starting to get a yellow cast. I simply haven't had any money to take her to the vet. If you can help her I'd be grateful."

The monkey let out a sickly squeak and settled back down into the squalor of the cage. Jim poked his index finger through the bars and ran it over its back.

"Feels like she's running a fever. They go through this when they're babies just separated from their mothers. Good ol' Muggs, the one I had when I was a boy, got this malaise when he was the same age. Nothing that some warm milk with a shot of brandy can't remedy."

"I didn't separate her," Miss Seymour said. "She came to me orphaned. One of those carnival barkers just up and abandoned her."

"Lucky for her that you rescued her," said Jim. "Some of 'em will sell these babies right to the slaughterhouse and none's the wiser... Fresh monkey meat in your hamburger and you never know a thing."

The boys looked at each other. Demian snickered, twisting his wiry body theatrically out of his seat like he'd been stricken with the plague. Mabelean stopped chewing. "I have to apologize for my husband, Miss Seymour. He's usually not this crude in mixed company but he does have a magical way with sick animals. Does she have a special name she responds to?"

"Daisy."

"Well you shouldn't blame yourself for her condition," Jim said. "If you don't mind my asking, do you have a church home at the present time?"

"I used to go to First Methodist over on Stapleton but my cataracts started acting up and they stopped running the van that used to pick all us on the eastside."

Jim cut himself another slice of banana bread. "We've just started van service for members that live far away or don't have transportation. If you're ever interested in coming to hear the service ..."

"I have to admit, I'm curious. You know, Reverend, you have a reputation for being a bit more modern than some folk would like."

"You mean ... messing with Negroes? That is what you mean right?"

"I'm being real frank with you. Some people will understand missionaries going down to blackest Africa to give the Good Book to the natives but they won't see why you and your pretty little wife here would want to ..." She trailed off, reddening as Jimmy lowered his head, picking at the shriveled banana bread crust on his plate. "I don't mean any disrespect, Reverend. I grew up in a community like this and seen good men in the clergy destroyed by the gossip and backstabbing of petty minds with no greater mission than getting a float in the Easter parade. I'll confess that I've never been in an integrated congregation or integrated anything. You're treading thin ice with that here. You got Negroes over there and white people over here and that's just the way it's supposed to be."

Jim nodded. "God tell you that?"

Mabelean looked uneasy. She took Jimmy's hand and rose from the table. "It's time we left. I don't want this baby hearing this—"

Jim held up his hand. "No, no. Stay there. We don't cut and run from no one." He brushed the crumbs from his minister's collar, beckoning Jimmy to come to him, pulling him on his lap. He turned to Miss Seymour, locking eyes with her. "My son has been excited all day because he got his first yo yo. Used to give me hours of satisfaction when I was lying up sick in bed with influenza."

"Oh."

He took out the yo yo from Jimmy's pocket and did a loop-de-loop. "You were saying, Miss Seymour."

"Just-just that—"

"You can understand that as a mother, now," Mabelean interjected gently, "I'm trying to build a better world for this little boy, for both my little boys. The Lord made all children innocent and it's we adults that corrupt them with prejudice and hatred."

Jim cleared his throat. He took the cutting knife from the banana bread and wiped it clean, carefully folding the wax paper around what was left of the loaf. "Now I don't know about all that. Some are just born bad." He handed the loaf to Miss Seymour, patting it with a rich smile. "That's not to say that sinners are beyond redemption."

Seymour leaned forward pensively, jowls shaking. "And would you say that being against ... being against Negroes and race mixing is a natural sin in the eyes of God, Reverend?"

"Yes, I would, Miss Seymour. Remember there is no difference between Jew or Greek, slave or free, for we are all one in Jesus Christ. That to me is one of the most important scriptures. If you don't live your life accordingly then how in the hell can you rightfully call yourself a Christian?" He nodded to Mabelean that it was time to go. "Pardon my coarse language, ma'am. Belief just gets the better of me. We thank you for your generous hospitality. Be rest assured that Daisy, who will be christened as Muggs Jr., will have a loving home with our family."

He hoisted the monkey's cage in the air, the boys hovered behind, fascinated. "And I'm serious now, whenever you want to market that baking talent of yours for the good of charity ..."

"Are you making a proposal, Reverend?"

"It's just that we're so lacking in the culinary quality department. Now mind you we have a lot of dedicated volunteers. We got women, and some men—because we don't believe in men sitting on their duffs letting the womenfolk do everything in the kitchen—making great meals for the members but they need guidance, a little more experience and versatility, some leadership. The kind I know you can provide, Miss Seymour."

"Well aren't you a born flatterer."

"I had a sense about you as soon as I walked in."

Mabelean edged toward the door, her arms around the boys. "Jim."

"There's strong energy here. Good energy. Not often that I walk into a place and feel that. You've done a lot in your life. Weathered a lot of hardship on your own. Lost a son in the war. I know how painful that is. My father was a war veteran. Came back home busted, isolated, died fighting demons. We welcome survivors with open arms in our church family."

Miss Seymour knotted the hem of her dress, glancing at the photographs slanting across the mantle. "I don't recall ever telling you about my son."

"There's no need for you to shoulder the healing experience alone anymore."

"How did you know my son died?"

"Daddy can tell the past," Jimmy said quietly.

Seymour looked at Jim then Mabelean, skepticism weakening into a moist smile of awe.

"My Calvin used to make little zingers like that," she said, a catch in her voice. "From the mouth of babes I guess."

Jim put the monkey cage down on the floor. He walked over to Seymour and took her hand. "Can I send someone to pick you up for Sunday service next week ma'am?"

It was the thirteenth night of roving. The big bad luck of witches and black cats and broken mirrors. Mabelean had intercepted Jimmy in the kitchen, taken him by the hand and led him back to bed, the labored plod of her breathing sending him down to earth again. The sleepwalking became their special night time ritual. Beyond Jim, beyond Demian.

It had started around the time of the death threats. His parents arguing about them in the night's winding down chatter. Whites and blacks couldn't mix in church. His daddy was going too fast. When Demian went to sleep the clowns in their toy chest directed Jimmy to leave. "Get out while you can," they said, drilling their glassy green eyes into his. Painted grins daring him to open his mouth and make a sound.

No one knew about his clown congress. On weekends the church bustled with planning meetings led by two white women named Carol and

Deb. They were lean, watchful, favorites of his father's; always there helping with food or giving advice or assisting the old people who fainted during services. He saw how his mother tensed in their presence, her hands fleeing to her hair, fluttering down her dress to the lump of fat left over from having Demian. As "first lady" Mabelean couldn't appear to be too proud or hoity toity. It distracted from the mission, Jim said. Trust was a premium. Thrift was a premium. 'Cause their eyes are constantly upon us, he told her, watching our example, taking notes, looking for guidance yes, but rooting out weakness too, always, always, always.

He demanded excellence from Jimmy at school, punishing his low marks with a teaspoon of castor oil or a brisk whipping.

"Your schooling is a dress rehearsal for everything else in life. It's a test. Black boys can't afford to slack off and be mediocre niggers like the world expects. White trash can get away with just being street smart but you got to be book smart and street smart on top of that." He made him sit in the dark and count to five hundred, leaving him to make a phone call or shower for his nightly planning meeting at the church. No matter what he was doing, if Jimmy was still counting when he'd finished he'd make him start over.

"Don't think you're fooling me with that speed counting and skipping over numbers 'cause I can hear you wherever you are. Your daddy knows every trick, scam and short cut you gonna use to get over boy cause I did all that shit long before you were a gleam in your mama's eye."

"It's harsh keeping him sitting up in the dark all that time," Mabelean said. She worried that Jimmy's vision would be affected, a squint already forming when he read simple sentences. "That's not the way to teach him to do his lessons right, Jim. He'll start rebelling against you, start to hate you for putting him through that."

"That what you think? Don't come whining to me with that naïve bullshit. He'll chafe at it now but in the long term he'll thank me for toughening him up. Boys are growing up quicker and quicker these days. Some of 'em are big enough and smart enough to do men's work as soon as they hit nine or ten. Hell, I was expected to fend for myself as early as six.

I didn't have a mama running after me wiping my behind or my nose or any other orifice. It stunts their character when you do every little thing for 'em and don't have any expectations."

"My expectation is that he be allowed to remain a child for awhile. And that he, that he not resent his brother."

"What kind of country do you think we live in, May?" He snarled. "Where the fuck do you think we are? There's no avoiding resentment. No amount of sugarcoating will change that Demian's white and he's black. No matter our intentions."

"I still worry about Jimmy. I don't care whether you think I'm being over-sensitive or over-protective. We can't know what's really going on in his head, whether he's really happy and whether this is the right home for him. People like Miss Seymour—they're the majority opinion. I've seen the way some of the whites in the church look at us when we bring in Jimmy from Sunday school."

"Fuck 'em and their judgments. And you make it sound as though this is some kind of experiment."

"Well isn't it?"

"That boy is my flesh and blood, May. His mama and daddy might have been Negro but he's mine and always was mine. Was destined to be. I willed him, just like we created Demian."

"How can you be so arrogant in the face of God?"

"God doesn't have shit to do with it."

She shook her head. Outside in the garage she could hear the doleful bleat of Muggs Jr. thrashing around in the cage. The phone rang twice then stopped.

"That's the second call today," she said.

"You've been keeping the log with the dates?"

"Yes."

"Like I said, I didn't want to upset you but Deacon Thomas intercepted a few letters last week, right before the March on Washington. Most of 'em were death threats. One even had a soiled rubber wrapped up in it. We got some real depraved individuals here, and dumb too, had the nerve to put their real return addresses and everything."

On the other side of the wall, Jimmy's room went quiet. The bed creaked with the small weight of his body. She could feel him waiting, straining for Jim's footsteps, the warm bath of his approval, his hand on his head, against his cheek, brushing his lips in sympathy.

She rose and went to the door. Jim looked up at her plaintively.

"We're getting under their skin, May. Every threat they make shows we're having an impact, just like Martin Luther King is doing with the redneck politicians in the South. That's the only reason I'm telling you these things. I don't want you to be afraid, to worry yourself too much about all this crap because we've got providence on our side. There's people in the community that don't even know that they have a voice and we're giving them one. Matter of fact, Ida Lassiter is coming Wednesday to interview me about the 3-2-1 food, clothing and shelter ministry."

"Again? Well she's certainly been a good advocate and platform for you."

Jim tilted his head canine, like he was listening to a far-off sound. "For me? For us, May, for us." He got up and stood next to her, pulling her to him as he burrowed his fingers softly into her hair, damp and coiled with sweat.

"What do you think I'm doing all this for? Kicks? Publicity?"

"I've got to get our son."

He took her chin in his hand, encircling her waist with his arm. The monkey sounds in the garage becoming more agitated as he kissed her eyes one by one. "I'm concerned about you darling. All this worrying. It's gonna make your back pain flare up again. First Lady Mabelean can't be bent over with back troubles. All the women in the congregation look up to you. Deep down all the wavering white ones who'd just as soon as run over hot coals buck naked than shake a black person's hand are inspired by your example in spite of themselves, May."

She wriggled from his grasp. "I've got to get Jimmy."

He stared down at her blinking, biting his lip, trying to keep still, to keep the dazed, besotted schoolboy who sat at the knee of Prophet Zeke years ago from roaring up and swallowing him. "Ok," he said. "Will you come by later for Bible study?"

"Jimmy has his spelling bee tomorrow. He's got twenty more words to get through on his master list. I want both boys in bed before 8:30." She took a stack of cue cards out of her apron pocket.

"I'll tell Miss Seymour to come up and watch them. It's important that the members see you participating in the evening sessions as much as possible."

"Why, Jim?"

"Makes 'em feel like everyone's equal. Keeps the women stimulated and connected to us. Makes 'em see that our family is their family and vice versa, that there's no separation among us. If one of their children needs something it's our duty to provide it. So many of these fake Christian ministries sink under the weight of false divisions because the church family never was a real family to begin with."

She paused, measuring her words. "I don't know why you need me to be there, Jim. Carol or one of the others could do just as well as me filling in. You defer to them anyway when it comes down to real decisions. If you want me to keep up appearances just say so." She broke away from him and went out into the hallway. "Jimmy! Jimmy! Come here, sweetheart." Jimmy stuck his head out of the door of his room, eyes stung by the musk of navy beans simmering on the kitchen stove as he teetered toward Mabelean, bracing himself against the wall like a parachutist scooping at thin air.

"I did all the way to 500," he said quietly.

"I know, sweetheart. Very good. We need to go over your spelling words for the big day tomorrow. Come sit at the table while I finish up dinner and we'll do them together."

Jim took the cue cards out of her hand. "I'll do them with him, May." He waved Jimmy down the hall toward the tiny cluttered study where he wrote his sermons, slept, caucused with church officials, doing counsel with distraught, insomniac members on the big black jerry rigged phone late into the night.

"Who's the one to beat in this competition?" He asked Jimmy.

"What?"

"Who're you most afraid of, who gives the most attitude that they're gonna win?"

"Gideon. He wins all the time."

"Wrong little man, it's you. It's you that the other kids need to fear. Hell, who's Gideon? Just another boy who pisses standing up and shits sitting down just like everybody else. He's no smarter than you, no better than you, and, in fact, I bet winning all the time's made him a cocky little bastard. When you win all the time you get complacent, lazy. It takes somebody knocking you down to make you remember how hungry you were before winning came easy."

He opened the door to the study. Outside, the next door neighbor sat slumped on his porch in his undershirt, sucking on a cigarette butt, stick-straight hair standing at attention, crusty feet peeking out of a pair of wilted slippers. Jim rapped on the window and waved at him, turning back to Jimmy, anger and disdain on his face.

"Bo over there hasn't had a job in two years. Got laid off and bounced around a few times now. No direction in life. Reminds me of my father. Got beat down early and stayed beat down. You want to do something that uses your brains so you don't have to bow to somebody else forever, control your own destiny."

He shuffled the cue cards in his hands and read off the one on top. "Celestial. Isn't that funny. Some people might say that card has something to do with our destiny."

"What does that word mean, Dad?"

"Of the heavens."

Jimmy looked down at his socks. Mabelean insisted that anyone who came into the house remove their shoes to minimize the noise on the floors or the stairs, telling people that Jim couldn't abide distractions that could throw off his thinking when he was writing or sermonizing.

"I don't believe in heaven," Jimmy said. Bo next door looked over at him and scowled, spitting a big gob of nicotine bile onto the grass.

Jim put down the cue cards, drawing Jimmy tenderly onto his lap. They sat and watched Bo scowl at them, smoking, spitting, his pale feet white as a dried out corpse.

CHAPTER 9

Ida Lassiter, Witness, 1963

THE LAST SUNDAY service brought out all the rubberneckers. The ones who thrilled at a car crash on the horizon, slowing down, salivating as they neared the blood, guts and gore. If they were going to get saved that week then 4 p.m. at Peoples Temple was their last chance. The church band and the choir were always crack, egging on audience members who'd gotten the spirit, accenting Jim's pulpit exhortations about apocalypse with a horn blast, drum roll or flute trill. Nuclear holocaust is a'coming, he screeched, and the only ones gonna get saved would be the Temple faithful.

This is what his visions told him, thrashing in his sleep with his thumb in his mouth and the night light on. The cowardice. The mama's boy shipwrecked in his own head.

I sat in the back pews and watched the afternoon's last dance of surrender. The musicians were black, white, mulatto, shiny untapped talent from the train track neighborhoods and bedroom suburbs, some barely out of high school, some recent drop-outs hot with disillusion; a fierce junior league hungry for the next breakneck chapter in their parched lives.

Jim called on me every month at the office with some new scheme for collaboration. The hotel strike years ago had galvanized him, raising his local profile as an audacious nigger lover with a jackleg church and a silver tongue. I could see him growing out of his puppy-hood as he got more confident. I could see him smelling himself, reveling in his youth, his novelty, his supernatural recall of the most obscure face and tortured personal history.

At night, the glimmer of something in him tugged at me, under the leaden waves of dream, a lamprey attaching in my sleep.

Elders from the white Pentecostal congregations sought him out as a whiz kid who could talk CIA spying one minute and the healing power of prayer circles the next. Jim began to ham it up, adopting a southern cadence in his confessional sermons, dropping g's, playing to the small throng of white women who hung on his every word and stayed after hours to clean up the church.

They were a grasping quintet which secretly jockeyed for dominance. Carol was the alpha who kept the assembly line of all the Temple's programs moving. She and Mabelean criss-crossed each other warily, avoiding duplication, maintaining a strict division of labor. Carol played the enforcer, supervising church finance. Mabelean channeled the Virgin Mary; sweet talking, soothing, her honey dipped voice soaring over Jim's during the hymnals.

The other white women, Sherie, Deb, the rest, monitored prospective converts. They tended to the curious who came for the faith healing, coordinating outreach letter campaigns to reel in ambivalent white seekers cockeyed about the Negro deacons hovering at the good Reverend's side.

On weekends, Jim plowed through our neighborhoods with his two little salt and pepper boys in tow. He dragged them to all the church picnics and summer ice cream socials, Easter egg hunts and autumn carnivals, talking integration and Moses beating back the Pharaoh.

"For example, just look at my little man Jimmy Jr. Top of his class and a genius in science and mathematics but them school board savages done barred him from the school his own brother goes to."

Outraged, the women in my historical society took up a collection for Jimmy's school supplies. More donations poured in after the feature story I ran in *The Gazette*. When it came to the beneficence of white folk some of us could out Tom Uncle Tom. Even the smallest, most perfunctory white gesture toward Negroes was deemed to be sympathetic. When they heard that Jim and Mabelean had been the first to adopt a Negro child in the state of Indiana they gushed with gratitude. These were the same ones who'd never lift a finger to help the boy's mother before she had to give the child up for adoption; the same ones who railed about loose morals and those triflin' country Negroes up from Tennessee spitting out babies in the slums. Forced sterilization should be provided at these clinics they go to for their birth control, one white-gloved Bethel Baptist steward told me. God bless that Jim Jones for doing what's right and setting a Christian example.

A small groundswell of Negroes joining Peoples Temple started. Some came after Jim's neighborhood canvassing. Some came after reading my articles on the church's work. Some were inspired by the hot spring of '58, when all the white homeowners' associations in the area tried to run a black doctor out of his new house on Cranston Street, and Jim participated in a meeting I set up with the family and the mayor.

I had made it a habit to go to the church once a month when I wasn't on deadline.

"When are you going to stay for an entire service?" he asked me one afternoon at the office.

"Sundays are work days, quiet time. This place shuts down and I can take advantage of a whole afternoon."

He leaned forward in his chair, stretching his hands over the worn knees of his pants, a leg hitched up to reveal the hairy scruff of his leg, the fat calf thick from walking the city, from running up stairs to lay hands on bedridden prayer patients. Outside in the common area Harrison grunted his departure, sweeping up the mail imperially as he doffed the colorless hat, coat and gloves he wore regardless of whether it was thirty or one hundred degrees.

"I've lost the yen for listening to preachers. It's tiring, dealing with intermediaries giving you their filtered version of the Lord's word."

"It's not out of vanity that I want you to stay. I'd just like some advice on whether I'm giving my people enough."

"Your people?"

"You think I'm being impertinent?"

"You sound like you want them on a leash."

"I want all of them, everyone, to feel like they have a home with The Temple."

"Home should be natural, not imposed."

"Where do you get that impression from anything I've said or done? The church should be a provider and I'm doing that."

"The way you said your father wasn't?"

"What gives you the right to judge him?"

"Boy, you've only taken me into your confidence for the past decade now. There's very little I don't know about you."

"I'm not a boy and I highly doubt I'm that much of an open book."

"No? You lap at black people's heels for approval and patronage. What kind of backbone is that showing?"

"Is that how you see me? As a lapdog?"

"No."

"Then how? How do you see me?"

I paused. The building drained of life around us. What should have been an hour of release and contemplation was sullied by his grasping, desperate presence. I had a paragraph left on a story about the mayor's latest capitulation to housing terrorists, then several hours of editing ahead of me, each wasted minute a squirming albatross on my neck.

He twisted a hangnail off his thumb, rubbing the scab beneath. I pulled out a bandage from my desk drawer and handed it to him. He smoothed it on, feigning absorption as he awaited my verdict.

"I grind my teeth at night," he said, "from the worry."

"And what do you worry about Reverend?"

"About building this congregation, about doing right by the community. You think because I'm a white boy I wasn't properly called—"

"I think no such thing. Let me see your thumb."

He stretched out his hand bashfully, blood encrusted under the bandage.

"You'll strip your fingers to the bone doing that. All that laying on of hands is giving you blisters. What is it that you think you're doing with that voodoo superstition?"

"People have legitimate ailments that need to be cured if they can't get to a doctor or aren't rich enough to afford one."

"You go to Seminary for that? You have a degree in hoodoo-ology? A doctorate?" I lowered my voice. "You're not a medical doctor, Jim. I know some of the effect is psychosomatic for folk. But the Lord will strike you down if you're pulling a con on those people."

"Oh will he?"

"Yes."

"I'm a healer. I don't pretend to have any special schooling or phony degrees. But what I will say is that there are men and women walking around right now who are cured of cancer, who can see, who are ambulatory for the first time in years because they went to The Temple."

"All because of you?"

"Because of God working through me."

"You don't really believe that."

He hesitated. "I do. I have to. How else do I build an alternative society and confront the endless war against working people and the Negro? Look at how they follow Dr. King. How they worship the ground he walks on. All because The Spirit moves in him, because he's called, walks the righteous path for justice. Come see us this Sunday. Stay the whole time. We've got a boy in the choir, a foster child, He's got a voice like an angel. Right out of the Sistine Chapel. S-say you'll come."

"I have deadlines and a paper to run."

He got up from his chair and knelt down in front of me, running his fingers through his hair, black strands falling.

"Say you'll come."

I inhaled the antiseptic must of hair oil, shampoo, and baby powder, residue from his sons' bath time. A scar threaded across the scalp where his hair parted.

"How are your children?

"Fine." He put his hand on my knee gingerly, probing the fabric of my skirt. I let him keep it there. The elevator dinged in the hallway, signaling the ritual delivery of the white newspaper's evening edition by an aging courier with a smoker's hack. We listened as the paper slapped across the floor. Jim stretched his fingers slowly out on my leg, averting his eyes.

"I hear you want to adopt more kids," I said, taking his hand.

"Yes, that's right." He wobbled off balance.

"Keep kneeling," I said, tightening my grip on his knuckles. "What is this thing you have about being everybody's daddy …"

"That's what a pastor does."

"Bullshit."

"Ida."

"Stay where you are."

Our fingers interlocked for a moment. The courier went back into the elevator in a volley of hacking coughs. I let go of Jim's hand. He settled on the ground, wayward, arms wrapped around his legs.

"Can I see you again?"

"Maybe."

I seldom thought about Mabelean. As a person she was simply of no consequence; only ghosting up unbidden in the grocery store when I walked past shelves of hair dye. Blond, frost, chestnut, platinum, auburn—the colors of the white ladies' stealth empire. If my cart was full with the better cuts of meat I was mistaken for a maid and given wide berth in the aisles, addressed respectfully as "Ma'am" while the checker searched hungrily behind me for a whiff of my white mistress or sniveling white toddler charges mewling for chocolate bunnies and lollipops.

Everywhere, the air changed with the faintest whiff, the hint, of a white woman. When it was crowded to overflowing Goldilocks couldn't dip a toe onto a train car north of the Mason-Dixon without a regiment of crackers overseeing every move, making sure no Negro man woman or child twitched, sneezed or batted an eye in her direction. Rape was what happened to white women breathing the secondhand air of Negro train cars or caught in the dead of night with their family's virtue, their good name, hanging on the line. Under the law Negresses could never be raped. And this kept white women safe in their kingdoms.

After our first physical encounter Jim had a standing appointment every week, arriving a half hour after Harrison left. Harrison always laid out the next edition of our paper on the center table for me to proof. Then, like clockwork, Jim would come in thirty minutes later with a cascade of questions. How would his sermon address problems of social relevance, should he tap this organization or that for donations, what was the key to keeping the youth he'd recruited motivated to come back.

At first I let him put his head in my lap, let him lie there silently, believing he was outside of time, his body coiled, simian. I could not say why I let him, why I desired him, what corner I'd turned inside myself. Desire battled revulsion as he lifted my skirt, nuzzled between my legs and licked me to orgasm. I would not allow him to speak, the sound of his voice otherworldly, unbearable.

This became the routine for our assignations. The slow motion recovery of afterwards, when the mundane shifts, starts, and creaks of the empty office steered us back into the rhythm of co-conspirators.

"I see so many who want to give and don't have a pot to piss in," he said. "There's this one woman, black as night, beautiful and dignified, in her 70s or 80s…she'd rather give me her whole army widow's pension than eat. Just a little slip of a thing too, but when we start doing our wrap up at the end of service with the Exodus story her face lit up like a diamond."

"I hear you've been doing door-to-door campaigns."

"Outreach. We're doing outreach in the community. Same as you do. I wouldn't call them campaigns."

"Are you promising your new converts a seat next to St. Peter?"

He got up and went to the window, pulling the curtain back warily, his profile hard as a mannequin's. "I know you like to test me Ida. I appreciate your doing that. Challenge only makes me stronger."

"You like to play the martyr with Negroes."

He shook his head. "The black pastors pay lip service to grand ideals they can't meet and the white ones are blatant racists or back-to-Africa missionaries."

"So you're a hybrid child then."

I got up and stood beside him at the window. Cold air streamed through a broken pane stuffed with cardboard and foil, an old souvenir from a brick that had been lobbed by a protestor after we published an anti-lynching editorial.

"The mayor folded again on the housing subsidies bill. It's not a major revelation. He thinks he can buy off the residents who were evicted with a few chicken dinner speeches at the Negro society functions."

"Is he right about that?"

"For some." I stood behind him, mouth against his ear. Stubble marched down the back of his neck where he'd shaved. The ever present baby powder scent rose offensively through the air, a noose swinging between us.

He turned, drawing me tentatively to him. "We can get The Temple back out into the streets again. Write a few letters of complaint to the editors of the major dailies about the rigged inspection reports. Those buildings will be falling down in a few years and they'll have blood on their hands."

"The main problem with The Temple is the reputation you've gotten with your faith healing."

"Our healing sessions are important, Ida. I get letters, invitations, I have a whole shitload of people just clamoring for me to give 'em relief."

"It's one small step up from sorcery. All those people, elderly women writhing around in a house of worship, lapping up false hope—it's unseemly."

He hesitated. "It's not false. It draws people, moves them. Some of them would be dead otherwise."

"It draws the less educated and the gullible."

"Maybe, yes, but they stay for our other programs, and hear the message of justice and equality that we're trying to promote. That's the anchor. Many of them believe deeply in divination and who am I to disabuse them?"

We stood shoulder to shoulder, excitement and anxiety radiating from his body as he considered each word, calculating, measuring their impact, eager to shock and please all at once. He had removed his minister's robe, folded it into a square and put it on the desk chair, his armpits rimmed with sweat. He pulled a smashed donut out of a paper bag and put the whole thing in his mouth, chomping through a cloud of powdered sugar.

"Don't screw up your face that way, Ida. Please. I don't want to be accused of running a benevolent dictatorship. And if my people want faith healing, then it's a necessary 'evil' for the here and now. Sometimes I don't have their full attention when we talk about fighting the discrimination at their door. I have seniors cooped up in these godforsaken nursing homes, swimming in their bed sores, and when they hear of a healing on our radio hour, it lifts 'em up, makes 'em feel like they have something to live for. The sickest ones have their eyes cast upward looking for something nobody in the world can promise. So the divine trick is getting them to feel a purpose that's bigger than any god can provide."

He smiled for the first time that evening, impish in his heresy. "My people...are open to anything you do. There's immense respect there. Your paper is one of the only ones that's saying anything of worth. Plus, we know your life is on the line every time you print something the establishment doesn't like." He stroked my hand. "I could get a few of my men in the church to provide you protection if you needed it."

"That won't be necessary."

"Don't be too proud... at least consider it."

There was the beseeching, and a germ of covert grandstanding. I pressed my knuckles into his cheek, down his jawbone, to his chin, holding his querulous face as he closed his eyes and leaned against the window. The last city buses of the evening left at 8. I kissed him, finding his tongue, sucking it, rough. I unbuttoned his shirt, pausing at the third button, a small hammer and sickle-shaped scar etched into his skin.

"Well I'll be damned. That part of your initiation rite with the good ol' boys in the Syndicate?"

He blushed. "It was years ago, an impulse right around the time when I was thinking about joining the Party."

"It's quite becoming."

"You're mocking me again."

"You're not that fragile."

"Maybe I am. Right now your judgment means everything to me."

"Right now?"

"Always. Why else would I be taking the risk to be here when I could fucking lose everything I'm trying to build, everything I want you to guide us on, be part of?"

"And admire unquestioningly."

"I'm not asking for blind allegiance."

"What, then? That I let up on you? Be the mammy? The nursemaid?"

"Ida."

"You've had a good run in the Negro press, Reverend Jim. That could change. I'm still not sure how I feel about you."

"You mean how you feel about this?"

"*This* is no more than these four walls. I meant I'm not sure how I feel about you politically."

He squared his shoulders, gathering his robe and the tidy sheaf of Temple pamphlets he carried everywhere, making as if to go.

"Don't be so dramatic," I said, waving him back. The last city bus wheezed from the end of the street. I sat down in my desk chair, resting my legs on the ottoman, as he bent down and kneeled before me.

CHAPTER 10

On the Road, 1964

THE TEMPLE BUS rolled into midnight, knocking Ida's head back, her pad, pen and indigestion pills clattering to the sticky floor. She bent to pick them up, wincing blearily at the tangle of sleeping bodies shoehorned into the cramped seats around her. Across the aisle, Jim's sons smudged up against each other, REM twitching, a green dump truck parked on their laps. The Temple was hitting sister congregations on an East Coast fellowship tour. Jim would speak at churches in Boston, New York, Baltimore, then join a peace summit in D.C. Ida had agreed to come at the last minute, flogging herself, bandying the decision back and forth over three stagnant days of deliberation when everything she wrote, everything she touched, turned to shit.

The affair was the least of it. They were running through the dregs, the snatched moments between services, the oral sex that ramped up in one fumbling session of fucking with a leaky rubber on the armchair in her office. It was a reptile brain drip that kept her enflamed, compromised, yes, in the eyes of God, but this was surely a small thing, a hiccup in the grand scheme of all her sacrifices.

She asked God for forgiveness, knowing Jim didn't because he didn't believe.

The boys shuddered and turned toward the window. Jim was in the back in the special air conditioned compartment his church board insisted that he have. He had to stay fresh for his appearances. Had to gather the inner strength to get direct communion with the Holy Ghost.

She saw Carol emerge from the compartment with a package of handi-wipes, staggering to get her balance as the bus coasted into a gas station so the driver could take a smoke break.

"Would you like a wipe, Mrs. Lassiter?" She asked.

"Thank you."

"I'm hoping we get into town before sunrise. It's going to be a hot one and Grace Tabernacle is an older building with notoriously bad ventilation."

"Jim is speaking to how many now?"

"Several hundred, it's one of the oldest black congregations in the East. You'll put that in your piece, your article?"

"That's standard information."

"It's quite an honor for us to have this platform." She smiled and wobbled down the aisle, checking for live ones, stopping just short of the front where Mabelean sat by the driver, talking weather and directions as he lit up a cigarette.

The tension between Carol and Mabelean was of no consequence to her. She was an outsider, an observer, and besides there was the more looming issue of her paper's woes; the soaring cost of printing, her editor Harrison's dwindling salary, rent, utilities, the refusal of several prominent Negro papers to run her "Inside the Black Church" series, fearful as they were of lost ad revenue. On the other hand, the Temple's star was rising. A few local white reporters were beginning to snoop around, morbidly curious, licking their chops at Jim's bravura, but none had yet latched on.

Mabelean got out with the driver, holding a road map over her lacquered head as she ducked into the drizzle, gas pumps gleaming in the soft humid light. A white couple made out in a car by the payphone, twisted against the door like wet salamanders. They disengaged for a moment, staring hard at the mix of people, black, white and in-between, spilling out of the Temple bus to stretch their legs, sucking on the sliced oranges passed around by Carol and Miss Seymour.

The toilet flushed in Jim's compartment. He sauntered out, fastening his belt bucket over rumpled slacks.

"What the fuck is this stop about, May?" He yelled. "We lost?"

"She's outside, Jim," Ida said.

He straightened up, startled for a moment, catching himself in her presence.

"Didn't know you were awake, Mrs. Lassiter. We could've been half-way through New York City if this driver had any sense of direction. Last time I get a temp driver."

He watched as the members outside scattered into the bushes to pee.

"You have places for everyone to stay?" She asked.

"The Tabernacle has its own youth center dorms which it's graciously offered us for the next two nights."

"Warm beds will do them good."

"Yes indeed. They deserve it."

She cocked her head toward his compartment. "And what about a warm place to use the toilet. They deserve that too?"

"Anybody that wants to use my personal bathroom is welcome to."

"Good, because they're holding us up using it out there." She looked over at his sons then smiled, patting his arm. "You've got some stiff competition going into Pastor Entwhistle's house. He's got some of his people believing they're levitating at the end of his services. You're going to want to be on your A game because miracles are in surplus there."

Jim blushed, frowning. He stooped down, lowering his voice. "Can you come here for a minute? I want to show you something."

She followed him to the back past a whole row of the Seymour family thrashing in a syncopated snore. The room was cool and dark. Books tee-tered from the edge of a writing desk jammed next to a hastily made twin bed strewn with tonic bottles.

"For after hours," he said, sweeping the bottles into a bag. "Sleep's a luxury."

"I get very little of it running a paper. But you seem to want bragging rights."

"I can't go up there preaching to over a thousand black folk and look a fool."

"You'll be part of the afternoon's entertainment, a curiosity at best, a sideshow at worst. In Harlem you stick to your programs, cut out that laying on hands mess. What did you want me to see?"

"Can you sit down for a moment please?"

"Your wife's on patrol out there."

He waved a magazine article in front of her. "You see this? It's a list of all the best places to be when those bastards drop the bomb."

"Northern California, Brazil…why are you obsessing on this at 12:30 at night?"

"We have to get out of Indiana."

"I've been telling you that for a year now."

"Naw, this time it's serious. Shh!" He paused, looking around. "You hear that?" He stuck his head out into the aisle then came back, shutting the door. "Christ. Some of our own kids shooting off firecrackers. I told Carol to take care of that mess. Works my nerves. Fortunately the more proactive men in the congregation have volunteered to be on security patrol."

"For what?"

"Threats. Attacks." He dug into a box under the bed and took out a .44 revolver. "My daddy was handy with a pistol. Taught me to bag gophers. I don't care much for guns but if one of them trigger happy peckerwoods gets it into his head to rush us I'll damn well use it."

Mabelean opened the door, stepping back, startled. "Oh, I'm sorry. I didn't know you had someone in here."

Jim cradled the gun in his lap. "What is it now, May? We going to get this rattletrap running before next year? We're sitting ducks for the police or anybody else wants to fuck with us the longer we're marooned here."

"Rodney is ready to go. It's just that a few of the kids got sick eating oranges and peanut butter sandwiches all day."

"Well we're promised hot meals once we get to Harlem. You know we have to keep costs down, May. I didn't promise anybody four courses out here on the road. It's all about the loaves and fishes, right Mrs. Lassiter?"

Ida stared through him. He shifted hopefully on the bed, black sideburns gleaming, an impish runt with a popgun waiting for his daddy to take his hand.

"I'll be sure and quote you on that," she said.

Mabelean fingered the cross around her neck. "That was callous, Jim. We've got growing kids here, they've been out all weekend with barely any room for a real rest—"

"Get off your high horse, May. You think you're going to sit up here and school me like one of them Hoosier hillbillies at the market? Jesus speaks through me and our mission, not you. You're gonna coddle us right into the ground. Besides, Mrs. Lassiter is one of the most esteemed journalists around and we're lucky to have an audience with her. I need to get my head clear for my speech this morning and I got limited time for distractions."

The bus started up around them. Jimmy Jr. came in rubbing his eyes, train pajamas bunched up around his gangly body. "Mom, I had a nightmare that I was falling."

Mabelean put her hand on his forehead, her eyes cutting into Jim. "That's the second time this week. It's ok sweetie, tomorrow night you'll be back sleeping in a real bed."

Jim put the gun back in the box and reached out his arms. "Come here, son. Tomorrow your Dad's going to speak to an important group of people. Now I have to admit I'm a little bit nervous. I've been up half the night thinking about what I might say. You know sometimes Dad doesn't get a lot of sleep right?"

Jimmy nodded, glancing cautiously from his mother to Ida.

"Sometimes it's necessary to go without things you think you need like a little sleep or good food when there's a bigger cause to serve."

Jimmy looked down wide-eyed at the box with the gun, awake now, curious. Jim winked at him. "Tomorrow when we get to the new church

I want you to sit right up in front where I can see you. You're going to be my inspiration."

The Tabernacle Church ushers freshened up the chrysanthemums on the altar, spritzing them with spray bottles, coaxing them from their mid-morning droop. The church was one of the oldest in Harlem, a crown jewel in the abolitionist movement, a post-slavery oasis. The ushers watched the Temple members file in, eyebrows raised at the whites leading black children, at the lines of black family after black family forming the advance guard to Jim Jones, who nodded greetings from behind dark shades as he waited to be introduced. In the early morning hours of their arrival to the Tabernacle dorms everyone had been instructed to be spit polish; teeth brushed to gleaming, hair combed austerely, slacks, skirts and button down shirts starched, steamed and pressed for decorum's sake, departing from the jeans and schlubby casualness of the Temple services.

Ida took a seat in the middle and thumbed through the program. It'd been years since she'd been in a traditional church. At her home church growing up in Memphis women couldn't have their periods when speaking before the congregation, giving witness or helping with Communion. It would disrupt the spiritual order, bring calumny on the church. They had special ushers to inspect the drawers of any woman or girl who'd been called to speak. Upright Christian women who wouldn't balk at any dangerous mission the pastor gave them, saintly so-called old maids who'd acquired a tolerance for dried menstrual blood; dubbed The Drop and Cover crew for their habit of making sure nobody's privates were exposed once their panties came down. Women and girls lined up in a basement room with a peephole chiseled out by the pastor's son. Clean panties meant you were cleared to speak to God publicly. Soiled ones meant you were marked for that week and had to wait, to sit in the special section for transgressors with the eyes of Drop and Cover upon you.

Mabelean took her place next to Pastor Entwhistle's wife as Jim bounded onto the stage with a handful of chrysanthemum petals.

"Can I get an Amen?" he asked exuberantly. "Good morning and thank you Pastor Entwhistle, First Lady Entwhistle and all the good people of Holy Tabernacle. I couldn't resist picking up these flower petals from the floor. The smell of these is so powerful and so sweet in this sanctuary it almost knocked me off my feet. I was reminded by these fallen petals of the trials of Job. How even when we're kicked way down low to the ground the Lord gives us little signs that he's with us if we just open our eyes. I want to introduce ya'll to my son sitting in the front here. Stand up for a minute Jimmy Jr. He came to me in the middle of the night tired, having bad dreams, in that ornery mood ya'll know five year-olds can get in. But you know what he told me brothers and sisters? Dad, I'm going to be happy because I'll be back in God's house in the morning. And you know that warmed my soul. That warmed my soul because we've gone through the ringer over the past year. Death threats, illnesses, a fire in our church kitchen, a few of our babies killed in a car accident on the way back home from Bible study. We're no different from any other striving to be righteous congregation bowing humbly in the light of the Lord's good grace. 'Cause you know He don't give us more than we can bear. He's testing us just like Job, brothers and sisters."

The Temple members broke into applause; one hundred on their feet, rapturous but mindful of the seated Tabernacle congregants clapping more guardedly as they took in the spectacle. Pastor Entwhistle smiled weakly from the dais, patting his bald head with a monogrammed handkerchief. He'd agreed to host Jones and the Temple after reading Ida Lassiter's articles on their service work with seniors and Negro foster youth. Ida had grit, integrity, if she championed something it would be to the death; but there was something in the air of the church that unsettled him, beyond the knee jerk ardor, beyond the faint dissonant stirrings of his own professional jealousy.

"I'm not too proud to tell you I was down on my knees in the bathroom every morning asking God for deliverance," Jim whispered. "After those precious little angels were murdered last year in the Birmingham church I thought my son and our other children might be next on Satan's list."

"We beat him back Reverend Jim, we beat him back!" A woman yelled.

"My insomnia comes from thinking of how best to serve Him and them … but now I sense that someone here in the sanctuary is struggling with this very same dilemma."

Ida kneaded the program in her hands, cringing, feet feeling three times tighter in the ill-advised heels that she'd squeezed into out of a last minute twinge of propriety.

"Damn him," she thought, as he broke into a smug little strut behind the podium.

"There's a sister here who's worried about where her family's next meal is going to come from. Who's come here for the first time off the New York streets sick in her heart, sick with worry about what's going on in this country. Now don't be bashful sister 'cause you're in the House of God, among family."

Jim stepped back waiting, soaking up the room's anticipation. "Gee, did we bring this hot sticky weather in with us, Pastor Entwhistle?" He asked, looking around for the parishioner. The pews shifted uneasily, seconds passing into a baited breath minute, Ida's shoes getting tighter and tighter around her sore ankles as the revulsion built in her and she was back in the office with Jim, lurching toward a bittersweet climax, his hand on her breast.

Entwhistle cleared his throat, his eyes seeking Ida out amidst the murmuring crowd.

A broom bristle-sized woman with a rusted cameo at her neck rose from the back pew, waving a piece of paper over her head.

"Yes, Reverend Jim, I believe you're talking about me. I just got this eviction notice the other day and I don't know what to do."

"It's causing your pressure to flare up."

"Why, yes."

"How long have you been part of Holy Tabernacle?"

"This is my first time coming, Reverend. I've been hearing about all the good things Pastor Entwhistle does."

"And he's as righteous as they come, practically Dr. King's right hand. Can I get an Amen!?"

"Amen!"

"I think we can all agree that this country is at a crossroads. That it's important for the faith community, Negro and white, to stand together in this time of tribulation." He grabbed the mike and jumped down from the stage, gasps of wonderment rising from the Temple throng.

"But this too, like the trials of Job, will pass. Walk with me sister—"

"Rollins. Joy Rollins."

"Sister Rollins your sweetness and sense of humility are big enough to fill up this room."

"Thank you, Reverend."

"You're raising two sons and a crippled daughter on your own?"

She blushed with surprise. "Why, yes."

"Is your daughter here with us in the sanctuary?"

"Yes."

Everyone in the church turned. Pastor Entwhistle stood, alarmed. Ida balled up her program, shaking her head with rage.

Sister Rollins helped the girl up. She braced herself against her mother in crutches, blinking at the stained glass replica of Moses and the Burning Bush on the ceiling.

"And she's been this way since birth?"

"Yes, Reverend."

Jim approached the girl, hands outstretched. He took out a bottle of holy oil and sprinkled the liquid on her.

"Help her Lord, help her Jesus," a man to his right muttered.

"Mama," she said plaintively, oil dribbling down her lips, down the front of her wilted yellow cardigan, every head in the sanctuary swiveled to face her. She took a step forward, unhooking her crutches.

"My angel," Sister Rollins whispered. The girl walked down the aisle unsteadily, a foal gaining balance, confidence. She stopped near the altar and picked up one of the stray chrysanthemums, burying her nose deep in it, exhaling, waving it in the air as she plucked its petals and threw them into the audience.

Jim beamed. "Pastor Entwhistle, we give thanks to you," he said. The Temple rose in unison, velvety voices climbing to the rafters, "Precious Lord, take my hand, lead me home", seducing the entire congregation into song, enfolding the girl as Carol bent down to pick up the discarded crutches from the side of the aisle.

Ida stormed out of the throbbing building, nauseated. The bus driver sat in the stairwell by the door, fat legs splayed apart as he savored a cheese steak sandwich, mayonnaise smeared in his fledgling mustache, eyes flickering with dull surprise at the sight of her.

"Got your Jesus quota filled for the day?" He smirked, pulling brown lettuce from the bun.

"You have a cigarette?"

"Sure." He reached into his back pocket and handed her his pack. "Need it bad huh? All that getting saved and talking to the Holy Ghost crap is way too much for me."

"Yeah, well we just had a bonafide miracle up in there."

"No shit?"

"No shit."

The door burst open and a group of children tumbled out giggling, followed by a weary trickle of adults and the dying peals of "Precious Lord".

"Looks like a whole lotta folk got burned at the collection plate," the driver said.

A man in a dark bowler hat approached her. "Are you Ida Lassiter?"

Ida took the cigarette out of her mouth. "Yes."

"I'm one of the deacons. Recognized you from your column in the *Amsterdam News*."

"Good to know they're still running it."

"Oh yes, it's one of the sharper ones." He lowered his voice. "What in tarnation was that all about in there?"

The service ended and the doors flew open again. "There's cake and punch in Fellowship Hall everyone," a blue-wigged usher announced, rushing ahead to prepare, the sanctuary emptying in a roar of babble. Temple kids raced out to the parking lot, launching into a game of tag between the cars and the bus, the sound swallowing up the deacon's voice. Jim walked out flanked by two young black men, a gurgling brown baby riding on his hip.

"Sure, sure we'd love to come back," he said to a group of women trailing him. "Just so long as you and your family are front row and center. In the winter you might just want a break from the cold for a little California sunshine. We're moving our ministry out West soon." He caught sight of Ida, bowing his head demurely. "Mrs. Lassiter this here's Sister Rollins' new grandbaby."

"I need to talk to you."

"Can't it wait?"

"Now."

He grinned at the women and handed the baby to Mabelean, who'd come up behind him. "Would you make sure she gets back to her grandmother?"

She nodded warily, eyeing Ida.

They walked to the end of the parking lot.

"So you're smoking now. Never thought I'd see—"

"What was that craziness you pulled in there, exploiting that mother and her daughter?"

"Exploitation is a strong word, Ida."

"Where did you get that woman from?"

"I didn't get her from anywhere."

"Your lackeys recruited her then. What did you promise her and the others? The best seat in your imaginary bunker?"

"We're closing escrow on two properties in California in thirty days."

Tabernacle members buzzed by the parked cars, hungry for a taste of Jim, a line of them forming to talk to him, held at bay for a moment by his two guards. Pastor Entwhistle watched the scene ruefully from the stairs, his deacons arrayed around him in dark felt hats, brooding like a freshly routed army.

Jim took it all in, edging as close as he could to Ida without it looking improper. "It's a big market out there, Ida. If you came with us the sky would be the limit for your columns, the newspaper. Indiana's a dead end, no pun intended." He chuckled limply, playing with his hair. "Seriously, I don't want to see you languish back there. You know how much I care about you." He waited a beat for a response. She stood, unyielding.

"Goddamnit I'm aching, Ida" he pleaded. "All these fucking people around watching."

"It doesn't make a difference, Jim."

"I'll get down on my goddamn hands and knees right in the middle of this parking lot and beg."

She waited.

"You'd like that wouldn't you? To see me whipped. That's what this has fucking been for you all along."

"If that woman will talk to me I'm going to expose you. It will be a headline story in all the Negro papers next week."

He straightened up. "To hell with you, then. She won't talk to you. None of my people will." He turned to the guards, signaling that he was through as he called to Miss Seymour, ambling by with a piece of chocolate cake. "Miss Seymour, would you see to it that Mrs. Lassiter is taken care of with a bus ticket back home. She's suddenly taken ill."

"Oh my, so sorry to hear that."

"That won't be necessary. I'm not sick, he is. And I don't need your damn charity. I'll be leaving on my own with my own money when *I* decide to."

Fat drops of rain pelted the car tops. The line waiting for Jim surged forward. Sister Rollins' family had been delivered to the front, the breakout stars of the raw morning. Daughter and mother stood arm in arm beaming, pristine teeth dazzling in triumph, faces candied with love for their newfound church family.

"Reverend, Reverend!" Joy Rollins called out in a strong voice scrubbed of the doubt and hesitance she'd displayed inside. "About what you said about coming to California for the weather and everything. That sounds mighty nice."

Ida intervened. "Sister Rollins can I speak with you?"

Rollins whirled around. "What about?"

Jim jerked with surprise, making a move to block the diversion, intercepted by the crush of seekers shouting his name, waving programs.

Ida led her by the elbow, away from Jim and the throng. "Can we speak in private, in the Fellowship Hall, or maybe we can meet somewhere else?"

"I'm sorry, I don't believe I got your name…"

"I'm Ida Lassiter, I write for—"

"Oh yes," the woman said drily. "Yes, I know who you are. I read the papers. You did that thing criticizing our churches. I'm sorry but I don't think there's anything you and I would need to talk about."

"Did the Reverend Jones pay you to come here this morning?"

Suddenly Mabelean and Dolores Frederick, a black greeter and Temple membership coordinator, appeared at Sister Rollins' side. Dolores inserted herself between Ida and Rollins.

"It took a lot of courage to do what you did, Sister Rollins. What an inspiration you and your daughter are."

"Thank you."

"All of our members will be provided housing when we get to California. Each family will have a space for a fruit and vegetable garden, plenty of fresh air and sunshine. Nothing like this cramped East Coast living."

"Sounds lovely," Rollins said.

Ida piped up, "Sister Rollins—" She broke off. The kids' tag game had escalated. They tore around the legs of the adults, the procession led by Jimmy Jr., Demian and three other boys who dove after each other, screeching manically as they barreled past Ida, knocking her backward into Dolores and the industrial-strength bible clasped to her chest.

"Boys, stop acting like common hooligans! That's no way to behave on a Sunday!" Mabelean yelled after them. "I'm sorry, Mrs. Lassiter. They meant no offense." She forced her lips into a smile, rubbing Dolores' arm protectively.

"None taken," Ida said. They watched Jim bend down to listen to an elderly woman in a wheelchair, his eyes gone dewy. "All things considered, they're not to blame."

CHAPTER 11

Mother Mabelean: A White Woman Speaks

WE NEVER HAD Negroes or colored working for us. Unlike some of the neighbors who were supposedly poorer and would scrape two pennies together for a day's worth of laundry. I never had the gumption to call a black woman mammy. Even as a child it was un-Christian to do so; those colored women who worked to the bone for whites were so majestic and dignified, balancing the world on their backs with barely a whisper of complaint. Or at least that's how it seemed from the picture shows.

Pinky. Imitation of Life.

The white women were long, lean, vexed and beautiful, while the coloreds stood dutifully by their side. How any self-respecting white woman could have allowed that is beyond me. But I loved the picture shows just the same.

Not the darkness, not the escape, not Hollywood, not the stories, but the proximity of colored up there in the forbidden balcony.

Jim would make a hobby of sitting up there and passing for colored. With his ink black hair and high cheekbones he could have been half-breed anything in the dark to a kid usher going through the aisles with a busted flashlight. As a boy nobody cared about me no how no way, so why would they give a shit whether I was white or Negro, he said once, knowing full well that it did matter to the world.

I never wanted my boy Jimmy Jr. to be taught to fear a white woman, to ingest it like poison, a waking nightmare every time he saw me. In the market white children would run up behind us with bananas, at the hospital white society ladies would say prayers for the mute African orphan.

Forgive them Lord for they know not what they do.

We left Indianapolis because the threats got louder and more vicious. We knew that nuclear holocaust was on the horizon too. We believed that the West, California, would be golden, would be safer. We didn't run with our tail between our legs like the town gossips said but with most of our congregation relocating as a unified family.

I found out about Jim and the newspaperwoman before we moved. I'd already seen her hold on him, seen the high regard he had for her in our services. She was older and had standing in the colored community, sang every number with the rest of the congregation, took great care with the matron ladies who Jim flattered and fussed over.

What would the colored world have said about her honor as a race woman if it had known she'd seduced a married white man? What would have been made of her reputation? I had no spies, just intuition. Intuition and the hopped up, desperate sense of purpose he showed when he came back home from her office; the way he took me later that night, fire in his eyes.

We are researching land in South America. Brazil and now British Guyana. My boys bubble with excitement about the prospect of our trip. Jim calls the new country the Promised Land.

After the bomb hits, North America will be unlivable. Water will be contaminated. Colored survivors will be made slaves. Race warfare will be permanent. We'll build the new settlement with our own hands. Brick by brick, stone by stone, crop by crop. Only then will my mind settle down and the lies, the betrayals, the march of cheaters that pollute my bed fade in importance.

This duty, not petty jealousy, is what God expects of me.

California Dreaming

THE BIBLE IS the thing that brought us, it's what they used to sneak us out of the rich lands of Africa and put us into chains, as we're still enduring four-hundred years later. So I question their Bible, and I question their god that said slaves obey your masters.

—Jim Jones, 1974

CHAPTER 12

Taryn and Hy, Fillmore, 1975

A MOUND OF grits glistened from Hy's plate, dense and gelatinous with melted butter, majestic next to two shriveled pieces of bacon impatiently plopped down by the waitress whose shift was about to end. Chester's Diner was always crowded and bumptious, brimming with the frenzy of missed collisions and stuffed tables, hawkishly monitored by restless customers queued up at the door. Hy had come early and gotten a spot near the back for herself, Taryn and Jess, Taryn's girlfriend. The two of them rolled in a few minutes later, arms primly locked.

"They served you quick," Taryn said, taking a piece of Hy's bacon. She turned to Jess apologetically. "I swear I'm off pork tomorrow."

Jess grinned and opened a menu.

Hy rolled her eyes. "So you guys have some kind of meat pact now?"

"No, I just want to eat healthier."

"Why? You love bacon."

"Times change. You have a problem with that?"

The waitress put down glasses of ice water for Taryn and Jess and rattled off the specials, watching the table turnover out of the corner of her eye. Every Sunday afternoon the restaurant swelled when the church services let out, drawing droves from Good News Baptist, Redeemer Methodist, Sanctified Apostolic.

A trickle came in from The Temple; new members not yet initiated into its prohibitions against the evils of gorging on high fat food, processed meat and refined sugar.

"There's no justification for such excess when people are starving right under our noses," Jim Jones preached. "We don't need to go to China or

Bangladesh to see poverty and hunger. We don't need to charter a jet to Africa or Vietnam to see how the imperialists have raped and profiteered off of their farmers, because its right here baby, right in our faces."

Jess and Taryn met during a Temple protest against the third police shooting of an unarmed black child in the Fillmore district that year. Jess' family had moved to Fillmore from Texas during World War II, chasing jobs on the bay shipyards, the neighborhood devastated after the government's removal of Japanese American citizens to internment camps. Jess talked with her hands, prided herself on the accuracy of her snap analysis, wore her therapy degree on her sleeve, and plowed through girlfriends with disdain. Hy had seen her dominate the discussion circles at the church and been wary. She acted like she knew everything and everyone in the Fillmore's black community and was quick to school the novice whites who thronged the circles dripping earnestness.

"These motherfuckers come out from Ohio, attend a few Temple services and think they're ordained to save us downtrodden Negroes," Jess remarked to Taryn and Hy during one session after a group of white students said they wanted to live with a black family in the projects for a week to get a feel for the lingo of "the people".

She had frequent run-ins with the white Temple volunteers who went door-to-door trying to sign up black people for the church food programs and free health clinics. The white ones were parasite tourists. The black ones certified victims.

"Some of these Negroes fall all over themselves with gratitude when whites show up in the neighborhood wanting to do something for them," she said. "Break out the welcome mat, serve them ice tea. All that shit. Then when we come around and they look at us sideways through the peephole and won't even open their doors."

Jess' black talk pissed off Hy. She'd been appointed a lead steward in the Temple's statewide recruitment bus rides, deftly steering every conversation with black members onto the subject.

"You going down to L.A.?" she asked Hy.

"I can't get off this weekend."

"Too bad, we need you. Jim still hasn't gotten fully hip to the fact that you can't have too many Kens and Barbies on the frontlines in South Central."

"I doubt that. There's always calculation in what he does," Taryn said.

"True. What do you want to order babe? One last hurrah until cold turkey?"

Hy tunneled through her grits, irritated by the little endearment. Jess rested her hand on Taryn's knee then took it off, stiffening.

"Oh shit, if it isn't Miss High and Mighty."

Carol, now the Temple's "information minister" and unofficial chief deputy for the Planning Commission, came in with three men in spit polish suits rippling from their lean bodies. They sat down a few tables away, her gaze fluttering in Jess' direction with a glimmer of recognition as she chatted the men up, straining to be heard over the din. With her upper middle class pedigree Carol had ascended from the frontline in Indiana, a key recruiter for new white members. Jones ate these converts for breakfast, stoking their white guilt as he pressed them into service as political gophers, admin assistants, and intelligence gatherers on potential members and known enemies.

Taryn surveyed Carol and her crew. "Order Jess, before you lose your appetite."

"Carol's probably fucking the black one," Jess said. "Getting down and going down for the Cause. That's how those white motherfuckers did it during the Black Power days. They loved to get them some black ghetto dick then run home to daddy's money."

"Carol's more savvy than that," Hy said.

The waitress put a plate of corn muffins in front of them and began taking their orders.

Taryn recognized the man sitting next to Carol as an aide to State Senator George Moscone. His boss was running for mayor and The Temple was backing him. He placed a freckled paw on Carol's shoulder as she cackled into her water glass in a rare unguarded display of mirth. Taryn could see that she enjoyed the attention.

The Temple had begun to buy up more apartment buildings and brownstones in the Fillmore district, getting below market rates through its nonprofit arm. Like Taryn and Hy's apartment, most were within walking distance from the church, housing a warren of communal living families entrusted with the care of multiple children; a point of pride to the Temple as it bucked the tide of gentrification.

Jess looked over at Carol. "The first time she gets one of those scraggly brown hairs in brother man's grits he'll slap the shit out of her."

Hy stopped chewing. "You got something against black guys?"

"No, just the ones that think white girls are the Second Coming."

"And what percentage is that in your mind?"

"Seems like a big one in this city," Taryn chimed in.

"How are you qualified to comment? You've never been interested in being with anyone black to begin with until now," Hy retorted.

Taryn cut a muffin in half and gave one to Jess. "Do you know how stupid you sound saying baseless things like that?"

"Go fuck yourself, Taryn. You lie, bend and twist shit just to make out like you're the pious one. It's you that's got issues."

"I've got issues with you saying I have this thing against black men when every man I've ever slept with or had a relationship with has been black."

Jess squeezed Taryn's hand. "It's Sunday, ladies. Cease fire," she picked up the program from that morning's church service and thumbed through it. "I may not agree with Jim on everything but one thing he did say today was powerful. That part about tending to your inner self before you do any kind of cultural work. That's when you're really tapping into God's strength right there to use it as a compass for everything you do. I tell my clients that all the time."

Hy winced. "You talk to your clients about God?"

"I talk to them about their spirituality and how it influences their mental and emotional state. That's a key part of assessing their mental health."

"If they're Christians."

"If they're believers. Most of them are religious or spiritual in some fashion. Buddhist, Hindus, Muslims, Christians."

The waitress set the food down. Taryn mashed her fork into the towering plate of bacon, eggs and biscuits in front of her as Jess bowed her head in prayer. The crowd continued to swell, shifting in disgruntlement at the wait. A tall woman with floppy brown hair spilling from a headband brushed past a clutch of people hovering like buzzards over a pile of open menus. Children jabbed their greasy fingers into the dessert display case as the cashier rung up table checks and stuck them into the metal bill holder, her round face sagging with fatigue. She brightened up when she saw the headband woman, whistling out to the kitchen.

"Thank god, the cat finally dragged Devera in! I'm outta here everybody. Girl you better look alive because this place is officially jumping today!" She swept Devera up into a tight hug, nodding toward Taryn, Hy and Jess' table.

Devera positioned herself behind the cash register. "Thanks for keeping the seat warm. Manny is going to take over the last part of my shift this evening 'cause I'm precinct walking for my church."

"Oh, so you're getting all political now with that crazy white man's church. I'll say. Think you'll be the first black transvestite queen out of Fillmore running for public office?"

Devera paused, biting back her words of rebuke to keep it light with her.

"First black Mexican *woman* and I never say never."

"Some of your church lady friends are here."

"They're not church ladies, they're soldiers," Devera laughed.

Taryn sopped up her last dollop of egg with a biscuit, while Jess and Hy settled into a silent truce, tempered by the plaintive wail of Al Green and the finger popping fury of an oblivious white couple locked in exhibitionistic embrace over a plate of hot links.

Bands of whites had begun to move into Fillmore, priced out of the tonier zip codes. College students, office workers and waitresses crashed on couches, bunching up in trios, quads and quintets in rent stabilized apartments, flooding local restaurants and markets, driving up the prices, thrill seeking for all the urban exotica they could cram into their hungry gullets after hours, when the police roamed the streets in search of black and brown bait.

The Temple was against the onslaught in public, but salivated over the prospect of juicy new acolytes in private, leafleting discreetly in the evening hours at the local bars. Carol reeled them in with her spiels on social justice, ditching the Lord Jesus and the Holy Ghost for riffs on the perils of nuclear holocaust, polluted water supplies and eating red meat. Hy watched her finesse the politicians' minions. It was rumored that Reverend Jim was gunning for a position in city government. In Indiana he'd sat on the Human Rights commission, a key part of his résumé and his claim to legitimacy as an activist and freedom fighter, the cherry on top to years of backwater organizing, amidst the death threats and nigger lover venom that he thrived on.

Carol was sharing a piece of sweet potato pie with the black aide. She took big bites, licking her fingers and bobbing her head in time to the Five Stairsteps. She scooped up the check when it came.

"What I wouldn't give to be a fly on the wall for that conversation," Hy said.

"I'm quite sure she closed the deal. I'll say one thing for Jim he don't promote no dummies. Or at least not one's that aren't teachable."

Devera walked up to their table. "Morning," she said.

"Hey Devera!" Jess got up and hugged her.

"Hey ladies, I'm back."

"How was it?"

"Good ... ok ... I had to read the same fucking tired Jacqueline Susann novel over and over again because they wouldn't bring me my bag with my real books. Remember I took that speed reading course last year? So by the end of the ten days in rehab I could've turned that crazy white shit into Shakespeare I had all those lines down so cold. Seriously, backwards and forwards and every which way. Fried my brain way more than any drugs."

Jess howled and clapped her hands. "You see Miss Ann over there right?"

Devera looked over at Carol, sucking her teeth. "God, spare me. How could ya'll eat without some Pepto."

"I wish Jim would dump her stuck up ass. I play it cool with her and the other weird sisters though, 'cause they're always looking for a weak point."

Carol glided past with a twenty-dollar bill in her hand. The minions followed behind. She nodded at Devera and stopped at their table, smiling at the women.

"I swear that sweet potato pie is heavenly. I was down in South Carolina protesting the jailing of a Native brother for allegedly shooting up a pig's squad car and we stopped at this little diner and I had a piece that melted in my mouth. Even that wasn't as good as this."

"Those South Carolinians haven't got a clue," Devera said. "Hell, most of the black South landed up here in California anyway."

Carol gathered up her purse. "You all walking precincts for Moscone with us Monday morning?"

"My shift starts now and I have to close," Devera said.

Carol leaned into her. "The Planning Commission really appreciates all the great articles you've been contributing to the Peoples Forum paper about our work."

"Thanks."

"I hope I didn't embarrass you."

"No, you didn't."

"It's just that Jim wants you, all of you, to know that you're an asset to the church. That the church is your home, your family, and that its strength is in you."

Her brunch companions had drifted off to the counter, pausing at the display case to load up on desserts to go, a few women in line gazing longingly at their suited sleekness.

"Looks like you had a good meeting," Jess said, noting the ripple of attention. "Those are supporters of the church from Moscone's office and a few on-the-rise city councilmen. They're falling all over themselves because they know we can deliver votes."

Devera nodded in agreement. "This is going to be a close one. Right down to the wire into the wee hours. I can see it. The Republicans aren't going to go quietly into that there night."

"Can we count on another brilliant article from you to that effect?" Carol asked.

"Well, I don't know. I've got the late afternoon to closing shift all this week and I'm doing the precincts on Saturday. Then I'm taking a short-hand community college class that starts soon."

"You can do all that through the church," Carol said proudly. "We're going to offer fully credentialed and accredited classes right in the community center in the fall. You ladies are welcome to check them out if you want to get your college degree."

Jess bristled. "I have a Masters in Social Work and I'm a licensed therapist. Would you like another business card? Maybe you can add it to the other two I've already given you."

"Of course. How clumsy of me. I-I didn't mean to imply..."

Jess threw a few bills onto the table and put her arm around Taryn, rising to go. "Just stop patronizing us, hear?"

"I think taking classes through the church would be neat," Devera said.

"Yeah, it'll be useful to have a degree before the world ends," Taryn said.

Carol blushed. She waved a limp goodbye to the government aides, brightening as her next appointment arrived; a family of four from a local black church who'd recently started coming to Temple services.

"What a fine Sunday," she called out to them. "Great seeing you all here. Lord, they've got sweet potato pie to die for."

CHAPTER 13

In The Sanctuary

JIMMY JR. WATCHED them from the stage, three hundred strong, eyes glowing with desire. The Soul Steppers had just sung Harold Melvin's "Wake up Everybody". Mother Mabelean reported on the progress of the new group home for fifty foster care youth. Turkey and gravy would be served to celebrate the congregation's twentieth anniversary. Congressmen were coming to speak at the jubilee dinner, deliver honorary plaques and fat donation checks to the group home fund. Lesser dignitaries had to be turned away because the rented hall only seated two hundred; but the poorest members would be given priority, would sit at the front and enjoy the ornate aperitifs donated by the city's culinary academy.

Jimmy watched the little kids fidget through the four hour marathon, playing peek-a-boo with each other over the tops of the pews, trading toys, bubble gum, Archie Comics as they watched the second hand chug slowly around the face of the clock. The clock was the last remnant from their church in Indiana. It was the one that he'd stared at with the same frenzy at seven, ten, fifteen and now sixteen when he'd celebrated his birthday with several other members who were having birthdays the same month. Individual birthdays were a show of egotism, an indulgence, a distraction from hardness and sacrifice. The last one he'd had all to himself was back home, in Indianapolis, heralded with a bloated chocolate cake topped by a white slugger hastily painted brown by Carol, the woman who'd become his father's main lover. It was the year Mother Mabelean had begun homeschooling him, snatching him "out of that Hoosier armpit, because a Negro child couldn't score higher than all the whites in trigonometry," his father raged. Not three times higher as he had done. Not slamming his paper down showing off like the test was a trifle ten minutes after it was given; his giraffe legs spilling impudently out into the aisle where any white girl could trip and fall and be disgraced for life.

Coming to California he daydreamed fields of orange trees, golden sunsets, scorched beaches, blue skies rippling into infinity right out of a Chevy commercial, his skin bleached not to white but to nothingness. Then he could walk invisibly among the voyeurs, the toadies, the Temple witnesses who sucked and fucked with every casual gaze trying to milk his heat. He, the Temple's young black prince, the tall inscrutable braniac virgin repelled by the simple flesh on flesh of a handshake or a backslap.

He looked out at the congregation, a patchwork of gleaming upturned faces. Mariah and Carol skulked at either side of the sanctuary like twin sentries, arms folded tightly across their chests, tapping their feet in time to the organ's soft drone as Mabelean read the final announcements.

"Congratulations to our new drug rehab graduates."

"Congratulations to Donel McShay who wrote the most letters to the governor this week."

"Congratulations to Nelson Fields who won the Benjamin Banneker science prize."

Children from the group home streamed across the stage and into the pews, lifting baskets full of tithing envelopes above their heads. They worked the aisles to the collective snap of purses, wallets and checkbooks being opened, the organ swelling as his father stepped back into the pulpit.

Jim waited for the noise to subside, microphone in one hand, an envelope in the other. He hummed into the mike and peered out at the shifting check-waving crowd, fixing it with the warm milk stare that had greeted Jimmy post-nightmare when he was a kid, tangled in soaking sheets, the stalkers from the white school crouching in the closet like a lynch mob in miniature.

"Brothers and sisters, thank you. Thank you for your generosity, but we got to keep it coming, we got to keep it moving … even when we think we got a fortified wall and a united front somebody's gonna try and knock it down. Before you go home to prepare for the festivities this evening I need to share something disturbing with you. We got this letter yesterday. Sister Carol brought it to my attention. Now, as you all know we get a lot of correspondence from people all over the world inquiring about our programs. Recently we even had some queries from aboriginal activists in Papua New Guinea and Melbourne, Australia who're looking to start a health collective like ours. I'm constantly uplifted by the example we've set for others in need."

A few women in the front rows stood, applauding.

"Thank you, sisters," he waved his hand for silence, adjusting his shades. "Unfortunately, there are those among us who struggle to find a place in our righteous mission for world peace. We've got some downright trifling individuals in our midst," He tapped the letter and lowered his voice. "According to this confession here one of our most talented musicians is having problems keeping his goddamned fly zipped. He's running around whoring and sinning and pointing the finger at everybody under the sun as an excuse for why his ass is dragging so low in the gutter. On top of everything he had the unmitigated gall to ask me to fuck him."

The women in the front rows sucked their teeth in unison. "Shame, shame," one muttered, fanning herself.

Jim folded the letter and put it in his robe pocket. "Brother, for the sake of the family I need you to reveal yourself."

Jimmy froze in his seat. A baby sucking a bottle on its mother's lap sputtered and spit up as a damp breeze wafted through the sanctuary. Cedric from his father's security detail stood and pointed to Felix the band drummer.

"C'mon brother, be a man and answer Father. Everybody knows he's talking about your shiftless butt."

Felix shrunk down then popped up stiffly in his seat. "I don't know what the hell you're talking about."

"Don't you, Felix? You're not exactly private about your shit," a white woman in a blue pantsuit shouted.

Cedric raised his voice. "C'mon stop playing games and wasting Father's time. After all he's done for you, sticking his neck out every time you needed something. You got some nerve playing this holier than thou innocent mess."

"I-I'm not going to confess to something I didn't do."

"You're living in a damn fantasy world, man."

The woman in the pantsuit stood, waving a train ticket in the air. "I saw you leave the Stone Street apartments at 6 a.m. Tuesday morning and go to the train station. You were supposed to report to the commissary for your work assignment, but you called in sick. One of your comrades in the house gave me this." She held the ticket out for Mariah to collect. "You sure looked healthy as a horse to me."

Jimmy watched his father. He'd settled into the stool behind the pulpit, following the interrogation with studied detachment as he sipped from a glass of ice water one of the ushers had brought him. The younger kids were getting restless; chirps, wails and shushed giggles filling the air. Cedric folded his arms across his chest and walked toward Felix's aisle.

In his spare time Cedric was the point man in an all-black detail that went with Jim to public meetings, patrolling the church grounds, ferreting out professional spies and hangers-on who washed up at the Temple's door. They were modeled after the Nation of Islam's grim regiments of stoic young Fruit of Islam guards. Jimmy had been trained to supervise them when his father was traveling, careful not to play up his authority, to quell any resentment about his privileged son status. His father half-jokingly branded them the Red Brigade, favoring recovering addicts, ex-felons who banged up against a wall of rejection from employers, former foster kids he wanted to give a chance at responsibility. They called Cedric Mr. Clean for his patience; his fairness and quiet resolve a symbol of the ride-or-die loyalty many of them felt protecting the church and Jim.

Cedric stood in front of Felix. "I don't want to call you out like this brother but you leave me no choice. After all Father Jim has done for you, to sit up here and disgrace him and the family like this. To sit up here and lie through your teeth in front of our seniors and in front of all these women who just spent the day making your sorry ass a feast? Naw, we ain't having that kind of abomination."

"He needs a beat down," a woman in the third row hissed as she dropped her offering in the collection plate. "For bringing disgrace on the Cause, for dirtying our name."

"We're not going to have enough time to get ready for the jubilee because of him."

"Cowardly, just cowardly."

"Playing silly little games like a child."

"Our children have better morals than him."

"That's right."

"Cedric spoke the truth, it's an abomination what he's done begging Father to screw him."

Jim rose, jumping from the stage, robe trailing behind him like a beaver's tail.

"No, no. Now that's not 100% accurate. Let me make something clear brothers and sisters. Messing around with men wasn't the abomination. We got to free ourselves from that biblical crap. All ya'll have homosexual tendencies, predilections you got to work out. Every last one of you. That's just natural. Animals in the wild are the same way. Felix's issue is messing around on his given partner and exposing her to disease and ridicule then having the fucking nerve to try and pull me into his mess by making unreasonable demands. Now tell me, how can you put all that energy into chasing every Tom, Dick and Harry so much as shakes his butt in your direction when you got a full time job, kids and responsibilities to our musical department? You must be Hercules, Superman and Mighty Mouse all rolled into one brother 'cause I don't have a goddamn clue how you do it!"

The congregation roared. Jimmy saw a few of the newer members glance around, torn with the fear and fascination of being strapped into a dark carnival ride on an invisible track. Some, who had passed the unofficial initiation period, and were familiar enough now to be recognized by Jim by name, puffed up, brimming with their newly granted insider status.

Felix opened his wallet and snatched out a few dollar bills, hands shaking. "Is this what you want? Here, take it all, take it. You want to bleed me dry? Fine. I don't have enough to buy you off, to buy my freedom. I've given my whole life to this place and I don't know what to do now...I don't know what you really want from me," He sobbed.

"Just cut the bullshit and confess!" The woman in the blue pantsuit jeered. "You've taken up enough time on this earth being sorry and trifling. Didn't your mama raise you better than that?"

"Next he's gonna say he's an orphan, a goddamn Oliver Twist!" an elderly man yelled.

"That's no excuse for what he's done. Demanding shit from Father! You better get your dumb ass in line!" The pantsuit woman retorted.

"So selfish," Mariah agreed.

"I-I'm not making excuses, I-I'm sorry. I'm sorry."

Pantsuit stood and turned, leaning against the pew to face Felix, her skin glistening with vindication and raw leonine youth, her normally slumped carriage statuesque in the moment.

"Ask Father for forgiveness," she said triumphantly, waving stumpy fingers with chipped candy red press-on nails.

Jimmy squinted. It was the same woman who'd come before the congregation dressed as an elderly spinal cord injury victim, pretending to be healed by his father a few months before. When he was little the imposters ruled the Indiana services, hobbling forth on canes in a flurry of wigs and makeup, croaking their testimonials to the rafters as the members swayed and begged for more. He saw a thirty year-old substitute teacher come out of their bathroom in full old lady regalia sucking a salted grapefruit to make her voice sandpapery.

He felt the eyes of the congregation on him, the people waiting for their black prince Jimmy Jr. to speak. Instead, he sat there immobilized. Mariah came on stage and handed him a collection basket filled with slips of paper. Familiar names stared up at him in chunky kindergarten writing. Each slip had the full name of a black man; the youngest, the darkest, the strongest, the most belligerent, the ones who talked epic smack, who could hang in the air doing supernatural dunks to the delight of white spectators, the chosen ones groomed to be Father's second string bodyguards, his righteous eyes, ears and fists when a first stringer fell from grace.

"Father wants you to pick a name," Mariah whispered, breath ablaze with cigarette smoke and mouthwash.

"For what?" He asked.

"The boxing match. Felix must be shown the light."

He looked down at the basket then back at his father. The choir started in with the first soft strains of "Precious Lord". Jim smiled gently at him and nodded as the music began, closing his eyes in reverie.

He swallowed and picked a name. Byron Markham. A shy boy he knew only by sight. Mariah motioned for him to read it out loud. He heard himself croak the name into the sanctuary.

Byron stood up and came forward. His face expressionless, mouth set into a thin gray line studded with fresh pimples. Cedric guided Felix up to the stage next to Byron. Mariah handed the two of them boxing gloves, the room going dead silent until a voice from the balcony shouted, "Go on beat the shit out of that whore!"

The first punch is a teaser. A fat drop in a stagnant pond, knuckle on cheek on bone, a spinning grace note.

The second punch is a wake-up. A reminder that the shit is real, the point of no return, the cold bucket of water for getting in the game right here right now before you go down, falling through the stars in ignominy, elephant herds dancing on your temples.

The crowd is poised to spring should Byron fall. The Indiana old guard clutching their hymn books. The ready-for-the-summer teenagers rooting for him between clenched teeth. The Red Brigade standing whip smart at attention as Jimmy paced the edge of the stage, damp with shame.

Felix is bigger and slower but agile from his tour in the jungles of 'Nam with all the other Negroes and Mexicans from Alameda who got caught in the draft.

He puts Byron into a headlock, murmuring, "I don't want to hurt you man, this beef is not between us, its them making us do this fucking crazy shit for show."

"Let him go! Let him go!" The crowd yelled, some spilling out into the aisles in white rage. Felix backed off, startled, panting, t-shirt riding up his hairy stomach. Byron seized the opening and reeled around and decked him, knocking him to the ground. Scattered applause echoed through the sanctuary, people in the first three rows returned to their seats, shaking their heads in disgust, nodding that's right, that's right, goading Cedric and Byron on as they locked arms to help Felix up.

Members of the Brigade swept onto the stage to lead Felix away. Jimmy staggered out of his seat, wanting to follow, cowed by his father's hard gaze.

Jim stood. He pushed his shades up on his nose, waiting for the din to settle. A pigeon flew overhead, settling in the rafters as a baby cheeped up at it, transfixed.

Jim smiled. "Now across town at the society churches they'd be talking about how Brother Felix is some kind of scourge," he said. "They'd be in high dudgeon about casting him out of the fold. But that's not what this is about baby. We gotta make ourselves whole." He unfastened the top of his robe. "I said I'd suffer right along with you and take my licks accordingly. Cedric, go get that paddle from the back."

A shudder went through the pews. "No Father, no," a woman in the back moaned.

"I appreciate your concern, sister." He paused. Pantsuit, Mariah and the whole choir jumped up in protest, pleading with him to reconsider.

"Nobody's above the will of our family. Brother Felix is no aberration. There are two-faced people sitting right up here in this sanctuary grinning and nodding at everything I say while they make a mockery of my work and think I don't know it."

He gestured to Felix's wife. "Oleta, come up here, sister." She rose trembling from the middle row, beaded purse pressed in tight armor to her chest, green rayon dress clinging to her legs.

Jim put his arm around her. "Do you forgive him sister?"

"I-I don't—"

"Now I didn't say *forget*, Sister Oleta, I said forgive. 'Cause there's nothing in the world weaker than a man. Not just in affairs of the so-called heart and sex, but in running this planet. Sisters, you know what I say is the gospel truth. I know I don't have to tell you twice. There's nothing weaker than a lowdown, two-timing, shit eating man! We look around and most everything that's going to holy crap is run by men. Thieving, greedy, warlike, rather go and drop a megaton bomb on some innocent third world babies than sit down and talk peace."

"Don't do it Dad, don't hurt yourself!"

"I'll prostrate myself right here if I need to. I ain't too proud. I'd lay my black ass down for every last one of you and get the shit beat out of me because I love you that much."

"We're all sinners, Dad!"

"Naw, naw… It's not about sin. That's those Christians selling Heaven to you! Heaven is the most lucrative slave game in the world baby!"

"That's right, yes it is."

"But did he need to be beat?" Jimmy strained to see who was speaking as the congregation rustled, heads turning in unison. A black woman he didn't recognize repeated her question.

"Was that really necessary?"

"Of course it was, Hyacinth," Carol said from the side of the stage, accenting her name.

"I'm surprised at you, Hy. Maybe you don't know Oleta's history," Mabelean said. "This woman came over with us from Indiana and has done every kind of service, every kind of volunteer work there is to do in this church. She's also been a devoted second mother and a mentor to many of our foster and homeless youth."

"We know that's right," Oleta's mother, aunt, uncle and cousins murmured in support from the back rows. "Deliver her Father from that trifling man."

Oleta looked down at her shoes, embarrassed at being in the spotlight, nervously fingering a charm from the Temple knick knack store around her neck, a lush picture with the rainbow family of multiracial kids arrayed around Jim.

Jim took another sip of ice water, gargled and set the glass down, narrowing his eyes at Hy.

"You expect us not to defend her, Hy?" He asked quietly. "Well what if it was you? What if it was any of you? Who's ready to stand up and pass judgment on how we deal with transgressors when you know good and goddamn well you'd be the first one screaming for justice if it was your tail on the line? Brother Felix had every opportunity to do right."

"Yes he did!"

Jim spread his arms, holding up a newspaper. "Ya'll saw the vile slanderous editorial that that woman Ida Lassiter wrote questioning our finances. She's been on us now for over a decade with the same lies. If we're under siege from outside we sure as hell can't afford to be under siege from our own people!"

"Thank you, Dad," Oleta rasped, suddenly finding her voice, turning her back to Hy. "Thank you. I don't know what I would do without you and the rest of the family here. Please just keep us in your prayers everyone."

Jim sneered, "Now sister what have prayers ever done for you other than keep you up at night wondering why the capitalist pig who never prayed a day in his life is getting richer and fatter?"

"Teach Dad, teach!"

Oleta blushed. "You're right Father, but it gives me comfort, helps me think, helps me clear my head."

Jess stood up. She walked over to Oleta and put her hand on her shoulder. "You're not wrong to admit it, Oleta. I still pray too sometimes. But prayer didn't get us out of Indiana or help us buy the new church in Los Angeles or help us stay communal doing it all for ourselves. Prayer didn't beat back the Democrat sell-outs who wanted to put an incinerator right in our backyard."

"Naw, and that's why we stay independent, stay above all that," Jim boomed. "The campaigning we're doing for Moscone is to make sure Fillmore doesn't get carved up and horse traded while we're sitting out in the cold with our thumb up our ass. They can buy some of these society churches but the Temple can't be bought, not while I have all of you behind me. Now Jess here is one of the most gifted counselors around. Any of you have issues, any of you feel yourself cracking up under the pressure from the liars and spies that want to tear us down let Sister Jess know."

He waved his hand in salute. "Now, let's get moving ya'll!"

The choir started up again. Jess smiled, her gaze flickering over to Hy standing awkwardly to the side fidgeting with the scarf around her neck. Jimmy rose from his seat, stooping to pick up the crumpled boxing gloves Byron had tossed off after his victory. He watched Hy as the congregation filed past her, abuzz about the Jubilee that evening, their eyes hot with pity and indignation.

CHAPTER 14

Ernestine Markham, 1976

THEY CAME OUT with pitchforks when we moved here. The women in their white pearls and pressed gloves, the men dressed to the nines in suits and ties; diminished after a day at the office, then fastening their lips to big orange bullhorns like it was the bottom of the ninth at a baseball game. The whitest white of San Francisco, out in the street for a tea party, pinkies raised at attention. We had just got in the week before from Tuscaloosa, Alabama. Hardcore FOB. And Lord Byron, my only son, was a tiny little thing, struggling even then to get away, to bust out and catch any sliver of the world that he could. A big-headed, curious, colicky little word warrior; babbling, questioning, as the Bay Area bluebloods tried to beat us back to Dixie.

When we got to California I wanted to kiss the ground and pirouette on Ghirardelli Square it was so clean and beautiful and open. The water, the bridges, the traffic, the life dripping from every corner.

It was the first time Byron had seen a white woman, and they came out in hungry packs; their babies tucked safely away in all those grand two-story stucco homes tended by black hands from sunup to sundown. They weren't cowering behind their men waiting to take direction; no sir. They weren't giving quarter to no one.

My brother bought the house from a black agent who was passing as white. He had Victorians all throughout Fillmore, Nob and Russian Hill. Bourgeois Negroes wanting to buy white capped off his career like Martians landing in Ozzie and Harriet's rosebushes. This is how Byron wound up being the only black boy on the block until it tilted black in the seventies. First chair in violin, first chair in trumpet and tuba, ace in the marching band when he wasn't daydreaming about something called Narnia. An introspective boy who never wanted for anything. How could he be suckered into beating that fairy down like a common street thug? How could he let himself be led by the nose by those miscreant white women panting around Reverend Jim?

There were women in our circle who got into the Temple in the early seventies. Left their home churches disgruntled by their pastors' empty promises, hooked on Jim's old school Pentecostal shine and his integration talk. Some packed up their houses, deeded them to the church and moved into Temple communes, taking on other peoples' children, cranking out three meals a day for the residents. Raising kids was supposed to be every-one's responsibility, a social compact that appealed to me. It was the end of the Vietnam War, and I was wrung out fighting to keep my teaching job at a school where black children were suspended for days if they so much as looked cross-eyed at whites. We could've damn well stayed in Alabama for that.

I joined the church in part because my son was in danger—mind, body, spirit up for the lowest bidder. All the years of music lessons, all the years instilling discipline and love for the classical traditions sucked into a vacuum of anger and self-pity when he dropped out of high school after the marching band leader tore him down for being effeminate. When the Nation of Islam rolled through the city that summer with their spit polish rap of instant brotherhood he fell hard. The pageantry, the easy rituals of manliness lighting a fire in him for a little while until he found out that eating bacon was an affront to Allah.

I wasn't in church the day they made him box that queer. Otherwise I would've stopped it. My students were reading the "Secret Sharer" and I had piles of final essays to grade. After the beating Jim's security boys closed ranks like it was an initiation rite and Byron had gotten his stripes. He was sky high with their camaraderie and nobody could touch him he was so big and bad.

But truth be told what did this boy have to prove? After all I'd lived and seen in Tuscaloosa he had a cakewalk. He never had to work for uneducated white people, never had a white policeman put a gun to his gut, never been made late to work watching buses packed with whites who could barely speak English pass him by. He was lucky to be born on the right side of history, when a black man had half of a fighting chance.

CHAPTER 15

MacArthur Park, Los Angeles, 1977

IN THE MIDDLE of the night, Ida heard moaning in the alleyway, the oppressive squall of cats scavenging around the trash cans ripe with trout bones. She was staying in a residence hotel of retirees living on Social Security and evaporating pensions, thinking what was worse, the howls of horny cats or sweating a menopausal river not being able to write a word or read without the horn-rimmed cheaters she'd bought for two dollars at the Temple thrift store.

Cats were as good as overgrown rats to her. Cats with their mangy ways were the hissing conspirators that killed her grandfather after he'd swerved to avoid hitting a pack of them and smashed into a tree, bleeding to death in the front seat of his Buick Roadmaster, nothing but segregated white hospitals for miles. This was one of the many anecdotes Jim had stolen from her when they were together, trotting it out when his audience was tired and on the ropes. In Jim's telling her grandfather was transformed into a battered old Uncle Remus, one of his grateful charges when he was a hospital orderly passing for Negro.

The cat rats continued their lament, rattling the trash cans, weaving in and out of the parked cars, clawing at her temples. She hadn't allowed herself to think of Jim intimately since she'd moved West in '72; the decades mocking her, his touch a shriveled ghost. After her credit was frozen and her Indianapolis newspaper folded she scraped by on freelance jobs from the black weeklies. When that dried up she begged former colleagues, bombarding editors and publishers who'd once feared her with pleas for work. Some threw her a few bones; an assignment on the fad diets of black celebrities, an "exclusive" on the naming of streets for long dead black politicians, a feature on the first cherry pie baking contest to boast a black winner. She took them and held her nose. When the bills buried her she sold the printing press, a few limited editions of the paper and finagled a part-time job freelancing at a paper in Riverside, California, a dusty suburb sixty miles east of Los Angeles.

It had not been her intention to follow the Temple. But now her life's work had been sucked up in it, the church movement roaring and untamable, powered by love, fear, the storm of naked violence a follower had told her about before she vanished into nothingness.

The last time she saw Jim was on TV. A slow motion local broadcast, a sliver of him chubby-cheeked and prematurely gray, hair dunked in Grecian Formula. Sputtering on to a reporter about the gracious thank you letter he'd gotten from First Lady Rosalyn Carter after the Temple packed one of her galas.

Every night she battled the gnaw and niggle of responsibility. If she'd been more persistent, sounded the alarm more loudly, refused to let him in her office the first time, in her bed, her consciousness. Every night, waiting for the world to go black, the clock drumming sleeplessly, she swallowed the fear that she was really one of them; the blacks who were always coveting white people, electrified by the smell, the taste, the idea of them.

She'd been interviewing current and former church members for weeks, disguising her request as a human interest story on black religion in America, reeling in anyone who would speak to her, her meager weekly budget demolished by doling out bus fare, gas money to induce the hesitant. The day before she'd talked to a woman named Ernestine, a teacher whose son occasionally served on Jim's security detail. Her house was a few miles from the Temple's L.A. church in a clutch of rambling Craftsmans that shadowed downtown.

Ernestine was one of the less guarded ones, an independent thinker who spoke with conviction but kept to herself, teaching modern literature at a local high school and courses at the church on weekends.

"Not a dry eye to be found when he started carrying on about passing for Negro to care for sick black patients as an orderly," she said. "Some of us knew a little about his work back in the Indiana hospitals but that anecdote really brought home how long he's been at fighting for black folk, how close it's been to his heart."

"Yes, he's quite the race man."

Ernestine laughed. "Don't think I've heard that term in a million years. Would you like some coffee? Whatever else he may be—and mind you I'm not big on the faith healing stuff—I believe that part is genuine."

"A lot of black folk in the congregation would agree with you."

"A lot of folk period. Some of my students' parents, people who've seen unimaginable things."

Ida looked at the faded salmon walls dotted with the outlines of picture frames that had been taken down. Travel books, remote controls, notepads and lotion bottles spilled from boxes on the formal mahogany dining room table. A sheet with a dime-sized blood stain flapped over the cracked bay window facing the driveway and a "for sale by owner" sign. A man with a sack of circulars walked across the lawn and stuffed one in the screen door.

"So you're in the process of selling your house?"

"Yes."

"Why?"

"I took the house note over from my aunt when she went into hospice care. We had a place in Frisco for many years and I thought being down in L.A. would be calmer, but I'll be glad to get away from this place. These ad companies hire Mexicans on the cheap who can barely speak English to cart all this stuff around for the five and dimes and it just creates more waste in the neighborhood." She opened the front door and snatched the flyers off. "I want to live more frugally, simply," she said, meeting Ida's skeptical gaze. "I have a unit reserved in one of the church's communal apartments on Hoover that I can share with a few other women. It'll be easier pooling resources, not having to keep up the payments on this place."

"Will you continue teaching?"

"Yes, of course. All of the women I'll be living with are still working their jobs. There are some secretaries, a few nurses, a court reporter, a chemistry teacher."

"And your salaries go directly to the church?"

"That's rather forward of you. Everyone is required to support church operations with whatever they can contribute."

"Are some of your new housemates on the Planning Commission?"

"Maybe. I'm not all up in people's business." She refilled Ida's cup. "I checked out some of your work before you came, some of the old stories you wrote about Vietnam and the draft devastating black families. You've had quite a distinguished career with your reporting."

"Thank you."

"I've dabbled a little in writing, poetry mostly, because I can get my thoughts out quicker. Next week my class is reading Lucille Clifton. I bought twenty of her books out of pocket. My school district doesn't think black women poets exist."

A street sweeper whooshed at the end of the street as Ernestine put her feet up on the bruised ottoman in front of her.

"You were involved with him I hear."

Ida paused. "Years ago."

"While he was a married man."

"Yes ... and why is that important to you?"

"I'm just trying to establish a chronology. He was a much younger *married* white boy and you got carried away. I suppose that kind of thing happens if you can't control yourself. If you were a black man messing with a younger white woman you would've been lynched—"

"Nobody gives a damn about the lynching of a black woman. I've spent my whole life fighting it, exposing it."

"Then why did you commit adultery with him?"

Ida was silent. Ernestine settled back into her chair, wisps of smoke rising from the dayglo "World's Greatest Dad" mug in her fist.

"I don't know. It wasn't a conscious choice. It happened and I have to live with it. On the other hand, let me ask you what attracts you to a so-called people's church that has no real black leadership. Why is someone like you, an outspoken educator with the kind of awareness that you have, so wrapped up in something you have no real ownership in?"

"You sidestepped *my* question."

She looked Ernestine in the eyes. "The thing with him was a whole lifetime ago, a whole political lifetime. He was and is a desperately needy person."

"But you saw something in him."

"Yes."

"Enough to spend time with him and leave your children."

Ida put her cup down. "I don't have any of my own children and it's none of your business what happened."

"Why not? You're calling our motives and intelligence into question, trying to portray this church as though we're stuck on a slave ship."

"Why did you join in the first place?"

"I wanted something more relevant to what's happening in the world. Jim was preaching on how the reality of this government, how everything we'd been taught in the history books about freedom and democracy was just a cover-up for all the government's legal violence against black and poor people. Of course that wasn't news to me but it was the first time I'd heard it come out of a preacher's mouth on a regular basis without apology, black or white. And the congregation was mixed, the programs were mixed. I wanted to expose my son to all that, California-style segregation being only slightly better than back in Tuscaloosa. Here I could go try on clothes in a department store and just get followed around like a common hoodlum rather than spit on."

Ida took a token sip of her lukewarm coffee, at once weary and wistful about Ernestine's candor, the familiar tale of desire and disillusionment. She'd been driven to leave Indiana by some of the same unrest as Ida. In different circumstances they could be comrades, soul mates maybe; but Jim was lodged between them like a bone in the throat.

The phone rang and then stopped. "Bill collectors," Ernestine said. "A ton of them grubbing for the hospital fees they claim we owe from my husband Paul's cancer treatments."

"Does Paul belong to the church?"

"Passed away last year."

"I'm sorry."

"He had no use for organized religion. But of course no one thought lesser of him, him being a man."

"Have you had any offers on the house?"

"No serious ones. I'd like to see it go to a black family, but that won't happen the way the Mexicans have taken over the neighborhood."

"Yeah, well that's what white folk said, and still say, about us. One of the first things Jim and I did together was help defend a family that was being forced out by the homeowners' associations in Indianapolis. They were no better than the Klan. You remember how it was. They created the blueprint for all of these areas being so ghettoized the way they are now."

"So he was your apprentice."

"Of sorts."

"To have a white boy running up behind you. Must've been gratifying. Given you a sense of power."

"I don't need a white boy to make me feel powerful. That *is* a slave mentality. So I'm going to ask the same thing of you—why do you stay when the church has been feeding off of black assets to survive, raking in thousands in Social Security and disability checks and 20% tithes every month. Not to mention all the black property that's been either deeded directly to the church or stolen outright."

"We're building a nation, Mrs. Lassiter."

"Yes, I know about the so-called Jonestown settlement."

"There's nothing so-called about it. It's going to be a nation of many races within a black-ruled nation. The Guyanese government is aligned with what the Temple is doing. Outside of going to Africa it's one of the safest places for black people on the planet."

"Who told you that, the Temple tourism propaganda board? That's insanity talking."

"And you believe that staying here where my boy could be killed at any moment, where I can't teach that we have a history, literature and a whole tradition of philosophical thinking without getting smeared by the school board as a dangerous subversive is sane? We have Nazis in the police department using chokeholds on us just because they get their kicks doing it, Mrs. Lassiter. I thought I left Tuscaloosa behind when I boarded that train to come out here in 1955."

Ida looked down at her hands, roughed up from the years, fingers an unrecognizable mass of calluses and bitten hangnails. "A lot of people thought that," she said quietly.

"So what's your answer, Mrs. Lassiter? Last week we had three dozen white women out in the Valley storming buses with black children trying to keep them out of the high school. In the Valley, here in Los Angeles. Just like in Little Rock and just like all those Irish housewives in Boston. For them desegregation is still a civil war. They would've formed a human barricade with their aprons tied around them if they had to."

"You don't need to tell me that. What I don't understand is all these black folk's urgency to dive into something that's untested clear out in the middle of nowhere."

"You can't tell me that you've never taken a calculated risk on something you believed in. Like publishing that paper on your own and getting all the mess you got, sticking with it because who else was going to speak for the race. You did that because there was nothing out there like it and all the doubters and naysayers were just noise."

"Right, yes, but I wasn't banking on a white man."

Ernestine took her feet off the ottoman and leaned forward, the cross around her neck flapping against her chest. "That's not what this is about. It's never been about blind faith."

Ida waited.

Ernestine looked down. "It's bigger than him, bigger than any one individual."

"The white women preside over the Planning Commission, operations and all the little secret tribunals behind closed doors. They are the power in the church and the public face. They go skittering around doing his bidding and call it a revolutionary act for the Negro masses. 'Father', as some of your comrades call him, sleeps with them and gives them the keys to the kingdom. How godly is that, Mrs. Markham? Where in the bible does it say a pastor can screw everybody in creation with total impunity to get what he wants on earth? Find that chapter and verse for me and justify it, tell me the ends justify the means, that you're willing to put your life on the line, after all you've seen and done, for this low down dirty treachery."

"Did you love him?"

The garbage truck droned at the end of the block, volume dipping into a robotic buzz as the stench of prehistoric trash roared through the window.

"Yes. Satisfied?"

"Well that didn't take much ... I've never felt it with a man. Certainly not with my husband, who was a good father, a good, dependable shepherd. There was none of that romantic, poetic love—"

"It wasn't romantic or poetic. It was over a decade ago."

"Some might say that your exposés are motivated by revenge."

Ida laughed. "For what? Do you believe that?"

"No, I think you found what you think is a good story and you're sinking your teeth into it to boost your relevance as a journalist. Gossip and innuendo, especially on the Temple, are going to be big hits when all people know about is black people and black organizations being in disarray. You've been out of the spotlight for the past several years and getting a straight job at your age with your reputation can't be easy."

Ida ignored the slight and pressed on. "Are you giving the money you make from selling your house to the church?"

"Now that's none of *your* business."

"Were you aware that one of the couples who followed Jim from Indiana is trying to get their property back?"

"That has nothing to do with me."

The door opened and a boy with a hood slung over his head ambled in holding a trumpet case. He grunted at Ernestine and started toward the hallway.

"Boy, get back here. Where's your manners?"

He turned sullenly to face Ida. "Hi."

"This is my son, Byron."

"Hello Byron. Are you coming from the church?"

"Who are you?"

"My name's Ida Lassiter. I'm a writer, a journalist—"

"Freelance," Ernestine added.

"Independent. Doing a history of the Temple."

"She's trying to dig up dirt."

"You were in a boxing match in the church awhile back?"

"No comment," he said.

"Well I hear you're an accomplished musician."

He rolled his eyes. "My mother tell you that? Yeah, I play a bunch of different instruments."

"He's been first chair for every horn that he's ever picked up."

"Mama!"

"No, you should be proud of that," Ida said. "I always wanted to play an instrument but my family couldn't afford it. It was considered an indulgence to teach black girls."

"It's only taken him a few months to master the fingerings on the trumpet, and that's a used one donated to the Temple by the Philharmonic. Practices his behind off. Going to be a professional musician one day, traveling all over the world. The Promised Land will just be the first stop."

Ida stood. "You mean Guyana? I'll be going. If you need to reach me at anytime…"

Byron plunked the trumpet case down on the floor, pulling his hood off as he turned to Ernestine.

"I need some money for the bus tour up North."

"That tour is going to take three days away from studying for the exam you have coming up."

"I can study on the bus."

"The church is paying for your travel and food, Byron, what do you need money for? What happened to the fifty dollars I gave you two weeks ago?"

"What if the bus breaks down like it did on the last one? Do you really want me stranded out in the boondocks with no money?"

Ida paused at the door. "I take it this is one of the whipping up the faithful and reeling in the converts tours. Is your band playing?"

"Yeah, in Ukiah, Sacramento and San Francisco."

"In partnership with some of the black congregations that are actually about something. He's also got a little girlfriend up there he thinks I don't know about."

"Mama!"

"You running up there better not have to do with getting away so you can knock up some girl like the rest of your trifling friends. I'm not trying to take care of any grandkids at this point in my life."

"You won't ever have to worry about that."

"What are you talking about?"

"Open your eyes mama, I'm a fucking queer."

"Don't ever say that. Don't you ever use that language in my house."

"What, are you embarrassed in front of her, ashamed that I've turned out to be a failure in everything you had planned for me?"

"That's a distortion, Byron."

"I really don't know how you can call yourself a Christian...not in the way Dad means it."

"Dad? You only have one father, Byron, and that's the one who raised you, God rest his soul. Jim is an atheist, says so now every opportunity he gets."

"Then why are you still there? If he's sinful, if I'm sinful—"

"I never said that, you're putting words in my mouth. The church is the people, it's not any one man. God gave me a purpose with this church and he gave you a purpose too. That doesn't mean I have to agree with everything one hundred percent. That doesn't mean that the Temple doesn't have flaws. You turning out the way you did, claiming you're a queer ... Well, you're either going against God or maybe he's giving you some other purpose that I can't understand ... I don't pretend to know anymore."

"You never did know," he said. "Can I have some money for the trip?"

CHAPTER 16

The Children, Jonestown, Guyana, November 1978

BLACK IS SURELY Beautiful.

The signs to our classroom float in the air, curling from the heat, rain and dried blood. We count down the seconds until recess. We tease and chant praise. We dance, doing disco, doing the splits, the poplock, all the crazy freestyle steps we brought from the States, strutting, showing off, running contests. We haven't seen TV in months. Free from its pollution. It's as bad as doing smack Dad says. Even the show *Good Times*, 'cause they always want to Stepin Fetchit, to zip coon a strong black man.

Not just the smart ones are encouraged to speak up in class. Our teacher makes even the slow ones participate. And naw, nobody is higher or better than anybody else. And naw, the blondies that were prettiest in the white American world ain't nothing here. Dad said it's the socialist way. Dad says everybody has a special gift to give. Anybody we see acting all big and bad we tell on them. Sometimes they get sent out to the jungle to get their attitude straight. Sometimes a hot pepper on the tongue does the trick. After that, they come back right in the head.

Mondays is science. Tuesdays is ancient civilizations of Africa, Asia and the Middle East. Wednesdays is geopolitics. Thursdays is public speaking. Fridays is music, crafts and creative writing. The walls are filled with poems of this better world. The walls are filled with pictures of bombs dropping, ghost white mushroom clouds spreading over L.A. and Fillmore, San Francisco.

We're lucky to have escaped in time. Lucky when so many were left behind. We know it's not right but we secretly pray for the left behind kids. We pray that they could be here with us in paradise. We know prayer is fakeness, magic and fairy tales. We know it's a con and a lie but we're scaredy cats, 'cause what if there's a god besides Dad.

The grown-ups are always watching for big breeches, big mouths, show offs. Any old grown-up can school you on the spot on what to do and what to be. We follow their lead, but have our own language for emergencies. We do youth council and speak in it just to rile them.

The white people rule, but everybody is equal. The white people say under the skin we're all blood. The white people say cut us and it's the same. Ché pricked her arm with a paring knife to prove it to one of the mixed white Mexican girls who was talking smack; a know-it-all with Laurie Partridge straight brown hair all down her back, trying to get out of slopping hogs like the rest of us claiming she needed novocaine for a sore tooth. Her little group puts on a show acting black at the meetings in the pavilion to please Dad. When the grown-ups turn their backs they're picking at us for weak spots, treating us like stepchildren.

The littler kids love the Sesame Street books with singing rainbow kids that look like us. They love how every month we adopt a new country, imagining how the children live there, performing Indian or Chinese customs, showing off our Russian greetings to all the adults as a warm-up to Dad's speeches. The adults clap and shout for an encore, proud of us, proud of how far we've come. Dad and Carol and the others are negotiating for us to move to Russia. Jamiah asks if there are black people there and is told to shut up.

At night we read the babies their favorite story about Grover the blue muppet before lights out and the bugs eat us.

There's a monster at the end of this book, Grover says, as the patrols start up outside. Rain rat-a-tats on the roof, rain leaks through the ceiling, rain drips into our mouths, making the sheets soggy.

There's a monster at the end of this book, Grover whispers, bugging out his googly scarecrow eyes.

There's a monster at the end of this book, Grover whines, toothpick arms waving.

Each page we turn there is Grover warning us not to go any further.

Each page we turn Grover puts chains over them to keep us from turning another page.

Each page we turn and turn until the last page and BOO there he is. Grover, the monster.

The lights shut off and we dive in our beds, waiting for the inspection. The guards pass, rifles clicking at their sides, noses poking into the dorms on alert for any kind of noise, any kind of stray cough, giggle or belch.

We are drifting, dreaming of the group of visitors coming the next day from America and how we will impress them.

They will sleep good tonight, the guards say as they leave.

CHAPTER 17

The Rebels, Oakland, 1977

HY LEFT WORK at the gift shop early to meet with the new group. She took the bus across the bay to Oakland, second and third guessing the trip, the stops bleeding into eternity, a river of lumbering after school bodies, teens smacking juicy fruit gum, fumbling with change, jamming into hard seats, every nook and cranny of the unspooling neighborhoods burned into her nostrils. Taryn wouldn't miss her that evening. For the past five months she and her girlfriend Jess had been swaddled in the brain dead love of the possessed. Most of their social time was spent at Temple events; lectures, films, rap sessions on politics, helping with the church's activism against apartheid in South Africa.

After the shaming and beating of Felix she stopped going to the services for awhile. She'd let herself be cowed by the congregation and it ate at her bit by bit. In between waiting on customers and doing inventory there was the constant besotted rumble of Guyana among her co-workers, excitement about the settlement the church was building from the ground up; a sense of urgency powering them through the gray days of selling knick knacks as though each transaction might be their last.

"Jonestown, they're going to call it Jonestown," they buzzed, letting it melt in their mouths like chocolate.

Felix had been the first in a tide of weekly reprisals. Her friend Alex called up for cheating on an exam. Two white girls for being snooty and flipping their hair. Cedric for sneaking three hours of sleep after an around the clock security detail. Ernestine Markham for letting Ida Lassiter into her house. Foster Sutcliffe for badmouthing the church's being in bed with the Moscone administration. Foster was one of the few young black men who hadn't been corralled into doing security; a dabbling blues rock percussionist and philosophy major who'd joined the Temple in the early seventies for the anti-war consciousness raising sessions and free grub. Hy had met Foster in a Zen meditation session, smoked a few joints, traded some Cream albums, the two of them collapsing in a giggly anti-Zen heap one night after a table top drum duel on the song "Toad".

A few years of being on the margins and he started questioning the hierarchy of whites, the lackey culture of clenched toothed control, the raise the dead faith healing rationalized as a necessary evil.

"The main thing is the power vacuum," he told a group of fellow college student dissenters he'd assembled in secret after the Felix beating. "What the church has become, is becoming, isn't what we signed up for." Some agreed, but weren't sure what to do about it. The Temple had paid for their tuition, room and board at the local junior college. Friends, couples, partners had met, found sanctuary in each other. Then there was the specter of Guyana, beckoning when they closed their eyes at night.

Jim got wind of the group and ridiculed their tin pot mutiny at every turn, derisively calling them rebels on "training wheels", amateurs influenced by the San Francisco media whores and Ida Lassiter.

After the umpteenth sullen teenager held up the bus scrounging for inexact change Hy weighed how much she was going to the meeting out of lust, how much out of curiosity, allegiance, obsession with the fine ass princely slope of Foster's buzz cut. Fucking him would be the cherry on top but not totally mandatory.

The rebels made sure to meet in different places. Members wanting to get in good with Jim had been tapped to spy on anyone who was disgruntled. "Some of our people have been beaten down so long they start to believe the press' lies. Down starts to look like up to them," Jim said. "Ain't their fault that they've been hoodwinked. Folk have been seriously fucked by the United States of fascism. It's our duty to lead 'em back to the light."

The group hunkered down in twenty four hour East Bay diners like Renata's, a broke artists' haven with wall to wall vinyl booths and zinc countertops, the world's best grilled cheese, mystery meat sloppy joes and the only black waitresses for miles. Most of the group had tried to keep their outside jobs and hang on to some scraggly thread of independence from the Temple. Still they funneled their incomes to the church to cover living expenses. Rents in the Bay Area were out of reach for poor and middle income families scraping to get by on half of what whites made. The Temple party line said why soldier on alone when we can all live together as an extended family.

When Hy got to the diner the meeting was in full swing over steaming plates of steak fries.

"They messed Felix's lips up so bad it'll take him months to play trumpet again," Foster said, acknowledging her with a nod. "No one will say a mumbling word about it or speak out against the beat downs to Jim's face. It's like dealing with a bunch of made people in the mafia."

"It's worse than that man, at least with them Don Corleone motherfuckers you can kill them, these assholes have nine fucking lives and the money to back it up," a hospital orderly named Marco said.

"How much are they giving?" Jonas, a grilled cheese junkie with a bushy ponytail curling down his neck asked.

"Thousands from stocks, investments, houses, trust funds, you name it. All I know is its shit we don't have," Hy retorted.

Marco shook his head, plunking his baseball cap on the table. "Naw, we got houses. That's all we got though. My auntie's whole block in South Gate down in L.A. is deeding their stuff to the Temple. Now, the white folk, they straight up buy their way into the church and the leadership and expect us to just roll over and not ask questions."

Jonas reached for a napkin. "Jim's doing speed to stay up all night."

"Yeah, but no one's forcing him to do it."

"Come on look at the way they run up behind him trying to outdo each other with how loyal they are."

"They got no politics."

"The politics is finding whose weak enough to fuck in secret and use as a pawn."

Foster licked ketchup from his fingers, dumping salt on his fries. "Ya'll are naïve. Nobody's twisting arms. There's a succession plan. The whites get positioned over us plantation style, load up their offshore accounts and live off the interest until Fidel smuggles them into Cuba or Brezhnev gives Jim the key to Ukraine."

Jonas attacked the last glob of melted cheese on his plate. "Shit, Russians are even more racist than the crackers we got over here. No way would they sponsor a thousand spooks in their country no matter how socialist they were."

Foster grinned, pushing his fries toward Hy, pleased that she had come. "Right, right. Hy, what does your sister say about the money that's passing hands over there?"

"Nothing. We don't talk about it anymore."

"Why not? I thought she was supposed to be the big skeptic."

"Once upon a time, before she met Jess."

"And got pussy whipped," Marco snickered.

"Lay off, asshole," she said.

"Ooh, touched a nerve. Bulldaggers are just too good for—"

"I said lay off, you shit for brains motherfucker."

"What part of what I'm saying is a lie? Jess is one of the main ones running up after Jim like she wants to lick his asshole clean and looking down on us like we're ghetto niggers she don't have to respect."

"Why should she respect an ignoramus like you?"

Foster stretched his arms out on the back of the booth, exasperated. "C'mon now, ya'll are getting sidetracked. Marco you better shut the fuck up before you wake up in a hospital bed. Leave Jess out of this. She's only a pawn, still coasting on the fumes of the movement and mistaking Jim for it."

Every time the door opened they paused, scrutinizing the newcomers for familiar faces, elaborate disguises, wigs askew, makeup slathered. Marco cut a pattern into his plate with a butter knife, Foster stiffened dog whistle alert. Renata's had been chosen because it was all over the top comfort food oozing the chemicals, dyes, saturated fat and refined sugars that the Temple brass railed against but wolfed down clandestinely at Jack n' the Box drive-thrus from Compton to the Bay. Members of the Red Brigade scored Jumbo Jack bonuses for every person they stalked and every head they cracked, fending off shadow enemies, intelligence gatherers, reporters from any meeting or public appearance Jim was attending.

Foster handed Hy a menu. "Eat girl," He gestured toward Marco. "No sense starving yourself because of this fool. My treat."

"The pecan pie any good in this place?"

"Probably the best you're going to have in a long time if you go over to the jungle with the rest of them. Put some whipped cream on it and it's a slice of heaven."

Hy rolled her eyes. "Too sweet. But it's the only thing on here though that looks even half edible. I saw you in the recovery group last night."

"Yeah, I go when I can. It's the one thing that still works for me. The college programs having devolved the way they have."

Marco snorted. "Man, the way you been talking I thought you were well on your way to getting a Ph.D. by now."

"Might've if the programs had stayed the way they started out. If the commitment to socialism had remained. I can take basic classes in American history and economics anywhere but shit, it's like they want to water everything down. Some of us have been organizing around all the cops they're dumping in the high schools, the Jim Crow curriculum. Nobody can move or do nothing independently without the white overlords giving the green light."

"Plus they're confiscating books."

"All the radical texts 'Father' used to reel in us poor Negroes. Gone, banished."

"What does Bernie, your wife, think about all this?" Marco asked Foster.

He hesitated, scraping a burnt fry up from the plate, black freckles on his cheeks shining with the heat of the dead air pumped by ceiling fans dragging overhead like pregnant tarantulas. Hy knew vaguely about Bernie, had seen her with Foster a few times, detected a whiff of disconnection between them, figured they had one of those Temple marriages that was more obligation and agreement than love match. During lulls at work her brain plugged into Foster, the air he gave off of the self-schooled, perpetually questioning academic; his lip curled pugilistically, ready to shut down the next dumb outburst from anyone within earshot.

"Bernie's doing her own thing," he said. "She's not trying to come down on any of the Temple's business."

"She even know you're having these meetings?"

"No, yes…she knows they're happening, Jim and his right hand woman Carol have made sure of that. Bernie's family is too deep into Temple shit though, this is the first time some of 'em have had a fair shot at any kind of stable employment."

"Better hope she hasn't bugged your toilet, man." Jonas chimed in.

"So how're you going to finesse this with her?" Marco asked, agitated. "In other words, what kind of a leash you got her on brother?"

"We don't have 'leashes'. We come and go as we please, if you know what I mean."

"She's going to be a problem," Hy said.

Foster looked at her. They had gambled on asking her to the meeting because of her sister's job at the Temple's accounting firm, figuring the information she might be able to get would outweigh the potential risks of exposure. Taryn was the highest ranking black person in the firm, the most likely to know about any financial irregularities; one of the few who actually came into the church as a non-believer, wary of the faith healing mumbo jumbo. Foster had heard her speak at an anti-apartheid meeting, noting her composure. Most of the time she sat in the back pews absorbed in spreadsheets.

"Don't worry about Bernie," he said. "She's not a snoop. She'd never sacrifice me for the Cause."

Marco looked irritated. "You think you got her trained, you're stupid. Look at what happened to chicken shit Tibbs and his lady. Look at what happened to Felix and Oleta—there's a reason why all the marriages up in this joint is 'communal'. It's to divide and conquer, to make sure the only one you have any allegiance to is Jim and the Temple."

"That's no big revelation," Hy said. "But clearly anybody who has umpteen relatives in the church like Bernie does is going to be compromised."

"Yeah, you better watch out if she gets mad at your ass."

Foster pursed his lips and looked at the table, pressing his finger down on an ant making its way up his napkin. "Ida Lassiter contacted me. She's making the rounds talking to people, doing research for a series she wants to write on the Temple."

"She better watch her back."

"What the fuck can Jim Jones and his ragtag goon squad do to break her?"

"He wouldn't do it directly. He'd arrange it so that it could never be traced. Maybe have that Negro doctor Goodwin that he's got wrapped around his finger slip some rat poison into her chitlins." Marco sneered.

A white man with hollow ghost cheeks sitting at the counter drowning his coffee in sugar cocked his head toward them listening. They stopped and waited, monitoring his movements. He took out a bottle of aspirin, opened the container and swallowed a few, coughing into his plate, making the elderly black man sitting next to him recoil.

Marco cocked his head in the ghost's direction. "Rat in the house."

Foster lowered his voice. "Goodwin sees what he wants to see. He's treating Jim. Probably writes him prescriptions to any upper he wants to snort, swallow or shoot up. They're thick as thieves. Much respect for what he did back in the day but he's no better than all those other fake revolutionaries Jim's sweet talked."

"I don't think he's that bad," Hy objected. "At least he's doing something for black people, providing free medical clinics and taking on the

Fillmore developers in his paper. The Negro establishment and the do nothing black churches hate him. That's gotta mean something."

Foster waved his hand dismissively. "They hate the Nation of Islam too. But that doesn't mean a damn thing. We got no natural allies, other than the people that hate Jim."

The ghost shifted in his seat, hummed along with the Muzak overhead, flipping through an Oakland zoo pamphlet with gorillas on the cover.

"Aww shit, monkey boy at 12:00," Marco said. "He's gotta be Jim's."

"I heard that animal shit was always his obsession," Foster said.

"You think he fucked any of 'em? I mean I'm almost 100% that he fucked his pet monkey."

Foster rolled his eyes. "Man, why would you even let that kind of madness concern you?"

"Unless you had some kind of personal interest," Hy said.

"Fuck you—"

"Alright, calm the fuck down," Foster said. "One thing ya'll need to learn is in-fighting is going to make them stronger. They bank on us being misdirected disorganized Negroes. I've been talking to some other people about making a break, going up to Canada."

"Where?"

"Vancouver. We could get construction jobs pretty easy with all the new developments they're putting in downtown. Devera has family up there and could maybe give us some leads."

Marco took some change out of his pocket and dropped it on the table for the waitress. "Devera? She's practically a lifer. How you going to go up against the Temple getting her involved?"

"She's not as hardline as you think," Foster said. "She's got working eyes and ears. I know she's got a soft spot for Mabelean but she's redeemable."

"What makes you think Canada is going to be all that better about hiring black folks?" Hy asked.

"There's no guarantee. I just know the unions and the building trades aren't as piss poor backward and black-hating as they are here. Seems they've mostly dumped on the Indians and left our asses alone. Nobody's saying its fucking utopia but it sure beats the hell outta here."

Hy looked doubtful, antsy. The buses started running every hour after eight o'clock and she didn't want to wait that long. "Right, cause that's what they're saying about Guyana. The people that are over there building Jonestown say you chop a tree down and it's got milk and honey for sap. Prime minister, the cabinet, everybody over there in power's black except for a few Indians who're taking orders from us."

The black man sitting next to the ghost at the counter stepped down from his seat with his bill in hand. He nodded a greeting to them and walked over to their table, an Oakland Raiders cap tucked down over his pendulous ears. "Afternoon. Sorry to bother you young people but would you happen to have a little change to spare so I can give it to the lady? Can't say the food's the greatest but the service is always top notch."

Foster gave him fifty cents.

"Thank you kindly...and you're right, Canada's beautiful. It always was a haven for us refugees. Not too many of us swinging on trees there." The man took out his wallet and put the change in it.

"God bless you," he said, as he walked to the door.

There was no twinge of Southern to Dr. Hampton Goodwin, no betrayal in his stiff clipped surgical tongue, no unraveling thread catching at the hem of his voice save maybe when he was laughing watching *Sanford and Son*, or eating black walnut ice cream, which he rarely did, in itsy bitsy monastic doses.

You from the islands, boy? The high class crackers who came to him on the sly for pain medications asked when he first started practicing medicine in Gainesville, Florida in the forties. 'Cause how could a home-grown nigger be disciplined enough to get two degrees in psychology and medicine?

He sat in his office, hunkered down in an imported leather chair with a view of the San Francisco Bay, yanked back to Gainesville for a second, mourning his earnest youth, his turn the other cheek Hippocratic luster. With all the bicentennial schlock over and done with, he could maneuver into 1977 with a new plan for boosting ad revenue for his newspaper, the *Sun Reporter*, the only serious voice of black news in the region.

It was unusually quiet for early evening and he liked it. The purples in the sky always did him in. The gray, gloom and sun at dusk mingling like a drunken kid's watercolors that chased away his homesickness for Florida and left him brimming, smitten anew with the city's fickle majesty. His editor Fleming was camping out at talks between the county and the long-shoremen's union. His two-person medical staff on the third floor was gone for the day and the cleaning woman would not make her way up to the newspaper's suite for another hour.

The advance guard for his next appointment would sweep in soon. The appointment himself would be five minutes late and not a second more, mindful of Hampton's time and impatience.

They'd been doing this dance for several years and Hampton was still dimly amused by it.

There was a knock on the door and Jamiah from the Temple Red Brigade came in trying not to look tentative, black beret slanted down over his smooth shiny forehead.

"Hello Mr. Goodwin, sir," he said, looking around cautiously. "Reverend Jim will be up in a second."

"If Jim sent you up here to look for bombs and assassins they went out that way."

"You serious?"

"Relax. Want something to drink, soda or something?"

Hampton took a coke out of the mini-fridge behind his desk and tossed it to Jamiah.

"Are you in school, son?"

"Yes, night school. Finishing up my GED."

"Good, keep on the straight and narrow. Here," he reached into his bookshelf and handed him a worn copy of W.E.B DuBois' *The Souls of Black Folk*. "Keep your mind sharp, read everything you can get your hands on, learn how to speak their language, know what the white boys are thinking before they even think to think it."

Hampton looked at Jamiah's blank face, growing momentarily despondent at the dullness, the incuriosity that radiated from it; his faith in the furtherance of the black race shrinking. Youth was surely wasted on the young. But then, he was just an old man to him, an apparition with an unknown allotment of hours, weeks, years to live.

He thought he felt the boy shudder.

Jamiah unclipped the walkie talkie on his hip and adjusted the volume. "Is it ok for the Reverend to come in?"

Hampton nodded.

The door swung open and two lanky man-boys with a dusting of red freckles on their noses stepped in, parting to let Jim by. He waved his hand at them and they sidled back out the door.

"Afternoon, governor," he said to Hampton.

Hampton nodded at Jamiah. "Him too."

Jim handed two dollars to Jamiah. "Ya'll go and buy yourselves something from the machine downstairs."

He sank into the chair in front of the desk, letting out a big yawn as he took off his glasses. Wide dark circles etched under his eyes.

"I feel like shit, guv."

"You run yourself ragged. You been taking the pills I gave you?"

"That stuff is like sweet tarts. Kiddie shit, goes right through me. Used to be able to go days without sleep now it's a fucking miracle if I can pull an all-nighter."

"You have to do the vitamins."

"Crap."

"It's cumulative, Jim. The benefits won't happen overnight. Are dark green leafy vegetables and anti-oxidants standard fare in your cafeteria?"

Jim paused. "They are guv, they are. We discontinued cooking in the collectives so everybody could come to the Temple for group meals."

"Doesn't sound cost effective."

"It's a dress rehearsal for when we make the transition to the Promised Land."

"That's a grandiose title."

"Maybe."

"Think you might want to slow down a bit now that the mayor just appointed you to the Housing Authority? Besides, are Guyana's prime minister and his boys still sweet on you?"

"Love our dirty drawers, thanks in no small part to your endorsement letters … now I just need something to stay awake, guv. There's too much to do and I'm fucking dying."

"We all yearn for a forty-eight hour day. From your lips to God's ears."

"Did you get the piece that Carol wrote?"

"I did. But I'm not going to run it, if that's what you're asking. Fleming can use it as background for his article. The *Sun Reporter* isn't a mouthpiece for white sympathizers, you know that."

"We need a rebuttal to the *New West* hit piece. That Lassiter woman is going to come out with her own load of horse shit soon. She's already approached some of the sisters in L.A. for quotes. Like I don't have eyes and ears down there."

"Evidently they're not 20/20. Look, you're not going to be able to control what she does. She's been outpaced, she's got a reputation—a very respectable one I might add—to uphold. Taking down the mighty Jim Jones. It's a matter of pride."

Jim grimaced, kneading his gut. Hampton got up from the desk and reached up into the top shelf of the bookcase behind him. He unearthed a bottle of antacids and handed them to Jim.

"Whatever she thinks she's got on you is pure hearsay. I see this as the last desperate gasp of a basically decent, honorable stalwart whose been marginalized. My recommendation is to sit down with her and see what she wants. You can use one of my offices if you don't want to involve Mabelean and the church."

Jim looked doubtful. "Right."

"Be proactive, man. Stop playing defense. We're circulating your paper all through the East Bay, down past Heyward and up to Napa Valley. The best thing you can do is keep your people on the ground promoting the charitable work and philanthropy of the Temple. That's the way you stem all this propaganda."

"I'm serious guv, what can you give me to keep me awake? Everything I eat just flows out like liquid. I feel like I'm fucking one hundred."

"It's psychosomatic, Jim. You've got to stop these fixations. You've got mental debris and it manifests itself in your body. Delegation, strategic, that is, should be your watchword."

"Yes."

"You've got all that youthful energy running around, marshal 'em. Our network of 'Negro' papers can only go so far."

"Moscone's not returning my calls."

"He's been abroad for the past week."

"I want to schedule the emergency Housing Authority meeting like you suggested. Those bastards in the sheriff's department are going to eminent domain all those folks in Fillmore without due process."

"Wait on that. You rush in you look like a zealot trying to deflect attention from the negative press. The sheriff knows he'll get his head handed to him on a platter if he so much as breathes without the community getting a hearing."

"It's fucking torture this waiting. All I've—we've done for this city and to get fucked in the ass like this."

"Stop being reactive. You practically delivered Moscone the mayor's office."

"I'm thinking about getting the clinics, service providers and teachers to organize a picket of the newspaper offices on behalf of the church."

"A picket ..."

"Crap like that story has potentially destructive consequences for our ability to get people the care that they need. Everybody that cares about racial equality in the city should be mad as hell when the press smears legitimate human services organizations. We demonstrated in support of those four reporters who were getting sweated for their sources by the feds and look how these chicken shits repay us."

"That's ancient history, Jim. You're not an Indiana bumpkin anymore. Moscone and our Democratic friends will hold their noses and cozy up to you because they see the Temple is a power at the ballot. If you keep delivering they'll fall in line and the media claptrap will inspire a backlash."

Hampton pressed his fingers together, mentally cataloguing the next day's appointments, deadlines, errands, the lab work he'd have his nurse assistant do. Jones had come in to get blood drawn and his prostate checked but here he was in full persecution mode, lips dessicated, the meticulously applied pencil dye on his graying lamb chops trickling down his cheek in black rivulets of sweat.

"You're being impetuous," he said. "Have a drink. I got a nice bottle of Dewar's from the Bay Area Black Physician's association banquet last week."

Jim went over to the liquor cabinet, taking a shot glass off the shelf. "Those sugar hill Toms know you're a dirty commie?"

"Watch it. Some of them got run out of Dixie and whitelisted here in Eden just like I did. It's tooth and nail being a black doctor with the whites not wanting you to touch them and some of the Negroes acting like only white folk are competent enough to practice medicine."

"No disrespect meant."

"A shot's all you need. Drink any more of it and between that and the meds you'll be passed out on my floor. We'll wait on the prostate exam until next week when you've settled down. Phyllis will do your blood work and have you on your way."

"You got some mouthwash? I can't go back with booze on my breath."

172

"There're some mints in the machine down in the lobby. How's Mabelean?"

"Good, thriving, gearing up for the relocation. Back problems she'd been having are virtually gone. Doing hospice care at a facility near Mercy General, coordinating all our senior homes and dealing with all the state compliance. In her element, couldn't be happier."

"She paid me a visit last month."

"Oh?"

"Expressed concern about your health, the sleep deprivation, etc."

"All of our people get very little sleep, her included. I'm not the only one."

"Right, it's an occupational hazard, the price of being committed to any business."

"The Temple's not a business to me, Hampton."

"Any church with substantial membership and influence is. The issue is balance, especially if we're claiming a socialist platform and structure."

"That's the first time you've used 'we'."

"You know I have more than a financial investment in the Temple. Why do you think I'm cranking out these editorials promoting your programs? When all the black pastors were speaking out against you Jim I defended you, not because of our personal or medical relationship, but because I believed this movement has traction, that it's *going somewhere.* Hell, in five years you've transformed some people, helped them transform themselves and that's something many of my colleagues in the business of religious emancipation can't claim. Most won't go an inch sideways beyond soup kitchens, clothes drives and job training seminars for the indigent. Ask them to get down and live the real ideals of Jesus? Forget it."

"And you say that as a good Methodist."

"I don't know about good. Better than some maybe."

"Well, the others lost their way, got seduced."

"Black folk aren't exempt from the lure of riches and private spoils, never have been. In fact, we've always had a bigger axe to grind because of white supremacy. Your mentor Prophet Zeke taught you as much. And yes all those earnest little white girls who flock to you are doing penance for their race's complicity in the looting and slow destruction of the planet."

"Zeke practically raised me back home. Gave me my start, my voice. He was honorable at core."

"And what about you?"

"I believe I am."

CHAPTER 18

Devera Medeiros, Fillmore, 1977

I WATCHED THE wrecking ball knock down our place like it wasn't nothing but a house of popsicle sticks. Boom, then there was a hunk of sky where Daddy's card table had been. Where he'd slapped bones and played poker on the weekends with his friends, where Mamí's relatives had had a high old time making fun of his wannabe Mexican black Spanish.

Mamí tried to stay in our apartment until the end, tried to hide, to stuff herself in the hall closet where I'd go to write stories when I couldn't sleep. All six feet of her curled into a fetal ball until the fire marshals and the sheriffs came in one by one swinging axes over their shoulders. She had what they used to call dementia praecox, an ugly name for hallucinating, for being fucked up in the head except for her it went two or three generations back, all the way to the Sinaloa women who couldn't afford a doctor, 'cause shit no way you could be mentally ill and be a Mexican.

We joined a lawsuit against the city with some of the other families that had been kicked out of their homes and that's how Mamí got involved in the church. Father Jim was sponsoring the legal aid attorneys, helping raise the profile of our case with the mayor's office. Some of the church people were doing translation to the small group of us from Mexico and Central America, making sure the city didn't fuck us over with jargon and fine print. None of my family was hardcore religious; screw the rosary beads and hail Mary's, the dirty sex addict priests never gave Mamí and the other women in the family nothing but venereal diseases.

So that's how we got here. Mamí's strong mind, her big crazy mouth, the pre-fab Temple family village where everyone had some kind of role, was always busy and if you weren't you'd best get on the good foot. Daddy said it helped her get over the shame about me.

Their fingers jab under my shirt. Poking caves into my skin. Down to the bone that once joined me to her, when I was the perfect boy, the sunshine of her life, the thing that made her legitimate in a world of men. They're panting like they're going to cum. Dying moose grunts filling the space behind the dumpster where they've cornered me just for fun, the he-she-thing they took for a spin after the basketball game they spent ogling the black cheerleaders' tits. Tell anyone and we'll fucking kill you.

Why would the pigs believe a black Mexican so-called trannie addict when my own mother wouldn't? There's no crime you can commit against that. No violation against the body of a thing that counts as an offense, the boys spat at me, running back to the safety of their warm beds, middle class thugs bored and on the prowl flexing their shriveled manhood.

Mamí is the top volunteer, the greeter, the true believer working the church doors with a smile, shiny spit curls, a program and a tithing envelope, tack sharp when she wasn't having one of her spells. Daddy said the Temple saved her, taught her to forgive, gave her a diversion, something to live for when she couldn't look at me anymore, the defeat like a butcher knife in her back. Thank the lord you wasn't an only child, he said, else I'd cut your balls off my damn self.

The last time I spoke to him it was that Friday, the day before most of us were set to go down to Los Angeles early the next morning.

You got Mother Mabelean running around like a chicken with its head cut off. You got all her assistants making sure the first aid kits are stocked on the buses and the repertory theatre kids have clean socks and underwear. Mabelean's a certified angel, a too-good-for-this-earth saint who's spent her life looking the other way while the sadity white trash from Palo Alto and the Berkeley Hills try to get it on with Father just to feed their malnourished little egos. I don't give a shit if they come from money; they got no morals, no common sense, no respect, no "sense of propriety" like Taryn says.

When Mother Mabelean goes down they'll pick over her dead body and pluck each other's eyes out to rule the roost those white harpies will.

There were about twenty of us in the strategy room where the Planning Commission met getting ready for the trip. Jess was sitting next to me. Pete Menken, a smiley silver-haired white man, was riffing on the new Rose Royce song "Car Wash", doing the hand claps, getting everybody dancing, stamping up dust on the floors while Father was sitting on a stool, filing his nails, grinning behind his shades. The group had just ripped little Viola Rombeck a new asshole for sneaking a Big Mac. We kept a strict health food diet to guard against impurities.

"Lean intestines make good socialists," Father said.

"I don't know how anybody gets shit done blissed out on the horse meat they put into those Big Macs," Mariah agreed.

After the harangue, Pete brought out this big jug of what looked like Boone's Farm and a stack of plastic cups, courtesy of Dad. He poured some for everybody in the room and we slurped it up, started to unwind, get happy. Cheap shit tasted like ambrosia after a long work week. Nobody questioned the hypocrisy of knocking back wine in the church when we were supposed to be all about abstention. Jess took a sip then went downstairs to check on the kids in the child care center. I could barely keep my eyes open from staying up printing flyers and stuffing envelopes till 4 a.m. Hadn't eaten anything but a package of peanut butter crackers so I sat there riding a little buzz, the walls climbing high as a beanstalk, opening onto a black heaven.

Mariah waited until everyone had had a few sips then stepped into the center of the room. The blip of a police siren flashing from downstairs passed over her face. The sound of somebody getting busted floated up to us.

"Fuck those pigs," she said. "Soon we won't have to worry about any of that shit."

"Yeah, we'll be over there, in the promised land," I said.

"Naw, I mean now."

"What?"

Father got off the stool and spread his arms wide. "I want ya'll to enjoy this drink, 'cause it's your last one."

"The wine is poisoned," Mariah announced all proud, batting those big black saucer eyes of hers. People froze up then gurgled, going sheet white, squirming like they were going to shit themselves.

"Savor it," Dad said. "Enjoy looking at each other. Reflect on all we've accomplished in this short span of time, of our lives, less than a millisecond in the grand scheme of the universe. We all think we're so fucking important, so central to the world. Well, we're not. Every damn one of us is disposable. Look how they plowed over all the serfs in Tsarist Russia. How they stuffed the blacks in South Africa into bantustans in their own damn country. Ain't no white sky daddy gonna save us field niggers. The world's gonna keep on turning and being unjust long after we're gone and that's the simple truth. It would take me a hundred lifetimes to achieve what I want to and I'd still be itching to do more. Remember ya'll are a part of me, every last one. There's no division. Anybody thinks there is get your candy ass out. We don't need your second guessing half-stepping. The weakest one in this room is the strongest. And the motherfuckers who arrogantly think they're the strongest are the weakest."

It got real quiet; the rank and file twisted in their seats, looked down at their hands, afraid to lift their heads and look at each other as Father had instructed. The higher ups pursed their lips, squinting knowingly, monitoring our reaction, eyes all over Father.

A thick bi-focaled woman named Eileen crocheting a sweater in her lap said, "You've always been the light for me, Dad. You and everybody else in this room are like a life raft for me."

Eileen turned on the spigot and they all chimed in, trying to be bad, not wanting to be outdone, one-upped, talking shit like why didn't this one or that one get the call to be part of the lucky vanguard that gets to see the mountaintop first.

"Cause we're chosen," the flunky Mariah sang. "Everybody in this room is chosen. Dad believed we were strong enough to take the hit. Don't disappoint him."

Pete starts whining that he wants to talk to his daughter one last time.

Eileen slurps extra loud from her glass. "I don't have anybody I want to talk to outside of the people in this room. You people have been my family when my own didn't want shit to do with me. I ain't afraid of dying."

"If we go out we go out as warriors not cowards," I said.

"I-I still want to talk to my daughter while there's time."

"And what the fuck do you want to say to her?" Carol had come in the room swinging, hair slick, big laundry basket piled with babies' onesies weighing down her bony arms, face two shades of righteous disgust. "That you're a damn deadbeat who can't work for more than four hours without going off to smoke pot? That you like to look at pornos with girls no older than she is? Or that you consistently write rubber checks to Father and expect everybody else in the commune to carry you?"

"Shit, you're lucky you're even here, man," Eileen said, trying to be badass, always the first one to pull rank because she had an adopted black grandson.

Pete got up and paced, pulling at the thin wisps of hair on his dome, "I don't want to be here. S-someone else could've taken my place. Should've taken it—whose going to look after my daughter?"

Carol laid into him, "Who's been looking after her, Peter? Who got her a decent place to stay, school clothes, books? Made sure she knows her Native heritage and not just that whitewashed garbage they shove down our kids' throats in the public schools?"

"Oh please, God, I don't want to die," he wailed, slumping onto the floor. A few of the others huddled around him, waiting for it to begin, willing it to go quick and slow at the same time.

I am five years old and watching my body from the rafters of the ceiling. A dark shell collapsing in on itself, three decades of human sludge soon to be stuffed in the back of an ambulance, every piece of my ass, balls, penis poked, prodded with mega sterilized rubber gloves for deviance, for a ten second jack off from the macho hide in plain sight motherfuckers living to annihilate me. Five and longing for Mami's sweet rough hands, waking me to get me up for the school bus on time,

179

forming a protective cage around my face when I come home from kindergarten with a bloody nose again. Mine all mine.

There are four of them on the floor quivering in a river of tears and spit, holding each others' saggy white skin for dear life. I want to drop on my knees and join them but I feel Father assessing, can taste his disappointment, the same lurking fear of abandonment he showed when we met in his office one night after Wednesday service. He over-praises my writing, swigging Listerine, reading lines from one of my articles out loud. It is shining truth, what we need to stem the tide of traitors. You have a gift, a singular talent, runs rings around any old journalism school stooge that got it all out of a book, he said, his gaze melting over me.

My hair is straightened for the day, parted on the side, the faintest hint of blush on my cheeks, lipstick cribbed from the Penney's makeup counter. Father says it's becoming. Sit up straight, he says, there's no reason to slouch. Start presenting yourself with dignity, he insists. He is the first one to do so when it became clear that I would not hide or bury myself to accommodate Mamí's shame.

A good man driven to the brink by bloodsuckers, I repeat, lapping up the sweet wine of his approval.

Ten minutes have passed and the police down below have hauled off a transient, the streets wriggling with foot traffic, muffled conversation, kids squeezing in stickball and hopscotch before the streetlights come on and mothers, aunties, grannies start herding them inside.

The white people on the floor clawed at each other, waiting as Mariah took the empty wine bottle and gave it to Father.

"Get the fuck off the floor," he said. "Fucking cowards, ya'll are a fucking disgrace. What are you people going to do when the real siege goes down and we need every bit of our nation to roll strong? Sniveling Mickey Mouse shit makes me want to vomit. I ask you to do one thing out of loyalty and you go and piss on me? You realize the FBI has tanks, a mini-arsenal stockpiled just to exterminate us."

"We-we thought—"

"You miscalculated."

"We panicked, Dad, we didn't know—"

"*You* panicked, Peter. You. Stand up and take responsibility for your own damn actions. Stop acting like a mealy-mouthed coward. Fifty-five year old grown man and you got on fucking diapers. Supposed to be gifted with testosterone, well having a set of balls don't mean a damn thing when it comes to real courage. Practically all the women here were ready to be tested and you had to show your ass. I can't have that shit in the jungle Peter. I just can't have it. You don't have the mettle to fight for the community then you better stay your ass here and lick envelopes."

"I didn't mean any disrespect to you, Father. I've just been under a lot of stress at my job."

"What kind of stress, brother?" I asked. "You're a white man, what do you have to be stressed about?"

Dad jumped in. "Some of these sisters here are three times as qualified as you and they can't get no cushy job in an office with a secretary and paid overtime."

"I think they're going to try and fire me because I belong to the Temple. My boss saw the piece on us in Goodwin's paper about the Jubilee with the Nation of Islam down in L.A. He brought it up in my evaluation."

"If he fires you without cause we'll get legal on it but we can't have you getting fired because you're slacking off or being too much of a basket case to function," Dad said. "That job and the salary mean too much to our bottom line, keeping up your household in the collectives and all of the other things we have to fund. Everybody's got to pull their own weight. You get out in the jungle with this capitalist entitlement attitude and your ass is going to get kicked."

Pete tried to crack a smile, still shitting himself with fear. Mariah cleared away the wine glasses as two low tier white women drag in duffel bags to pack up the clean laundry in Carol's basket, whirring with the seriousness of their task like nothing had ever happened. Mabelean sits humming "Down By the Riverside" at the window, lost in another world as Jimmy Junior walks in, holding the hand of John Boy, a foul-mouthed imp with dark hair rumored to be Dad's spawn from one of the bourgeois white women.

Mabelean shakes her head with her eyes closed like she's channeling Rosetta Tharpe.

"Join me, join me brothers and sisters," she sing-songs, glancing around hopefully at the group, the white people on the floor recovering from the shock of the drill, Father sucking on a tangerine, a dozen children tramping in and out from daycare downstairs with tambourines, kazoos, caracas.

"Join me and let's get in a joyful mood in preparation for our trip tomorrow."

CHAPTER 19

— ⚜ —

Insurrections, 1977

To CANADA, FOLLOWING the North Star like generations of black fugitives had done before them. Though Foster knew it was not so dramatic as that, their escape would be noted by a select few, savaged and brooded over as the petty rebellion of sell-outs by Jones and the inner circle of white Temple sycophants.

Against Foster's wishes, Marco brought his white girlfriend Zoe and her brother Avi, an ex-serviceman starry-eyed over the prospect of a Beat poet road trip adventure fueled by persecution. A white boy in the car would make it easier for them to get through border patrol, Marco had rationalized. Even though being Jewish Avi and Zoe loved to argue they weren't really white.

"No one has noticed this other than ya'll," Marco quipped.

They let Avi take the wheel with Zoe sitting next to him in the front seat. Four black people crammed in the back posing as members of a junior college basketball squad. The white border agent winced groggily at their i.ds, grunted a few questions about who played what position on the court then waved them through. The night sky stretched before them, blue-black, pockmarked with tiny lights from the next town, the grinning windows of farm houses floating out from dark open fields.

A beautiful sight, Foster thought, regret banging in his stomach, keeping him awake amidst the snores and rhythmic wheezing of the others.

He'd been almost certain that a car had followed them from Blaine, Washington to the border. It had kept a methodical distance behind them, just far enough that he couldn't see the driver. He imagined one of Jones' higher up henchman, one of the plucked-from-the- ghetto enforcers he was so proud of, first in line when the next suicide drill was staged, hellbent on showing their manhood. It would be Byron running away from his gayness, or Cedric puffed up craving acceptance, purpose, place. Marco had been there before, scavenging for a father figure amid the rubble of his own father's desertion; or so the sob story went during the grinding into dawn purging sessions where they were forced to confess the deepest, uncharted corners of their lives, one-upping each other with lurid flourishes that sent Jones into orbit.

They'd decided to drive straight through instead of stopping at a motel. His Dodge Dart shit box shuddered out of control if it went a few miles over seventy, the heater kicking in when it felt like it. When night fell they'd cocooned themselves in wool blankets stolen from the Temple, swaddling every inch of exposed skin, virgins in the bitter cold. He'd only dreamed of Canada, had never really traveled anywhere except for the out-posts near Tallahassee where his grandparents lived; shriveled up pinprick towns that stood stock still like Emancipation had never happened, all the black families watchful and armed to the gills.

After they crossed the border the stalker disappeared, doomed with-out a white escort to help grease the way through the checkpoints. Foster had hidden a gun in the wheel well, recklessly banking on border patrol being conned by their basketball routine.

The white Canadians weren't Southern rednecks but they were still scared of "Negroes". For that reason, Hy claimed she wanted no part of their trip. Why travel all that way to a mini version of America where they fucked over Native people.

"None of us can be free if all of us aren't free," she said in their last conversation the night before he left. Somehow, in the month since they'd met at the diner, staying in San Francisco had become a defiant gesture for her, a life line and burning source of clarity in an otherwise clouded existence.

He'd picked her up a few blocks from a Temple meeting in the Dart, wanting to say goodbye properly, to touch her, to see her quizzical kaleido-scopic face harden and light up one more time, hoping to sway her, afraid he'd be recognized by the church faithful streaming into the night.

184

"You're only staying because you're afraid to leave your sister," Foster said as she sat beside him, stabbing the onion rings he'd gotten her with a plastic fork.

"Not true."

"Aren't you tired of her calling the shots?"

"What gives you the idea that she's calling the shots? She doesn't control me."

"Certainly seems that way."

"What do you know about me, about us and the way we live? You're running because you're too scared to stick it out and fight."

"Why should I stick out being abused, Hyacinth?"

"It's Hy. Nobody calls me by that other name. So you run up to Canada and then what?"

"We clear our heads, get jobs, cut the umbilical cord once and for all. Just fucking live without being told where to go and what to do."

"Nobody tells me where to go. Ever. I got into this thing of my own free will and I can leave it the same way. Taryn followed me into this, not the other way around. I sure as hell didn't want any fucking church to be the answer when we moved here. That was my mother's crutch thirty years ago."

"So you're just going to ride the wave and not question the shit that goes down, ship out to Guyana and do unpaid manual labor in the middle of nowhere for the rest of your life? That what you envision for yourself?"

"I can work for the daycare or write for the paper."

"What are you going to do with a bunch of kids, Hy? I mean, seriously? Are you just interested in taking care of kids 'cause that's what's expected of you as a female? They got a million other people who can do that, a whole army of 'em. It's a waste of your talent. Sounds to me like this *is* a crutch, a way for you not to think about what comes next in your life."

"Unlike you I'm not holding myself above anybody, being judgmental. I'm not trying to separate myself from the people. Whatever I do is tied to what happens to this community—"

"And when did you have that revelation?"

"Going to Canada is just a stopgap."

"That's not what you said last month."

"Things changed."

"What, exactly? Is it because Marco's involved?"

"I don't give a shit about him."

"Then what is it?"

"You were in the Panthers right?"

"Not formally or anything."

"Why?"

"Too heavy into my music. Making big plans that never panned out. Fear. Brothers were getting killed left and right by the police. But the Panthers were the only ones around offering solutions and a framework. My mother was practically going blind with cataracts and she got some special eyeglasses through their free medical care program."

"She suck you into joining the Temple?"

"Nobody sucked me into it. You didn't answer my question." The headlights of an off duty garbage truck swept over them. She gathered up the stack of library books she'd put on the seat. Two manuals on Plumbing Basics. A copy of Nella Larsen's *Quicksand*. He reached over and took her hand.

"Just because we slept together once doesn't mean you own me," she said.

"That what you think this is? A ploy to control you? Give me more credit than that."

He picked up the Larsen book, squinting at the back cover. "I haven't read a novel in ages."

"It's about a mixed race woman confronting stuff in her life. I special ordered it, did interlibrary loan. They claimed it was out of print."

Foster shook his head. "The greatest country in the world, where you can get a thousand kinds of junk food on any street corner and this woman's book is out of print. They should have it up in Canada."

"Is that your utopic sales hook? How many books the Canadian library system has that the U.S. doesn't?"

He smiled and looked down at his lap. "If it'll get you to come with me, I can dream."

She leaned over, kissing him slow and hard, savoring the familiar taste of bubble gum and Lipton tea, laughing inwardly at his schoolboy Black Panther hard-on, imagining him skulking on the sidelines, Mattel machine gun at the ready to repel the fascists.

"Christ...why do you smell so good," she whispered.

A group of bikers rocketed past on ten-speeds, bumping the car's side mirror. Foster rolled the window down.

"Watch it motherfuckers!" He got out and surveyed the damage. "Let's go," he said.

"Where?"

"Richmond, Albany, somewhere where we're not going to be hounded. I'll get you some real food. Need to get away from here for a minute so I can think."

"I've got to go to work at 5:30 in the morning."

"Right, the chain gang. What the fuck have they got you doing that early?"

"I have the first shift at the Laundromat. I don't go in to the Temple to fill resident supply orders until the afternoon."

"Call in sick."

"Can't."

"Please."

"You can come upstairs to my apartment for an hour. My sister will be back around 10."

He shook his head and started the car. "Let's drive."

They drove the hills. Down, up, the city a vertiginous swirl of molten light, the last gasp of the dying weekend panting breakneck 'til Monday when a new group would launch for Guyana, dragging into the Oakland airport with one way tickets and their lives smashed into a duffle bag. They parked in a cul de sac by Golden Gate Park and lay together on the back seat, his heart hammering against his chest, breath coming in the asthmatic bursts of his childhood, back raw on the cold seat cushion softened by a thousand ass imprints, the Stylistics their spiritual guide as they made love for thirty minutes, parting at the distant hint of a siren, yoked together in damp silence, tracing the arcane scrawl of previous owners on the car's ceiling.

They lay head to head for a minute, moored in their tiny speck of earth, their significant insignificance, one hundred years from then when they would be less than nothing, less than marrow on an ant's behind. He shivered, dug his fingers softly into the crook of her thigh, slid them up to her waiting clit, rubbed her to climax under the static of DJs barreling through disco-pissing midnight playlists.

"Marco's a snitch," she said, rising to put her shirt on as raccoons skittered across the lawns of the bug-eyed Spanish houses fronting the park.

Foster sat up, "Those are some violent fuckers," he said, watching the animals run past. He stroked her cheek. "Marco's a little fucked up and stupid sometimes but he's not a snitch."

"You don't know that."

"That's fucking crazy. I've known him since fourth grade."

"He's playing you."

"What do you base that on?"

"A hunch. His criticism of Jim is too hyped up, plus he's always volunteering for something. It's like he never sleeps."

"That's 90% of everybody in the Temple, you included."

"He follows you too closely, like he wants to be you."

"Marco's no fucking groupie."

"I can't help you if you're too blind to see it."

"I can't see it because it's not there. You give me some hard evidence, something tangible then maybe I'd take you seriously...besides, you keep deflecting on why you want to stay around here."

"Let's go. I need at least six hours to be functional tomorrow morning."

"Come with us, Hy. You see what those biker assholes did to my mirror. That was a sign. They're tailing me and it's only a matter of time before they come after you."

"They won't try anything. They mess with me then they got Taryn talking to auditors about their group home funding or all the property that got deeded to the church from seniors with bogus conservators."

"You have a lot of faith in her."

"What are you implying?"

"That you shouldn't be so invested in the illusion that she's going to rescue you."

"She's not going to throw me over for some church."

"Funny, you're so quick to question Marco's motives but Taryn is sacred space."

"She's my sister."

"Ever heard of Cain and Abel? Jesus and Judas? Family doesn't mean shit."

They drove back to Fillmore, past crumbling Victorians, dark storefronts twinkling with neon liquor signs, dives issuing last call, bands of veterans sifting through clothes in front of a homeless shelter, a woman huddled on a bus bench in a green sleeping bag whistling to her dog.

If she died that night would she miss these things? If she were told she'd have to choose between dying or living with them, what would it be? If someone said right then that there was no possibility of change in her lifetime and she'd have to bow down to groveling acceptance. Canada loomed clean, pristine, a blank slate for vacillating blacks like Foster, a temporary haven for him to ride out the storm, lick his wounds, find adoring snow bunnies to fuck while playing the exotic expat in the undertow of a dead revolution. He had escaped Vietnam by a hair, a quirk of birth, a low lottery number, a cosmic accident that he nursed like a badge of shame, haunting the endless memorials of the lost boys in the neighborhood he grew up in, afflicted with war envy.

His profile flashed lovely and desperate in the street lights as they approached her apartment.

He pulled up short at the curb, hands tight on the steering wheel, the engine drawling underneath them.

"Can I write to you?"

"If it makes you feel better."

He paused, smiling wistfully as he tapped on the dashboard. "How about one last drum duel for the road? I know you can smoke me on "Toad", or what about 'The End'"?

She rolled her eyes at the limp irony. "Yeah, the Beatles, I always thought that solo was lame."

He turned to her, grabbing her arm, pulling her into him. "Come with me Hy. Please."

"What the fuck are you doing?!"

A shadow fell over her side of the car as a woman appeared, knocking hard at the window. "Hey, is he hurting you? Let her go asshole," she said firmly in a smoker's rasp.

Foster sized her up, shouting through the crack in the window. "Fuck you! And you can run back and tell massa I said it."

The woman dug in her purse and pulled out a vial of liquid. She opened it and threw it into the car, the smell of lavender filling the air. Hy recognized it as one of the holy oils the Temple sold to members who were still into faith healing. It was Father's secret sauce and classified recipe, the sanctified juju that the Sunday seekers lined up to see round out his sermon's final bit of theatre when his marathon lamentations began to exhaust the most diehard best beloveds.

"You shut your mouth you dirty bastard. You're nothing but a dirty primitive pig and if there's a hell you're gonna burn in it!"

She was clearly in disguise, dark bird's nest wig with silvery streaks askew across her lined forehead, tinted glasses dwarfing a miniature face splattered with brown freckles peeking from a layer of pancake makeup. The voice was familiar, but it too was distorted with practice.

The oil had gotten on Foster's pants, dribbling from the radio console, the maw where the heating panel had been ripped out, then shoddily reconfigured. He jumped out of the car cursing as the woman ran. She dropped the vial, clutching at her capsizing wig to a chorus of barking Dobermans pacing behind the fence of an auto shop.

Hy got out of the car. The light in her sister's room had gone on. She picked up the broken vial and turned it over. On the back was a small mass-produced picture of Jim, his pet monkey Muggs and a smiling black child.

The Emancipation of Muggs
Jonestown, Guyana 1978

The fearless wizard girls are the first to hear about White Night from Muggs.

In the hush of late afternoon, lessons done, chores half-begun, Get the Monkey was their favorite pastime. The wizards liked to ogle him when he was asleep; marveling playfully at his majestic human teeth, his tittering Popeye the Sailor snore, wondering how and what he dreamed; was it of Father, Mother Mabelean or escape into the jungle to meet the other monkey brains barred from Jonestown. Behind the grown-ups' backs they made him the lab rat for their experiments. How does wet chimp fur conduct electricity with paper clips? Would he react to the medicine stolen from the infirmary doctor's medical bag, the weird stuff that stunk of bitter almonds? The doctor had a pig for that purpose. A hairy shit-colored sow who irritated Muggs with her dumbness. The wizards had a pact with Muggs not to tell, plying him with secret stash chocolate kisses and apologies, the odor of their mischief all over him.

Monkey memory is longer than an elephant's, their teacher Mrs. Ernestine told them. It's because they're the closest kin to us. Strip us down to the bone and we're apes without the glory of tails. Strip us down to the bone and it's the humans that have always been more dangerous.

Muggs would let them know if the killings were real or nightmare. In the white of night he would give the wizards the signal to levitate into the darkness and join the other monkey brains.

CHAPTER 20

The Talk, Fillmore, 1977

ON A RARE Sunday when they weren't in church, they lay next to each other, back to breast, listening to the lazy fits and starts of the morning. For the past hour Taryn had pretended to be asleep. Jess had gotten up, used the bathroom, picked up the paper from the front step, then clambered noisily back into bed, resting her hand on Taryn's hip.

"Rain's coming," she cooed into Taryn's ear, sliding her fingers down her thigh in invitation. They had stayed up late listening to records, watching the news with the sound off, working in manic bursts, fucking languidly when the fatigue swallowed them up and the phone calls from her mother, Jess' clients and Planning Commission people died down.

Taryn squirmed under her cold fingers. "I should get up."

"I thought we were going to take it easy this morning."

"I've got a report to turn in tomorrow."

"On what?"

"The performance of a few new accounts."

Jess kissed her earlobe, "You're lying."

"No I'm not."

"You're a bad liar."

Taryn looked around the room, suddenly repelled by the mess of half-empty wine glasses, smeared Chinese takeout cartons, ashtrays clogged with Jess' lipstick stained cigarettes and grocery store receipts. Disorder disgusted her, the residue of a sleepless semi-drunken night and all Jess' personal effects swirling and encroaching, tightening her throat.

"If I don't get on this now I'll be up all night."

Jess put her arm around her neck playfully, "Relax, you just can't hold your liquor."

Taryn flinched. "Not true. You know I don't like the stuff, never have, never will."

"Don't worry you didn't reveal anything earth-shattering when you were in a drunken stupor," she laughed. "You just don't like not being in control."

"What's wrong with that?"

"You need to lighten up, T. This is our world in here. Temple rules have nothing to do with what goes on between us."

"I can't fuck this deadline up fooling around today."

"Fine. I'll leave." Jess put her pants on and bustled over to the center table, gathering up her bag, notebooks, a faded bottle of homeopathic cough medicine the color of sewer water. Taryn watched her numbly, her gaunt face knotted with determination as she took stock of the last vestiges of her stuff and whittled the clutter down to a few stray pens.

"Babe, Jess, come on, I didn't mean you had to leave."

"Your priorities are pretty clear to me."

"If I don't get this in on time it just gives them more ammo, more of an excuse to give me some clerical, busywork shit they'd never give to the Stanford white boys on training wheels. I don't even know why I have to explain this to you of all people."

"How come you didn't want to move into the communal units with the other sisters and brothers?"

"I'm not ready for that."

"You have so much to give, T. As long as you hold yourself apart from everyone you'll never be ready."

"You sound like my sister."

"She finally dragged in early this morning you know."

"I heard."

"She was with that Foster person."

"He seems ok, reasonably smart."

"He's smart alright. Likes to instigate, play the field. Smug mf fancies himself as some kind of oracle of all things black. Just like Hy to fall for a jive dilettante like that when she should be applying herself, doing something in life."

"Back off."

"You've got to stop coddling her. She's a thirty three year-old grown ass woman, T."

Hy had gotten up and was outside the door in the kitchen, washing her hands in the sink. She made a show of shuffling dirty dishes as she strained to listen, aided by the gray dolor of the building still entombed in narcoleptic sleep at 9:30.

Jess had become more manic as of late, more cloyingly insistent about being right, her client caseload growing along with new responsibilities on the Planning Commission and the workaday stream of anguished hotline callers seeking guidance, sweet relief from the rogue memories, the three ring circus raging between their temples.

I can't help them, can't contain them, a lot of them could do with meds but black folk don't want to hear nothing like that, she'd murmured semi-conscious, drifting away in Taryn's arms after they'd come home from a classical concert the night before arguing about the red light Jess had run.

"You got a death wish and want to take me down with you, ask me first," Taryn said as they undressed each other with the detachment of emergency room nurses.

Taryn had the sense that Jess was always taking stock of her, calculating whether she was worth the gamble and the time, whether their ambitions meshed. Part of her believed she was a project Jess was undertaking; the sex, the halting intimacy between them a source of ambivalence.

The tide of planning for the move to Guyana was rising and Jess had only dipped her toe in it personally, counseling others on how to make the transition. She sidled up to the subject with Taryn in unbidden moments, Jonestown brochures bright with pictures of verdant country sides always at the ready.

"The sooner Hy snaps out of that fantasy of mock rebellion the better her head will be. You know this. You don't need any adult children to raise."

"I told you to back off."

"When we leave for Jonestown—"

There was a knock on the door and Hy came in.

Jess snapped her belt buckle on. "Ever heard of asking before you barge into a room?"

Hy brushed past her and handed Taryn a roll of bills. "My half of the rent and utilities for the next two months before I split."

"Split? Where? And where did you get this?"

"Work."

"Hy they barely pay you and they're never on time when they do."

"Times change and people change."

Jess smirked. "Interesting how you got all that cash when you're supposed to be tithing it to support the settlement. Or did your revolutionary sugar daddy give this to you for a blow job? If you lived in co-housing you wouldn't have to whore for it."

"Eat me."

"Not if yours was the last pussy on earth. You know Foster's only agenda is testing to see whose got the biggest one, him or Jim. He's got no program, no method and no cause other than himself and being skeptical for skeptical's sake. Beyond that he's flailing—"

Hy continued to ignore Jess. "I have a friend from City College who might be interested in renting the other room. Or will you be moving her in here?"

Taryn put the money on her desk. "Nobody else is taking that room. I don't understand why you didn't talk to me about this first."

"What's there to talk about? I'm obsolete in this place. You don't want to fuck up your mental health by 'coddling'."

"C'mon, Hy."

"She feeds you your lines like a fucking ventriloquist's dummy."

Jess slung her bag over her shoulder and pecked Taryn on the cheek. "I'll see you later, T."

The phone rang. Taryn picked it up and said hello. There was a long pause, as though the caller were waiting for an invitation to speak.

"Hello?" She repeated.

"Can I speak to Jess please?" The caller asked.

"Who's calling?"

"Can I speak to her please?"

Taryn handed the phone to Jess. "Some woman. Won't give her name."

"Hello? Yes, yes...hi Zephyr. How did you know I was here? No, I didn't plan on coming in today."

Zephyr sighed on the other end. She was an engineer, a weapons designer laid off from Lawrence Livermore lab after being accused of stealing a bag of potato chips from the commissary. She'd flitted around looking for another job, unraveling, seemingly branded for life as a high-achieving black klepto until latching onto the Temple and a renewed sense of purpose beating swords into ploughshares.

"There was a meeting last night about preparing for Guyana," she said.

"What? Nobody told me about it."

"We saw an orientation film about the people and the weather and they talked to us about liquidating our stuff."

"We've never discussed that in our sessions. Listen, Zephyr, I need to talk to you later in private. Call my answering service and make an appointment."

Zephyr paused. "Actually, Mariah gave me this number. She expressed concern about you. Said your girlfriend's sister had gotten in with some screw ups and it might be compromising your ability to serve clients."

Jess tightened her grip on the receiver, digging into it like it was black rubber. Taryn watched her quizzically, annoyed at the flutter of jealousy in her stomach.

"I see," Jess said. "So Mariah recruited you to deliver the message instead of telling me to my face."

Zephyr was silent.

"I'm surprised that you'd allow yourself to be sucked up into her games. She's a petty uneducated little white bitch with too much time on her hands, understand?"

"But—"

"Why is she getting into my business and how does she even know where the fuck I am on a Sunday morning when I told them I wouldn't be coming in?"

"Tone it down, she didn't mean any offense."

Hy went back out into the kitchen, leaving the door ajar so she could hear. Taryn sat with her arms crossed on the bed.

"One last thing," Zephyr said. "You need to watch your back with these chicks you're hanging with. Evidently Hyacinth's boyfriend left town overnight and stole one of the Temple's check registers. Tried to use them in a massage parlor off the I5."

"And how do they know that?"

"Security had a tail on him."

"Please call my service and make an appointment. You're not mentally ready to go to Guyana." She hung up the phone. Taryn had begun pulling the sheets off the bed, rolling them into a prim ball in the center of the mattress as she reached over to the window sill and flicked dust off the bare ledge.

Jess watched her coolly. She walked over to the bedroom door and shut it. "You overhear any of that? Seems Foster hightailed it out of here last night and financed his shenanigans with checks he stole from the church. Right after he dropped off missy out there. No wonder she was so indignant."

"That hardly seems credible."

"It's very credible. The man had no steady job. He thought his shit was too superior to work for the church. He's a pathological liar and closet case who probably wanted to do Jim."

"That what the tea leaf reading repressed white women you just slammed tell you?"

"No. That's what I know. He reeks of it, reeks of impotence. Self-hating black queen with a constituency of one."

Hy pushed open the door from the kitchen holding a bowl of cereal in one hand, the water running in the sink. "You know damn well Foster didn't steal anything. They're framing him just like they did the others. The reason he left is because he wasn't allowed to have an independent voice as a black man. Didn't have any family to tether him here so what would be the point of trying to 'reform' from within? Toms like you drove him out."

"That's a convenient theory, and I'm sure you spent a lot of time on your back formulating it with him."

Hy threw the cereal at her. Cornflakes dribbled down her cheek and onto her jacket.

"Christ," Taryn said, shaking her head as she handed Jess a towel from the dresser.

The phone rang again. Hy picked up the receiver and slammed it back down.

"And tell your minions not to fucking call here again."

Demian rolled out of bed anxious that morning, skin crawling with imaginary tics, every cell in him alive and screaming like little electrode pustules firing a million different messages. He'd come in late from a showing of *Taxi Driver* the night before. Snuck off with three non-Temple friends he'd met in his acting class at City College. They chided him about doing a prison break as they scavenged the greasy bottom of the popcorn bucket they shared in the back row. Everything was good until Monk, jealous and sky high on glue, said I heard your daddy got busted jacking off at a porn theatre for queers. Then it was on and cracking and the ushers had to haul them out right when Travis Bickle was going ape shit in the mirror.

"Do you want to press charges against that nigger?" One of the ushers muttered in the back room where they let Demian mop up his bloody nose, gave him an ice pack, sympathy and shrugged shoulders even though he'd thrown the first punch, circling around him in wolfish solidarity. All they could see was his white skin, not his black brother, not the Temple's principles of black struggle, not the real him; quivering with love.

And he'd been secretly glad.

Glad that the manager had let him go quietly off into the night with little more than a Band Aid and a wag of his finger. The better so no one in the church would know that he, the role model, had been in a fight over Father's honor.

He snorted, turned onto his back, wincing from the pain of the night before, determined to delay the inevitable, making small talk with a bronze-winged roach trying to take flight from the ceiling. This, the commandanté of his pathetic four walls, witness to all his secret longings, the marginalia of his independence.

His father had integrated a whole theatre chain in the fifties in Indiana. Did it through sheer force of will they said. Mobilizing three hundred blacks to go see *Auntie Mame* in matinees downtown every weekend after Sunday service. Even though it had been a free state north of the Mason Dixon it was just as klannish and black-hating as Dixie. Just as fixated on race purity and licking old Confederate wounds. Growing up hearing it invoked as distant legend he'd learned to loathe it and long for it.

Today was the picket of the newspaper that had published an exposé on the Temple. He got there late on the bus and the members were already massing. Some had come to the newspaper headquarters before dawn, shivering in faded overcoats and ratty sweaters, a smattering of the old faithful and a sprinkling of the new out to test their mettle for the first time. Newspaper employees veered around them, annoyed by the ruckus, the sidewalk brimming with bodies. A woman pushing a shopping cart filled with bottles scowled and navigated through the throng, ignoring a member who tried to hand her a brochure.

He stood off to the side and watched for a while, grateful for the moment of anonymity, fearing that his father would descend any second and part the sea. Reporters from the local TV station wandered haplessly in and out in stimuli overload looking for a salacious quote.

"Fucking robots. Who's in charge here?" One muttered, tearing into a lemon jelly donut in a grease-stained paper bag. He eyed Demian.

"Are you part of this? Can I get a quote?"

"Naw man, I don't do press. Where did you get that donut?"

"Stan's, place next to the dry cleaners. Want one?"

The reporter offered him the bag. Demian dug into it and took one, letting the sugary forbidden goo melt luridly on his tongue. The man watched him, grinning, recognition dawning over his cynical face.

"You're the son, aren't you?"

Demian paused. Carol, Mariah and Zephyr had appeared and begun directing some of the picketers, chiming in with chanted rebukes to the publisher, fists raised, heads down in solemn affinity. He could feel them watching him, waiting for him to join the procession. It gave him a thrill to hold back, to have them see him talking to the reporter, to keep them teetering in suspense.

"Yeah, maybe. What's it to you?"

"I was thinking maybe I could get an off the record interview with you about what's happening here. What the end game is with all of this."

"The end game's pretty easy to see man. Our organization is under a microscope, unjustifiably so, many people think, and that's why folks have given up their work morning to be out here."

"Is that your opinion too?"

Demian flicked his hair out of his face. His mother had warned him against keeping it too shaggy and long lest it be a magnet for cops itching to bust hippies.

"Yeah, sure."

"You think there's any merit to the allegations in that story?"

"Which allegations are you referring to?"

"That the church punished and ostracized members who were critical. That you had two so-called problematic congregation members die under mysterious circumstances over the past several years and no one was held accountable for their deaths."

"I can't speak on that."

"These were members with families. Good people. Loyal. Don't you feel some tiny obligation to care about what happened to them?"

Demian watched the picketers flow by him. Moist-eyed earnest newcomers, thrill seekers, parasites, acquaintances he'd hung with a few times, talking, laughing, dreaming about what was next in their lives, stealing a joint here and there in the knuckle dragging death hours of the night when they were scrambling to get food and toiletry orders filled for the communal apartments. Some smiled, pained, searching his face for clues; others looked past him, shrinking in the pistol whipping cold. He wanted black coffee and the succor of his warm bed, to regress maybe even, to the soft tomb before birth and the anointing of names; the stink of a rose is a rose is a rose.

"I do care ... I-I just don't know what you're talking about."

"Lindsey Chappel. Merrick Kruger. Got a nice list of names supplied by the relatives' group. Look, I know you all have done good things. A lot of good for poor people. That's undeniable. No one can take that away from you all. I just want to see if there's any light you can shed on why all these folk are claiming that there's been foul play."

"I can't help you."

"I saw your mother at the library the other day with a whole battalion of little kids jumping around her. You look a lot like her. It'd be a shame for her to get dragged down into this if there were any indictments."

"What are you talking about? She had nothing to do with any of that shit."

The reporter held out the paper bag. "More? Look, you're just a teenager. Bright, advanced, well-spoken. You have your whole life ahead of you. There's no reason why you should be judged by what your parents do. You're your own person just starting out."

"You don't have to tell me that."

"If you don't want to talk here or can't talk here why don't you meet me at Stan's? They have killer French crullers."

Jamiah approached them, toothpick poking from his mouth.

"Hey, Demian. What's up?"

"Nothing much."

"Who's your friend?"

"He's not my friend."

The reporter stuck out his hand. "Kip Hayashi, KVTR Channel 5. You one of Reverend Jones' bodyguards?"

Jamiah grunted. "You don't need to worry about who I am. I'm a friend of Demian's and I look out for him when there's a need to."

"Reverend Jones coming out this morning?"

"I don't have no crystal ball on Reverend Jones' schedule. Dig?"

"Sure, sure. What did you say your name was?"

"I didn't, later for this." He pushed through the crowd. More newspaper staff had begun to arrive in a flurry of briefcases, thermoses, high heels, mousey middlebrow suit coats slung in garment bags over hunched shoulders, the white editors swinging their Volvos around to the company garage for the black valets to park.

"You don't know anything about me and my family," Demian muttered.

"You're right. I don't. So why don't you give me your version. Off the record. I'll even throw in a dozen donuts."

"That's a cheap bribe."

Kip laughed. "Hey, I'm in public television. Look, I know it's hard for you with all these people here. I'll cut out and you can meet me there in ten minutes ok?"

Demian waited until the crowd was distracted by a passing ambulance then slipped off, liberated by the brisk walk to Stan's, the glorious slide back into anonymity, the normal drone of people going to work, school, the ploddingly familiar places their bodies had memorized. He drank it all in, envying them.

When he got to the donut shop he saw Kip sitting at a table with a tray and a cup of coffee. He motioned to the display. "Take your pick, courtesy of KVTR."

"Just a cinnamon roll."

"That's it?"

"Yeah."

"Cheap bribe, cheap date."

Demian glowered.

"Lighten up. I respect your asceticism."

"If that's what you want to call it."

"Fancy term for giving up things. I suspect you've been doing that all your life. How old are you by the way?"

"Seventeen."

"About to graduate from high school?"

"Yeah."

"And your brother?"

"He already graduated."

"Sharp guy I hear."

"Uh huh."

"I hear he's just at genius level."

"Some say that I guess."

"Your parents adopted him when he was a newborn."

"Yeah."

"You two pretty close?"

"Yeah, sure."

"Being that close in age you could either be tight as wet pantyhose or wanting to shit all over each other."

"Yeah, a little of both."

"Must've been interesting him being black."

"My parents took him in when he was little. They took in a lot of kids from other races."

"That's real honorable. I'm an only child. I would've loved a posse of adopted brothers and sisters running around my house. Must've been cozy."

Demian shrugged. "That's just the way it was."

"So it was all Kumbaya, or copacetic as the brothers say. Excuse me but I grew up in black neighborhoods in South Central Los Angeles. Whole community of Japanese tucked away."

"We have a church down there."

"Yes, some of the Temple basketball team is recruited from that congregation right?"

"Yeah."

"I hear you have a pretty mean jump shot."

"I'm decent."

"More than decent, you're the captain of the team and the top scorer. You interested in a career in basketball?"

"No."

"Or are they grooming you to take over from your father when he gets worn out from saving lives?"

"Nobody's grooming me. There are plenty of other people who'd do a far better job of it waiting in line."

"Like the white man who's co-pastoring in L.A.?"

"Yeah, him, I guess. Although my dad doesn't have a lot of respect for him, thinks he's trying to break away and start his own church."

"He either spends his life being your father's sidekick or strikes out into the world. I sure as hell don't envy anybody who thinks they've got a calling from God to preach."

"My dad didn't have a calling. The religious stuff was just a stepping stone for socialism."

"And what does that mean in your mind?"

"Equality, man. Freedom from the corruption of private property. Freedom from everything being about one person, one family, 2.5 kids, possessions, kids as possessions, women and men as possessions. If you've got a fancy new Schwinn bike and nobody else in the neighborhood has one we all get a crack at it provided we agree to share, put air in the tires, not bring it back fucked up."

"How do you keep the neighborhood rabble from stealing the bike?"

"I don't accept that term rabble, that's offensive. I mean the main reason poor people steal is because they don't have anything, or the crazy TV commercials create a need in them to have all these things they don't need, then people mistake superficial material stuff for life or death."

Kip nodded, watching the women behind the counter scoop cake donut grease bombs up into white bags. They counted change out in rapid fire, trading idle pleasantries with the morning regulars.

Kip emptied the glazed sugar at the bottom of the donut bag into his mouth.

"So there would have to be some kind of, some kind of contract that the community agreed on to make sure the bike didn't get so-called 'fucked up'."

"Yeah."

"And you have that type of understanding in the Temple 'family'. Isn't that what you call each other?"

"People feel an obligation to do right by each other."

"How? What makes you guys more saintly and utopic than the fifty million other congregations on the planet?"

Demian licked his fingers, a gaggle of weather-beaten old men playing Black Jack at the corner table let out a raunchy harmonized whoop as one of them smacked down a winning hand. Kip capped his pen and leaned forward, the blood vessels in his eyes scissoring out at Demian.

He glanced at the men in the corner, his face going still. "No disrespect meant to your Temple. I'm genuinely curious. My mission in life right now is to not wind up like them, holding court in a donut shop booth. Older I get the more it sucks to be an agnostic, man, so anything you can tell me about your mojo for keeping a thousand people from all kinds of different races and creeds together will be an education."

"It's just something that my parents and other folks who were involved at the beginning valued. They were working in poor neighborhoods with black people who were getting dumped on by racists, they invited blacks to the services and—"

"The white people and the church elders didn't take kindly to that."

"Vandalized the church, threw rocks in the windows of our house, used to follow me and my brother around the grocery store calling us Buckwheat and Alfalfa."

"And how did you feel being the white brother to a black orphan?"

"It made me see the ugliness, the insanity of prejudice and whites thinking they were superior."

"Didn't you sometimes wish you were him to get your parent's attention?"

"What?"

"When I was little I took a big box of band aids from the medicine cabinet and stuck them all over me. Smeared on Mercurochrome to make my 'bruises' look more authentic and went to school looking seriously fucked up. Fine ass white lady teacher fawned over me, made me her pet 'chink' for the week."

"You're Japanese though."

Kip chuckled. "C'mon now Demian, what difference does that make to them? Didn't being the white brother to a black orphan teach you anything about the way your people think? The way they want to put us colored folk on pretty leashes so the neighbors can see how kind they are to the animals."

"I don't identify that way."

"And your parents certainly don't either right?"

"Our parents don't what?"

Jimmy had walked up from behind him. He stood over them placid-faced, arms flat at his sides, head cocked as though he was on a school playground poised for the bell to ring. Demian stiffened, pointing to the donut case trying to be cavalier.

"Hey, Jimmy. Remember that time when we threw up all those donut holes we snuck on the bus going to Texas?"

Jimmy stuck out his hand to the reporter. "I'm Jimmy, Demian's brother. And you are?"

"Kip Hayashi from KVTR, Channel 5." He gave Jimmy the once over. "Damn you boys are tall! What kind of growth hormones have you been hitting? Just kidding, I've heard a lot about you. A whiz in the classroom and on the court, most likely to be a nuclear physicist by twenty."

Jimmy looked at Demian. "That what you heard?"

"Not entirely from your brother, we just met in front of the newspaper building and I lured him over here for the donuts. I want to do a human interest story on the Temple spotlighting how it's giving back to the community."

"What are you doing here?" Jimmy asked Demian.

"What do you mean?"

"They were looking for you on the picket line."

"Who? Mariah? Carol? They sent you to hunt me down?"

"Nobody sent me to hunt you down. I didn't know where you were and Jamiah said he saw you come this way. We've got practice this afternoon remember?"

"Right. Sit down, join us."

"No. I have to study for my Calculus exam before we head to the court."

"You'll ace it, Jimmy, I don't know why you even pretend to sweat it."

Jimmy moistened his lips, wincing at his brother's words, the praise bending into envy. The card men in the corner cackled uproariously again, jeering at a squat man in a pork pie hat for dealing too slow. Jimmy glanced at them distastefully then put his hand on Demian's shoulder, his voice deepening into the gentle lull of their shared bedtime deep in steamy Indiana summers, in the moments before the goblins descended and his arms were heaven for Demian.

He thumped him softly on the forehead and nodded to Kip. "Later."

CHAPTER 21

The Sons, Fillmore, 1977

THE BASKETBALL SHOT punched into the backboard, flipping off the rim, taking a millennium to land back. It melted all buttery in Demian's hands as he turned it around, did a quick layup and manufactured the swish of an invisible net in his head. How you like that, genius, he thought to his brother standing across from him, his eyes obscured in the velvet dark of right before the streetlights fluttered on, the court stretching in front of them, oceanic.

Was it true that their mother dressed them alike right down to the underwear? Was it true that she'd tried to get their picture taken for Christmas at the neighborhood Woolworth, and been turned away? That she'd hired one of the church members to play photographer at the last minute, bouncing Demian on one knee and Jimmy on the other. The photo shoot was captured in a collection of amateurish black and white pictures rammed behind the birth control herbs in her dresser drawer. The top of his head is torn off in one of the pictures; his arm around the adopted refugee sister who'd died in a car crash right after being baptized.

Dad hadn't been able to bring her back from the dead like he had Jimmy when he'd gotten crazy sick.

"There is no fucking God, boys," Dad said. "Get that in your head. Look what he did to your innocent little sister."

Demian had kept the Woolworth picture all these years, fascinated by the symmetry of their bodies, how nature had spared them but devoured their sister, hovering above them, babyhood's bitter emissary.

On the court he and Jimmy always had an audience, a wise ass regiment of snickering eleven year-olds from the Catholic Brotherhood's after school program. They ran color commentary on every fuck-up and half-step Demian and Jimmy made, the two of them circling each other like queasy suitors. They jeered at Demian's bow-legged free throw, Jimmy's ponderous dribble and hard fakes, playing the dozens as though their lives depended on it.

Pretty boy, honky tonk, Bambi, they yelled.

Jimmy ignored them. Demian gave them the finger. He hadn't changed clothes from that morning. He took off his terry cloth shirt and put it on the park bench, marinating in the ripe smell of his own must, the soggy remains of his anxiety seeing his brother at the donut shop.

Jimmy waited for him to get back on the court then thrust the ball at him. He caught it in his chest, cradling it for a second, faking, throwing it back with the same brute force that they'd learned when their father stood over them with a stopwatch, timing them on who passed the ball the fastest, goading them with sweet talk about his imaginary career as a mongrel untouchable high school hoops star.

At the tenth cannonball pass, Jimmy stopped, conceding. He chucked the ball lightly at Demian, bending down to tie his high top sneakers, a floppy pair of green Converse on loan from one of the Temple thrift stores.

"That reporter took a real shine to you," Jimmy said.

"How do you mean?"

"You know what I mean."

"He's not a homosexual."

"Whatever he was, he was putting the moves on you and you fell for it."

"I have the right to speak my mind."

"Speaking your mind is one thing, getting played for a punk is another."

Demian gripped the ball, holding it over his head, breaking into a hard dribble. Jimmy's breath hung in the air, a lingering rasp leftover from childhood asthma.

"You ok?"

"Of course."

He passed the ball to Jimmy. He drove down the court and did a layup, squeals from the Catholic boys crackling from behind the gate.

"Time for ya'll to go home!" Demian shouted to them.

"Fuck you, snowflake!"

Jimmy waved his hand dismissively at Demian. "Leave 'em alone. They don't know any better." He stared coolly at his brother, starter mustache droopy with dew. "Dad wants us to leave for Jonestown in a few weeks."

"I'm not going."

"You tell him that?"

"In so many words."

"He expects us to show leadership over there, we're the only ones who can really be trusted not to screw up his vision."

"I don't really care what his vision is for that place. I have a life here that I'm not going to ditch just because he wants to play king of the fucking jungle."

"And what life is that? Smoking weed? Staying out late, getting up late, screwing your way through every zip code in the Bay?"

"No, that's Dad's thing, get your propaganda straight."

"Get serious. We go over there for fifteen months, clear the land, get supplies, supervise construction and establish relationships with the locals. You'll pack a career's worth of experience into just one year."

Demian shook his head. "I don't want that kind of career. I don't want to waste one second of my life busting my ass doing shit work for his pipe dream."

The first tinny peals of an ice cream truck jingled through the street, sending the Catholic boys off in a gallop.

"Look," Jimmy said. "I know he's not perfect. He's done some messed up shit. This move is a chance for him to make it right, to atone. Not only for him but for everybody. It's bigger than any one person. If you see it as just his pipe dream then you don't get it."

"What do Ernestine, Cassandra and all the other little old black ladies who've given Dad and the church their homes and life savings have to atone for, Jimmy?"

Jimmy took a step back. "Nothing. Not a single thing. I just know some people have been waiting their whole lives for this."

"Then let them go in my place."

"What are you going to do then?"

"Take some acting classes. There's a few theater groups I want to check out."

"Theater? Dem you've never acted in your life. You know how hard it is to make it in that industry? You'll get chewed up and spit out. People will judge you right out the gate because you're Jim Jones' son."

"I don't have the same kind of negativity as you."

"What do you have to be negative about when you've been sheltered all your damn life? You say jump, the world says how high?"

"Get off it Jimmy, I didn't get any fucking special privileges. If anything..."

"If anything what? Mom and Dad bent over backwards for a poor little black orphan and left Homemade, their own flesh and blood, out in the cold? Was supposed to be the other way around right?"

"Yeah, that's right."

"You don't believe that."

Jimmy put his hand on Demian's shoulder. Demian tried to pull away, his brother holding him firmly. "Remember the summer we spent at Grandma's when everyone was out on the road at the Wings of Deliverance thing."

"Yeah, I remember. What about it?" Demian asked tartly. Muddy water gurgled up in his throat. Baby frogs suctioned up his leg, tiny glow-in-the-dark toys. Down, down, down, he'd gone, landing in the seat of a rusted trike. Down, down, down and this was surely the end, he'd thought, of his stupid eight year-old self. Never be able to eat spaghetti with melted cheese again, never be able to press up against Kira's thigh and pretend like it was an accident, never be able to fly a plane to Brazil. He would sit at the back of the funeral home, drinking in his parents' laments at yet another lost child. But then his brother's hands were around him, snatching at his collar, grabbing hold to the scruff of his neck, pushing past the hail of leaves, twigs and bone imploring them to stay and play for a while.

He'd jumped in the creek on a dare from a neighbor boy.

Betcha Sambo can swim better'n you Stringbean, the boy taunted, cramming strips of baloney sandwich in his hatchet face. He was captivated by the spectacle of he and Jimmy; tall, gangly, selectively protective of each other. Now here was Demian taking the bait, trying to be bad by jumping into the glorified piss hole he'd feared since he was a toddler.

"That time in the creek. Boy, were you scared. Grandma—little bitty grandma—wanted to beat your butt afterward. Went on and on about this kid drowning in the summer of '48 that they didn't get to in time."

"You want a fucking medal after all these years for rescuing me? That it?"

"It's not about me. It's about why you needed to prove yourself to that little asshole who was teasing us."

"I wasn't trying to prove shit."

Jimmy took a towel from his duffel bag on the ground. He reached over and wiped the sweat off Demian's cheek, handing him the towel. "Didn't want Sambo to upstage you. Right, little brother? I forgave you that then. I forgive you now."

Demian balled up the towel and threw it back at him. "Fuck off."

"Before she died grandma used to say that we were the church philosophers, always in our heads thinking heavy, like it was us against the world. She loved it when I took up for you. Too bad she didn't live long enough to see what we're going to do over there."

"Don't go trotting her out to make me feel guilty."

"The bigger vision Dad has is partly because of her. She couldn't do a fourth of what he's done because society wouldn't support a dirt poor white woman. You were the dreamier one in her eyes, more like Mom I guess. I defended you then, told her you could be counted on."

Demian turned away from the court and spit. In the distance he could see cars flitting by across the iguana's spine of the Bay Bridge. He thought he saw someone scaling it, waving a white flag into the barreling headlights.

Could he cut himself open and quarantine the genes that were his father's for an hour, a day, a year.

Jimmy followed his gaze, looking impatient then bemused. "There you go daydreaming again. C'mon, let's go get something to eat."

Jim sat at his desk on the phone with Hampton Goodwin, grimacing between slurps of spinach juice. "The Nation of Islam will support us on this. Glide Church will support us on this. What remains of the Panthers will support us. Trust me Hampton. Those motherfucking pigs wake up cracking our people's heads in the morning and go to sleep cracking 'em. There's no fucking way that little shit Ayers is going to get away with greasing the palms of the Police Benevolent League to crap on the affirmative action initiative we're backing. Take a seat and let our Peoples Forum paper handle it. After the buzz we got from yesterday's picket at *The Chronicle* they're gonna think twice before fucking with us."

He paused, holding the glass out in front of him. "Christ, this colonic cleanse stuff is some nasty shit."

"Alright Jim, you handle it. I've got enough on my plate this week what with going to DC tomorrow to make sure those boys in the Congressional Black Caucus don't screw up the subcommittee hearing on South Africa."

"Then we can depend on your trucks to distribute to more newsstands in the East Bay? Some of our people are going door-to-door in the a.m. I want to make sure that edition gets shoved in front of six hundred more eyeballs than we usually have."

"Will do, my friend. But you know those trucks don't run on air and the drivers don't put food on their table with their good looks. You'll send my office a check from the Planning Commission before I leave, correct?"

"You got it, guv."

"One more thing, Jim...I've gotten several letters from this aggrieved relatives' outfit, so-called Temple defectors and such. I had my girls dispose of them."

"Right, guv. Thank you."

"You've got to handle this, Jim. We can manage the newspapers, politicians and volatile folk like Ida Lassiter for a little while. Yes, the community needs you right where you are on the Housing Authority, applying pressure. Otherwise they're going to keep selling the Fillmore to the highest bidder and next year we'll be watching them serve caviar at sidewalk cafes to white dilettantes from Sausalito. But you've got to handle this business with the relatives. Meet with them, or have some of your people meet with them. Listen to their sob stories and neutralize them."

"It's all gutter trash Hampton, politically motivated fabrications we shouldn't have to dignify—"

"That's the nature of the game, Jim. I'll speak to you when I return."

"Godspeed," Jim said. The phone clicked on the other end.

He could hear the rumblings of activity downstairs on the first and second floors of the church. The end of a rehearsal; the ingredients of the morning's breakfast fussily assembled; the slip of an argument over an unpaid bill; toilets being flushed, scrubbed, disinfected. Back in the day, even his elementary school teachers had been awed by his dog whistle ears. Sharp enough to hear a tick's fart, his father had said.

Carol walked in holding his calendar. "What did Hampton want?"

"Nothing I hadn't heard before."

She settled into the chair in front of him, resting the calendar in the folds of her denim skirt, assessing him with a tender wariness. "You know you like his little counseling sessions. What did he want then?"

"Wants us to run an appeasement campaign with the defectors and disgruntled families. To sit down and have tea and crumpets."

"The best way to deal with these people is to step up what we've been doing—put a little more pressure on those whose relatives are loud and meddling and saturate the media with our good works."

He pursed his lips in irritation, popping a pill into his mouth as he motioned for the cup of water at her side. "That's not winning us the war. Where's Mariah and Sally?"

She stiffened, noting the feline longing in his voice. "They're downstairs doing accounts receivable."

"Have them come up."

"What for?"

"I want their opinion on this."

"They're little more than children, Jim. What insight could they possibly have?"

"They've more than proven themselves."

"Bullshit. They've proven how good they are thinking while they're on their backs with their legs spread."

He leaned forward, rolling his index finger over her lips. "Stop being so self- righteous, Sweet Pea. You were only twenty four when I saw the potential in you. Next to Chiang Kai-shek no better general ever lived."

She took his hand, spreading the fingers firmly against her skirt. "Don't forget who got those two and all the other whores you've laid in this church."

He rubbed her thigh, tracing down to the ankle, suddenly bashful. "May is out tonight. Thought maybe I could come over—"

She cut him off. "Hampton approve of our plan to expand circulation?"

"So long as we pay his gas."

"I'll have Mariah cut a check."

"See, they're good for something other than fucking."

"Cute. Devera is almost done with the new article."

"Jealousy doesn't become you, Sweet Pea. You can fuck whoever you want, you don't see me lording it over you. Long as you protect yourself against all the new venereal diseases floating around."

"How charitable of you, Jim."

"I'm serious as a heart attack."

She glared at him. "So what about the Red Brigade. Jamiah is looking pretty ripe these days."

He screwed the top back on his bottle of pills and shoved it into the desk drawer. "Naw, you need a Protestant, a WASP boy, or maybe even a Jew. Somebody closer to your own species."

"Someone non-threatening, is that what you mean?"

"Jamiah's just a baby."

"Listen to how you sound."

"Look, you're a privileged cunt from a rich white family."

She jumped up, fists squeezed into lead at her sides. "Don't ever call me that again!"

"Ok, ok, sit the fuck down … I meant to say that's how some in the church see you."

"Oh?"

"You're a woman and you gotta play it down. You've done pretty good at that. I've got a dick, testosterone, I can ride people and they'll be like, can I have a side of ice cream with that Massa? Pretty please? Makes me wanna puke."

Carol smiled weakly. He rolled his chair around to her side, pushing it up to her knees as he pulled her into his lap.

"I like it when you smile, Sweet Pea. You look so heavy all the time."

"I'm planning for the future and those pills are affecting your ability to think straight. Mariah and I have already started booking the first flights to Georgetown through Kennedy airport like we talked about. Some of the members are balking about all the secrecy with folk they're leaving behind. We've got to keep morale up."

"Then give 'em a picnic or something. A big thingamajig with music down in Golden Gate Park. Aren't the Soul Steppers putting a revue together with James Brown's greatest hits? Do anything, I don't fucking care."

"No, that's not going to cut it. You've got to talk to them, Jim. Touch them, make it real to them, make them taste it. Especially your sons."

"What about them?"

"Demian's been talking to outsiders."

He took off her sandals and put them up to his nose, inhaling the leather straps, then the damp insole. "He's manageable. Boy's got his head in the clouds and his mother's thumb up his ass."

"He's not entirely sold on this. And if his wishy washiness spreads ..."

"Shit, what kid was ever sold on anything their parents wanted, Sweet Pea? One minute he thinks he's fucking James Dean, the next he's one of them muppets from Sesame Street. He'll fall in line the moment the purse strings are cut."

She got up and went around to his side of the desk, opening the top drawer. She sorted through the jumble of pill bottles, gathered a handful of them up and smacked them down on the desk. "I'm confiscating these."

"The hell you are," he said limply. "Alright, go on then. I'll just have Jamiah get me some new ones."

"They're going down the toilet. And the prescriptions too."

"I'm dying, Sweet Pea."

"Shut up."

"When I piss it's like liquefied guts in the bowl."

"Here's the to-do list for the week."

"They poisoned my eggs the other morning at that jive prayer breakfast at Glide Church. The pepper those sonovabitches put in it was pricking my stomach like a dagger."

"That's gas, Jim. When Devera's article is finished I need you to review it before we go to press. We have twenty families who're being processed for a January departure. I'm moving around some of our offshore money so we can buy a new tractor, bulldozer and a backhoe without depleting the stateside account. Then we need to decide whose going to stay behind to oversee the nursing homes on Geary and Divisadero."

There was a knock on the door. Lance Schuler, a white doctor trainee poked his head in, face flushed, blond hair clumped in seashell whorls on his leathery neck. Jim had groomed him for a medical career after he'd started hanging around the Temple services drugged out and distraught over a break-up.

"What is it Lance?" Carol asked.

"Muggs has pulled through from his fever."

Jim perked up. "Finally."

"Gave him a mild tranquilizer. He'll be out for another hour or so."

Jim got up and walked over to Lance, giving him a pat on the shoulder. "Excellent work. Your flight to Georgetown is tomorrow morning?"

"Bright and early. I'll be armed with laxatives and other meds to treat the assorted gastrointestinal complaints we've been hearing about."

Carol folded her arms, resting her gaze on Lance. "Everyone will be fine Father. The tropical climate just takes some getting used to."

"Well no one expected all these city people used to gorging on saturated animal fat and refined sugar to adjust overnight," Lance retorted.

"You got decades of that crap in your system it's only natural there's gonna be a recovery period." Jim sat back down, motioning to Lance. "Sit down. I'm real proud of everything you've managed to achieve in such a short period of time, Lance. When you came to the church you could barely put two sentences together, could barely think straight that dope had burned through your brain so much. Now look at you—aced all your internships and ready to blaze a new trail with our medical center at the settlement."

Lance looked down at his feet, avoiding the sight of his forearms, a mess of rutted track marks. Carol stood very still. Cheers and applause cascaded up from below. The fourth graders in the after school program had mastered a complex passage in Frederick Douglass' "What to the Slave is the Fourth of July" speech.

"I don't know what I would've done without your help, Dad," Lance said.

Carol swept Jim's meds into a paper bag. "And you think you'll have ample time to build up the infirmary for the second and third migration?"

"Lance can do it, what with the nurses, the internist and other personnel pitching in. I have supreme confidence in him."

"It's a lot of work and it shouldn't be taken lightly," Carol said.

Lance perked up. "I really don't think you're qualified to lecture me on how to do my job."

Carol crumpled the bag closed. "The ink hasn't even dried on his diploma yet and we're expecting this former dope fiend to be entrusted with the lives of our kids and seniors??"

"Aw hell, lady, you've got some nerve. I earned every minute of that degree, studying terms and procedures you have no concept of."

"And so now you're an expert overnight on running a clinic in a third world country with limited supplies and potentially hundreds of lives at stake." She turned to Jim. "This is his first work assignment. It's crazy to expect him to manage this level of responsibility without a a more experienced supervising doctor."

"That's all well and good Carol except for the simple fact that we haven't got anyone like that who we can just pluck out of thin air to send down to South America."

"What about Dr. Goodwin?"

"Hampton isn't going to take a year out of his life and running his businesses to hold our hand." He walked over to Carol and put his arm around her. "I'm three steps ahead of you. There's no need to fixate on this. You're overworked and overtired. Go get some sleep, get rid of that nervous energy. Or better yet go sit in on the choir rehearsal. That'll loosen you up, get you out of that uptight space in your head."

She put her hand on the doorknob, staring at Lance melting into the chair. Jim picked at his discolored teeth. The news about Muggs had enlivened him, setting him aglow with nervous energy.

"I hope you're right about this," Carol said. "Talk to your sons."

He waved her out the door and locked it. Lance gestured to the two empty bottles Carol had left behind on the desk. "She trying to chuck your meds Dad? That's a pretty half-assed detox."

Jim grinned and walked over to Lance's chair. He rested both hands on the arms of it, leaning down, nuzzling into Lance's hair, drinking in its moist funk. Lance arched his back, turning his face up to meet Jim's, kissing him slow and deep.

"Dad," Jim said, opening his legs. "Gives me goosebumps when you call me that."

The Promised Land

WE DON'T BELIEVE in religion, we don't believe in God, we don't believe in reincarnation, we don't believe in [the] impossible. We are not concerned with the beginning, the end or the hereafter. We are only concerned about today.
                    —*Peoples Temple Eight Revolutionary Defectors, 1973*

Dover AFB, December 11, 1978

THE NIGHT WATCHWOMAN does not drink coffee. She never pees. Never leaves her post for a smoke break, a phone call or a fart in the subzero weather that's kicked in the teeth of Dover, Delaware. She sits behind the air force base security console with gloved fingers, eyes darting from screen to screen, scanning for shadows, her desk stacked with packages stamped Classified.

Their arrival here has been a sensation. A few reporters descended in earnest. Locals banded together to gawk and complain. They say the cold, the snow, is the worst it's been in a while. That it's an omen of something bad, that it's a fitting greeting for the nine hundred of them.

When we were over in the Promised Land we secretly dreamt of a white Christmas, of snowmen, of ice angels.

The watchwoman's shift begins at midnight. She takes the bus back home at 8:30, passing the morning shuttle crammed with airmen off to training. She watches them on the banged- up TV set that only has three clear channels, getting her children dressed as the heater rumbles on, shielding their eyes from the bloated bodies while she tries to turn to Woody Woodpecker, to Bugs Bunny, to ordinariness and animals bashing their brains in.

We don't blame her. It's a mother's instinct to protect her young from bad things.

They have identical lines on their necks. Baby from birth, Mommy from age, the slow creep to thirty-eight. She was still young but spiraling downward, an older woman having a baby for the first time thousands of miles from home. She changed Baby's diaper on a folding chair in the pavilion. Sat in the front row waiting for the performance to begin. A good seat means a plate of hot food at the end of the meeting. It means recognition that she is dedicated. It shows the leadership that she is serious. The nurses delivered her by C-section, the first one in the settlement. Cleaned her then plopped her on Mommy's chest, couldn't pry open her clenched pink fingers, her tiny Black Power salute fist.

She doesn't have to participate in the drills because of the C-section. At night we lie together cheek to cheek, listening to the rain blow through as our people rip and run, rehearse and fortify.

The takeover could happen anytime.

It will come in a flood of parachutes, blazing military guns, contaminated water. Best to sit on the edge of preparedness than to be caught off guard, slack, flabby, complacent.

Her voice is too hoarse to sing Baby a lullaby. Her body too heavy from the painkillers. Her brain too tired from the crashing chaos. But secretly, really, she is not that kind of Mommy. So she holds Baby like a fine cut piece of steel.

Does the watchwoman know this as she walks through the morgue inspecting the surnames, lingering at familiar ones, the long and winding road of church families, generations' deep, the crazy quilt of birthdates stretching back to Indiana, Texas, Chicago, Tennessee, Alabama, Mississippi. She eats her dinner alone in the cafeteria, the transistor radio by the cash register burbling about hit squads, spies, Negro fanatics that go bump in the night. Be careful down there, the cashier says, banging a roll of nickels into his drawer. Them spooks are liable to snatch you up.

Does the watchwoman know that when Mommy spoke there was no trace of Amarillo about her? That her accent was clean, with no upturn at the ends of a question, no licorice sucking drawl like that of her grandparents who'd followed Father to California after Newark burned in '67, their dry cleaning business destroyed.

To own anything and be Negro was criminal. But this is what the watchwoman doesn't know, counting the mountain of steel coffins stacked to the ceiling in drill formation rows.

After a week the press has left, bored by the absence of revelation, fireworks, by the clawing and scratching of next of kin bent on revenge.

When they begin the grind of identifying remains who will come forward to claim us, Mommy and me, lying intertwined, as though I'd never left her to venture on my own into the outside world?

CHAPTER 22

Fillmore, 1977

ROLLER SKATING IS for fags, the jocks hanging in the quad at the continuation school told Demian. Like, what you tryin' to do son, qualify for the disco roller derby?

It was the white ones, always the white ones, half blissed out on weed and looking at him askance, bleary-eyed when he was lacing up his skates about to go home. The blacks, the Asians, the Latinos left him alone, uninterested in his so-called showboating, uninterested in his rangy ambiguous looks.

His father was waiting for him in the parking lot. He seldom drove, allowing himself to be ferried around by the Red Brigade.

"Get in," he said.

"What are you doing driving?"

"Never mind that, come on."

"I'm skating home."

His father took off his glasses, dark eyes sparkling.

"C'mon, Dem. I'm flying down to L.A. in the morning and I wanted to see you before I go."

Demian climbed in, keeping his skates on, his gaze fixed ahead.

"I didn't know you still knew how to drive on your own."

"It's a lifelong skill … who were those ruffians?"

"Nobody."

"Don't lie to me. I won't let you be taken for a punk. People are going to play you for a punk if you give them the slightest little opening."

"Like you really give a shit how people see me aside from how it affects your reputation."

"Watch your fucking mouth." A group of boys skateboarded through the light, crisscrossing diagonally to the other side of the street. Jim waited then pulled cautiously out into the intersection.

"Look, I didn't come here to lecture you. I'm just worried. I can't sleep anymore. Close my eyes and the carnival starts. We're spending thousands of dollars a day trying to get the settlement up and running before the first big relocation and the crew can't cut it. Got a lot of heart, but don't have the skill or the discipline. I'd send your mother down there but she's too weak with her back issues. And I have to manage this situation with the goddamn local press and these relatives and defectors whoring for publicity."

"They're not all whores."

"Well they're not doing shit for our people. Who feeds 'em and gives 'em medical treatment when they're sick? I fucking do. If they keep up this nonsense and shut us down three quarters of San Francisco will go down the fucking toilet."

"So you have to smear them to try and make us look good?"

"They started this war, and, by the way, that little cub reporter who sucked up to you the other day at the donut shop is one of Ida Lassiter's boys."

"Jimmy came back to you and blabbed."

"Jimmy told me as a brother who loves you and doesn't want to see you get wrapped up in some mess you don't understand."

"He's a snitch. The reporter said two people down in L.A. committed suicide."

"They were troubled individuals in need of psychiatric care. I helped one of 'em, Lester Sims, get put on a 72-hour hold when he was threatening to take hostages at one of the senior centers because they were wire-tapping his cereal. Brother was collecting counterintelligence from his Cheerios. Now that isn't too farfetched given what the feds are capable of, but you put a guy like that next to a trigger happy cop and he's dead meat."

"Why should I believe you ... and how do you know Kip has a connection to Ida Lassiter?"

"They all do." He scowled, adjusting his seat, the steering wheel cutting into his ponch. "Ida was always secretly an elitist, showboating around with all her awards and trips with white women's groups overseas. I was never more than a trained Indiana porch monkey to her."

"I don't believe Kip's down with her. And besides it doesn't matter if he is. Whatever the truth is it will come out on its own."

"That's fantasy, boy. When it comes to the press, and the fascists that run it, the truth is malleable, less than a load of pigeon crap on a park bench. If they want to paint Jim Jones as a peckerwood exploiting poor Negroes then that becomes gospel."

Demian was silent. They were approaching the Temple building. Children from the elementary school down the block streamed through the church's doors to the after school program. He shuddered.

"I don't want to go in there."

"Why not, son?"

"I don't want to see anyone. Mariah, Carol … Especially not Jimmy."

"Don't blame Jimmy. You can be mad at me and everybody else but he doesn't deserve it. He was only trying to protect you. I can drop you off at that place of yours if you want."

"Drop me off at the court. I want to shoot some hoops before practice."

Devera and Jess walked past. Jim blew the horn and waved. He stopped the car, rolling chapstick on his cracked lips. "I need you, Dem. I'm not too fucking proud to say it."

Demian scraped a piece of gum off the window. A group of girls gathered around the Temple steps, taking turns doing daredevil hula-hoop moves, glowing, crowing about who was the best.

"I'll go if you stop cheating on Mom," he said.

"Those women are insatiable, I-"

"Stop with the bullshit lies! You can't justify your crap like it's some kind of saintly sacrifice with me like you do with everybody else. I don't know why Mom accepts it and pretends to look the other way but it's killing her. Stop shitting on her and I'll go, on my terms, then I want to come back here and do my own thing."

"Fine."

Demian opened the car door to go. Jim cleared his throat. "C'mon, don't go. I'll drop you off at the court."

He sat back in the seat, picking at the laces of his sneakers, tied together in a knot on his lap.

"Believe it or not you were always more of a country boy," Jim said. "Ever since you were little, when we took you to Brazil and I was looking to start a congregation there. You were right in the thick of it, eyes wide as day in wonder over the beauty of nature. It's virtually pure wilderness over in Guyana. You're going to love it, son."

Demian could feel the heat of his father's reverie, enraptured with his own pitch. Part of him wanted to swoon with him, to trust unconditionally and be swept away by his faith as he had when he was a baby and his father's body, his lulling voice were the known universe.

"You had the smallest feet," Jim continued. "Almost like a doll's. Your mother was scared you'd never grow beyond a few pounds big, must've fussed over you and measured you every hour that first month after you were born. Then you sprung up like a Redwood and she was so proud ... I know I've fucked up Dem. If I believed in a god I'd get down on my hands and knees and repent right here. Your opinion is the only one that matters to me now."

They come through the airport gate with one-way tickets to New York City, solemn, hushed, huddling close to each other, steaming on two hours sleep but ripe for the journey; poets, teachers, nurses, clerks, letter carriers, engineers, lab workers, dancers, janitors, torn lovers, old marrieds, doe-eyed newlyweds, families three generations deep pantomiming a unified front.

The letters they never receive are marked return to sender.

The milk they leave on the kitchen counter goes sour.

The morning and late edition newspapers wither in their courtyards.

The cars they have abandoned are fined, towed.

At the schools their children left their classmates survey the half-empty rooms during roll call—the best friends, the bullies, the teacher's pets, the class clowns, the ones voted most likely, the ones voted least likely, the wallflowers, the nerds, the jocks, the smart asses and cross your heart hope-to-die ace boon coons snatched right from under them overnight in a ghost exodus.

Ida arrived at her appointment with Hampton Goodwin twenty minutes early to check out the area and make sure she wasn't being followed. That week someone had tried to break into her car. The thief had jimmied the lock then quit midstream, unwilling or unable to make a more definitive effort.

The street tensed in front of her, trolleys chugging up and down, taxis discharging fares, smokers peering from doorways, puffing dully into the Hare Krishna procession rippling past in a blast of tambourines and orange robes.

She went into Hampton's building and waited for the elevator, calming her racing thoughts with a nursery rhyme, a falsetto round of Jack and Jill.

She'd met him in the fifties covering a strike by the Brotherhood of Sleeping Car Porters and Maids. The train workers' headquarters had been bombed in every Southern city they struck in. Hampton was a reporter and sometime union negotiator; a lion, hard charging with a twist of genteel reserve, always assessing, always pushing. His network of black newspapers was a respected force on the West Coast. Over the years they'd run her syndicated pieces, her byline disappearing as his relationship with Jim Jones deepened.

"Yes. I belong to several boards, Negro and white," he proclaimed into the phone as his secretary showed her in to his office. "Your boy graduated summa cum laude I see. I can give him a reference. Tell him to take the adversities on the chin, but don't fold. Those white boys in the academy are drawn to weakness like sharks to blood."

He hung up and stood, extending his hand to Ida. "Temple woman," he explained. "Has a kid who's applying to medical school. Good to see you again, Mrs. Lassiter."

Ida sat down. "It's been awhile."

"Augusta, Georgia, 1966, The Buggy Whip restaurant. Caught you trying to order a rum punch on the sly." He paused, eyes twinkling. "Now you're hot and bothered about our Temple friends."

"That's what I wanted to discuss with you. As you know, I've done several pieces on the church over the years. My next one is on this so-called Jonestown settlement in Guyana. Last week I had an appointment to interview Zephyr Threadgill, a Temple member and a former engineer at Lawrence Livermore."

"Good God, the things some of these misguided Negroes name their children."

"She pulled up stakes shortly before our appointment. Vanished into thin air. Didn't say a word to her family."

"And?"

"Why is Jones relocating these people to Guyana, Hampton?"

"Because Cuba and the Soviet Union weren't available."

"Don't be glib."

"Now Ida, surely you didn't track me down to interrogate me about something so picayune."

"Hundreds of people's lives aren't picayune."

"Guyana is a virtually black nation that's amenable to the Temple's politics. If you want some deeper insight into why they're going over there you should ask Jones himself."

"Why are you aligned with them, Hampton? What are you getting out of this? Jones intimidates his followers, has them beat up, does surveillance on defectors and there are a string of mysterious deaths on his watch."

He let out a dry cough and leaned back in his chair. "That's ad homi-nem attacks manufactured by the right wing to discredit this movement."

He tapped a folder on his desk. "These are receipts from payments made to three of those so-called defectors by a private investigator. Some crackpot hired by a rich Marin County society lady whose daughter got mixed up in the Temple. A lot of these people are being paid handsomely for their services, Mrs. Lassiter."

"Surely you're not suggesting that everyone who steps up to complain is being paid off?"

"Come now, Mrs. Lassiter. You can't be naïve enough to believe the cooptation of left radicalism went the way of the dodo, or King and Malcolm for that matter. No doubt the FBI has a dossier on you that's as long as the Golden Gate Bridge."

"Listen to yourself. Jim has got you wrapped around his finger."

"Don't patronize me, Mrs. Lassiter." A call lit up on one of his phone lines. He glanced at it and frowned. "Hold it please!" He yelled to the secretary across the hall.

"*Ida*. After all these years just call me Ida."

He got up and went to the liquor cabinet by the window and took out a bottle of brandy. "Can I offer you something to drink, or is that against regulations?"

"A gin and tonic."

He mixed the drink and handed it to her. "I got a nice bottle of brandy when I was in Turkey for the UN human rights conference. Barbarians still won't budge on the issue of the Armenian genocide. One of the Temple's attorneys is of Armenian descent. Whole family escaped the slaughter and came over here with just the shirts on their backs. Anglicized their last name like most of the smart white immigrants did."

"Must be nice to have the luxury of reinvention."

"Yes."

"Like traveling thousands of miles to a country where you can't be tracked. No trace, no footprint."

"Same human desire." He finished the brandy, gripping the glass tightly, "Don't rush to judgment on these folks, Ida. Hell, if I was younger and in different circumstances maybe I'd be on the first plane out there too."

He leaned against the cabinet, glancing at the wall of college degrees, medical licenses, the framed first edition of the *Sun Reporter* newspaper yellowing under glass. "You know, I can still hear the laughter of that first cracker who doubted I would make it through medical school. An Irishman. Naturalized citizen with god given rights as soon as he stepped foot here. Master of the split infinitive, could barely speak English but he knew he wasn't a nigger and that's all that mattered."

"That was then."

"Meaning?"

"These people have lives here, Hampton. Families, jobs, homes. Are you saying they should throw all that away at the whim of Jim Jones?"

He shifted, the lines on his forehead hardening. After all the decades of intersecting, tripping around the margins of each other, his quiet steeliness captivated her in a way.

"Jones as puppet master," he said. "That's only the small picture. This isn't the first time in history black folk have dreamt of repatriation and acted on it. If we can't get our forty acres and a mule here, then…"

"Wide-eyed idealism is an unexpected shade on you, Hampton."

"Wide-eyed? That's a bit melodramatic."

The phone line lit up again. A note appeared under the door. Hampton went over to pick it up. He skimmed it, shaking it triumphantly in the air.

"The IRS, in its infinite wisdom, has closed its investigation into Temple finances." He crumpled the note up and threw it in the trash, turning his attention back to Ida as he glanced at his watch. "What's next for you, Ida?"

"I have a few more people to interview."

"If you don't mind my asking, how are you getting by?"

"I have resources."

"Social Security will kick in in a few years, then what next? Writing your memoirs and chasing after some scruffy publisher teetering on bankruptcy for a piddling advance? I have a proposal. Come work with us."

"What about Jim and the *Peoples Forum*?"

"My relationship with them would have no bearing on your position. Jim knows his boundaries with me. This is not a co-optation move. I wouldn't condescend to tell you what to write. That would clearly be suicidal." He hesitated, watching her grave face flicker to life, unsure if he'd overplayed it.

She leaned forward. "I need benefits. Medical. Retirement."

"Of course."

"Where is the contract and when can I start?"

CHAPTER 23

The Jonestown Pioneers

To CLEAR THE land for the pavilion in the center of the Jonestown settlement it took ten men. After 72 hours the citified among them were broken,
burnt and babbling as the sun spread in scorching middle fingers across the
plain. The blueprints for the center building were pored over and revised
according to new population totals. Every day there is a fresh estimate
of the number of emigrants who will be coming through Port Kaituma,
the closest town to the settlement. Every hour an exuberant report from
Central Command in the capital Georgetown about the progress made
back in California marshaling documents, donations, clothes, immuniza-
tion records, bodies short, fat, thin, tall in preparation for customs.

Back in the States those who have never flown before squirm in
bed at night in cold sweat anticipation, circadian rhythms broken.
Half a world away the working men sing Top 40; catching harmonies
here and there, trilling come-on-people-now-smile-on-yer-brother
everybody-get-together-try-to-love-one-another-right-now.

At 6:30 in the evening the workers scramble for the showers. To save
energy the hot water is turned on for only ten minutes under orders from
Central Command. Central Command is a bunch of loyalists, inner sanctum women headed by Mariah. They work the radio, communicate with
Father, dispatch Jonestown's pioneer message out to the world. Central
command oversees the budget and monitors the tiniest expense, keeping
the construction timeline on track, bracing for the glorious arrival of the
whole Temple family, antsy over the utilities' bill.

But the working men, the boys, ignore the directives belched out
through the radio and cavort in the hot water, bound for the glory of heavy

235

sleeping nights, mummified from head to toe under miles of mosquito netting. Any millimeter of exposed flesh is a pulpy bug feast *out here in the perimeter where there is no stars*, they sing. The heat is an aphrodisiac to the ripe smelling teenage boys sneaking peeks at each other as they lather up under the black sky, rinse down, dry off, unwind with the last monster joint of twilight.

First time you've gotten stoned immaculate, son?

Naw it's the first time he's dared to sit down and take a shit without a permit from Father.

Daddy 'O says he's the only true heterosexual.

Well if he is I'm Doris fucking Day.

And you certainly ain't that fo' sho.

I'd like to see her prissy white ass out here dying in this heat.

At the Georgetown office they got air conditioning brotha man.

That's not for the natives, meaning us.

So we natives now?

Anywhere there's poor black and brown folk we're natives, brother.

Shit, I ain't black, I'm Creole, motherfucker.

Acting like a dumb jungle bunny. This is the right place for you. Get you back to your roots.

I hear a whole lotta Negroes here trying to speak the King's English.

It's all about caste. You can smell it soon as you roll off the plane, man.

Colonials in the sticks always try to be more British than the British. That's part of the disease.

Blacks and Indians staying at each other's throats trying to keep a pecking order of liberated slaves. Just like in the States.

This is nothing like the States, brother. At least we got our own country here.

Who's we? I hear this shit is fixin' to implode.

We got a whole country riding for the Marxist socialist cause.

Even as fucked up internally as they are.

Price of freedom, brother. Everybody ain't gonna agree on the same things—long as there's equality in the free market of ideas.

Yeah, but what do the women and the real Indians have to say? I don't see any of them running anything in this place.

They're at the bottom like they are everywhere else.

Well Dad's going to change that, he'll liberate everyfuckingbody.

Watch your mouth.

That's the reason we're over here right? They call this place the country of the swamps and now we're trying to make gold out of swampland.

Man I don't care about the bigger mission I just wanna get some before the Central Command Puritans come and shut us down.

With your little pencil dick?

Got his eye on some of those Indian girls in the bush and they don't give a shit what the circumference of his dick is just as long as he's an American fresh off the boat white boy 'cause your asses are exotic down here.

After years of being under the Brit's heels a few white boys from Kansas symbolize freedom to the Indians? Stop toking, fool.

Hey I wouldn't mind taking a Guyanese wife back but they ain't trying to get with something brown as me.

Back? You planning on going back?

Soon as my black ass is done over here putting up this new building.

You clear that with Dad?

You know decisions like that go through committee.

I ain't scared. It's my life.

Why would you want to go back? I mean everybody's coming here. This is gonna be the spot once we get finished with it.

This little puppy's homesick that's why.

Misses hamburgers, fries and Donna Summer coming for him on the radio.

Before I came to California to check out the Temple I'd never been out of Ft Worth.

There's a whole lotta world out there I still want to see. Things I wanna do.

We all have things we want to do.

I put getting my degree on hold for this.

I'd just sent away for info on training to be an EMT. You know how long it takes ambulances to get to the ghetto? If there were more of us on those calls that shit wouldn't be happening.

So what about Jimmy Jr? When those Jones boys get over here they gonna try and play overseer?

Jimmy's nobody's fucking goon.

Boy's got a big brain like Dad.

Mastermind in the making.

Heard the Guyana president himself took a shine to him.

Shit that's all fine and good but at the end of the day money talks. Father just wrote Prez a fat check with a lot of zeroes right?

Don't know how much he paid, brother.

Well we know it wasn't with a promissory note.

They just dig our ideology.

Word is people are trying to get the fuck out of here. The economy's shit and the blacks and Indians are at each other's throats.

Blacks and Indians screwing it up on the inside, Venezuela screwing it up on the outside. Government thinks Jonestown's going to be a buffer zone just in case Venezuela tries to invade the western border.

Glad you're on the case smart ass.

No reason to come to a new country ignorant about what's going on in it. That's a slave mentality right there.

CHAPTER 24

The Station, San Francisco, 1977

A RARE FRONT of humidity swept through the city, sucking at the jubilant end-of-the-day surge of bodies flowing through the turnstiles at the train station where Jess waited holding an envelope full of donations. The mayoral campaign signs Temple canvassers had posted for Moscone over a year before wilted from the station beams, embroidered with peeling porn stickers and train grunge. She, Hy and several others from the church had been assigned to solicit that week for donations. Jim buttonholed her to be the lead, taking her aside after the collection plates from Wednesday service had been counted, his voice softly conspiratorial as the Soul Steppers dance troupe thundered through a Funky Chicken routine in the hallway.

"Now I know how busy you are counseling members, Jess. That's real important work. Real important to our family's mental health. Your people have been here in Frisco awhile and you have the greatest knowledge about what's gone down in the community. After all the campaigning we did to get Moscone in office we still have to go around begging for our projects. Folks are so tired of being fucked they don't want to hear no honky politician promising them a few more food stamps."

Jess hated politics, hated glad handing and the tedium of going door-to-door, business-to-business hustling for money. Jonestown was being powered by the members' tithing, benefit checks and property but there were still big holes to fill with ballooning construction, travel and supplies' costs.

She would meet the rest of the group then take the train to Sacramento for a lobbying session with other progressive religious organizations. At the far end of the platform a man sucking a cigarette butt squatted on a bench doing drum rolls on paint cans. A mime balanced on one foot across from him, knocked suddenly off balance by boys in school uniforms rushing to make the L.A.-bound train upstairs. She liked watching the passengers coming on and off; pumped up, in spite of herself, by the skittering randomness of the crowds, the warm pounding shitstorm of fuel, incense, fried food and tunnel breezes sweeping across the platform in juicy homage to her grandfather, who'd worked as a Pullman porter for thirty years until two of his fingers got sheared off in an accident.

The drummer announced a pending "set break" then ripped through Iron Butterfly's "In a Gadda Da Vida". Jess saw Hy's owlish face pop out from the flurry of people coming down the stairs. She'd balked at being paired with Jess on the fundraising outing, pissed that Jim had singled her out for a leadership role. After the fight in the apartment they avoided each other. Hy did her shifts in the gift shop, hanging out at after hours' disco clubs in the little spare time she had, dancing, drinking, dragging her feet on moving, brooding as Jess climbed up the ranks; higher than any black woman had risen before in the Temple. Therapist Jess had a halo of practical beneficence around her, guiding each session with the firm yet calming touch of a daughter and confidant who listened, empathized, understood.

Devera, Zephyr, Demian and other Temple members followed Hy down the stairs. A group of skateboarders gathered by the drummer, flailing around him in sweaty multi-colored tank tops, vaulting off the benches spasmodically. Jess waved to the Temple members to move to the side of the staircase away from the uproar.

"How'd everyone do?"

A Droopy Dog-eyed white man hoisted his envelope in the air, "Did ok all things considering. There were a few idiots that tried to give me shit, dropped pennies in my envelope. Other than that it was a peaceful afternoon in the city."

"Peaceful and hotter'n hell!" A woman behind him blurted, tugging at the drenched bandana on her forehead for effect. "But there's a lot of love out there for Father. A lot of people wanting to see what we're all about."

Hy grimaced at the sales pitch. "I didn't get any of that."

"Depends on where you went."

"Some of the news stories they're running on us are having an effect."

Jess collected the envelopes, snapping them briskly onto her clipboard. "So we work harder to counter them. We've been over this several times now. The more visible we are the more leverage we have with Moscone and all the other politicos."

Hy stepped back and tuned her out. The drummer had drawn a big zealous crowd, an undulating line of ragtag white boys banging their heads in time as he launched into Cream's "Toad." She looked at the drummer more closely. It was Foster.

"Foster?" she gasped.

Devera came up behind her, fanning herself. "Well, well, it sure is. Asshole's got talent on those paint cans."

Hy braced herself against a station beam, feeling sick. "He was supposed to be up in Canada."

"Must not have been able to cut it up there if he's down here busking. All I know is he got his ass beat real good for what he did in the L.A. church stalking those babies like he did."

"What?"

"Preyed on little girls half his age. Knocked up one of 'em."

"That's crazy."

"He's nasty, girl. That's why he hightailed it out of here. Lucky you didn't get in too deep with his mess," Zephyr added, giving her a bug under a microscope stare through fogged up Ben Franklin spectacles. "It's bad enough some of these pervs are teaching in public schools where they don't even screen for shit like that. All the undercover abuse that goes on is disgusting."

"I don't believe it. What proof is there that he did it?"

"Proof that he did what?" Jess stepped between them, wielding her clipboard like a sceptre.

"We were just talking about Foster over there."

Jess followed Zephyr's pointing finger. "He's back huh?"

"That the one who got some rough justice then tried to stage a coup running up to Canada?" The white man blurted out. "I wasn't in the audience that night but I heard he sho nuff got put in his place, as the sisters say."

Hy rolled her eyes, the man's pink gelatinous face going slack with doubt. "What *sisters* are you talking about?"

Jess inserted herself again. "Stay focused people. I need you to give me lists of everyone you spoke to. Yays, nays, addresses, household backgrounds, the works."

Foster finished the solo and threw his drumsticks in the air in a final flourish, catching them to the oohs and aahs of the writhing crowd. He whistled a warning to a fan boy taking pictures then stopped, catching sight of Hy.

She broke away from the group and walked toward him. He was drawn, gaunt, his knuckles plastered with bandages. He'd grown his hair out, masking the sculptural head of serene beauty that had driven her wild.

He rose from his seat. "Hello, Hy."

"When did you get back?"

"A few days ago." He squinted past her, irritated at the sight of Jess and the others following close behind.

"Aw fuck, if it ain't the cock Nazis from the Temple. Here to do a citizen's arrest on me, motherfuckers?" He fiddled with his drumsticks, nodding thanks to the trickle of passengers who filed past and dropped change in an upturned baseball cap he'd laid on the ground.

"Why did you come back? I-I thought you were gone for good." Hy said.

He winced. The vein that she'd once licked, traced to infinity, jumping on his swan's neck. "I couldn't get work up there. Any real work that is. Nobody's hiring black men unless it's under the table scraps with no protection or longevity." He stood over her, hard eyes going momentarily tender.

"How you been?"

The wind picked up in the tunnel as the light of the oncoming train punched through the darkness. The fan boy kept shooting pictures, fascinated, twisting his body to get Hy in the frame.

"I said cut it out!" Foster shouted. "He with you?" He asked Jess.

"No, but what's the problem? I thought you wanted publicity? Or maybe it's not so comfortable being in the spotlight after what you did to that kid in L.A."

"She wasn't a kid."

Hy stared at him. "You know what she's talking about??"

"She was a seventeen going on forty two year-old cock tease. Knew exactly what she was doing reeling me in. Craftier than shit." He turned to Jess. "Look, I don't have any church secrets to leak. I'm of no value to you, don't even have a job, stable address or phone to tap so just leave me the fuck alone." He lunged at the boy's camera. "Gimme those pictures asshole. I know what you're doing. Hypocrites! Jim Jones can fuck anything that moves and I so much as touch my dick to pee and get crucified."

The boy jerked away from Foster. The camera flew out of his hand and smashed onto the tracks. At the end of the tunnel the train loomed, inched forward, then stopped. The station manager announced that it was waiting for a trash barge to unload in a connecting tunnel. Foster jumped onto the tracks. The platform exploded with shrieks and snickers, the skateboarders egging him on, craving theatrics. He grabbed the busted camera, prying it open to get the film, innards flopping out onto the ground as rats skittered around his feet, nosing through a fried chicken bucket stuffed with gym socks.

"Man, you betta get your ass outta there!" Somebody yelled.

Foster ignored him, holding the film up incredulously to the light. "Dumb motherfucker this entire roll is of me! How long you been following me boy? Huh? How much did those assholes on the Planning Commission pay you? Trying to character assassinate me in front of all these people? Where were you going to run this shit? That fucking rag they print up every time Daddy Jim gets an itch? I'm not for sale you candy ass!" He unzipped his pants, letting out a cascade of pee on the mangled camera. The station manager barked dully through the intercom as a new crop of riders came in, eyes bugging at the sight of Foster pissing on the tracks.

Devera crouched down at the edge of the platform, frantically offering him her hand. Hy kneeled down slowly, the shock of the revelation about the girl simmering in her.

243

"Jesus Foster, what the hell are you trying to prove?" Hy pleaded. "No one's spying on you. Get the hell out of there before you get killed!"

He snorted, stuffing his penis back into his fly. "God … Hy, darling, they got you bad." He smiled sourly. "You patsies have no credibility. You're the emperor's mouthpiece and the fucking emperor has no clothes. I got all these people down here who want to hear my music and they don't give a flyin' fuck about what I did in the past. They don't care how low on the totem pole I was to the great and all powerful Oz. Down here is beautiful, there's no judgment, there's no patsies in my ear telling me I can't have ice cream 'cause it's not fucking revolutionary."

Silly string spraying elementary students ran past, hopped up from a field trip, nearly colliding with Demian as he kneeled down next to Hy and Devera. He eyed the tunnel gravely, "Fos, come on man, seriously, stop trippin' and get up out of there."

"Got the crown prince here too? Ain't that fitting. It's a regular family reunion. Where's Daddy Jim?!" Foster yelled. "Bring him down here. Let him see all these people who paid to come see me."

"He's out of the country, man."

The crowd surged restlessly around the platform, a growing chorus shouting at Foster, angry that he seemed to be holding up the train.

"Hey braniac we've gotta get to Sacramento by six o'clock!"

"Go fuck yourself, puppets." He flipped them off and started walking toward the staircase. The station manager squawked a warning through the intercom as two transit police officers rammed through the crush of bodies to get to Foster.

"Aw shit here come the pigs, brother you better get to steppin'!" A man in a PG&E utility uniform shouted.

A pair of hands hoisted Foster's paint can drum up over the crowd and hurled it at him. It bounced off the chicken bucket and onto the third rail. Foster lunged, slamming against the rail, his body jerking like a paper doll as electric current ripped through him.

Devera grabbed Hy's arm, face ashen. The screams of the crowd rained around them. Hy covered her ears with her hands, her legs buckling. More police swarmed the platform in slow motion, barking at the crowd to stay back; guns drawn, walkie talkies blaring. A white woman scooped up her brood of tow-headed children and pushed them away, the youngest pointing, blubbering into the soiled belly of his teddy bear. A photographer sprang from the darting bodies and jumped up onto the bench, snapping rhythmically over the chaos as a burly man with a Giants cap smashed onto his head dropped his shopping bags on the ground, bleating, "It's a sign from God! It's a sign from God! Lord have mercy on him!"

Years later Hy would be able to summon Foster's beseeching voice at will, the burning smell from the tracks a spiked tide keeping her on the edge of wakefulness in the monstrous nights when she grieved, gnashed over his betrayal.

Jess came up behind her. She put her hand on her shoulder, watching as the police fanned out and set up shop, waving their guns over Foster's limp body.

Hy flinched. "He's dead dammit what do you need guns for!" She screamed.

Devera pulled her away. Jess whirled around, hissing, "Stop it, do you want to get us fucking killed? Let's go," she said. "We'll have to see if there's room on the Temple bus for us in the morning."

Devera bit her lip, blinking back tears. "But, but what about, shit, poor bastard's got a fucking twelve year-old kid—"

"Let's go," Jess repeated. "I'll see that the child receives something from our survivors' fund."

Marin County, California 1977
They found the noose hanging in the garage after breakfast, finishing up their poached eggs and black coffee, cruising through the drive time shows on talk radio.

The body was laid out on the floor, hands clasped in rigor mortis prayer.

Our brother Pete, they told the earnest policemen. Must've snuck in last night through the window while we were sleeping. The shame of a suicide happening here, in such a tony neighborhood, to such an upright family.

We'd lost track of him all these months he'd been so swept up in the church and its weird rituals. Loyalty tests. Marathon meetings. Beatings.

Still, he was one hundred percent dedicated. Married to a woman Reverend Jones chose for him. Raising a passel of orphan kids. Traveling up and down the state. Panhandling all through the city.

There is no rhyme or reason.

He only wanted to help people, they wrote, in their letter to their local Congressman.

CHAPTER 25

⚜

Taryn and Jess

In winter, 6:15 was Taryn's savored time of morning, when the light was still pale on the empty sidewalk, the downtown office buildings barren and unmolested, free from the coffee drips, the toilet flushes, the chugging of typewriters, copy machines, file carts. If she got in early enough there was time and space to catalog all the things she had to do before the departure to Jonestown, bracing for the shattered quiet when the junior executive barnstormed in at 6:30 sharp, shaking his dirty blond bouffant out from his motorcycle helmet.

She'd left the Temple's new account statements on her desk in a folder from the day before. The plane tickets for five hundred people had been itemized as a lump sum, miscellaneous travel expenses for a "religious mission".

"You're on the frontline of making sure the feds don't stick their snouts into this," Malloy, the lead supervisor, said to her and the other accountants. "It's a shame when genuine charitable and philanthropic organizations have to operate under a cloud of fear. But that's the American way."

Telephone calls from a group of church members' relatives claiming tax fraud and stolen property trickled in. Press queries followed. Malloy and his staff handled them gingerly with no comment, keeping a hermetic seal around the Temple's business dealings.

Carol and Mariah alighted every week bearing cookies and bright smiles. They chit chatted with the file clerks and flirted with the middle managers, spreading airy charm, transformed from the terse overseers of the Temple into spry conversationalists. Malloy whisked them into his office with high deference, demanding that all calls be held and intrusions kept at bay.

When they departed an hour later he had his personal assistant quietly dust for electronic bugs.

The mass relocation to Jonestown was an open secret in the office. Guyana loomed, distant, flopping awkwardly off flat American tongues. The rumors of Taryn's involvement with the Temple were confined to the white secretaries, tossing them about on their lunch break. A few of them with black or Mexican boyfriends had dipped their toes in the church, been turned off by the demand for life commitment, the militancy, asceticism and whiff of white-shaming. Others went to a few weekday services as part of their foray into local tourism, basking in the city's glut of spiritual exotica.

Early morning was her refuge from that vortex, time to gird herself for the snubs at staff meetings, the circus of Malloy making a show of Noah or Stan or Josh; the trio of golden boys from Stanford who offered their robust heterosexuality up on a platter for all the partners teetering on retirement to drool over, rightful heirs anointed.

Shame flowed through her as she tried to will herself to start working. A tiny niggling part of her had already begun to countdown. Jess had started packing for the trip a month before; her studio apartment overrun with hoarder's debris, letters from old lovers that she'd tried only feebly to hide from Taryn. All discussions, fevered, languid, in between, began and ended with the question of whether to stay or go. In each other's arms with the TV on, they loped through the pros, cons and intangibles.

"If you're going nowhere with the firm why stay?" Jess asked.

"That's not a good enough reason to move thousands of miles away."

"So you agree."

"Didn't say that."

"Unless you take some kind of action at that place you'll never make what the new white boys make, never be respected, much less be promoted."

"I'm not ready to do that."

"Then why waste your time, Taryn?"

"It's easy for you to sit up and suggest all these militant things I should do when you don't have someone who depends on you to pay the rent and put food on the table."

"You can't continue to use Hy as a crutch forever. Besides, you guys wouldn't have to struggle like that living in Guyana. It would do her good to get away from here after what happened to Foster."

"You don't know that."

"I know no one will steal the credit for your work. I know you won't come home feeling like a fucking Russian serf."

"Or a House Negro? Just say it. That's what you think I am."

"Your words."

"There's no way in hell I'm going over there to work just for a dorm bunk and the good of the Cause."

"That's a limited view."

"Yeah? What's the long range view, Jess?"

"You work over there for the Temple as a financial planner for a year or two then we leave to start our own consulting business in Brazil or maybe even Cuba. There's a big need for trained therapeutic health care professionals in both of those countries."

"Leave with what money?"

"I've been saving the money I get from my private clients. I haven't given everything to the Temple. I knew we'd need our own cushion when we wanted to make a transition from Jonestown so I've been socking away a few hundred a month."

"Ooh, that's sacrilege."

"That's right baby, I'm a heretic." She smiled, putting her arms around Taryn, nuzzling her neck. "Stick with me for a while won't you? We've always had to be three or four steps ahead of everyone else anyway. Let's treat this like an adventure. Our first one together. If our investment doesn't pay off then we bail, do something else."

Taryn rubbed her cheek against Jess' arm, swallowing her uncertainty, basking in the ripeness of the moment, the spring sweet taste of forever, her dawning love for this woman who'd shaken her life. "Well this is a turnabout. When did you become so calculating about all of this, incorporating 'we' so liberally into your vocabulary and such?"

"I always have. You just haven't been listening … Just love me, will you?" She asked, gentle, plaintive.

Taryn laughed, moving her hand up Jess' thigh as they kissed. "Always."

"I love you," Jess said.

Taryn sat, now, waiting for the drip of the office coffee machine to begin. When she wasn't meeting with clients, Jess spent every waking moment in Temple meetings, scrutinizing the character, interests, dispositions, relatives and sex partners of each member, from the tiniest child to the octogenarian women who signed their Social Security and disability checks over to the church.

Jess saw some of them for depression. They called her late at night for furtive consultations, ashamed of their need, felled by the candor she coaxed them into. They were betraying God by worshipping at the Temple. They were betraying Jim by secretly believing in, calling upon God. Daria Townes, her oldest client, had ten family members who were preparing to go. Her daughter was reluctant to leave. Her sons veered between apathy and curiosity; wanting to experiment with the novelty, the openness of a new black country where they wouldn't have to prove themselves. The division among them wore Jess down, replicated in family after family, the grist for her overtaxed client notebooks.

The copy machine clicked on, then the overhead lights, flooding the office in sickly Chiffon yellows. She could hear Bouffant the junior executive making his first in a series of showboating calls to East Coast clients. He knew she was there but would never formally acknowledge her until the paper was delivered at 7:00 when he sidled from behind his cubicle, slurping chocolate milk as he trotted through the headlines.

"Bus fare hikes, the PLO is making mischief again and fucking Anita Bryant is coming to town to rally the flat earth troops," he said over the cubicle walls. "Whoop de fucking doo, Jesus is turning on the cross."

"Good morning, Noah."

"Ever been to Florida, Taryn?"

"Once."

"Depressing fucked up place. A bunch of Brooklyn and Jersey retirees like my grandparents running around with their orange tans, golf clubs and midget dogs all mixed in with the crazy Bautista-ites and Anita Bryant Republicans. What a steaming shithole."

"Are you working on the Wisnant account today?"

He angled over to her side, a bottle of Nestle's Quik in hand. "Possibly. You want a section of the paper?"

"I'll take the Metro section."

He peeled it off from the fold, his eye catching on a column on the bottom right.

"Interesting … looks like Congressman Luke Reardon is launching an investigation into our very own Peoples Temple church. Malloy's little pets are going to have a shit fit. Interesting group though. Few months ago I donated to a street kid who came through my neighborhood claiming to represent some kind of sports league they run for group home kids."

She dug her fingers into her keyboard, ignoring the reference. "Wisnant needs a quicker turnaround on the audit. They want everything wrapped up by next week instead of the end of the month."

"They can go fuck themselves on that quicker turnaround."

"Nice. That what you're going to tell Malloy?"

"In so many words. What's he going to do, do it himself?"

"Must be peachy to have that kind of veto power over the boss."

"Yeah, you should try it sometime."

She took the paper and put it on top of her desk, turning back to her work. He lingered at the partition trying to look absorbed in the headlines, agitated by the stillness.

"This Reardon probe should be a real trip. What do you know about that bunch?"

"Not much."

He picked up a paper clip, balancing it between his thumb and index finger. "Come on, I saw one of their papers on your desk."

"What were you doing snooping around my desk?"

"Malloy needed the Landesman file and you were hogging it all week. That newspaper actually looked like a fairly quality production. I thought it was just one of those grubby Berkeley throwaway rags at first."

"This one is put out by writers who can actually write, unlike the hacks from *The Chronicle.*"

"I agree. Their racket hasn't been relevant for years, especially where you people are concerned. Blacks have every right to create their own independent press."

"The *Peoples Forum* isn't an exclusively black publication."

He pored over the article, pale lashes blinking furiously. "They mention possible abuse allegations. Kids being taken away from their families and what not."

She rolled around in her chair to face him. "They're unsubstantiated allegations."

"Malloy is really going to be hot about this."

"Look, I've got a ton of work to do. I don't have time for a fireside chat with you."

He plopped the paper down on her desk. "Thinking about getting saved this Sunday, Sister Taryn? Got your dark shades ready? Seems to me someone around here has a little conflict of interest."

Taryn stiffened. One of the secretaries had come in the front door, walking carefully down the hallway to the break room in a bustle of grocery bags. She could feel the woman straining to listen, waiting for the rest of the show.

"Get out of my space," Taryn said.

"Sure, whatever ... you might want to talk with Malloy first. Pays to be proactive." He yelled down the hall. "Becky, did you get some Danish?"

She turned back to her desk. The family collage Hy had made in fifth grade stared down at her from the dingy partition wall. It was the only personal effect she had allowed herself. The only remnant of their failed past as children. Mother, father, sister, all smiling through dried wads of glitter and glue. What had the ancestors done when faced with daily obliteration? What tiny desperate acts of resistance had they committed—spitting into cornbread batter, snorting snot wads into steaming plates of collard greens, sprinkling garnishes of sugar dandruff into the plantation mistresses' mint juleps, firebombing their late afternoon lynch house aperitifs with earwax.

She imagined Noah splayed out across his desk inanimate, bouffant wilting in the caffeinated haze as she let the monkey Muggs raid his files, slurp up his chocolate milk.

Above and below the office myrmidons stirred on every floor, trapped in their ant tunnels.

Consider yourself supremely fucking lucky that there's an escape hatch, she thought. There would be none of this noise when she got to Guyana. The begging and scraping would be over. The cardboard clowns of the firm would recede into nothingness. She could look at her life with clear eyes. There'd be peace with Jess, and, possibly, Hy.

She laughed out loud, suddenly pitying the two or three buttoned-down Negroes stuck in the third floor accounting offices with their actuarial tables and color-coded Rolodexes nursing delusions of gliding up the corporate ladder.

She took down the family picture, crumpling her sister's lopsided smile into her fist as the front doors ushered in a flood of anxious bodies, the first client calls of the day beginning in earnest, chatter clogging the air, stealing her breath.

CHAPTER 26

⚜

Devera, Jonestown, July 4, 1978

TODAY IS THE Jonestown youth squad's big day. Twenty of our babies, the brightest second and third graders, lined up around the microphone reciting Frederick Douglass to kick off the morning broadcast:

What to the slave is your Fourth of July? To him, your celebration is a sham; your boasted liberty an unholy license; your national greatness, your prayers and hymns, your sermons and thanksgivings, are, to him, mere bombast, fraud, deception, impiety, and hypocrisy—a thin veil to cover up crimes which would disgrace a nation of savages.

"Thank you, children," Dad said over the loudspeaker after they've finished. "Today there will be no stars and stripes forever. No rockets red glare, no bombs bursting in air, no finger licking falling off the bone BBQ pork ribs greasing up our lips. All across the U.S. they're having a high old Bacchanal. A flat out orgy in saturated fat doing what Americans do best; eat, drink, get shit-faced and tell the world how much better they are than everybody else. Well I'm here to tell you brothers and sisters that we was busting our asses and getting beat down to a nub out in the fields when them honkies proclaimed their freedom from British tyranny. When they were singing about being under the Redcoats' boot heels they was raping our sisters, our mothers and grandmothers with their Yankee Doodle dicks."

We wake up to Dad's voice in the morning and go to sleep to it at night. Doctor's got him pumped up with pain meds so he slurs his words sometimes. We know his secondhand dispatches from the Soviet Union front and back; the long bread lines in Leningrad, the hostilities with

Ukraine, the Belarus temper tantrums, the trumped up American claims of Moscow graft.

Every day a whole lot of new people come in from the States. When they get to the pearly gates of Jonestown they blink, pinch themselves to see if this is real, look for their buddies then brace for the pat down. They give up their personal stuff to Mariah, Everett, Kenyatta, the foot soldiers who usher everyone in, confiscating toothpaste, sanitary pads, floss, zit medicine. They toss everything into a big wheelbarrow and take it to the commissary.

I heard some of that shit turns up in Dad's cottage for him and Carol to use or gets traded on the underground supplies market the sneaky kids got going.

When the shine of getting here wears off some of the new ones bitch about how different things are. Piss and moan to high heaven about the heat, the bugs, the hard work, the humidity, having to crap in the outhouses with no privacy. I tell 'em to save that mess until they're 90% alone. Hold your tongue comrades until the wee hours inside your head when only God can hear you scream.

They rounded up a man I had my eye on. Lean mean sweet Greer from hick town Antioch got snatched up by the brothers from the Red Brigade one evening after I spoke to him.

"Things are goin' down the tubes back home," he told me, flirting up a storm during his shift in the laundry room. "President Carter's gonna pass a bill to keep blacks from voting. The Mexicans and the Chinese will be next, then they'll probably start herding up niggas, issuing government i.d. cards. All's said and done brothers out there might need to export weapons from us."

The shit sounded crazy, but sexy dangerous too coming out of his mouth. He wasn't afraid of me. Didn't smile in my face then gag behind my back like some of them, playing like I was a sideshow freak. Even Jess and her magpie girlfriend, the Heckle and Jeckle of Jonestown, have turned against me since we've been here. The shit is not even subtle. All the mock unity of when we were struggling together in the States is over and done. Jess gets off on her promotion to head counselor, barreling around in a tank top with her tits hanging out acting like she works so much harder than everybody else, like she's the thin blue fucking line.

Greer wanted to be in the Brigade but was told he couldn't cut it because of his allergies.

"That quack doctor Lance gave me an antihistamine for 'em a few months ago, one of those super drowsy pills just for a runny nose," he said. "Knocked me clean out when it was time to go to work. Made me look trifling when I was promised a trip to Georgetown to help with the Black History show if I did twelve hours straight in the laundry."

"Word is Dad's fucking him," I said.

"Oh yeah? Why am I not surprised. Boy is shakier than jello."

"Dad paid his way through med school."

"Must've been nice to have that kind of deal at first, but now he's the one payin' for it. Can't say I feel sorry for him though 'cause he sure ain't shy about throwing his tin pot credentials around."

"Scratch the surface and he's a Texas good ol' boy, but being Jewish complicates it. And you know he wears that shit as a badge of honor."

"They all do."

He lowered his voice, bundling clothes into packs for delivery to the dorms. "I hear they want to dope up troublemakers."

"Where'd you hear that?"

"Zephyr said she heard it from Hy. She stays over there by the piggery, is on the list to pick up some clothes today. Dr. Lance is going to take a stick to anybody who gets out of line. So everything we say is on lockdown, Dev. You better watch your back. What're you planning on writing next? Can you do something on this and maybe keep it on the qt?"

"I don't know," I said. I could barely concentrate on what he was saying because there were people flowing around us outside, the washing machines were churning loud and a woman who'd ratted on her cousin in

256

confessional for keeping a stash of candy in her mattress hovered close by, dunking soiled underwear into a basin full of bleach.

"You think about it." He leaned in so close he could nibble my ear, watching the woman out of the corner of his eye. "You write good. People look forward to it."

"You look forward to it?"

"Yeah," he blushed. "I-I used to do a little writing myself before I dropped out of school. Poems and stuff."

A group of children ran past outside, squealing and teasing each other, racing to get a good place in the 12:30 lunch line. I figured they must be new kids, uninitiated into the dorm- by-dorm protocol for lining up, foot-loose, fancy free.

Greer looked up at the door. "Speak of the devil," he said. Hy came in lugging two sacks of dirty clothes. I'd always thought she was beautiful. She'd lost a little of her pep since she'd moved here; what with Foster getting killed back home before we left, a fucked up job assignment that cheated her mind, plus her sister and Jess ain't no picnic.

I helped her put the sacks on the counter. "Hey girl, how you been?"

"Surviving. You?"

"Same. Think I made a new friend though," I winked at Greer and he blushed deeper. The other woman edged out the door, flagging some of the kids down outside.

"I ain't new." He started folding onesies into tiny squares. "We was just talking about that thing you noticed going down in the infirmary."

Hy backed up a little, skittish. It was only us in the room now but she played with the drawstrings on her pants, mosquito bites dotting her long brown arms.

"Dr. Lance is trying to calm excitable folk."

"Excitable? Damn girl," Greer sputtered. "Who they think gonna be excitable in all this fucking heat?"

"Yeah, that ain't Dad or Mother Mabelean's call. Sounds like something Mariah and Carol cooked up with Lance," I said.

"Maybe. That pill he gave me was pretty foul."

Hy shook her head. "Jim knows. Give him more credit than that."

"True, only reason why they'd be jerking around with meds is to look good in his eyes."

"Possibly," I said.

"Yo, brother, you got that order for the nursery?" Jamiah and Cedric came in. Cedric nodded hello at us, slapped five with Greer. Jamiah spritzed himself with the spray bottle he was carrying then turned it on Hy.

"Cut it out," she said.

"Girl, you know you like it. We're picking up diapers and, what's that other stuff called?"

"Onesies," Greer said.

Cedric watched us for a second. He was always packing a piece now, eyes in back of his head.

"Feels heavy in here. What ya'll caucusing about...Hyacinth you look a little uptight."

Jamiah sprayed a blast of water in the air, giggling. "I don't know why, it's the Fourth of fucking July."

"Jamiah's got a little G-town weed."

"For an exclusive party like we used to do back home."

Greer folded up the clothes and put them in a plastic bag. "I wouldn't mind a little taste. Ladies?"

"Hy ain't getting ripped," I said, trying to keep it light. I took the bottle from Jamiah and sprayed water on my face then on Greer's neck. "It'd be good to get fucked up and unwind."

"You on deadline though," Greer added.

Jamiah perked up. "That so?"

"Not really."

"What you writing?"

"Just a short thing on how the babies nailed the broadcast this morning."

"Right on."

Jamiah edged over to Hy. He was getting under her skin. "John Boy and the rest of 'em tore up some Frederick Douglass on the radio. Were you listening, Hy?"

"I've only heard it a million times."

"A million and one is golden baby, 'cause it's all about positive vibes," Cedric said. "They got a delegation from the States coming in a few months to check us out and their delivery has to be tight."

Jamiah took the rest of the laundry from Greer. "What time you off, homeboy?"

"Same as everybody else, right before dinner."

Jamiah cupped his fingers to his lips like he was toking a joint. "We'll swing by and get you. You can do evening patrol with us."

"You don't need to prove yourself to them," Hy said. "I thought you had issues being out in the jungle for a long time."

I felt Greer tense up, like she was calling him out. "Don't know where you got that from, sis."

"It ain't no state secret," Cedric said. "Dr. Lance been giving you medication for your allergic condition, brother?"

"Yeah but it ain't no big deal."

Jamiah rolled a onesie into a ball and threw it up in the air, catching it two-handed. "He helped me when I had the stomach flu."

"We got some of the best medical care around," Cedric said, keeping his eye on Greer. "But yet you think they got our folk coming out of the clinic all drugged up. That don't make no sense, brother."

Greer was silent. People were starting to come in from lunch to pick up clothes orders, hand wash socks and underwear in the big rusty basins.

"I overheard something like that."

"From who?"

"I forgot." He didn't look at Hy. She picked at the bug bites on her arms. I gave her the spray bottle.

"If they're itching use this."

Jamiah curled his lip. "Just like you to be spreading rumors like a little sissy."

"Why does he have to be a sissy?"

"I didn't mean no disrespect to you, Miss Devera."

Cedric waved his hand. "Cool it. It's just noise anyhow. All this chatter going around is like a fucking disease. We'll swing by later. The kinda grass we got works wonders for healing."

CHAPTER 27

In the Pavilion, Jonestown, August 1978

THE TWO WOMEN sitting next to Jess in the pavilion whispered as they ate their dinner. Look at him. No doubt he's kin to Dad. When he grows up he's gonna be something else. A leader, a nation builder, a great speaker. There's a spiritual resemblance. That cute as a button nose of his. Those strong white teeth and black hair.

John-Boy the little emperor strode through the aisles picking petals from a lily. He climbed onto the pavilion stage and plopped down next to the drum kit, aware that all eyes were on him. The women watched amused. They ate their rice gruel in breathless slurps, sopping it up with a pair of biscuits, taking turns waving the horse flies away from each other.

Jess couldn't tell whether they were friends, relatives or lovers; intrigued by the easy symmetry of their movements, their sentence-finishing pauses and glittery-eyed recognition of favorite turns of phrase. She'd never noticed them before. They were part of the third wave of immigrants, secretly resented by the first and second for their neediness and naiveté. They took up too much space, asked too many questions, reveled in being just plain lazy, ill-prepared for the sunup to sundown work regimen. As therapist she was assigned to conduct psychological evaluations, taking inventories of every quirk, habit, fantasy and predilection from children to adults. At the end of the week she presented her findings to the Planning Commission. The group digested each individual's case for hours, Carol pacing, Mariah chewing her nails ragged as dawn broke. Cases would be placed into one of two categories: definitive action or watch and wait.

The women's fascination with John-Boy irritated Jess. Their covetousness was shameful, as though he was a figment of all the unborn children they'd never had. She would never be so pathetic a caricature of a lesbian. Even though she knew nothing about them she couldn't stop herself from thinking this, from being repelled by their solicitous yen for the little white boy, by the way they were whispering loud enough to try and ingratiate themselves with Father.

The pavilion had begun to fill up. She saw Taryn come in and sit in the middle row. After moving to Guyana they had drifted into a stalemate. Like most couples they were housed in different dorms. Separation was for the greater good of the community. It bred moral strength, loosened the bonds of dependence, reduced the distraction of sex, Father said. They avoided contact during the evening mass meetings when the community would gather, dead tired, to hear announcements, music, work detail changes, news of the outside world.

Still, she liked seeing Taryn there among the crowd, face smudged, fresh wrinkles swirled under her eyes from the dust and heat. She wanted to look forward to sharing the day's revelations with her; but Taryn was envious of her time with her patients, scoffing at her new reporting responsibilities, branding them invasive. Taryn had been assigned to library and archive duty three times a week, working in the fields the other days like everybody else. She complained that her accounting skills were going to waste, that she hadn't moved there to be a common field hand.

"What, you too damn good to work in the fields?" Jess asked her later that night, after they'd clumsily attempted to make love for the first time in months in one of the small cottages reserved for seniors. They lay shoulder to shoulder, unnerved by each creak and twig snap outside, brooding over the threat of exposure. Shortly after they'd arrived a couple who'd been caught having sex behind the infirmary was traipsed out into the pavilion in the middle of the night half-naked, shamed for selfish fucking, for doing it and betraying socialism. Everybody had had a grand time with the spectacle, fearful of, tantalized by who might be next.

"They messed up their heads," Taryn muttered, settling under the covers. "Damned disgrace."

"They deserved it. That will never happen to us," Jess said.

"Don't give me that. How can you defend that crazy shit?"

"Lower your voice."

"Why, if there's no danger of detection?"

Taryn moved to the end of the bed, Jess' presence was at once unbearable and necessary. A warm stillness nestled over the cottage. Cats moaned and scuttled outside, scheming to get in.

"I don't know why I'm here," she said. "For some reason I thought this would be better for us."

"Babe, at least here you have a job and a niche, *a role* ... back there working doing numbers all isolated for the white man ... what kind of destiny was that going to be Taryn? Nobody said this was going to be a cakewalk. I asked you to have long range vision. Otherwise, we'll be like the women who used to live here. Worn out and going back and forth to the hospital with nothing to show for it, with no legacy or claim to anything that outlasts us."

"I don't care about that anymore. You were the one obsessed with all that. When I die I'm dead. That's it. I never wanted to tether my afterlife to kids or grandkids or any of the other common shit we're supposed to be so desperate for."

"Nor did I." Jess sat up suddenly in the dark, profile bloated in shadow against the wall.

"I overheard two of the newcomer women whispering about John-Boy tonight," she said. "They were carrying on about him, staring at him like he was something good to eat, like they were coveting him."

"What's strange about that? He's the so-called chosen one."

"I think they're infiltrators."

Taryn shook her head. "Why?"

"Vibes. Their affect was off. They knew I was listening and started acting up a storm with all this mock concern. So many of the new ones are trying to prove they're down by slobbering on about how talented he is and just like Father and all that crap."

"So what, are they special agents then? Sent here by the government to kidnap John-Boy and take over?"

"Is that so farfetched? That's how they brought down the Panthers, AIM and all the rest of them. Why not us? It's all about installing people on the inside. Getting middle-aged ladies who supposedly wouldn't hurt a flea to take us down."

Taryn shivered under the damp sheets, stomach lurching as though she was falling, tangled up in Jess' creamy self-assurance. The cats continued to moan and cajole by the door, staking their claim, simpering in league with the monkey Muggs and the cult of animal reverence that had sprung up around him.

"That's paranoid," she snapped. "Nobody cares about this place enough to do that. We're the only ones dumb enough to leave the States en masse without a plan for a way back. In fact the government is probably saying to Jim, why can't you take some more Negroes with you? While you're at it, take all the ghettoes of Watts, Newark, Detroit and Harlem and dump them in Jonestown. What the fuck do we care about a bunch of spooks."

Jess stretched out her legs impatiently. A battered Donald Duck clock in the corner ticked eleven o'clock.

"I bet Carter's State department people are laughing right now about how they'd like to pack up every last nigger from the inner city and do a special repatriation program to Guyana."

"Who's sounding crazy now?"

"It's no crazier than your paranoia about those two women. You've let yourself become a cog in this fucking machine. I know you go to the Planning Commission and tell them every little last thing about your so-called patients. How can you justify that Jess? How does that translate into fair and righteous? Some of those people look up to you. They see a black woman in an authority position and automatically you've got their trust, at least with the new ones who don't know how things are run around here."

"They were coveting him, Taryn. Favoring him because they're already jockeying for something. In a few months Congressman Reardon, the

Democrat who sits on the Armed Services Committee, is coming from San Francisco. These women are connected to him."

Taryn got up from the bed. Her back ached from hours of bending and hoeing in the fields. At 5:30 the morning broadcast would begin with an inspirational pre-recorded poem from Pyong Yang kindergartners, then news of Fillmore's further decline into anarchy, food bartering, gas rationing and arson; whole blocks gutted by fire, mosques, temples and churches ravaged. Father had had a revelation that this would happen. And now the prophecy was coming true, verified by anguished reports from members who had benevolently volunteered to stay behind to manage the church's affairs.

"I'm going back to the dorm," Taryn said. "I won't be a party to this, whatever it is you're trying to do."

"Don't act so high and mighty. You signed onto this with both eyes open. You're implicated in whatever the fuck goes down here. I know you. If it benefited you and your bourgeois ambition you'd be right here with me."

"You sound like a cartoon, a sad vindictive one."

"I wasn't a cartoon last night when you begged me to make love to you."

"That was an error in judgment. One of many that I won't make again."

"You just remember who protected you, who took care of you as a semi-out black 'dyke' when all those fundamentalist fuckers were in the streets coast-to-coast screaming about deviancy trying to make sure we couldn't work. We've got a country here. A real shot at building it from the ground up. Go run back to the States and see how long you last over there."

Mariah decided who would be brought up on the floor:

Wisdom copied Nancy's math test when she wasn't looking.

Janet masturbated in the second bunk three nights in a row.

Greer spread rumors about drugging in the infirmary.

Stanley and Levette plotted about saving money for plane tickets to Miami and leaving in the middle of the night.

Chloe and Sterlinda talked about raping and kidnapping John Boy.

The minor charges would go first, then the most heinous. A list would be made of offenses in one column and recommended punishments in the other. The informants were rewarded with special privileges; allowed to sleep in on meeting days, served meat instead of rice gruel, given a few hours reprieve from fieldwork. They basked in the golden haze of being in Father's good graces for a day.

"Maybe you need some corrective instruction from the Education Crew," he said, looking down at Stanley and Levette from his chair on the stage. "'Cause I'm not sure why you'd do such a blamed stupid thing like try and sneak and get plane tickets out of here when you didn't have a pot to piss in to begin with."

"We were just joking around, Father. It's-it's hard getting used to living like this."

"You should've fucking thought about that before you moved here," Zephyr Threadgill volunteered. "You're taking up space that could've accommodated somebody who really wanted to be here and make a contribution."

William, the man sitting beside her, nodded in agreement. "Yeah, if you can't cut it maybe you *should* leave or go on Education. Everybody who came here knew it wasn't gonna be no peaches and cream at first. Rome wasn't fucking built in a damn day. Shit, I'm grateful to Dad for giving me this opportunity at rebirth 'cause I was dying in the United States of Assassination."

Jim rose, the buttons of his shirt popping open, his chest slick and gleaming.

"Naw, Brother William, these two know better than us. Hell, they're no better than Greer spreading lies or Janet getting her rocks off and making everybody in her dorm privy to it. In fact, they're ten times worse because we expended all this effort and energy developing them for this mission and they've proven themselves to be unworthy. Makes me sick to my stomach. I got a call this morning from the Prime Minister thanking me for all the progress we've made clearing the land and making crops grow. We've got good communications with the local indigenous people who see us and think, hey those American motherfuckers ain't all bad. They ain't all terrorists, racists and thieves. Hell, some of the Indians are even thinking about joining us here in Jonestown because the government is trying to encroach on their farms. See, that's that superficial do as I say not as I do kind of socialism. The ones at the top are profiting big time, driving fancy cars, smoking Havana cigars and fucking every piece of young tail in sight. Sound familiar ya'll? Sound like the religious and government pimpocracy we got back in the States?"

"Down to a T, Father! That's some bootleg bullshit right there!"

"Indeed, indeed brothers and sisters, but we digress...Stanley and Levette and them want to undermine our livelihood with their little games. But we love them all the same don't we? I love every last one of you so much I'd be willing to lay down my life to any wild beast in the jungle wants to eat my nuts for dinner. Hee, hee, hee. That's what Jesus did. That's what he was all about. Total sacrifice in the face of destruction."

He paused, watching, gauging the reaction, conjuring the hungry teenage boy in the back of Prophet Zeke's church.

"What's your recommendation Zephyr for their penalty?"

Zephyr plodded up to the microphone. She wiped her palms on her t-shirt and took a deep breath. "Put 'em on Education like William said. Put 'em on there for at least a week. They'll see what real hard work is."

The crowd jeered in support. A group of toddlers that had been brought in from the nursery by Mother Mabelean to see the gospel performance later that evening bobbed and cooed in response.

"Oh sister, you're such a strict disciplinarian," Jim squealed. "I would've hated to have had you for grade school! We'll show 'em a little more compassion this time around and assign 'em to Education for a few days instead of a week."

"That's the tip of the iceberg, Father, what's more disturbing is what sister Jess found out."

"Come up here, Jess."

Jess walked up to the stage past Taryn, avoiding her gaze. Mariah swung down from the drum kit and took the microphone. "Jess overheard two of the new sisters talking about kidnapping and assaulting John Boy."

A gasp rippled through the crowd, then silence. Jim dabbed at his eyes with a tissue. The last breathless stream of people came in from the machine shop, the kitchen, the sawmill, the nursery, laundry and infirmary, their shifts blissfully ended for the night.

"I need the culprits to come forward," Jim said quietly. "You know who you are. You ain't fooling nobody. I gave my goddamn eyeteeth to get you out here and now you want to whore for this white politician motherfucker who's tryin' to take us down. Don't look all surprised like you don't know what I'm talkin' about. I'm not going to drag you up here. I want you to act like you got a fucking spine and come up and face the music on your own."

Jess stepped to the mic. "They were covetous of John Boy, Father. I felt it was disrespectful, like there was sinister intent."

The audience looked around, waiting for the revelation. Sterlinda swallowed, raised her hand and croaked. "We were talking about John Boy, Father, but we were only complimenting him on how much he favored you and what a good leader he'd be when he grew up."

Jim settled back into his chair. The new arrivals scrambled to find places in the packed rows. "Well now I appreciate that. I appreciate that you were making a favorable comparison. But it's not compliments that move us, right brothers and sisters? It's good works. It's being able to see our children thriving and waking up to the bounty of this sacred place. It's seeing our seniors revitalized and dancing and being constructive, not cooped up ghettoized in some chicken shit nursery home."

"That's right!" The crowd shouted.

"So we don't need idle flattery. That don't cut it. John Boy ain't any more special than any of our other children. They're all precious jewels.

Only thing I can figure out about you revering him over the others is you been told something about his status. Somebody been whispering in your ears. Correct?"

"No, I don't know what you mean."

"Zephyr, enlighten her."

Zephyr walked back up to the stage, spreading her freckled arms out wide, a yellow flower wilting behind her ear. Muggs stirred and jumped up and down in his cage, baring fleshy pink gums as the toddlers squealed, eyes trained on a bulbous cockroach skittering under the chairs.

"Ya'll know I don't need a microphone, right?" She hollered. "That's what I like about this space. All our voices can be heard here brothers and sisters. What Dad is talking about is envy. It's one of the deadly sins in the Bible. And I know we don't believe in that slave book no how but even a broken clock is right twice a day. John Boy may be one of Dad's natural born sons but we don't treat him no different. See, evidently Congressman Reardon has planted some spies here. Didn't even have the common sense to train them proper to know you shouldn't be too eager, too, too—give us a twenty dollar word, Jess."

"Overzealous."

"That's it. You shouldn't be too overzealous and show your hand when you're trying to be undercover. Obviously these two didn't take our history class on the CIA in Vietnam, Chile and Angola. Those fuckers messed up big time. Moles all over the place and double agents spilling classified information."

"So you've got some dummies who don't know how to spy worth a damn? That what we're dealing with?" William said, offended.

"Why get some old white man to come in here and take us over without an advance guard? They're the jigaboo brigade."

Sterlinda fidgeted, eyes locked onto her sneakers, hand-painted with sprite's glitter from Monday art class. Five rows back, Taryn sent a silent message of support to the woman, her challenges to the interrogation bubbling up, dying in her throat. She did not know where Hy was, wanting, needing to see her face to save herself.

On the perimeter of the pavilion the Red Brigade brooded, guns at their sides, watching Cedric for cues on when to move.

Sterlinda took off one of her shoes and held it up. "Look, see, I decorated these the other day ... they say 'With love for the children', *all* the children ... I love John Boy. I would never say anything to hurt him. We came straight from the neighborhood in L.A., just like everybody else. Lived on Budlong and Exposition right over there by the train tracks. I-I was cleaning houses and taking the bus to Miss Ann's on the Westside when I started going to the Temple in '73. Got saved by Jim and stopped going to this Methodist church that was trying to take every cent I had. Two of my grown kids are here, Jackson and Ebony. You can't claim I'm anybody's spy. We lived right next to them!" She pointed to an extended family of ten sitting in the third row; a woman flanked by her children and grandchildren. "Ya'll know me. We lived on the same block since the '65 riots in Watts. Working two jobs the way I did when was I going to find the time to be anybody's spy?"

The family sat silently, shifting in their seats, watching their mother for cues.

"Don't try and drag us into your mess," she said.

Sterlinda lurched forward, shaking the shoe at Jess. "Why are you doing this? Why are you telling these lies? You call yourself a social worker or whatever it is you claim to be. It's you that's the traitor. I've given five good years of my life to this church, been on every trip and campaign. Even wrote letters against that ballot initiative putting down the queers despite my being a Christian and not believing in those nasty things they do. So you can't sit up here and say I've been disloyal. I'm not going to let you paint me as a traitor just 'cause you're the only black woman with any so-called authority position."

Mariah jumped in, her quivery voice rising into the gloom of the storm clouds; a boldness to her posture borne of years of preparation, rehearsal, watching and waiting in Carol's shadow. "You should be more careful about what you say in front of the entire community. It's obvious why you'd want to attack sister Jess to try and get the spotlight off of yourself. But guess what, we got other witnesses, right Ebony?"

Ebony peered out from the crowd, a pacifier gnawing infant struggling in her arms. The baby clawed at her eyes, her breasts, wriggling to get free in the sopping heat. "I'm sorry mama," she whispered, as Mabelean rose from the brood of children to help her with the infant. "Sorry."

"Your son went to Georgetown with the other kids to get donations," Mariah continued. "He was too ashamed to be here tonight to see this."

"C'mon, let's get on with it," Cedric chimed from the sidelines. "We got five more cases to run down. What's going to be the penalty and what about her accomplice?"

"Since Zephyr was such a good prosecutor I think she should decide," Jim said. Muggs clapped his hands at the pronouncement.

Two Jonestown service trucks pulled up outside the pavilion. Red Brigade guards jumped out shouting, rifles drawn.

"They're coming, Father! We need to secure the area!"

Gunshots cracked through the air from the jungle. Jim staggered backward on the stage into the drum kit, the cymbals falling in a dissonant clang as he clutched his chest, red fluid gushing from his shirt, fat face turning to chalk.

"Dad's been shot!" Mariah screamed. Cedric ran down the aisle and leapt in front of Jim, shielding him while the other guards pulled him off stage.

Jimmy and Demian wandered in dazed, clothes mud-caked from slopping pigs. They stared pop-eyed at the chaos, the fish tank scene of screaming toddlers being herded back to the daycare center, their father launching into a gobblydegook chant of "White night".

"Come on!" Cedric yelled at them. "Follow me! We gotta get those motherfuckers!"

The crowd burst out of the pavilion.

"Everybody report to your drill captains please!"

"Is Dad ok?! Is Dad ok?!"

"They'll never be able to lick him! He's bulletproof!"

"Closest thing we got to God almighty."

"Look at what that bitch Sterlinda put in motion. We'll be up for hours doing the patrols because of this."

The guitarists and drummer from the band clambered back onstage to their posts. They readied their instruments, counted three, thumping out the first few notes of Buffalo Springfield's "For What It's Worth", the whack and the twang steeling them against the onslaught of the monsters.

CHAPTER 28

White Night

PLAY ME LIKE Dirty Harry, the gun said to Jamiah.

He'd always wanted to shoot one, just to hear the sound. The only ones he'd seen up close and personal were in cops' holsters; lean, gleaming, black and mean.

Nigger killers, his boys in East Oakland called them. Pig talismans taking out whole families with one clip, maiming the able-bodied, silencing the innocent, swallowing a clutch of his running buddies well before sweet sixteen.

How did he get here, patrolling the fringes of the compound with a semiautomatic he could barely hold straight, his knees rattling in time to the soft spit of jungle drizzle?

In the distance he could hear the announcement. The White Night was upon them. The ghost dance for Jonestown's lifeblood.

"We all must stand up and fight," a voice crackled over the loudspeaker. "Every man, woman and child. Until the last breath."

"They tried to kill Father," Cedric yelled, running toward Jamiah. Jimmy and Demian were on his heels, flanked by Casey and Malik, Brigade guards since March.

"Shit." Jamiah whispered.

Cedric squinted hard at him. "Nicked him. He's gonna be ok. You know how to hold that gun, boy? Don't look like it."

"Don't fuck with him. He's Mr. Rough n' Ready," Casey said.

Malik snickered. "Looks like he'd be better off handling a pea shooter."

"Shh, ya'll hear something?"

"Me and Demian'll go check it out," Jimmy said. They took off to the west, sleek as rival sprinters. Cedric barked into his walkie talkie and headed in the opposite direction.

A figure darted through the brush behind the rest of the group. In the silence they could hear the swish-thud of a gun reloading.

"Wait ... Motherfucker there they go!"

Jamiah crouched, following the others toward the intruder, heart punching out of his chest, mouth swimming in nausea, the sky filling suddenly with purple birds trying to escape through a hole in the clouds. He wanted to go back to bed, burrow down into the cool sheets, the lumpy mattress of his bunk looming like a hidden oasis. Back in California he'd done minor shit. Strutting and glaring from behind dark glasses, looking Stagolee bad and untouchable like a frontline soldier for the Panthers, taking care of small things; crank calling Temple members who were getting out of line, putting the fear of Jesus in the press vipers that followed them around. Father had noticed his diligence and rewarded it with a prime position in the Vanguard corps, an elite cell in the Red Brigade trained to gather fringe intel the higher ups in the Planning Commission didn't want to deal with. Mostly, though, he watched on the sidelines as his friends, his adopted family, ratted on each other, panting at the opportunity, daredevils of tongue.

"Think it's spies sent by that dickless congressman motherfucker they were talkin' about? Or maybe the CIA?" Casey hissed, hoisting his gun to his shoulder, pumped up from months of hauling logs and clearing brush.

"Speaking of dicks I see your girl is about to bust out," Malik said to Jamiah.

"Yep. She's due any day now. She's gonna be one of the first to give birth here. My little man is gonna be a Guyanan."

Jimmy and Demian ran out of the brush. They swayed into each other, neck to neck, Demian a hair taller. The rest of the group drank in their intimacy.

"Be still, be quiet," Jimmy commanded. "We've repelled them. Whatever's out there in the jungle will take care of them."

Jamiah leaned over and vomited, just missing Malik's Converse sneakers.

"Aw shit, he lost his dinner. You'll be ok man," Malik said, patting him on the back. "It's just nerves."

Jamiah recoiled, feeling their eyes on him. Show me what you're made of boy, his father had said, after he'd mumbled through a Civics speech at school and come home crying, wilting in his father's arms.

"I'm gonna be a daddy soon," he whispered.

"Yeah, that's great, man," Demian said. "That's great." He motioned for Jamiah, Malik and the others to go ahead, glancing wearily at Jimmy.

"We'll stay here to check the rest of the area out to make sure they don't come back."

"Ok."

Jimmy watched them walk away. Shouts reverberated from the direction of the pavilion. Stray dogs adopted from Port Kaituma barked and bayed in unison.

Since they'd moved to Jonestown, he and Demian spent nearly every waking moment together, serving on the security detail, the Jonestown basketball team, plugging in for the more strenuous work shifts when needed, stealing moments with their mother away from Jim's chaos. Still, Jimmy kept Demian at a mental distance; afraid he would pick up and leave like he'd threatened to in the States.

"All's clear here, I think," he said.

"Of course it is. You've gotten to be a better shot."

"So have you."

"I hate these fucking guns, Jimmy. I hate fucking pretending."

"Keep your voice down. Just think of it as a dress rehearsal."

"For fucking what?"

"For when the real invasion happens."

"You sound just like him."

"These people are coming in a few months, Dem. This shit is real. You can't put your head in the sand and pretend like it's not happening and play the on-the-fence moralist."

"I'm not playing at anything. I just don't see why we have to lie for Dad and pretend we're getting shot at when we're not."

"You're being short sighted. This is how we survive. This is how we, you and me, come out on top. By outsmarting, outwitting the outsiders and being Dad's right hands, his eyes and ears like we've always been. This is how we protect Mom and the others. It's the only way, Dem."

Demian shook his head. He kneeled down in the dirt, covering his face with his hands, the rifle flapping against his bent leg. The dogs had stopped barking and their father's voice echoed from the loudspeaker.

Jimmy kneeled down next to him. "You know I don't agree with him one hundred percent. Even about the decision to come here. I know you think I took his side to coax you here. But you have to keep it in perspective. This is temporary. He's sick, spaced out on drugs and painkillers half the time. Pretty soon he's going to fall apart. When that happens they're all going to be looking to us for direction. If Carol and Mariah and that lot are allowed to take charge it'll be anarchy." He paused.

Angela Davis' voice came over the loudspeaker. Then Huey Newton's. They rang out bold, otherworldly, sages urging Jonestown to stay strong for the umpteenth time. A loop had been made of their recorded greetings, the radio room workers interspersing them with the daily news digest.

The White Night was winding down.

"Nobody respects them," Jimmy said.

Demian got up from the ground. "They have their supporters."

"Yeah, but nobody's gonna follow them. My bet is if all this crumbles they'll hook up with one of their rich relatives and fly the coop like the other two white girls whose daddies bought them tickets to Europe."

"Carol said Jamiah's parents are coming as part of the Congressman's group."

"Jamiah will never leave here as long as his child is here. Besides, he worships Dad."

"Maybe."

"There's no maybe to it. Even as weak and incoherent as he's getting, the white women will never have the kind of power he has over these people."

The trees parted. William, gun in hand and out of breath from running from the pavilion, barreled up to them.

"Is it done?" He asked gruffly.

Demian looked away, tired, disgusted, pants sticky with tree sap, beetle carcasses. "Yeah, it's all clear," Jimmy replied. "There's no more threat."

"Good, then everybody can have a sound night's sleep till the next time around."

Ernestine Markham
Jonestown, August 1978

She had the most majestic voice, Sister Angela did. I'd heard her speak once at a rally at the university before they shackled her and threw her into prison like a zoo animal or a vicious hardened criminal, not like the brilliant beautiful mind she was, not like the world traveler who spoke five languages and could debate Marxist philosophy in five more than those LAPD crackers ever heard of. I told my son Byron, boy, you better love this black brilliance, better savor the sound while you can because Jim will twist it to meet his own ends.

Her voice is my secret, my special potion to get us through the day sliding into night and the endless siege drills, the animals screeching unsettled in the trees, willing us interlopers gone.

I aborted a daughter with your name, Angela. The best gift I ever gave to myself, back when I believed in a God because it was convenient. He could help me get where I wanted to go in my teaching, my dreams of a learning institute, a freedom school for our children; a training ground for the revolutionaries I could never be, stuck with a conservative asthmatic husband and an excitable child who I had to groom to greatness. I was always working, watching on the sidelines, making food for protest marchers, giving books to their children, opening my home up to women prisoners who got out of jail and had no place to stay.

Fifty years old, watching and waiting. The church was a chance to remedy that, Angela. All my life I'd looked for its likeness in other places and been disappointed. It was the lost limb that my marriage, my pregnancies took from me.

We must stay the course against the thieves like Angela did when they left her to rot in the jails they built to dump us in after slavery, the twentieth century solution to the Negro Problem. She says that this is just one part of a longer journey to reclaim ancestral homes and inheritances, a worldwide coming together of African peoples after the holocaust.

But did she see Sterlinda's eyes peeking from the bottom of the pit they threw her in after she was accused of treason? See her yellow teeth, the skin peeling off her fingers. All of Jonestown could smell the surrender of this simple woman who was learning to write poetry after doing menial labor all her life. See how she was forced to defecate on herself just like they did in the hull of the slave ships while massa plucked a few of us to fuck and throw overboard.

What I wouldn't give for real toilet paper, Sister. Soft white scented floral please-don't- squeeze-the-Charmin ethereal. The two ply kind I had in the bathroom of my house in MacArthur Park, all baby blue tile and matching vanities.

They'll never be able to count me among the thieves Angela, though I fell just as hard and as deep and as long.

The Pit was as big as a city elevator. It had its own memory of inmates, their nightmares rubbed off on the wings of wasps. The Jonestown pioneers dug it as a horny hiding place; a way station for bong sessions and furtive hook-ups, the monsoon rains turning it into an incubator for new bug species.

The Pit was where they dumped the most recalcitrant and compromised, the strongest who strayed, the hardest cases of disillusionment. Sterlinda made the record for staying in it. One week with water and gruel, conspiring with the wasp larvae, praying to Wile E. Coyote; no way you gonna fucking break me.

After she was released they sent her to the Extended Care Unit for more rehabbing.

"She's hearing voices," Carol said at an emergency meeting of the Planning Commission. Mariah, William and five others sprawled out on the floor, struggling to stay awake. Jim lounged in a wicker chair by the window, fully recovered from the staged assassination attempt, red guayabera painted onto his pale skin.

"Voices of the ancestors? Voices of Reardon? Bitch came here delusional."

"Go easier next time."

"Yes."

"Listen to the letters the third graders wrote. Tough fuckers. Tough as nails. Bet if you put 'em down there in The Pit they'd keep on truckin'."

"I will screw a thousand government agents for socialism. I will go back to the States and poison the food of any friend or relative who speaks against us."

"So precocious for their age."

Lance came in the room with his medicine bag. He shoved a stack of patient charts at Carol. For the past few months he'd floated through the settlement conducting chemical experiments on the pigs with shipments of potassium cyanide from the States, gauging how long it would take for a reaction, watching them squirm, flop, die. Between shifts at the infirmary he tended to Jim, dispensing an unending supply of painkillers to silence his moans, appearing spectrally at his bedside, a rusted stethoscope garlanding his stooped shoulders.

"There," he twanged. "These are the most high risk."

Carol flipped through the charts. "Most of them are new like Sterlinda."

"We have to do a better job of orientation," Mariah said.

Jim waved them aside. "What have you got for me, Lance?"

Mariah looked pained. "The new ones are the most impressionable."

Lance took a thermometer from his bag. "You gotta slow down, Dad."

"We've got another batch of letters to relatives leaving in the mail tomorrow," Mariah volunteered.

"Give it to me, boy," Jim said, opening his mouth to get his temperature taken.

"102. Low fever."

"Sweet mercy." He flicked the thermometer out of his mouth, grabbed a piece of guava from a bowl on the table and wheeled over to Muggs' cage. "Them letters ain't getting our land cleared or our crops grown and sold fast enough. Prime Minister Burnham is breathing down my neck asking me to justify why we need another government subsidy."

Carol kept her eye on the charts. "He'll give it to us. Don't worry about him. Paula is working on his deputy minister."

Jim stroked Muggs on the head. "White pussy. They always fall for it. Even the most pro-black ones are brainwashed when it comes to their dicks. Paula better reel that chicken shit motherfucker in. If he gets it on the regular maybe that'll keep his buddy Burnham off our backs." He fed the guava to Muggs. "There you go baby ... Lance'll take good care of Sterlinda and them."

Mariah walked over to the table. She dug her hands into the fruit bowl, restless, savoring the coolness, the smell; the faces of the people in the room shifted distortedly before her.

"I don't think she was actively spying for Reardon."

"You know that doesn't make a whit of difference," Carol said sharply. The door opened and Jess came in, the sounds of the midnight patrols following her. Volunteers clanked through the grounds with lanterns, bats, sticks and any makeshift weapon they could get their hands on.

Jim stopped, listening. "Jess had it right. It's all about intent. You think Mao's Red Army slept at night? Think they whined about loyalty and family when Hunan was being invaded?"

"The children were upset when we brought Sterlinda up on the floor," Mariah insisted.

"Let 'em see how the real world works when traitors get called to justice. That's as much a part of their education as the book learning they're getting."

William turned to Jess. "Well you're certainly making a name for yourself."

"Jess is a good soldier," Jim said. "We need more of 'em. Lance, c'mon now, get on it, I need at least an hour before I get on the horn with the Prime Minister this morning."

"The welcoming group at our center in Georgetown is holding it down but we have to make sure they stay on message with any outsiders from the local press."

Lance handed Jim a vial of vitamin tablets. He snatched them and threw them on the ground. "Vitamins?! Get this Mickey Mouse shit outta my face! Where are my fucking pills?

"Here's a Valium."

Jim closed his eyes and swallowed it down. "Monitor Georgetown close, Sweet Pea."

"You haven't called me that in a while," Carol said, bile rising in her throat. She panned the group, bodies melding lethargically into each other. "We've got a few months to get ready for Reardon's little regiment."

"And I can't have ya'll farting around getting sidetracked."

"Of course not Dad," Lance said. "All the shipments are in and the supplies are in place."

"Good. And the animals are responding to the chemicals the way we anticipated?"

"Yes."

Mariah started cutting up an orange from the bowl. She fed a slice to Jim, letting the juice drip into her palm. Carol handed her a napkin, the rhythm of desire, secrecy among the three of them charging the room.

"You damn well better make sure that anybody who needs to be corrected is transitioned into the reorientation program," she said to Lance. "We don't need anyone going off while the Congressman is here."

"We've successfully reoriented ten people in the ECU program who made threats to Dad. Aside from that, bug bites, upset stomach, diarrhea and complaints of collick among the babies are down twenty percent this week. I had one voluntary request for Thorazine for heart palpitations. Other than that we're in tip top shape."

"Tip top?"

They turned, startled. Hy stood in front of them. "Dr. Schuler you need to come immediately. There's a patient in the infirmary with bad cramps and vomiting."

"What? Who sent you here?"

"One of the nurses, she's taking care of the patient."

Lance looked at Jim. "Go on," he mumbled, the Valium kicking in. "Mariah, darlin', can you help me back?"

Hy watched them stagger out. The group's eyes fastened on her. Lance remained rooted in place, biting his lip, foot tapping.

"Come the fuck on, the woman might die!"

"Don't be silly," Lance said.

"She's one of Jim's conquests."

"Stop ranting."

"He was trying to fuck her."

"No, you got it the wrong way round."

Carol put down the patient charts. "Unless you're on patrol with the others you're not authorized to be out here anyway. Jess, can you handle this?"

"I don't need to be handled."

Jess rose from her seat. "C'mon."

"I don't fucking need to be handled."

Jess led Hy out of the room past the front door toward the library. Lance followed on their heels, cradling his medicine bag. He turned to Hy in mock salute, grinning sourly at her as the patrol light lanterns flickered across the fields, scouring between the dorm buildings.

"Goodbye," he said.

They watched him disappear through the trees. A group of women with shovels and garden shears greeted him. They ticked off a list of people missing from their dorms.

"What the fuck do you think you're doing Hy?" Jess spat.

"This reorientation shit is all about drugging people to neutralize them. You know it and everybody on that goddamned commission knows it."

"I don't know shit, Hy, and you don't either, you hear me? You want to fucking jeopardize our place here? Get Taryn and me put on the Education Crew or exiled in Port Kaituma?"

"Yeah, right, like they really want to fuck with their cash cow intermediary. I know you're keeping everybody in line with that so-called therapy shit so they can keep signing their checks over to Jonestown."

"That's sick. I have a lot of people who depend on me."

"It's no sicker than what you did to Sterlinda."

"Sterlinda came in with wrong thinking."

"She came here looking for a better way just like everybody else."

"She lost her way worshipping false idols. Remember what the Bible says."

"Oh man." Hy reeled. She broke away from Jess and started toward the light of the patrols.

"No, listen—" The voice was small, forlorn, secreted from someone else's body. Hy ignored it, making her way to the infirmary. Lance was a few yards ahead, his desolate figure a blond firefly bobbing in the darkness.

She turned the corner and saw Jamiah and Demian step out of the cafeteria latrine.

"Evening Hy," Jamiah said. "Where you headed?"

"The infirmary."

"Can't go through there," Demian said apologetically. "We're doing inspections."

"For what?"

"Listening devices."

"Around sick people?"

"We're just following orders, sister," Jamiah said. "Go back to your dorm."

"Those people are drugged out of their minds, what threat are they?"

"Go back to your dorm, Hy. This is for everyone's protection."

She started toward the infirmary. Jamiah blocked her.

"Don't get crazy," he said.

Footsteps sounded behind them. Cedric ran out from the side of the building, exuberant, extending his arms to Jamiah. "Come on man! Your girl just went in to Dr. Lance. Looks like the baby's coming!"

CHAPTER 29

San Francisco, September 1978

THE BILLINGS SAT at the breakfast table reading their son's letters together line by line. She drove a city bus from early morning to afternoon. He worked at a shipping yard, had a bad hip, stayed tight with the union and was biding his time till his pension. They hadn't heard Jamiah so excited, so hopped up since he was a little boy, a giggly six year-old with no front teeth contemplating his first trip to the ocean; a treat to savor for weeks, landlocked as the family was living right on the spine of the new freeway.

Mama, he said, *the fruit here is like from heaven. Everyone has a job. Everyone is taken care of. At night it's so quiet. Like you can hear straight to the other side of the world.*

His girlfriend was eight months pregnant. A boy, he was sure of it. The child would be one of the first to be born in Jonestown. They'd name him Atticus, after his great-grandfather, a freedom fighter during World War I who had come home and tried to integrate the local college.

I can feel him kicking Mama. Sometimes when I put my ear to her stomach I can hear his heartbeat. Our baby revolutionary is coming soon, our African and Seminole warrior; he'll probably have the same birthday as Marcus Garvey. But where Garvey faltered leading our people back to Africa we've been successful. We did it with our sweat and blood, the living capital of the people.

I wake up every morning and see their beautiful smiling faces at work, everybody pitching in, everybody doing their part, everybody struggling together. I can't say that it's been easy. The bugs are bad. Sometimes I get dead tired out from the heat. But my boy will never know racism. He'll never know police beating his head in. He'll never know that private property divides and kills. Mama I wished that could've been my life from the beginning but surviving America's evil has made me stronger.

There were certain things Jamiah said in the letters that didn't sit right. Certain phrases they knew weren't his. Their boy never liked to write to begin with. He was into drawing pictures, loved watercolors, Buck Rogers' kinda tapestries of buildings and flying machines from space age neighborhoods he made up, obsessing about alien races living in harmony with humans. That was the part of their boy they wanted to remember, they told Ida when she came to call, looking for a new angle on the exodus of young black men from their street.

She'd set up a meeting between the Billings and Congressman Reardon, paid them two hours' leave time with an advance she'd gotten from The *Sun Reporter.* Since starting his probe into the church Reardon had taken testimony from a stream of relatives, met with journalists working the Temple beat; lobbied for disclosures about its finances in the undertow of the Carter administration, which flicked him off like a manic flea.

Reardon kept an office downtown in a swamp of congressional buildings.

"A close friend of mine contacted me about a year ago, said his son had been harassed by these people after leaving the church," he told the couple by way of introduction, a stocky white man powering a big oak desk and two roomfuls of pencil pushing staffers. "If this could grease the 1980 election in some way Washington would be all over it. Unfortunately politics always trump principles."

"That ain't him writing those letters on his own, Congressman," Mrs. Billings said, erect in her chair, drizzling cream into a cup of coffee.

After all, he was going somewhere in life as a genuine creative artist with God-given talent and the Temple was going to help him. Then he'd gotten mixed up with this fake Indian girl with curly hair down her back. Didn't want anybody to think she was too black so she claimed Seminole heritage. Their boy just straight up lost his mind over that madness.

I've got a whole lot of new responsibilities, Mama. In addition to being on my way to becoming a Daddy I'm helping lead security with some of the other brothers. We do for ourselves and don't have to depend on nobody else. No handouts. No begging. A man has to protect his family, especially when you have so many on the outside trying to tear this community down, when you have people who don't believe in the dream as strong as we do.

"He was excited about going over there," Mrs. Billings said. "He was always carrying on about how he and that girl of his were going to get a new start. But this thing, this living *all* the way over there … That was supposed to be temporary."

Reardon leaned forward, shaggy salt and pepper comb-over falling into his hard blue eyes. "I've seen about a dozen of these letters now and they all spout the same best-thing-since-sliced-bread shtick. It's been virtually impossible to get real uncensored information out of them from the beginning and I'm starting to lose patience with the obfuscation."

"Mr. and Mrs. Billings have been trying to save money to go out there. We thought you might be able to help," Ida said.

"Yes, that's possible. Before he left the country Jones wouldn't sit down with me one-on-one to account for his people's actions so I'm organizing a delegation of press outlets and families to go over and investigate. We can certainly help you with all the paperwork and some of the travel expenses, provided it's just you two of course."

Ida frowned. "They're not asking for charity, Congressman. They've already saved up half of the airfare for two plane tickets."

"I meant no offense, Mrs. Lassiter. Naturally we'd like to take everyone who has a vested interest but the cold reality is we have limited resources. Like I said, the State Department, the boys in the Bureau, you name it—don't give a damn about what's going on down there."

"We understand that," she said, glancing at the Billings. They nodded soberly in approval. An aide scribbled notes on an industrial strength clipboard.

"How many of the families that you're sponsoring to go over there are black?" She asked.

"I'm not sure I understand why that's relevant."

"It's very relevant. Three quarters of the church members and the Jonestown population are Afro-American. Yet, you'd think from the media coverage it was mostly white people."

"I certainly hope you're not suggesting that I'm guilty of bias. I'm well aware of the demographics of the church. I've seen plenty of coverage of black and minority Temple members. In fact, just last week there was an article on a couple from Lynwood who gave their adult daycare home to—"

Ida interrupted him. "We didn't come here to argue the merits or lack thereof of the press. I'm unable to travel to Guyana myself for financial reasons. So Mr. and Mrs. Billings just need assurance from you that they'll have safe and legal passage to Guyana under the aegis of your office."

"Of course. We offer the shield of the U.S. government to any constituent that goes over there. You can rest assured Mr. and Mrs. Billings that this office will work with you to ensure your trip is productive. But based on the testimony we've gotten about the apparent fanaticism of certain church members we can't guarantee that your son will want to come back with you."

Herman Billings grunted, exasperated. "Fact is if my wife hadn't gotten mixed up with those people in the first place the boy would be back here in school or working, toughing it out like I had to, not holed up in some countrified fantasy world pissing in the woods. I was always suspicious of them churches. Even as a kid way back."

Reardon nodded. "Mr. Billings, I'll be candid with you. I'm not partial to them either. I always figured men, excuse me, people, came into this world wanting to work at whatever they were good at, and, through a combination of talent, industriousness and luck, sometimes in that order, they made it or they didn't. God was for the most part peripheral. The fact that there's so much evil around tells us there's just as much a probability of God not being real as there is that he is real. I'm betting on the latter just to be sure."

288

He chuckled and winked, sweeping his hand over the piddling tufts of hair nursing his pink scalp. The sound of wind chimes tinkled from the open window behind him. "Lovely things huh? They're a token of sympathy from my Native American friends in the East Bay. Took pity on this square old white man after a long campaign night a few years ago when I was fighting for my political life. Like I said, I don't believe in good luck charms but maybe I'll take them with me on our trip to South America."

CHAPTER 30

Georgetown, Guyana, October 1978

HY STIRRED, STRETCHED on the lopsided twin bed. Her dreams are bite sized, snatches from conversations, music from taxi windows, the bump stall bump of fruit peddlers trundling over the cobblestones, church bells sounding on the hour, babies wailing; bottoms powdered, diapers changed, fat fingers sucked by fretting mothers.

The woman inside her couldn't remember where they were; whether they were back in the States in the greasy postage stamp sized apartment she'd once shared with her sister or jammed in the coach section of an airplane with fifty other black women or abandoned to a fitful sleep in an attic room swimming with old shoes and rotting newspapers. The woman inside her decided that it was the attic. Yes, that was where they were. They'd come to Georgetown to run an errand and stayed late, talking and laughing freely for the first time in months with a group of traveling ecology students from Venezuela; downing glass after forbidden glass of diabetic coma-inducing white wine while Sherie Allen catalogued her every move for her morning status reports to Jim Jones.

Sherie was the head of public relations in Georgetown. She ran Peoples Temple's headquarters from a house near the town square, a one woman command post who oversaw every press dispatch, government meeting and informal communiqué while managing her little brood of mixed children like a grand vizier tending a royal garden. They assembled obediently every time she so much as raised an eyebrow, addressing her by her first name, the promise of being just Mommy a coy treat she offered up when they were especially compliant.

290

Hy had been cleared by central command in Jonestown to wait out the rash of electrical storms that lashed the night. The confrontation over the drugging program put her on their watch list. Each day she waited for the rebuke and inquisition but got nothing except the deliberative smiles of Jim's enforcers; the silence, the waiting, rattling her more than the viper's coil of potential discipline.

There were several others either marooned or stationed in Georgetown for official purposes. White kids from the beggars' posse clustered in a room downstairs. Members of the Temple basketball team slept off a rout by one of the provincial squads. Demian and Jimmy Jr. knocked around in their fitted shorts and muddy high tops, alternately sulking and joking about the loss.

Hy had never noticed before how much they looked alike. The years of living under the same roof, of imbibing, rejecting their father's reign, of stumbling abortively forward on their own; ambivalence and defiance etched in their long limber perpetually in motion bodies. Part of her admired their hard fought brotherhood. Part of her shuddered at the thought of being adopted like Jimmy Jr.; shackled by the constant house arrest of thirsty white eyes.

She had not spoken to her own sister Taryn in a week. The sight of her was repellent, a lemming sucked into Jess' vortex of steaming shit, the two of them bonding showily over the care of Nkuli, a sullen thirteen year-old girl whose grandmother had shipped her over from L.A. for attitude adjustment. It was whispered that she was Foster's child, that she had been placed with them because Jess had wrangled a small relief check for her from the Temple survivors' fund after the accident. Hy avoided the girl out of shame, anger, watching her from afar, as though Foster lurked behind the girl's hot, reproachful eyes; as though he would appear and envelop her with his probing, lying.

Ever since they'd come to Jonestown Taryn had taken a sudden pious interest in children, fascinated by the bustling nursery and the pell mell groupings of preteen boys who pounded their boredom out with clannish games of stick ball when the pavilion was empty. She had requested to teach math, to be placed with Ernestine Markham in the high school classes. The Planning Commission put off making a decision, toying with her, she believed, because of Hy's outbursts.

"They want me to bargain with them, to beg," Taryn raged. "I can't take digging up weeds and turning over top soil all week anymore."

She'd watched her sister devolve into a voyeur, gutted of purpose, her brittle rigor sliding into the mush of algebra equations scribbled in a journal she carried around in her back pocket, insisting that she was hot on some big revelation, that every movement had a formula; every interaction hid a matrix of occult alternatives.

When they were kids she told Hy there were codes that could predict the future.

If Taryn could just find the correct one in time Jonestown's children would be set for life.

Hy lumbered off the bed, jolted back into the house's squirming menace by the drone of Sherie's voice downstairs. Sherie coordinated all the jobs and roles in the house from a big board in the radio room. Every resident had to sign in and out. Curfew was 9:00. Rap sessions, review of the day and assignments for the next were at 9:30 sharp. Sherie luxuriated in her authority as satellite commander, snapping the permanent residents in line when anyone overstepped, niggling the temporary ones with rules and regs.

"She'd run into a whole block of burning buildings for Dad," Devera commented to Hy over dinner before she'd gone to Georgetown. She and Devera could still trust each other, their friendship sheltered from the betrayals and backbiting. Devera did daily write-ups for the settlement paper, reporting on weather, events, achievements, fab facts of history, dotting it with witty marginalia and children's riddles to appease the voracious readers who'd plowed through most of the books in the library. Only Hy knew she was writing her memoirs. She was supposed to do a story on the Reardon visit. Word was they didn't want her on the frontlines interviewing.

"Because of my so-called gender issues. Those rotten bitches are trying to make sure I stay tucked away and quiet because it's gonna ruin their public relations with this fascist?! I helped build this motherfucker, my writing helped make it real in people's minds before they even came here. Who the fuck are they trying to fool! They're just as bad as any man with their damn pecking orders."

"They shit at his command."

"If Mother Mabelean wasn't so giving she'd kick their asses. There's a white woman who's worthy of respect. All the crap she's had to put up with over the years with them trying to walk all over her to see whose pussy could rule Dad."

The morning sun filched through the attic window. Hy got up and went into the hallway to the tiny closet bathroom. It was blissful being able to close the door and sit on a real toilet instead of doing the squat piss ritual in the common outhouse in Jonestown. The woman inside her agreed provisionally, reminding her that slaves had no such luxury. Downstairs Sherie's children bumped through the living room playing hide and seek as the residents slurped down bowls of lukewarm oatmeal, listening to the morning's first broadcast of group calisthenics moves. Sherie ordered everyone up to do jumping jacks, windmills, toe-touching, lunges, the room echoing with pants and groans. Hy hovered near the staircase, waiting for the regimen to end.

"Come on lazy bones," she heard Sherie bellow to a slacker. "Dad wants everyone in fighting shape when the outsiders come. We have to be lean and mean like our brothers and sisters in China and North Korea. They get up at the crack of dawn and do this a thousand deep all synchronized. That's how they stay strong. The physical and mental working together. The West doesn't understand that and never will."

Demian walked up the stairs, smiling faintly when he saw Hy. The last time she'd seen him was during the White Night, looking miserable as a gun-toting toy soldier. He jerked his head in the direction of Sherie's voice.

"The drill sergeant's at it again, huh?"

"She always like this? This is my first time staying here."

"She takes her official role real serious. Especially since the defections."

"I'd say she's earning her stripes."

Demian paused, taken aback, stimulated by her bluntness. "She's like the central nervous system of G-town. Sorta like the computer in the cave in one of those old *Twilight Zone* episodes, if you ever watched those."

"Yeah, I did," she said. They stood listening. The calisthenics had ended and Jim's voice came over the compound's speakers, outlining the schedule for Reardon's visit. Demian tensed, tree limb arms shrinking, dark eyes shallow inscrutable pools. Standing there, she saw Foster flicker up in him for a moment, his contemplativeness and brooding, his wary skeptic smile. They stared at each other, bracing for Jim's torrent of directives.

She had never wanted to fuck a man more than she did now, right there in the drear of the stairwell, the salt of his ear on her tongue, damn the consequences.

"I have a game tonight," he said.

"You feel good about it?"

"Sorta. Jimmy's playing center. My dad's desperate for us to win."

A cat skidded out from one of the bedroom doors, chasing a mud-colored lizard, a frequent denizen along the floorboards of the rambling turn-of-the century Georgetown houses. Demian moved to give them room, his Father's voice crescendoing from the speakers:

"We're ready to fight, to die if we need to. We've lived and loved like no other people have before, brothers and sisters. I don't need to tell you about our history. I don't need to go through the litany of struggle. Moses battled the pharaohs, Toussaint fought back the French, the Bolsheviks stamped out the Czar and his thieving oligarch lackeys. We're standing on their shoulders brothers and sisters, giants, all of 'em, slingshot Davids never to be underestimated. And all of you just as beautiful and precious as my natural born children. And you know I don't see any motherfucking difference. We field niggers will never be cowed by the empire."

The lizard vanished into the cracks of the floor, the cat pawing and whining after it in frustration. Demian hesitated, red and white tube socks crumpled up under his knobby knees like toadstools, jersey flopping over his waist, his mother's ghostly gauntness rising up in the shadows of his troubled face. She turned and looked up at him.

"Ya'll are still playing in light of this?"

"Yeah."

She put her hand on his cheek, skin old and rough, Methuselah's years. "Come here," she said. He followed her into the guest bedroom. She shut the door behind them, sliding the metal bolt through the latch, the clamor growing louder downstairs as the residents joined in with fevered call and response to the broadcast, drowning out the bustle of the marketplace. The woman inside her balked, raging about slaves and brainwashing and Miss Ann sitting on the veranda sipping iced tea while Topsy toiled at her feet. Hy turned the volume down on her, liberating Demian of his shirt and shorts, the socks staying put, his feet dangling from the end of the bed as they kissed, his penis a mast through his boxers. All the years she'd watched him from the audience in the Temple, playing the part of the repentant white son. All the years she'd only had a fleeting, morbid interest in him, and now Foster beckoned from the back of her mind, his cagey resolution intoxicating in the midst of the prone boy's tremulousness.

"No time for doubt or second guessing," they heard Father say. "That's way past. Who can we depend on to keep the Underground Railroad safe? All our ancestors looking toward the North Star. This is the desideratum. Ya'll have heard me talk about that. If I can't depend upon you now, If our *family* can't depend on you we got nothing."

Hy looked at Demian. Tears of anxiety rolled down his cheeks. He wiped them off in shame, turning away from her. She held him, turning him back to face her, guiding him inside her, stifling his soft moan with wet fingers.

The cat scratched and fussed outside the door.

"We'll be found out," Hy said, their hips locking together, her leg coiled around his ass, thighs; the minutes dying in the sweaty sweet small of his back as his father's voice rattled around them.

They'd be brought up on the floor, beaten in front of a thousand jeering inquisitors taking special delight in the fact that it was she and Demian. Jess would be in the first row. Taryn lurking grimly in the back. Jim, rotting from within, would send away the children and make them fuck in front of everyone as he had in San Francisco when a couple was caught being "licentious."

"He's fucking Ariane, my friend Richard's girlfriend," Demian said, staring up at the ceiling as they disengaged. "She's nineteen. There's no way she'd agree to having him put his dirty hands on her if she wasn't forced to."

Hy scowled. "Rapist."

The stairwell creaked in the hallway and the sound of Sherie coaxing the cat over to her echoed through the wall.

"They're done. Come on, get up and get ready for your game."

"What about Sherie? If she sees me coming out of here ..."

"I'll deal with her."

The house stilled as the noise from the broadcast subsided. Sherie went through the hall pushing doors open, inspecting, the cat following along at her heels. She tried their door then shook it, rapping loudly in irritation, calling Demian's name.

Hy got up and opened the door.

"Excuse me why the hell was this door locked?"

"I didn't know I needed your permission to lock it."

Demian appeared from behind her. Sherie looked him up and down in disgust.

"You've got to be on the bus with the rest of the team in thirty minutes and you're messing around up here," she turned back to Hy. "When you're under my roof you need to abide by my rules or be on your way."

Demian snarled, "There's no need for you to talk to her that way, we're not fucking children."

"Fine. If you lose tonight we'll know why."

He brushed past her. She bent down and picked up the cat, ruffling its tattered fur. It snuggled against her, licking savagely at her fingers, eyes darting, radar on the lizard's return.

"I told them not to send you here. I don't need any more troublemakers or distractions while we get ready for the outsiders' visit."

"Last I checked, you don't own this house. You're expendable just like everyone else. I don't care how many mixed kids you adopt."

Sherie tightened her grip on the cat. It shifted, edging up her freckled arm, the purring receding. "Easy girl, easy," she whispered. "No cause for alarm. None at all."

A thin-faced white boy gnawing on a carrot bounded up behind them. "Carol, Dad and Mariah are on the line. Reardon's people want to stop by here next month before they go to home base."

She recoiled, dropping the cat. "Fuck. It's the end of October! I need more than a few weeks to get this house functional for outsiders! Everybody needs to get their shit together immediately. All the work I've put into making this place just like Father wanted it, keeping it running on a fucking shoestring. My *biological* kids, straight from my vagina, thank you very much, are just now starting to settle in here and I'll be damned if this fascist honky is going to fuck it up."

Hy turned to go. "Central Command is going to get a detailed report about your smut-mongering with the boy," Sherie said. "We got witnesses that'll testify to your unexcused absence from Father's broadcast this morning and the boy is only going to back us up so you might as well initiate a confession."

"I have nothing to confess to. We're consenting adults and nobody owns us."

"He may be eighteen but he's still impressionable. It'll come out that you forced him, we have witnesses to that. Nothing's private, nothing's personal here. You left all that behind when you came over here. Remember all that's given to you is given by Him. You think you can go behind closed doors and do your smut without detection you're sorely mistaken. This is a world class operation Miss Hyacinth. I entertain people of international influence from all over the world on a regular basis, people who know and appreciate just how much the Temple is giving back to this country and to the cause of socialism globally. The prime minister even let some of us vote on the referendum in the last election he was so impressed with how I run my operations here. So we can't afford any internal distractions. You want to play the slut with Dad's son do it for the whole family to see and pay the consequences."

CHAPTER 31

Jonestown, Midnight, November 17, 1978

HUSH BABIES, COME to Mother Mabelean. Use your words. Your inside voices. Calm now, don't fight, don't argue, keep order in the line. The world is watching. I know many of you are hungry and tired, are eager for the special dessert I promised to celebrate Frederick Douglass day. Be patient beloveds. The good doctor Goodwin, who's treated Father for insomnia, says he's ebbing by the second. Says we should still look to Him for guidance in his lowest hour.

Says we should treat his flaws like chinks in china.

Says we should walk by faith, not by sight.

Darlings we should recognize this life for what it is, fleeting, undeserving of our goodness. There's no shame in facing the truth. There's no shame in saying we've reached the limits of what we can do on this hell on earth. Our last meeting together will be one for the ages, not a death but a rebirth. Another sign that we've been chosen like the Israelites were. Mariah has turned on the tape recorder for future generations. The talented Lenny will do background accompaniment on the organ. The Congressman, with his lies and accusations was not enough to suppress us. After all of his proselytizing and unholy snooping only ten brothers and sisters will ask to leave here. Only ten and most of them are white people with petty grievances. What is ten in a movement of multitudes?

How will they live with themselves when the world finds out about their treachery?

In the twilight hours the natives are getting restless. I hear them when they're sleeping. The things they say in dream are at odds with the

299

confessionals, the warrior love letters and brave oaths of allegiance they scribble to us on paper.

We are a strong but sometimes needy people, my darlings.

They lauded me as a saint for what I did for my boys. Though I didn't want their praise. I did what any real honest to God Christian woman would have done. And now I come to you beloveds, not as a Christian anymore but as a lover of Jesus; a disciple of his selflessness, his suffering, his model of community. This is the example that I've secretly kept in my heart in the midst of the betrayals going back decades.

I'd like to believe that I haven't betrayed you best beloveds. I was a simple Indiana girl plucked from whiter than white obscurity by fate.

But maybe that's being too modest. Jesus will forgive me if I allow for a little pride in what we've built here. The nursery, the library, the school, the serenity room for our seniors to sit and meditate in when the heat gets too intense. The kitchen fully-equipped to feed over a thousand a day. The Winnie garden, where our babies can experiment with anything they want to grow, unfettered by what we adults deem to be possible. To have all this nature around us, to see our image reflected in it is a blessing.

I initially had my doubts. In the early days when we were nomads and Jim dragged us to Brazil and Philadelphia then here to Guyana when it was still held by the British. I clung to the old insular ways of being; wanting the life of a settled minister's wife, the easy path of baptisms and christenings and lunches and dinners, bridge games and bingos and prayer quilts. There is a tiny corner of my mind that wanders there. To what if and what could've been; but I only shudder to think, best beloveds, what if I had been one of those regal white women, a stiff blue-eyed distant queen, afraid to get dirty, to take chances or risks, rising, maybe, to be the toast of Indianapolis and accepting it as my one true destiny.

Through all the unintended cruelness, I've remained grateful. Look how many of you I've watched grow into bright teenagers, young adults, doting parents ready to take up the fight from us older folks. Father has seen, *I* have seen death for you on the streets of Fillmore, in the ghettoes of Los Angeles and across occupied America always hounded for never being what the establishment says you should be; docile and bending not gloriously fearless like I know you to be.

Through all the mini crucifixions I've had hope, found sweetness in our work, basked in the small every day gifts I've been given. I've turned the other cheek like the righteous leaders, Gandhi, Reverend King, Martin Luther. Even when I saw our people bruised and beaten, witnessed hordes of disgraced members chewed up and spit out like rotten meat, a corner of me protested, but said *Yes*.

I have a taste for key lime pie beloveds. The ladies in the kitchen are making a special treat for our culmination. Thick, fresh, cream with the best condensed milk.

It was all for a higher purpose beloveds.

It is all for a higher purpose.

Hush, remember, use your inside voice, the world is watching.

Trust in Mother.

They meandered around the settlement mumbling when spoken to, eyes glazed, a sub class of zombie dissenters created pill by pill; a lawyer who'd been one of Father's closest consiglieres; a teenage girl who'd rebuffed Father's advances; an Indiana follower who'd been baited into defending the smear journalism of Ida Lassiter; a Nat Turner dreamer who'd tried twice to run away. It was understood by all that they were among the most recalcitrant, the most in need of correction and a tailored life plan, their wraith bodies cautionary tales.

Mother Mabelean ordered a woman on the banana crew to take a special one-way trip to Dr. Lance after she'd refused to give her place working in the shade to a white woman.

Her fair skin will blister and crinkle into pieces, beloveds.

"The world's battlefields are fertilized with the bones of ingrates, whiners, weaklings and misguided upstarts," Father declaimed through the loudspeakers. "We can't have any deviation from the mission. Remember why you're here. It's to build up a new black civilization, not to fuck around and act like spoiled dilettantes. You want to play Marie fucking Antoinette go back to the ghettos like they want you to. We all gonna be put into concentration camps while whitey sits back and mans the plantation."

When inmates were liberated from The Pit, Jess was assigned to keep tabs on them for any signs of backsliding. She took her expanded enforcement role seriously, a disciplined pupil to Carol, whom she'd disdained as a groveling power monger years ago. Now she logged long notes and carried out stealth observations, patrolling the settlement with three minions borrowed from the piggery in tow.

"Relatives are our point of entry," she lectured them. "Leave no stone unturned, no lead unexplored." The families of newly reinstated upstarts were given strict instructions to report any irregularity. Jess pioneered a whole smorgasbord of incentives for snitches; sleeping late, movie nights, relief from working the weeding crew, relief from outhouse cleanup, relief from crack of dawn catharsis sessions. When the minions got desperate they plowed through the settlement in lightening pursuit, dangling Snickers bars in the faces of children to get them to report a suspect conversation or random filthy-mouthed epithet.

Taryn watched the mini-inquisitions in the margins of her ten-hour work shift, her contempt for Jess' militarisms gnawing at her. In the morning breakfast line they avoided each other. Taryn sat on the far end near the children's garden while Jess took her place with the eagle-eyed core of Jim loyalists. Jess' therapist duties had dwindled down to once a week. Instead, she supervised residents' letters home, every detail edited to the bone, scrubbed of any hint of homesickness, doubt or regret.

When Nkuli's family wrote trying to find out about her status Carol intercepted their letters and gave them to Jess. The family worried about her diet, her sleep, wondering if she'd had to repeat the seventh grade, pleading that she be kept away from idle boys and their un-Christian ways. We know she's a handful. At first we believed that going to Jonestown would be a good environment for her but now we want her back home. Could you please have her call us collect as soon as she can? Her grandmother is sick and might not live through the month.

"These are ploys," Jess said to Taryn on a rare night when they were together, bunking in the seniors' cabin. Meetings had been cancelled. The hours loomed blankly before them in uncharacteristic quiet as a warm rain fell.

"That woman is healthy as an ox," Jess muttered brusquely, sprawled out in the room's only chair.

"They have a right to get information on her. Are you questioning that too?"

"Hell yeah, the mother gave up that right when she let her become a drug addict and run the streets all hours. No daddy. Thirteen and running the streets. Think that's acceptable? That's the case with most of these parentless kids before they came. If they weren't here their asses would be dumped or left for dead in juvenile hall. This is the last hope for them to get their lives together."

"And of course only you know what's best for these kids."

"Keep your voice down." She went to the window and looked out. "I wanted to help this girl because of what happened to Foster. Now it's clear you've developed an obsession with her and you're trying to disguise it with some bullshit advocacy for her fucked up mother."

"You're just as fucking sick as the cabal is if you think that."

Jess went over to Taryn and kneeled down in front of her. "Look, babe, I'm sorry. I'm under a lot of stress. Like I keep saying, I think you need to find something, some kind of role for yourself otherwise you'll just be out there flailing, going crazy fixating on little things." She picked up the notebook full of equations by Taryn's side. "What is this?"

"Stuff. Put it down."

Jess flipped through it, dropping it on Taryn's lap.

"How long you been doing that?"

"What difference does it make?"

"A lot."

"Since we got here. I've always kept some kind of math journal."

"That's beautiful, baby." She stroked Taryn's hair. "I've been talking to them about you teaching, about you wanting to work with Ernestine's group of kids."

"Ok."

"Remember how we talked about moving back to the States in a few years and starting our own business? I think Carol and Mariah would be willing to help us with seed money if we just hang in and work at this for a little while."

Taryn pulled away. "You're spinning your wheels. They're not going to invest jack shit in any business of ours no matter how much you play the good Negro."

Jess sat back on the floor. The rain raged against the thin roof. Garbled laughter bleated from the loudspeaker.

"I heard Hy got into a fight with Sherie out in Georgetown over her 'conduct'."

"What conduct?"

"She fucked Demian in one of the guest rooms then lied about it, claimed he raped her to garner sympathy with the other residents."

"She wouldn't do that."

"Which part? Fuck him or lie about it? The way Sherie tells it Hy was the aggressor. They're going to put her on the Education Crew or in The Pit when she gets back. I have to decide which."

"They told you that?"

"Yes."

Taryn got very still, Jess' voice coming slow and heavy, an imploding drip of motor oil on her ear. Her heart seized up in her chest.

Jess picked up the journal again, examining the cover, dotted with gold stars, drawings of brown stick figure girls. "I've protected you," she said quietly. "I tried to protect her but I can't now, not after this latest violation."

"Don't give me that shit, Jess! You like this, you like being the front line of discipline. You get off on it. You always have." She snatched the book away from her. "Listen to me, goddammit! If you do this, if you allow this so help me I'll—"

"You'll what? Excommunicate me? Baby you have no allies here. You've isolated yourself. The only reason why they haven't put you in The Pit or on the Crew is because of the buffer I provided."

"So it's all about indebtedness then, right? Bowing down to you because you've been such a staunch advocate for us? That's really what the therapy and counseling have been about all these years, leeching off of other people, getting off on their helplessness to bolster your sick, impaired ego. I always told myself, lied really, that that couldn't be your motivation, even when you and Hy were at each others' throats and she told me to get away from you—"

"Now you admit it. Good. You know she never wanted us to be together in the first place. Hated you for being a lesbian, wanted you all to herself because she could never stand on her own two feet. Can't cut it here or anywhere else," she shook her head. "Fucking that white boy ... Her shit is latent to the nth degree but you haven't been able to see it because you're so far up her ass trying to keep her from dealing with the real world."

There was a faint knock on the door. The knob turned and Mabelean came in, damp, pale, smelling of lilacs, a sack of clean diapers in her hand.

"Excuse me Jess but we need you in the pavilion."

"This late?"

"We have a situation developing with a group of teens in the eighth row dorms. They smuggled in some smut magazines they probably got from the day laborers."

Jess waited.

Mabelean put the sack down, rubbing her back. "And two of them have been writing in code back home to their relatives."

"I don't think so. I would've detected it."

"Evidently you didn't dear. They have an aunt and uncle coming with the delegation."

"You're slipping," Taryn said.

"Be quiet," Jess said through her teeth.

"They can't take those children away from here," Mabelean pronounced. "They'll be lynched if they go back to the States."

"That's ridiculous," Taryn replied.

305

Mabelean's eyes bugged in shock. "Are you questioning Father's predictions?"

"Yes."

She turned back to Jess. "Looks like you have several problems on your hands. Please report to the pavilion immediately."

She started to leave, bumping into Hy as she came in the door. She stood aside, stewing, and let Hy go in.

"You're wanted in the pavilion, Hyacinth."

Hy ignored her, speaking directly to Taryn. "I need to talk to you."

Mabelean picked up the sack of diapers, tying the drawstring primly with raw fingers.

"Perhaps you didn't hear me. You're wanted in the pavilion. Please report there immediately. If you're unable to make it on your own I'll have escorts come retrieve you."

"I don't need any fucking escorts because I'm not going."

She shook her head in disbelief. "You have some nerve … with all the strain we're under preparing for the Congressman's visit." She paused, fixing her with a hard gaze. "I know what happened in Georgetown between you and my son. He's probably not blameless but you should be ashamed of yourself. You need to make serious adjustments if you're going to stay in this family."

"I only have one family, and that's with my sister. Whatever happens to me happens to her and vice versa."

Mabelean nodded. "So be it." She opened the door and walked out into the night. Outside, people trickled in small groups toward the pavilion, yawning, shielding themselves from the rain with old copies of the *Peoples Forum*, dark circles carved under their eyes. Lance Schuler rushed by against the foot traffic in the direction of the infirmary. A Red Brigade guard wheeled the sleeping form of Muggs on a mini-stretcher, arousing the delight and curiosity of a thumb-sucking child holding her mother's hand. She broke from her mother and followed the stretcher, singing softly into Muggs' ear, coaxing at him to wake up.

Hy watched them pass. Jess folded her arms and looked down at the ground. "Taryn, I need to talk to you in private," Hy insisted.

"Jess was just leaving anyway. She was given a direct order. She's good at following direct orders from superiors."

"Baby … I didn't mean all that shit."

"Please. Spare me. Just go, please."

She walked over to Taryn and stroked her cheek. Taryn grabbed her hand and stepped back. "Don't."

The nightly broadcast had started up again. A woman's voice read the news and California weather report in crystalline tones. Rolling blackouts, food rationing and prison detentions of dissidents had begun, she said, as electrified snippets of the "Star Spangled Banner" pounded through the air.

"Aw naw, at least give us some fucking Hendrix!" a voice from the moving crowd yelled.

Jess brightened. "Seems like a million years ago, seeing him at the Fillmore. Just out of college, just got my degree and the sound was atomic. A lot of fine sisters there that night. You trumped them all though."

Jess pulled Taryn close, kissing her full on the mouth. Taryn faltered, aware of Hy's eyes on them, a clammy paralysis gripping her.

"There's no way I'm going down there," Hy said.

Taryn disentangled herself from Jess. "You've got to call the dogs off."

"She's in too deep. It's already in motion."

"That's it Jess? That's all you've got to say?"

Jim Jones' voice blasted over the speaker. Preparations for the visitors' tour would begin bright and early the next morning.

Hy opened the door to leave, glancing back at the two of them. "Jess pissed away her clout a long time ago," she said.

Rumor from the kitchen had it that dinner the night the outsiders came would be real macaroni and cheese, baked chicken cutlets sautéed in lemon sauce, green beans with almond slivers and potato rolls drowning in melted butter; a regular gourmet paradise. There'd be key lime pie with gobs of whipped cream and sweetened condensed milk for dessert. There'd be crisp white dinner plates and electric fans to cool the humid cafeteria. There'd be open seating, like in the old days, to catch up with friends, connect with loved ones.

The rumor fluttered through the pavilion on angel wings as they waited in the darkness for the meeting to begin.

Taryn watched the crowd for Hy. If there was an interrogation she would offer herself up in Hy's place, snatch her voice back from the sludge of doubt and fear.

Groups of children tittered and fidgeted restlessly behind her. They'd stayed awake all night fantasizing about the meal of paradise. It had been ages since they'd had a real meal, their ribs hidden under recycled smocks and baggy t-shirts, teeth yellowing from an underground market of smuggled junk food and Day-Glo corner store candy.

"This is the kind of fare we have every night," Carol briefed them to say, standing on stage with a list of priority items. No one could claim commune living was a failure after beholding the riches of their sweat equity. "We're aware that some of the teens have resorted to trading sexual favors for candy. There are also other cases of sexual misconduct that have come to light. This is reprehensible. We intend to take care of all the offenders after the Congressman's visit. For now, for the next twenty four hours, we must have unity."

Taryn pressed her knees together, relieved, applause swelling around her.

The film projector was wheeled out and a short on air raid drills was shown, then the people were dismissed by rows.

After the gathering disbanded the Jonestown chorus and the Soul Steppers practiced deep into the night, harmonies sharpened, dance moves synchronized in cut glass precision.

Ready, steady, get in position.

CHAPTER 32

❖

November 18, 1978

WHEN THE FIRST truck of outsiders pulled up a hush fell over Jonestown. Six white families and Jamiah's got out, blinking in the dead sun. The press and the Congressman came in a separate convoy, guided by Guyana soldiers. The camera crew disembarked and clanked around with their heavy he-man equipment, shooting anything that moved. Jonestown aides, huddled up in youthful interracial pairs, rushed to escort them, as the Red Brigade roved around the front gate, patting down bodies, scrutinizing identification. School was scheduled to stay in session for a half day; then the oratory of star pupils would be showcased in a noon assembly followed by a presentation called "From the Middle Passage to Integration?" in the pavilion.

Jess spent the early morning hours strategizing about the impending visit, briefing escorts and guides on vital Jonestown stats, revising the itinerary of sites each outsider would be allowed to see. She said yes and no when spoken to, mustered the proper venom about the superhuman strain the visit put on Father. She watched him hobble through the grounds in a bloated web of despair, clutching his gut, growling for Lance to work his magic, every inch of him dive bombed with aches, pains, tics, indigestion, his skin flapping, shredded like trout innards.

She tried to be fully present, to keep her finger on the pulse of the relentless movement, gnawed at by the scene the night before and the mystery of Hy's whereabouts. Taryn would not speak to her. She'd returned to her own dorm after the pavilion meeting broke up.

Zephyr walked past, pushing a wheelbarrow filled with paper towels and toilet paper. She nodded briskly at Jess, impatient, face drawn, concentrated on her precious cargo. Since the incident with Sterlinda she had locked up her loyalist status but been less vocal in the meetings. Others had eclipsed her in urgency and zeal.

"That for this evening?" Jess asked.

"Yeah. We'll have enough to last the entire shebang."

"I hear you and some of the Dorm 10 group want to take off for a few hours this afternoon."

She looked up at the sky. "Thought it'd be a nice day for a picnic."

A white cameraman with a soggy mustache clanked into view and shot their picture.

"I'd smash that shit if I could," Zephyr said.

Jess reeled around on him. "Hey! Cut it out!"

He raised the camera from his face, grunting an apology.

She turned back to Zephyr. "I'm supposed to get ya'll a chaperone."

"Make it somebody cute."

"Right, by the way have you seen Hy?"

"Not since before the meeting yesterday."

Zephyr wheeled away. Before their fight Jess had recommended to the leadership that Taryn chaperone the group. Now the thought set her on edge. Taryn would run off out of spite. Or use the opportunity to challenge her. She brooded over that scenario as she walked into the pavilion, watching Mariah and Carol double team the families who'd come to meet with their loved ones. Jamiah's parents brushed the two women aside. When the guards led him in seconds later his mother broke and ran to him, waving a grade school picture he'd drawn of a rocket ship. "I found this just before we left sweetheart. We're here to take you home if you want to leave here."

Jamiah grasped her stiffly. He put his lips to her head, looking past his father's gaze. "No mama. I'm happy here. This is the best thing in the world to happen to me. My girl just had a baby."

Jess touched his back, murmuring words of praise. She went from group to group, monitoring the testimony. When a member went off topic she chimed in with a history of the settlement, keeping her eye out for Taryn and Hy.

Outside, the lunch line swelled to the hundreds. Residents decked out in their Sunday best milled together restlessly, enveloped by the stench

310

of burnt chicken. They strained to catch a glimpse of the outsiders. The women from the nursery traded bets on which white man would fold first in the heat. Reporters scribbled on the sidelines, tape recorders whirring. Applause tinkled from the elementary classrooms as the children finished their full-throated show and tell.

Hy stood at the end of the line. After riding out the night in her dorm she was starving and queasy, the shiny new food beckoning like an evil mirage. The picnickers gathered to her right as the cafeteria workers handed them a few samples from the feast to take with them. Zephyr had told her fleetingly about the outing, planned by a group of fifteen, black, in their late teens and twenties, most of whom had never been called up for anything. She knew she had a small window before the leadership came down on her for the drugging claim and sleeping with Demian. They'd already started plotting creative punishments for her transgressions. The delegation's visit was a temporary reprieve. Every hour she stayed increased her risk of being publicly shamed, medicated or imprisoned on Jess' vindictive watch.

Taryn joined the group of picnickers. They moved away from the crowd, bags of food and paper goods from Zephyr's wheelbarrow on their backs. They waited in a collective pause, Jonestown's light of the future: Nkuli, gum smacking and sullen in a blue sundress, Autumn Dixon feeding her little boy peanuts, Ernestine Markham's son Byron nuzzling up to his boyfriend, defiant under the stares of the haggard camera crew.

The crew argued with the Red Brigade over the position of the filming equipment.

"C'mon now," the soggy mustache white man said, lifting up his rumpled plaid shirt to smear the sweat off his forehead. "This is your golden opportunity for the whole world to see what you're all about."

"Move it back, move it back," Carol ordered. "You can set it up for the evening's performances but we can't have this constant interruption of the flow of the day."

"Whatever you say, lady."

The sky blackened, close to breaking. In the pavilion Jess excused herself from the interviews, pushing through the lunch line. Jamiah followed her, spotting Devera and Greer from the laundry room with a reporter by the central outhouse.

"They're talking to those motherfuckers," he croaked after Jess. "What the fuck are they talking about?"

Jess looked back at Jamiah, peach fuzz glistening on his long chin, a soft sad quizzicality under the desperation, his abandonment of his parents and the alien country they'd come from. She grabbed his arm. "Let's go."

They made their way to the front. Taryn and the picnickers had reached the gate.

"Where do ya'll think you're going?" Jamiah asked.

"We have permission to go on a picnic," Zephyr replied.

"From who?"

"From Dad through Carol and Jess. "We'll be back to see the show later."

Taryn narrowed her eyes at Jess. "What are you doing here? I thought you were part of the welcome wagon."

"You haven't been cleared to go."

"What are you talking about?"

"I'm hungry," Nkuli said, stretching. Jess followed Taryn's gaze, lingering too long on the curve of the girl's arched body. In the distance the Congressman's delegation wended its way from the classroom to the library.

She turned to Taryn. "Babe, you're not well. You're overworked. You need medical attention. I made an appointment for you with Dr. Schuler."

"Fuck that, she's not going to any appointment." Hy walked up. She put her arm awkwardly around Taryn.

"Hy, it's ok. I can speak for myself." She looked at Jess. "You're really amazing trying to pull this eleventh hour crap." A pair of stray dogs wandered up to them sniffing around their feet, crazy at the scent of the paradise meal steaming from the picnic baskets. Taryn bent down to pet one, kneeling in the dirt, fingers full of its hot fur, the must of all that it had witnessed. It panted and whined, snout to the sky.

"Let Hy go with them instead," she said.

"You know I can't do that."

"You can if you want to, with all these distractions here. Please." She squared her shoulders, meeting her eyes. "You owe me that at least."

Jess paused, considering. Taryn pulled out a plum from the basket and gave it to Nkuli.

"Here, eat." She bit into it, ravenous. Taryn leaned forward, whisking the plum meat off her dress.

Jess watched them, slayed by the gesture, transporting her to when she'd first seen Taryn and wanted her, captivated by her reserve, her hard-tender leanness, the numbers dancing in her head.

She motioned suddenly to Jamiah. "Go back to your family. They came all this way to see you. Spend a little time with them before they leave. Show them the baby. Then get the rest of the guards. This area shouldn't be unmanned for this long."

He opened his mouth to protest then nodded, backing away behind the convoy vehicles.

In the distance the school bell sounded to muted cheers. Jess turned to Hy, steadying her voice, cut glass, deliberate. "In a few minutes the guards will be back wanting to know where you are," she said. "You should go before they come."

The group had already started out past the gate. Hy hesitated. "Taryn?"

"Go," she said. "I'll be ok."

Hy kissed Taryn on the cheek, holding her face in her hands. They breathed together, back again in their twin beds on Myrtle Street, bodies intertwined, waiting for the first beast of dreamtime, each trying to keep the other from falling asleep.

Hy turned and walked toward the jungle, the dogs following, their hungry yips rising over Jonestown.

Port Kaituma, Guyana

First the townspeople saw the birds. Gliding in a shimmering black arc, the sun boiling between the rain clouds in the wrath of high noon. Thousands, millions, gazillions in big Kahuna bird congress, flapping in unison far as the eye could see. They dipped and dived, swooping back up again. Flesh gleaming in red ribbons from their beaks.

The gunman hid behind the Congressman's plane. He dropped under the wing, waiting as the passengers boarded. The press delegation lusted aloud for Big Macs. The Jonestown residents and their families laughed in agreement. They turned one last time to see the country from the ground as the pilot finished fueling, flashed a thumbs-up sign, put on his shades.

No more threat of rain, boys.

The girl hummed to herself on the staircase of the plane, telling her stuffed animal not to be afraid, pressing into her father's trembling body. She hadn't had a chance to say goodbye to her friends. The big girls from Mrs. Markham's literature class who let her do the chalkboards and called her little squirt; the hopscotch girls who liked to French braid her blond hair. She fingered the good luck charm in her pocket, a prize ribbon from her teacher: Most Improved Oratory, 1977.

Behind her, Devera clutched at the guard rails, her entire life crammed into her jeans and a carry-on bag, the prospect of home bittersweet on her tongue. She would come back and get the others. She would help them rebuild. She would pass the church's true heritage on. She would find a real heaven on earth.

"God's smilin' on us," she said.

"The congressional shield of protection is around you," the Congressman promised as they stepped onto the plane. He paused, gave a politician's pat wave to an invisible crowd, grinning for the rolling cameras.

A row of birds settled onto the rickety control tower, watching the trucks pull in from Jonestown.

Bullets ripped through the air, taking the passengers down in midsentence. Mangled bodies formed a chain from the cabin to the tarmac. The living played dead, gagging on the funk of diesel and blood.

By the time the assassins were through they'd blasted out the roof of the plane. Devera could stand up and touch the clouds from her seat.

314

She could see clear out over the trees, past the bowing rainforest, past the valley of the shadow of death to her people, eating each other alive in Memorex.

Jonestown

They took turns watching each other sleep. Jess sitting in the desk chair, Taryn propped up on the bed with her math journal, crossing out pages of fledgling proofs.

The delegation had left and gone back to Port Kaituma. The trucks rumbled off in single file, pachyderm-style, holding each other's tails. No one was to leave their quarters until Mariah gave the word. Day bled into evening, the sour milk of waiting.

In Taryn's dreams they made love, suctioned together afterwards in conjoined twin telepathy.

"Believe me baby when I say that I never meant to hurt you … or Hy."

"She'll come back for me."

"Maybe."

"No maybe, definitely."

"What do your equations tell you about that?"

CHAPTER 33

Ernestine Markham, Nighttime, November 18, 1978

I NEVER LEARNED how to swim. Some primordial part of me knew, had kept the skill in embryonic memory from the womb. My brothers were champion swimmers, had always teased me for my timidity. Prim, proper Ernestine, they said, wouldn't put on a swimsuit unless it was a turtleneck. As Coloreds there were no teams that would take them. Not even in Los Angeles, our counterfeit paradise, where the white surfers brayed that their blackness would wash off in the water and contaminate.

This was the last thing I told my students before the Congressman's delegation came. Black babies were going to be drowned. Snatched up and thrown into the shimmery Olympic-sized pools of the capitalists. The adults rounded up and taken to concentration camps.

I did not want my young people terrorized by this revelation, handed down by Jim. But they took it in stride. It made them more defiant to the outsiders. Toughened their spirits. Strengthened their resolve.

"We ain't surrendering," my brave tenth grade commandantés said.

The black Spanish cross dresser Devera and her boyfriend from the laundry slipped a note to the Congressman asking to leave. Rumor had it that they'd been planning for a long time; tired, homesick, unfit for the kind of living that only the tough of mind can hack.

Later that afternoon a few more followed to go back to the States with the delegation; Jim's frontline soldiers, families that had been with him from the beginning, braving the crucible back in Indiana.

"The whites have abandoned us," Jim raged. "Look at who walked out of here today. White bourgeois who always had one eye on the door and a finger on the trigger."

The chorus gathered as he spoke, nursing the a capella song of a girl from Dorm 10, the only one who hadn't gone on the picnic. When the white men from the delegation came they gorged on the earnest soul shake, the Negro pomp and circumstance we put on for their benefit, the Congressman congratulating us on our solidarity, our pioneer spirit, as the cameras rolled for posterity.

"There's been an incident at the airport," Jim announced when the chorus finished. "They laid old man Reardon out on the tarmac for the buzzards."

"Rat bastard deserved it," William muttered, insomniac eyes gouged out of his face.

Jim walked into the crowd. He picked up a baby in the first row, cooing into her ear as she fussed against him. "Hush now. We are a people out of due time." A shudder of agreement went through the congregation, a thousand souls in cataclysm. "Right now the opposition is readying itself. I can feel it, brothers and sisters. They're gonna parachute down on us in the middle of the night when they think we're sleeping. Mother Mabelean knows I've never been wrong. Brother William and Brother Cedric know I've got the sixth sense. Everything we've built, everything we've sweated and strived for will go to shit. Our babies' destinies, our seniors' lives."

A woman named Rosalie stood up, "Naw Dad we won't let them dictate how we're gonna live!"

"Or how we're gonna go out!" Jamiah yelled.

"No that's right, that's right sister Rosalie." He walked over to Jamiah, touching his forehead. "This warrior here is my pride and joy. Parents came thousands of miles to hoodwink him and he said no dice." He turned back to the congregation, his voice breaking. "Remember our beginning."

Mabelean threw up her hands, sing-songing, "Those of you that have been with him, with us, from when it all started in that ramshackle little church in Indiana."

"Think how they, the whites who were afraid of their own fucking shadows, fought us almost to the death on this."

"And you showed us the light, Dad. You stuck up for me when nobody else did."

"Yes he did, yes he did."

They are crying in the back of the pavilion. Babies dance barefoot in the mud, rubbing it on their chubby little faces.

"All this crying and carryin' on is for the birds," Rosalie said, raising her voice. It is bigger than the mike, the soft plodding organ, the clang of the vat of poison the Red Brigade has dragged out from behind the stage.

"Better to go down fighting than on our backs, ya'll."

"Yes!"

"Are we black, proud and socialist? Better to go down as revolutionary suicides than cowards. We die now and cross over to the other world together."

My boy, my baby, my island in the jungle, is safe. Watch him now God. Guide him. Take his hand. He was a whiz at classical trumpet, a quiet one who was misunderstood, underestimated.

"They're going to nail us to the cross for murdering the Congressman. Going to try and tell us that one politician's life is worth more than our entire family."

More came to the microphone to testify, phantoms thirsting for sleep. The stench of almonds nearly knocking Taryn off her feet as Jess moved ahead with the procession of speakers.

Mabelean floated past, handing out flowered Dixie cups.

"What about Russia?" I ask. "Is it too late? What about all the Politburo higher ups who were supposed to believe in us? Can't they take us in?"

"Well, now, there's a call in to Russia as we speak," Jim said. He returned the baby to her mother, a cloud of white powder rising from her diaper. Gunshots popped in the distance. He cocked his head, listening to the dog whistle song of the animals in the jungle, waiting their turn.

"Anywhere we run, though, anywhere we go on the planet, Ernestine, we'll be hounded and hunted down."

"That's always been the case but why concede?"

"It ain't concession," said a Red Brigade guard, barely eighteen, stroking his side piece.

"Apostle Paul was a man out of due season. He was sent by God to bear special witness," Jim remarked. "I'm speaking as a prophet. The only obligation we have is to ourselves. To lay down with dignity, to cross over with an ounce of self respect."

"Yes but everyone shouldn't be asked to make this choice. The children, the babies have a lifetime ahead of them."

"A people out of due season," Jim repeated, staggering. Mariah and Carol appeared on each side, steadying him. Muggs paced and clapped in his cage by the organ.

Jim stood, straightened to his full height. "Line up, line up. Lay it down, you gotta lay it down with dignity. From the time you're a child 'til the time you get gray you're dying. Mother, mother, mother, give the medication to your children. Stop this cryin' and carryin' on. We go in peace."

"We all have our own destinies. Everyone from the littlest to the oldest should be allowed to choose."

Some ran, desperate, gathering their children, biting into the darkness for freedom as they pushed past the rows of friends, lovers, family lining up at the stage with cups raised, the guards close on their heels.

A woman tore out of the pavilion with her baby and is dragged back screaming.

A group of cousins, junior orators, the cream of Jonestown, rushed toward the gate as the men tackled them, readying doses of poison, the night ringing with the youths' pleas.

Jamiah approached Taryn with a cup. "Here you go, sister."

She slapped it out of his hand and angled around him, watching Jess move forward in line, enfolded by the waving arms, the bodies of the people aching for home. A woman beside Taryn fell to the ground, sucked under by the vortex, hands locked in prayer. Taryn stopped to help her up, parting her hands. "Let's go," she whispered. They clung to each other for a moment, rocking silently, wedded in the gap of years past, when the woman had stood before the congregation, blissful, delivered from cancer, the world tight in her fist.

At the head of the line, Jess looked back at Taryn. She pressed her fingers to her lips in a kiss and raised them to the sky.

To you, my one and only. Cross your heart hope to.

The tape recorder clicked forward.

"Sounds like you're making excuses, Ernestine. Sounds like you're afraid to die."

Jess turned to face me, lovely eyes aflame, opening the floodgates to the jeers and lamentations of my last family on earth, the roar of dank Atlantic tides lapping at a slave ship, the rumble of bald tires cutting past the Mason-Dixon.

Now Sister Jess stands in the middle of the floor, oblivious to the guards on the hunt. They whip across the grounds and into the fields, lost sons brandishing rose-colored syringes dripping death in the children's mouths, envoys from God herding up strays and would-be messengers, seekers gulping down the last dregs of night air as she puts the Dixie cup to her lips, and drinks.

Author's Note

THIS IS A work of fiction and imagination. Although based on historical events, I have at times re-imagined places and people, as well as invented characters and situations, in order to give voice to perspectives that may not have been captured in the voluminous body of literature on Peoples Temple and Jonestown. Coming from the vantage point of a Black woman writer in a field—Jonestown scholarship and fiction—where African American feminist analyses are few, I have sought to creatively illuminate (and problematize) what is still a turbulent and evolving historical record and signal event in the "psychic space" of African American migrations.

Acknowledgments

I'D LIKE TO express gratitude and appreciation to the following individuals without whom this book would not have been possible: to Juanell Smart, Jordan Vilchez and members of the Peoples Temple survivor community for graciously allowing me to interview them about their lives and experiences with the church movement. My thanks to Fielding McGehee and Dr. Rebecca Moore of the Jonestown Institute, formerly of San Diego State University, who were unwaveringly helpful in providing archival material and feedback on the history of Peoples Temple and Jonestown. I am greatly appreciative of the invaluable editorial commentary and feedback provided by my friend Dr. Kamela Heyward-Rotimi and writer/editor Diana Gordon. Many thanks to my parents, Yvonne Divans Hutchinson and Earl Ofari Hutchinson, my brother Fanon Hutchinson, daughter Jasmine Hutchinson Kelley and friend Heather Aubry, Esq., for their support and encouragement of this project. And finally, my deep appreciation to my wonderful husband Stephen Kelley, who was a patient and thoughtful sounding board, reading early drafts of this book, lending his considerable literary expertise to help sharpen its vision, and encouraging me, always, to go further.

Made in the USA
Charleston, SC
13 September 2016